HUMBOLDT CUT

HUMBOLDT CUT

Allison Mick

an imprint of Kensington Publishing Corp.
erewhonbooks.com

Content notice: *Humboldt Cut* includes depictions of horror-level violence, death/dying, pregnancy (including abortion, traumatic birth), infant death, sexual assault, suicidal ideation and mental illness, and references to ablism, racism, sexism, and antisemitism.

EREWHON BOOKS are published by:

Kensington Publishing Corp.
900 Third Avenue
New York, NY 10022

erewhonbooks.com

All Kensington titles, imprints, and distributed lines are available at special quantity discounts for bulk purchases for sales promotions, premiums, fundraising, educational, or institutional use.

Special book excerpts or customized printings can also be created to fit specific needs. For details, write or phone the office of the Kensington sales manager: Kensington Publishing Corp., 900 Third Avenue, New York, NY 10022, attn: Sales Department; phone 1-800-221-2647.

ISBN 978-1-64566-221-1 (hardcover)

First Erewhon hardcover printing: February 2026

10 9 8 7 6 5 4 3 2 1

Printed in the United States of America

Library of Congress Control Number is available upon request.

Electronic edition: ISBN 978-1-64566-223-5 (ebook)

Edited by Diana Pho
Interior design by Leah Marsh
Interior images courtesy of Andromeda2064/Wikimedia Commons, Doug Kerr/Flickr

The authorized representative in the EU for product safety and compliance
is eucomply OU, Parnu mnt 139b-14, Apt 123
Tallinn, Berlin 11317, hello@eucompliancepartner.com

To everyone who's still here, especially
when they didn't always want to be

"But of course it's not the world that needs saving. Only the thing that people call by the same name."

—Richard Powers, *The Overstory*

HUMBOLDT CUT

PROLOGUE: THESE WOODS

1951

A MILLION-MILLION IMPERCEIVABLE EYES barely registered the golden-shine pollen dancing through the forest air. It sparked into blazing comets passing through a column of sunlight. Some things were too important to watch too closely—everything cast off will return to the forest if someone doesn't steal it first. These woods operated on a timeline too vast to acknowledge urgency; when death feeds life feeds death in concentric rings across millennia, there's no real difference between the two, between anything. Only increasing complexity toward what happened before creates the potential for the present.

The woods here were Potential embodied at its purest: quick-growing *Picea sitchensis*, fire-resistant *Sequoia sempervirens*, lightweight *Thuja plicata*. All beautiful, useful, and profitable in their own ways.

THE FALLERS

The blue truck slowed to a stop along a steep gully, kicking up nutrient-poor dirt and sawdust. An unsmiling old man stepped out, staring across at the dense mural of variegated green. Impassive, the forest returned his gaze. He opened the passenger door and carefully lifted a small Kodak Vigilant from the passenger seat. Adjusting the lens, he looped the strap around his neck. Snapped a picture of the expanse. He loved the woods with his whole heart.

He looked down the incline where the dozen or so men on his crew littered the grove. The foreman's stomach dropped a little when he thought about the responsibility he had over them. The most dangerous job in America. For good reason. Especially in these woods.

There's a small glade, long and narrow like the inside of a church. The canopy's branches reach across to shield this place from the sun; it forms a wooden cathedral of gray and green shadows. The old man scuttled down the gully toward the coast redwood at its altar.

Above him, cables thwanged arrhythmically. He squinted up at the high rigger. All these young men, so drunk on their own vigor they don't even realize they're spitting in death's face. If the high rigger has got time for acrobatics, he'll have finished putting up the cables needed to drag this mother down to the yard once she's been cut down.

In no time, the old man was at the trunk. Thirty feet across, the titan towered over him. A living thing so alien and yet more of this world than him, his truck, this road, and anything he considered part of his world. So old it predated the arrival of Europeans on this continent. An entity so large as to be rendered faceless, stripped of individuality, becoming one of those things that are so big we have no choice but to call them "places," a forest rather than a tree. It made him feel like one of his daughter's baby chicks, who were so small that they barely registered the human legs around them as more than pillars that occasionally showered them with grain. This pillar's grain was a thick, pale yellow pollen that had already started caking on the spittle in his beard. Released to ride the fog to open spaces and seed a new generation of giants. Not for much longer.

The man rounded the tree to face the nave of this forest chapel. Above his head, on either side of the redwood, stood a young faller. Two boys, both named Tom, with thick arms and strong backs, were going for the Humboldt cut: a wedge cut into the trunk at an angle that suggested a slack mouth. The strong boys bounced as they swung their axes while balancing on flimsy springboards. The springboards were jammed into the tree ten feet off the ground. The cut doesn't work on a human scale, so these boys stood on lumber, bobbing up and down to hack into the neck of a thousand-year-old giant.

"Boss." The leftmost of the Toms tipped his cap to the old man, his sleeve lifting enough to show a peek of what the foreman felt was an idiotic line tattoo of an axe head. *Not even a Humboldt axe at that. If you're going to get inked up like a syphilitic sailor, at least get more than a little hatchet head that won't even fell a Wisconsin pine. The little punk's only worked timber for two seasons. Ridiculous.*

A nod and a grunt served as enough of a greeting to the fallers. The boss had a greenhorn today. A gangly fifteen-year-old skulked up to him from the other side of the *S. sempervirens*.

And the boy *was* green. Wide eyes. Soft hands. The boy's obsequious slouching made the old man want to smack him on the mouth. *He'll probably die in these woods*, he thought. *Or turn into an old man like me. Or worse.* The forest takes all kinds, especially those that mean to harvest her parts to build a more efficient means to kill the rest of her.

The skyline cable thwanging above them percussed to the logging crew's symphony of shouting, grunting, sawing, and a couple expensive gas-powered chainsaws. Noise upon noise.

The old man started his spiel about how this whole thing's about to go. More noise for the noise.

"Sir?" The boy even yelled like a servant. *Where the fuck do they find these guys?*

The man gestured for the boy to follow him. Handing the kid an axe, he demonstrated how to chop down the smaller trees colonnading the glade. The two worked side by side, chiseling wedges into the spruces and pines. They worked together to push the trunks over, hefting them down the center of the chapel with dozens of others to fill the nave with pews.

From the high-up cables, a harness-less young man in his early twenties tightrope-walked quickly down a line. He barked down: "Oy!"

Half of the men stopped chopping. Gas chainsaws powered down, sputtering to silence. The greenhorn could barely see the high rigger against the blackened canopy.

"We're good! That's enough!" The man scampered across the line and hopped off onto the bough of the nearest tree.

The old man was annoyed. Dirty sweat and pine needles lodged in the furrows that radiated outward from his nose and petered out around his ears. "Ach, Whipple," he grunted.

"He's the skyliner, right?" asked the boy. Still dumb enough to be impressed. By Whipple, of all people.

"Yeah. We say high rigger. He don't need to be up there, but he never comes down less'n it's to eat. He's a wee shart fuck who don't want anyone to see how small he is down on the ground. He ain't died yet so I don't give a shit if he sleeps up there."

Whooping, bellowing, the Toms hoisted their axes in triumph.

Another man yelled, "Picture!"

The half of the men who didn't stop working at Whipple's signal stopped at this. All the men looked to the foreman. The old man nodded. Most dropped their axes as they swarmed the giant tree, now sporting a slack-jawed grimace across the width of its trunk. The boy hung back, keeping slightly behind the old man.

Whipple, the impressive high rigger, shimmied down a Sitka spruce, landing and kicking up a cloud of dirt, dust, pollen, and sawdust.

The man in charge picked up his camera from the stump where he had stashed it. The boy leaned in to admire it.

"That an Ensign?"

"Kodak."

"I had a similar one in San Francisco. Sold it to get up here."

The old man nodded. He knew all about sacrificing what you love to bet on your future. Everyone here had a similar story. Jettisoning whole lives to come to the middle of nowhere to do the most dangerous job in America. No one joins a logging crew if they already have the life they want.

"If you want, I can take the photo. So you can be in the picture too," the boy offered.

"No, s'all right. You get in the pitcher."

"It wouldn't be right, sir. I've only been here a few hours. This is your all's tree. I can be in the next one."

His smile was so earnest and optimistic that again the old man had to stifle the urge to hit him. Instead, he responded using the road much less taken: He smiled back. Eyes only.

The crew clambered up the springboards into the gaping mouth of the death-row redwood. The dozen and a half men stood in the mouth, as big as any whale's, as alive as any whale's. They smiled big whale smiles. The old man leaned against the tree below them, squinting even in the low light, which the boy accounted for as he adjusted the lens.

Even with this huge wedge removed, the tree breathed; nutrients, water, messages of warning rising and falling in its organs. Trees hundreds of miles away knew her to be screaming while a handful of organisms one half-millionth their weight stood smiling in her wound. With just a scant touch more gravity, she could crush them in that mouth. She could bite down on those industrious men who would kill and sell her body. They shuffled around in it. Pushing each other. Arguing about who gets to hold which axe. Should anyone be holding axes? Can the chainsaw be in the picture? But she was unable to bite down.

They were good at their job, killing her. The only thing left to do is fall. And even that's not her choice. They knew exactly how to cut so she would fall down exactly where they wanted her to. They'd set down a bed of smaller trees to cushion her landing. So she'll fall. When they're ready for her. After the picture.

THE BUCKERS

The boy snapped the photo, and the men climbed down to get ready.

When the boy handed him back his camera, the old man snatched it, fearful for his treasure. He wrapped his buffalo plaid jacket around it and returned it to his vault stump. More metallic thwanging rang out from the cables above him. He didn't even look up, but in his spiteful ignoring of the gymnast, he noticed Whipple still climbing up a nearby hemlock. *Taking his sweet time too. Must be wind in the cables. A bad omen. We'll have more'n a few logs falling off the haulback lines today if that keeps up.* As it is, a tree takes an hour to reach the lumberyard, bouncing down the mountain like a shit ski lift.

The bed was set. The cut was done. The men took up ropes and chains hooked into the giant *sempervirens*. A hundred years ago, these same men's great-grandfathers would have sailed from New Bedford, Nantucket, and Providence. They had used the same motions to cull the Atlantic's humpback whales. The tree groaned its own cetacean song. The men grunted in reply; heave, ho.

They pulled over and over, feeling more give each time. The old man heard that up in British Columbia, they were using tractors to do this work now. Wouldn't need all these men in that case. Pity. Every time man builds an industry, another industry comes in to take man out of the equation. Or the industry reaps until there's nothing left. He'd never seen a humpback, even back in New England.

The telltale CRACK. The men released their chains and took cover behind trees, bushes, each other.

One would think a tree falling in the woods would start to feel anticlimactic after a while. Despite ten years at this job, the old man's spine still tingled watching a hundred tons of thousand-year-old wood as it sailed noiselessly through the pollen-dense air.

He didn't even hear the Toms yell, "TIMBER!"

The felled redwood smashed to the ground, turning the bed of thick logs into matchsticks. Splinters the size of drumsticks rode a cloud of sawdust outward.

The impact was tectonic. His wife and daughter said they never heard or felt the trees falling. He wondered how. How can something so colossal just not even register only ten miles away? He wondered if one day he might fell the wrong tree and crack the Earth in half.

There were only a couple injuries from the fall. All minor. Men who weren't good at shielding themselves always caught a little shrapnel. It was what he deserved for being too old for the war; one way or another, he was going to have to watch young men get hurt and die. He'd only lost one kid this season, though, hence the gawking greenie next to him.

"I knew it was a big tree but . . . wow," the kid rightly stammered.

The old man inspected the log. No breakage along the whole two hundred feet. Good. He never got sick of this. He imagined himself a modern-day David gloating over the hulking corpse of Goliath.

"Grab your saws!" he called.

Jonesy used an axe and white paint to mark the tree into forty-foot lengths. The buckers carefully produced two-man saws fresh from the filing shop.

The old man clapped the boy on the shoulder and warned, "B'careful with these. Too long a look at the saw teeth can draw blood. And keep your wits about you. Fallin' this tree probably loosened some of the other branches above us. Falling branches killed more'n tree trunks ever did."

The old man pointed above them, to the trees he deemed caution-worthy, and the boy was nearly blinded by the newly created hole of sky in the canopy. Its nakedness struck him as obscene. The boy quickly abandoned the thought for the spectacle in front of him. Regarding the bed of shattered logs, he found it funny that the things he previously thought of as "logs" didn't even survive what he now knew as logging. It's all so much bigger.

He and the old man began their sawing. From what his roommate told him, they'd be at this for hours.

THE CHOKER SETTERS

Three hours later, the foreman showed the boy how to set the medieval-looking spiked choker around the now-manageably sized tree trunk. The boy's hand fit in one of the smaller furrows in the furry red bark. They hammered in the spikes with the side of an axe. The tree would fall, many times, on her way down the mountain. But the choker, its spikes, and its torso-length chain links would make it easier to pick her up again.

They strung her up, pulling her down the haulback lines that Whipple saw to. The cables led down the mountain. The trees were half dragged, half hoisted, bobbing along like clumsy ghosts, floating in ugly parabolas before touching down on the ground, scraping at the soil before bouncing back up again.

Before setting to work on the next section, the crew crowded around a tin water tank with an open top, letting water spill down their faces until their beards and mustaches dripped with wet sawdust.

The boy took off his gloves to pour water on his hands. The skin was mangled and bloody.

The men on the logging crew smirked at each other, knowing from experience that pouring water on a first morning's blisters would only make the afternoon's more hellish. They all went through it so there was no reason to warn the skinny kid with the big eyes and wispy mustache. There'll be a new greenie soon enough and then he'll be one of them. Probably even before he'd broken in his spiked boots.

No time for that now. "Get your gloves back on. We got a long day." The old man strode back toward the log.

"We've already had a long day," the kid jibed.

Since the kid couldn't see his face, the old man smiled.

The boy at least had enough sense to wipe his hands on the inside of his shirt until they were completely dry before putting his gloves back on, flustered, stumbling after the foreman. Still getting used to boots with inch-long spikes on the bottom.

Nearly back at the log, the old man softened a bit and decided to throw the kid a bone. "It gets harder, you know."

"What's that, sir?"

Christ, this fuckin' kid. I said what I said. No, he's just a stupid kid. He don't know nothin'. "The skin. On your hands. It gets harder and don't bleed as much. Over time."

The boy smiled. "Oh. Thanks. I never—"

The boy disappeared.

The old man looked around, but his vision was all red for four good blinks until he could take in the scene before him.

The boy's body lay crushed by a branch the size of a couch.

His blood had splashed onto the beard and clothes of the foreman, who just stood there. Shell-shocked.

All around him, more gunshots cracking. More branches plummeted from the trees. The old man looked around for cover, trying to find somewhere safe. Another man—one of the younger buckers—pushed him to the ground and immediately got impaled through his back. The bucker fell to the ground, slightly elevated by the leg-sized branch in his chest. More men fell around them.

The old man stayed on the ground and thought about his daughter and her chicks. The tears streaming down her face after he accidentally crushed one with his caulk boot. *I'm sorry, Alice.*

Sounds came from above him. A hoarse barking like the coughing yelp of a deer. He lifted his head to locate the sound and saw another branch falling at him. He scuttled across the ground toward his vault stump, kicking up pine needles. In his periphery, a figure descended a trunk, but when he looked to follow the movement, there was nothing. Just a redwood.

It was at the stump that the old man realized everyone else was dead.

The branches kept falling like gunfire, then suddenly stopped.

The old man's ringing ears drowned out the eerie silence of the redwood forest until more sounds emerged.

From the quiet came another deer-cough. Answered by another, deeper bark near another tree. Jesus Christ. From behind the stump, the man could barely make out a figure moving through the trees. Then another. Their skin was hairless, moist, and covered in rusty leopard spots that camouflaged them perfectly in the tree trunks. Their bodies were too alien to be human. Eyes too black, arms too big, legs bending at the wrong angles. Monsters. They climbed the trees even more gracefully than Whipple.

Paralyzed by fear, the old man ducked back behind the stump until the cough-barks faded into the distance. He closed his eyes so tightly his head hurt, and he felt he might go blind. But blindness was better than seeing those hairless, coughing things again.

Behind him, a twig snapped. They were back. Instead of adrenaline, the man's veins flooded with the absolute certainty that he would die in the forest on this day. *I'm sorry, Alice. I'm sorry, God.* In his final moments, he realized his daughter would be the one to tell the future generations what he was like. He hoped she would be kind. That she knew how much he loved her and wanted her to have a good life.

Another snapped twig. Closer this time. Maybe six feet away. The old man, resolute in his fate, didn't even bother to turn around.

"Boss."

"Whipple? What the fuck?"

Whipple warily approached the old man, who hugged his legs, happy to see him for the first time ever.

"We gotta get you out of here," Whipple whispered to the foreman, pulling him up.

Huddled together, Whipple and the old man stepped gently through the gully toward the road where the foreman's truck was hopefully uncrushed and serviceable. They passed monstrous burled stumps whose woody protrusions reminded the old man of the cancer that had killed his father, warping his skull until he couldn't breathe. The burls' brown marbling reminded him of those . . . creatures. The barkers.

"What were those things?" the foreman asked, whining more than he cared to but too terrorized to care.

The look Whipple gave him said it was more whining than Whipple cared for too. They let the forest sounds fill the awkwardness as they shuffled through more leaves than the old man had ever noticed were in these woods.

At an escarpment overgrown with tree roots, the younger man roughly pushed the elder through the roots into a makeshift cave. The old man tried to escape the root cave, hoping his truck was nearby, but Whipple grabbed him when a scream echoed off the stone walls of the gully.

"Stay in here," Whipple warned gravely. "Do not leave."

"Where are you going?"

"For whoever that was." Whipple flashed an apologetic smile before darting back into the trees, immediately disappearing into the heavy brush.

Beneath the roots, the old man started to wilt. Wooziness overcame him as all the strength he had left oozed from his body like maple sap from a still. He leaned against the cave's back wall, cushioned by the soft soil, finally able to rest. The boy, the Toms, Jonesy . . . Every man he had talked to today was now dead. While cradling his head, he noticed that his hands had taken on a pale, mottled look in the cave light. *What is happening out there?* he wondered. He strained to listen. To pick up a noise—any noise—in the silence.

He didn't know if he heard or imagined the hacking deer-cough from off in the woods, jarring, like a kick to the face. Either way, he was terrified. He pressed harder against the back wall, praying he could stay hidden by the roots.

Ninety-nine years ago, a tree fell in the woods. As its wood decayed, successive waves of moss, mycelium, and other plants grew on it. Its roots grew for a few decades longer, reaching across the forest floor and falling over a small escarpment, forming a cave. More plants grew on the nurse log, thriving from the dead tree's nutrients: a line of Douglas fir saplings, twenty kinds of mycorrhizae, and by 1951, magenta tree mallows were in bloom.

The mallow didn't belong here, of course. But in 1931, this particular plant's great-grandparent rode up from San Luis Obispo, pinned to a hat. The car took one of the looping turns of the Redwood Highway too quickly. The hat flew off and fell down a gully onto this very nurse log. The weather had only gotten better in the past twenty years, becoming more like Southern California every day. That pretty flower's descendants lived and died on the nurse log, and now they fed *Vanessa annabella*, the West Coast painted lady, a butterfly with nothing but beautiful names. After eating its fill of tree mallow leaves, a *V. annabella* caterpillar—at this point not a lady but still painted with white and ochre impasto speckles—went on a walk.

While the trees slaughtered the loggers, the caterpillar sauntered down the tree mallow's vines toward the roots, each section of its spined body tensing and releasing. Unhurried, its forked hairs swayed to and fro. It was on these roots when Whipple thrust his supervisor into the cave and knocked the caterpillar to the ground.

On the ground, the fuzzy gray protagonist had nowhere to go but up. The nearest and most graspable surface in the cave was the old man's denim cuff. Luckily, the caterpillar evaded the steel spikes lining the bottom of the foreman's caulk boots.

The man's terrified shaking was natural to the caterpillar. She'd been shaken worse by stronger winds than this and had hung onto smaller targets than this. She inched up, spines tingling as she perceived the change in altitude. Higher. Higher. She reached something like the tattered bark fibers of her home *sempervirens*. The man's beard. Using every foot, she climbed from hair strand to strand over chunks of dirt, sawdust, pollen, blood. Suddenly, there was an opening.

When the caterpillar crawled into his ear, the old man jumped so high he banged his head. He could feel and hear the caterpillar's rough body entering his own. He shrieked and scrabbled, falling to the ground as he batted fruitlessly at his ear. Blind and afraid in the cave's darkness, he kicked against the ground until he was out in the open, bawling and pawing at his head.

The caterpillar, shaken free by the man's hysterics, landed hard on a pine twig. Unbothered, she continued her climb upward. She'd been through worse than this in her short life.

When the old man stopped shaking, his body was tense all over. Of everything that'd happened that morning, this was the thing that made him cry. This made him lose his calm so completely that he jumped out in the open where smooth-skinned freaks of nature would surely hear him and kill him. This. He wasn't even surprised when he heard the crunch of leaves behind him. He'd done this to himself, worrying more about a caterpillar in his beard than his own life, 'pparently. Such stupidity deserved death. He hoped it'd be fast.

"I told you to stay in the cave." Whipple again.

Laughing, the old man flopped onto his back. Always looking up at the high rigger. May as well let him feel like a big man now, standing over a silly old man crying over bugs. The men always talked poorly about Whipple—the almost-midget with the Negro wife hidden away somewhere. But from down here, the man may as well be king of the forest.

The king looked displeased. "Now you've done it."

"Done what, Whipple?" The old man was still giggling incredulously as he lumbered up to his feet and shook out his adrenaline-soaked limbs. *Saved twice in a day by fuckin' Whipple who—now that we're both standing—isn't that short. Shorter'n average for sure, but a far shot from the little men of the Wizard of Oz.*

Whipple's eyes widened as he looked up at the old man. No, past him.

Above them, that metallic cable noise sounded again.

Whipple grimaced.

The old man turned to follow the skyliner's gaze and barely saw more than teeth as one of the hairless creatures with the speckled amber skin crushed his skull with a wet crunch.

THE SKYLINER

Whipple uncovered his eyes. Next to him on the ground lay the old man's corpse. Strips of skin and beard were all that was left of his head. He should've stayed in the cave. Might've been better. Whipple fished the man's keys from his pocket, then scooped handfuls of leaves and dirt and pine needles over the man's body. The mound squirmed with bugs, already there to feast.

"Mmmm!"

Whipple heard the whimper not too far from the foreman's final resting place. He stood to locate the sound. It sounded close, but sounds and distances could distort in these woods; it could be coming from anywhere within three hundred yards.

A flash of a white hand in his periphery alerted Whipple to this new man's location at the lip of the gully. The skyliner hopped up toward him, deerlike, until he stood over one of the hotshot fallers. Tom, maybe?

"Whuhh," Tom croaked. His legs were crushed. His face was swollen. His lower lip was missing. His strong arms were streaked with blood, forming a forked river around his hatchet tattoo.

Whipple nodded down to him, and Tom exhaled blood bubbles of relief. Whipple grabbed the man's arms and yanked. The big man yelped like a hurt game animal as his arms nearly dislocated from his shoulder sockets.

Tears streamed down his face. He babbled, pleading incoherently with Whipple, who continued to drag him down the gully to the root cave.

Denuded of other men, the forest was dead silent but for Whipple's grunting and Tom's moans. Whipple pulled Tom past the old man's burial mound, which had become barely a heap. Its height was half what it was before, the human body quickly reduced to rich, black loam. The speed with which it happened would be unnatural outside of these woods.

At the cave, Whipple pulled the faller between the roots. He pushed the man up against the soil wall and left him there.

Whipple was already a few hundred yards away, picking up the old man's camera, when the screaming started. In no time, Whipple was in the old man's truck, throwing the shattered Kodak into the passenger seat.

Tom's life leached out until his skin took on the same reddish mottle of the other forest wraiths. The faint blue outline of his tattoo remained on a thickening forearm that quickly lost its other human qualities.

Whipple drove his dead boss's truck down the logging road. Through the window, he heard Tom's screaming go hoarse as his life drained, his yells rasping into a hard coughing bark.

At the end of the logging road, the skyliner didn't turn toward town. He went farther into the forest, heading home to his wife. He loved her and these woods with his whole heart.

PART 1

THE WORLD

1 JASMINE

IN OAKLAND, CALIFORNIA, CONTAINER ships gently carved the Bay's choppy waters. Cormorants perched on the remains of the old eastern span of the Bay Bridge, silhouetted against a morning sky reddened by wildfires up in Sonoma County. Behind it, the new Bay Bridge's modern white buttresses reminded commuting transplants of their bridges back home in Boston, Dallas, St. Louis, Croatia. Even though it was built to be more seismically sound than the old trestle bridge, people said this new bridge wouldn't survive the Big One. But neither would anything else. That's what made it "the Big One."

A ship slid through the entrance channel and approached the peninsula of westernmost Oakland, a crooked finger that pointed at San Francisco as if to say, "I didn't do anything, blame *him*," in accusation against its richer, colder, hillier big brother. San Francisco already claimed an outsized share of the blame for the insufferableness of the Bay Area. Humble Oakland saw itself as a more genuine version of that city—it even called itself "the Town"—full of culture and community and history. There was plenty of all of it in both cities. Oakland just had poorer people who still cared about shit like that, people who cared to make it themselves instead of just consuming it. But not for much longer.

Everything was disappearing everywhere. Nowhere in the world was safe from civilization's devastating Shermanian march toward . . . whatever it was they were destroying the world for. In Oakland, it was obvious that the end goal was not progress. There weren't even any of its namesake oak trees left. BART trains hummed through the tunnel under the Bay, which separated the Port of Oakland from a walled-in patch of buildings surrounded by homeless encampments. In the middle of those buildings was a large green lot, and in the middle of that lot was the H.

The Hewes Hutton Hospital—known to its staff and patients as "the H"—was one of the last large mental health facilities left unmolested by Governor Reagan's budget cuts. Besides the gothic flourishes filigreeing the facade, the compound was all sane right angles. A checkerboard of identical courtyards was latticed by an arcade of walkways of yellow, eroding sandstone. During the day, groups of patients gathered in the interior courtyards to smoke cigarettes, mill around, shake, and yell.

Outside the building, around dawn, the psychiatric staff gathered to smoke cigarettes, mill around, shake, and yell.

Jasmine Bay didn't smoke. She was the only nurse who didn't. Instead, she crouched between a hedge and a window, leaning against a bust of the big man himself, Hewes Hutton. *This Teddy Roosevelt–looking motherfucker*, squinting in bronze above her, was one of the robber barons who flocked to California throughout the 1800s to make their fortunes. Ruthless, then moneyed, these were men whose mausoleums commanded the best views from Mountain View Cemetery.

The hospital budget came from a trust he had set up for the care of an older wife, shut away to make room for a younger one. At the time, it was said the older wife suffered from "hysteria," which was the name psychiatry painted over the effects of her husband's abuse. His single-minded pursuit of wealth-by-exploitation had presented itself in every aspect of his life. Hutton had insisted on naming the place after himself so his other businesses would benefit from the name recognition in the event that any money-rich, sanity-poor blue bloods found themselves at the H's portico. He certainly wouldn't be caught dead near the place. The first Mrs. Hutton had been one of the hospital's earliest patients but, like so many others, had not lasted long. The money did, though. So the hospital did too. Anyone who knew the history just called it the H.

The H had been a marvel in its heyday, but diminished budgets and institutional inertia left it looking like most of Oakland's grand, old buildings: a graying reminder of the ways the greed of the very few lays waste to a landscape over and over. The exterior had cracked noticeably. Inside, peeling linoleum was more common than not. Dirt pooled in the corners of every room. They didn't do internal medicine at the H so there was no need for sterility, but the grime on the place was insidious.

Jasmine slipped down the granite plinth that probably cost a year of her salary. Her knees shook. She stood up, briefly, to crack her joints and make sure no one was looking at her, scanning around while smoothing her hair down. Before resettling, she noticed that a corner of the statue was crumbling at the bottom. Jasmine knew better than to lean her full weight on that. If she knocked it over, even a little bit, she'd be villainized. Or worse, have to pay for its repair. She moved over to balance against a thin tree.

If there was still money from the Hutton millions, it wasn't going toward maintenance. Or the statues or the institution they represented. No one bothered to teach anyone how to do their jobs, so most tasks went undone. There were two hard-and-fast rules at the H: (1) Don't let a patient get the upper hand on you, and (2) Know which website to use to report your hours.

Jasmine leaned back, forearms on her knees, texting, careful not to let her pristine scrubs touch the ground. Twenty feet away, her coworkers smoked and laughed. She made sure to stay clear of their eyeline.

It wasn't that she didn't like her job or the other nurses, but a decade in the field had taught her that the best way to protect her paycheck was to keep her head down and do her job. No matter how much she'd tried to get along with people, go the extra mile, be congenial, go out for after-work drinks, she still felt separate from them. After a while, she had stopped trying.

She tapped out a text to her best friend:

> Two more hours of this longass shift then im on the road. cya at the wake.

She wasn't completely alone in the world, but it felt like it often enough. The other nurses made her feel inadequate, even as she pretended to be her best self. And right now, her best self was a frizzy, flat-ironed bob and overgrown eyebrows. On someone less tired it would be called natural beauty. But Jasmine barely had it in her to wake up and come to work every day, and just enough left over to make it home and have exactly two ice-cold beers while watching TV before passing out in bed.

The H was a decent enough gig. Or at least hellish in different enough ways than the ways she'd promised herself she'd no longer put up with.

Jasmine's phone buzzed in her hands. The avatar showed a young Native girl in a trucker hat sucking on a joint and flipping a bony middle finger.

> **Tilly Blackman**
> Be safe.
> It's a long drive.
> I don't wanna bury you next.
> :-P

Jasmine smiled, then:

> How's the funeral?
> Fun?
> -ereal?

How's the funeral? Banging her head back against the tree, Jasmine exhaled. "What the fuck is wrong with you?" *Why are you making jokes right now? Fucking kill yourself, idiot.* With one hand, she smoothed her hair against her neck in frustration.

Tilly replied:

> Funerals can suck my dick.
> Hurry up and get up here.
> Your aunt's friends are being weird.

Jasmine smiled, then—

"Are you taking a shit back there?" Carlos, a Filipino nurse with beauty-influencer eyebrows, looked down at Jasmine from the walkway. He sneered at her like he couldn't wait to tell Sarita about this.

"Goddammit. No!" Jasmine shot up to stand and huffed. "I'm not."

"Okay, whatever." The smugness hugged his honey voice, a little high-and-mighty, Jasmine felt, for someone who'd tried out for *American Idol* seven times and never even got on TV.

But by the time she was able to think of a comeback, he'd already walked inside, laughing with his friends. Her ulcer thumped inside her. She guessed it was an ulcer. Some kind of abdominal pain that she didn't have the bandwidth to deal with. Jasmine didn't want to imagine herself on the other side of the medical staff/patient divide. The doctors were disrespectful to her now, but at least she wasn't a patient.

And the ulcer only really bothered her when she was stressed. Or had been working a lot. Or on the BART a lot.

Jasmine imagined it growing and growing until one day it exploded all over the other people on the train, painting the inside of the car red. Then she'd be gone and wouldn't have to worry about it anymore. About any of it. And it wouldn't be her fault because it was an accident. *No one could be mad at me anymore because I'd just . . . be gone.*

Two more hours until her shift was over. After checking in on her favorite long-term patient, Jasmine smoothed her hair and opened the door to the room to extend Fifty-One-Victor's sedation by another four hours. The drugs were a temporary fix, but the man couldn't be trusted with consciousness until he could go two seconds without trying to kill himself.

Victor's legs bracketed the door, still and silent.

Shit! Jasmine quietly backed out of the room to find some help. The intestinal hallways went on forever, like a labyrinth. Her mind had to work hard to shut down the part of her that was sympathetic and a little jealous. *He doesn't have to deal with any of this anymore.*

Two orderlies, Henry and Toussaint, followed her back into the room wheeling a gurney. Together the three of them cut down Victor's body from the pipe visible through the drop ceiling. The H's management knew the pipes were a suicide hazard but never did anything about it.

When the body was safely on the gurney, Jasmine cleaned up the puddle of urine below where Victor had hung. Luckily his bowels hadn't emptied. She was a good nurse and took her job seriously, but shit was still disgusting. Her skin crawled imagining the leavings-behind of past people who had died by suicide.

"Thank you," Jasmine whispered to the two men.

"Anytime, Nurse Bay." Henry winked at her, which sent a shiver down Jasmine's spine, bouncing over her bones like a wrought iron antique doorbell she'd seen once and ringing a little bell at the base of her tailbone. Memories of his soft hands and strong fingers seized her.

Jasmine blushed and followed him out. Still smiling, walking into the hallway, she ran into Freddie, Victor's roommate.

Freddie looked over Jasmine's shoulder at Henry and Toussaint disappearing down the hall, their backs obscuring the contents of the gurney. The patient had always reminded Jasmine of Big Freedia, except for Freddie's androgynous twang. "What's going on? Why are you in my room?" they asked, wringing their hands over their dingy sweats. "Where's Victor?"

Jasmine winced. She might've been inured to the chosen deaths of her patients but informing the people they left behind never got easier. She hadn't even known the two were close. Victor had been sedated since he got here. "I'm sorry, Freddie. He's gone."

Freddie's eyes filled with tears, a wall half an inch thick. They kept staring into her eyes, even as the tears rolled down their cheeks.

Jasmine was unsettled by the eye contact, but remembered rule number one and didn't back down.

Then Freddie spoke. "This place is trying to kill us all."

Suddenly, Jasmine felt hot tears trying to needle their way into her own eyes. The truth bubbled up from the knot in her guts, to her lungs, her throat, her mouth. "I know."

Freddie nodded, finally feeling heard. "I knew it. I'm not crazy. Victor let the world get to him, but I'm not letting it get to me."

"Sometimes going crazy is the appropriate reaction to un-sane circumstances." Jasmine shrugged. "This world is sick, and you're not sick enough to fit in with it."

"You are," Freddie countered and shuffled away.

Jasmine watched them walk away from her, and in that moment, she wanted nothing more than to die. Did she want to die because she was too much a part of this world? Or too apart from it? The why didn't matter. Imagining herself gone, that brought relief.

As they entered the community room down the hall, Jasmine heard Freddie yell, "Nurse Bay confirmed it. They're trying to kill us all and that ashy bitch is part of it!"

Ten minutes later, Jasmine was filling out an incident report for Victor at the nurses' station.

"Orderly?" A male voice cleared his throat just out of eyeshot.

Jasmine looked around her. Oh. He meant her. She dropped her head toward the big RMN letters on her lanyard and sighed. *And now I have to deal with this guy. Fucking kill me.* Jasmine swallowed an eye roll as she turned toward Dr. Williams, an old white man who considered himself God's gift to medicine. He'd gone to Yale. Or the Yale of the Midwest. Something.

"Can I help you, Doctor?"

"Actually, I think I can help you. I observed what occurred there in the hallway, and I sincerely believe you'd find the patients easier to deal with if you weren't so aggressive with them." Dr. Williams tilted his head toward Jasmine in a parody of concern. "Orderly, here's what you need to do."

Off to a pretty normal start already. He was always imparting asinine advice by framing it as a command. She'd reminded the doctor many times that she was a registered nurse. She surreptitiously flipped her ID lanyard over to display the big blue letters that declared her a full-ass nurse.

Jasmine blinked. "I'm sorry, sir—"

"Doctor."

"Doctor . . . I think you might not have seen the whole interaction."

He leaned in conspiratorially, looming over her. "I didn't need to. As a black woman, you have to be more mindful about how your actions appear to others." He winked.

"Dr. Williams, I've been in mental health care for over twenty years. My mom—I'm just here to help take care of people and help them get well."

"That's what doctors are for. Your job is to provide a welcoming atmosphere and keep things cheerful so we can do the real work."

"Okay." Jasmine pressed her back against the nurses' station, trying to escape. "So . . . Are we good here?"

"No," he said, voice clipped. "You cannot tell patients that they're not crazy. If they're in a psych ward, it is because they belong here. Unless their insurance runs out." He laughed way too loudly and patted her on the hip before walking away.

Jasmine stood there for a moment, stiff with shock at the audacity of the man. She wanted to call after him, tell him to chug a hundred dicks, but she pushed it down, coiling up the fiery threads of her indignation like a garden hose and hanging them in the spot under her rib cage where they were slowly metastasizing into a stress ulcer.

She smoothed down her hair and power walked to the next room on her list.

2 FUNERAL

Jas (duh)
How's the funeral?
Fun?
-ereal?

Tilly Blackman peeked at her phone in her dress pocket, hidden by the curve of an early pregnancy bump. Leaning on her husband, she tapped out a response. Her low heels dug into the brown grass, and she leaned further into her sobbing husband. James's shoulders jerked next to her. Tilly dropped her phone back into her pocket and slid her hand up under his jacket to rub his back. Her husband was normally quiet with everyone but her, but Gin's death was making everybody act differently.

The . . . minister (or priest? Something?) droned on about the body's return to the forest. Tilly wasn't really listening. Instead, she was shooting daggers across the burial mound at a quartet of equally sour-faced old women.

The Witches would be the type to judge a man for crying at his own godmother's funeral. Like, how dare he mourn? Those Witches probably see it as an admission of Gin being gone gone, rather than being all around us in the trees or some shit.

Tilly wanted nothing more than to forget the time they had spent caring for Aunt Gin. A woman whose dementia had gnarled her into a sneering bully who'd focused her sights on the one person she could still control and hurt: her dutiful godson.

Aunt Gin had always reminded James of how "lower'n shit" she found him as an entity, and by becoming an "ain't-shit lumberjack," he'd further debased himself. As fellow drinkers of the Mother Earth Kool-Aid, the Witches had sung backup for Gin's lamentations during their frequent visits. They were the ones who'd planned this . . . event. A standing funeral. Bitches.

The Witches were Nancy Hsu, Charlyne Blackman, Victoria Mooney, and Ellen Zeller. Most of them grew up together in Humboldt County and had worked at the high school at some point. The women had been Gin's best friends, forming a community within a community in Redcedar, an island in the sea of overwhelming whiteness. A nice idea, even if it was centered around their weird hippie church. They were constantly in Tilly and James's house, eating all their snacks and generally oppressing the two of them with their version of "being helpful."

Nancy Hsu's family had been in the area since the building of the railroad, starting out as loggers, then later owning small businesses in town. They were driven out, then came back and opened even more businesses. Mrs. Hsu and her people were on the tail end of a generation-spanning feud with her great-uncle's family, the Xus. They did business together but still talked relentless shit about each other. Tilly couldn't imagine not talking to members of her own family. Didn't have to imagine it, with James and Jas.

Mrs. Hsu taught history and never failed to mention the many contributions of the Chinese people to the economic growth of the region. Neither she (nor any of the history books) mentioned how all that economic growth had tried to wipe out the Wiyot tribe and their centuries of flourishing culture. *But sure, there was nothing here before the railroad.* Mrs. Hsu had brought over tray after tray of food for her sick friend, but each item required very specific preparation, and the woman never took any of the hotel pans back. Even stacked under the dining room table, James was constantly tripping on them, clanging metal and wincing "shit"s echoing through the small house. Tilly planned to drop them off on Mrs. Hsu's doorstep later in the week, after things settled down.

Charlyne Blackman owned the Skyliner, the only bar in Redcedar, which made her the unofficial queen of the town. She was also Tilly's auntie, whose giant, red-shellacked brontosaurus lips dominated Tilly's childhood memories of the woman. While Charlyne's proportions varied wildly across Tilly's memories of her—between her yo-yo dieting and boob job—her pink beehive always stayed the same size. Charlyne's son, Buck, hulked behind her but looked genuinely scared of James's tears. *Macho asshole*, Tilly thought at him. Charlyne taught electives in shop and home ec. For someone who owned a bar, one would think that Charlyne would get enough booze at work and wouldn't need to drink the last of whatever James kept in the fridge. But at least she had closed the door when she sat with Gin to chat, giving Tilly the illusion of an afternoon of peace and quiet during her visits.

Ellen Zeller was newest to the group and taught English. The last of the "real" hippies, in that she stank of patchouli oil and that she abandoned her husband and kids in the '90s to grow weed and worship Mother Earth at the forest church with Gin and them every Sunday. She was the one who'd booked the minister, who'd gone on about the whales and Gin's special connection with the ocean. Gin had hated the water. Junior varsity–ass freaking priest. Whenever Ellen had brought some disgusting-smelling witchy tchotchke to clutter Gin's room, she had nudged Tilly and asked if she was pregnant yet. Real *Rosemary's Baby* shit. For three years, Tilly hadn't been. Now that she was, Ellen touched her belly without asking every time.

Victoria Mooney was the official queen of the town, a lean and tall former beauty queen, scion of the Mooney family, and, much less importantly, the mayor. Before she was Mayor Miz Mooney, she was just Miz Mooney, the principal of the high school when Tilly and James and Jasmine had been there. Tilly winced at the memory of a staticky loudspeaker blaring Miz Mooney's clipped, condescending "Go Bearcats!" Miz Mooney didn't need to work, but she used her inheritance to never repeat an outfit, spending her time bossing around teenagers. She'd leveled up when she'd realized she could boss around the whole town. *Well, we Wiyots were here long before you, ya stuck up old bitch, and your dried-up family tree. And we're still here.*

It was hard not to hate the Mooneys, who not only had founded the town, but also were compelled to remind everyone of it by putting their name on every building. Some legacy. There were barely any Mooneys left. Victoria certainly wasn't having any kids. Tilly alone knew the truth about her relationship with Aunt Gin. If James suspected, he never mentioned it. Victoria openly criticized Tilly's caretaking, but she had paid for a nurse to come twice a week.

Gin was their black friend who had been the newest to the group before Ellen joined. She was a secretary in the school office for fifty years or something crazy like that. Tilly couldn't remember what the students had thought of her back then.

Most of Tilly's memories of her from before were faded, bleached out by the sharp white pain of the old woman's abuse over the last three years, including more than a few physical altercations between the two women. Tilly rubbed the scars on her forearm from the time Gin drew blood when Tilly tried to administer eye drops.

But now Gin was a pile of dry dirt. According to the box Victoria showed them, Gin would grow into a redwood tree in a few decades. Right now she was the Gin from the big framed print of her last school yearbook photo. She had been a spry and lucid eighty-three-year-old wearing a loud print caftan and giant wooden beads. Then the walls of her mind caved, no longer able to stop the dementia from flooding in. And then she wasn't Gin anymore. Tilly tried to remember that: The woman who'd hurt her and her husband eventually had lost her mind and reverted to something more primal, all wants and demands and taking; it wasn't his godmother anymore. Hopefully she was herself again. Somewhere.

Tilly made a note to remember to tell the baby about the tree. They'd need things to look forward to that took time.

The service ended awkwardly. Buck picked up a shovel to fill in the grave. In the house, there would *not* be refreshments for the guests, but that didn't stop the Witches from trying to follow Tilly and James inside.

Tilly turned to stop them.

Tear-faced, James waited for her on the porch, but she nodded to him that she'd be fine. She could handle these bitches.

"Ladies."

The gaggle of them approached in a tight group like a smoke bomb, no less menacing for their slow, unwieldy creeping.

"Tilly, hello. Did you like the service?" Ellen asked, her eyes hungrily targeting Tilly's pregnant gut.

"Sure. Listen, we're pretty tired and—"

"Jasmine is coming home today, isn't she?" Victoria nailed her in place with a well-quirked eyebrow, just like she had when Tilly was in high school.

Nancy asked, "Do you need help cleaning up for her? She's staying with you, right? In Gin's room?"

"It'll be nice to see your little girlfriend. Reunited at long last," Charlyne gushed.

Tilly bristled at the word choice. *Jasmine is* not *my girlfriend.*

"Are you sure we can't help you?"

Tilly nodded. "We're good. James and I just need to rest a bit before the reception." She didn't know what it was about these women that turned her into a deer in headlights, unable to escape from their blinding attention.

Ellen caressed Tilly's belly and said, "Well, it's never too late."

"Ellen!" Victoria snapped.

"Too late for what?" Tilly asked.

"To join us," Charlyne purred. "In the woods, for forest church. I think you'd like it."

"There's a lot to learn from the forest. It's all about regeneration. Life feeding death feeding life."

Okay... "I'll think about it," Tilly mumbled while thinking, *Over my dead friggin' body.*

The Witches released her, drifting away like smoke.

Gin used to say their house looked like a 19-year-old boy had decorated it: one futon, no lamps, and the only pictures in frames were handed-down family photos. It hurt her to remember Gin, and it hurt her more to try to relax. Aunt Gin had had the two of them in a chokehold of fight-or-flight for so long that she wouldn't admit, even inwardly, how much relief she felt that the woman was gone.

Tilly and James passed out in their funeral clothes on the futon.

James woke first and was at the fridge, putting up his warm, soggy ice pack, when Tilly arose, uncomfortable folds of her dress digging into the backs of her thighs, pressed in by the cheap futon's frame. Crossing the room from the kitchen, James placed a glass of water on the cable spool table and loomed over Tilly, his body silhouetted against the bright sunlight. Tilly smiled back at him, realizing how rested she felt. Between her morning sickness and Gin's night terrors, the couple hadn't gotten a proper night's rest in almost two years.

James said nothing and leaned over Tilly menacingly. She blinked. "What the hell are—?"

He pounced on her and pulled her shirt up. She screamed.

He blew raspberry farts on her stomach while she laugh-screamed and struggled. "Pfft pbbt pbbt. Baby, you have to stop farting. It's bad for the baby!"

Tilly screeched, "You dick! I'm gonna kill you!" She then glanced at the clock: 3 p.m. "But not yet. We gotta go."

James slumped over Tilly's lap and sighed heavily.

She rubbed her eyes. "I can't believe we slept for so long. I feel amazing."

Her husband slid across her softly and mumbled into her legs. "Me too! So why ruin it?"

"I told Jas we'd meet at the bar at four. It's three now so I want to factor in time for you to drag ass and try to get out of going." Got him.

Pushing himself onto his elbows, James blew one more belly fart on her, then stood up. He handed her the glass of water. "It's only three miles down the road, but I gotta stop at the office real quick and pick up some paperwork."

Tilly's eyes narrowed. "Oooh, paperwork?" she mocked. "I'll grab your briefcase, Mr. Bay. Or would you prefer to go with the valise today?"

They both laughed, and he pulled her up off the creaking futon. Tilly smoothed down her black dress, and James pulled on his BIGFOOT LIVES trucker hat. The way he smiled at her lit Tilly up inside, as if their unborn child could feel his love as well. No matter how bad things got, they still had each other. Together, all the annoying little details and injustices didn't hurt as much. She loved him with her whole heart.

3 HENRY

HENRY SAVAGE WAS A regular-shmegular dude from East Oakland, and he liked it that way. He worked at the H because it paid $3 more an hour than working security, and none of these crazy people had guns. He'd played football at Bishop O'Dowd High School, then at Saint Mary's College, but he lost his scholarship when the Gaels dropped their football program in '03. He had survived on work-study and loans for a bit, but when his dad got sick and he needed to work full time, Henry dropped out entirely. And after his dad died, he'd kept working because paycheck to paycheck was hard enough without tuition on top of it.

He wasn't Jasmine's boyfriend, but he wanted to be and hoped that by the end of this trip they would be. Henry tried to be congenial and chill (chill, more than anything—life was hard enough without him causing friction for others) so he didn't dare admit how much he wanted Jasmine, even to himself. But there were flashes of what it could look like. Cooking for Jasmine. Reading in bed next to each other. Kissing his head as she spooned Sunday dinner onto his plate. The way his mom used to with his dad. Wholesome, old-school love.

It wasn't a proper courtship. More of a situation-ship. They were work friends who hung out on occasion. One time she'd kissed him in the supply closet, pulling him in close by the waist and kissing him deep and desperately. Then she had just stopped, smoothed her hair down, and ran out. Despite that—or because of it—Henry harbored an embarrassing, fluttering crush on his coworker. He would probably feel differently after he slept with her, but maybe he wouldn't.

He liked her but liked his job more; he wasn't trying to overstep his way into a harassment complaint. He was flirty but kept things strictly friendly and professional. Unless she wanted more. If she wanted more, she'd let him know. Probably. Toussaint clowned on him about it. His gaming friends were encouraging, but they'd never met him in person so they didn't know what the fuck they were talking about. Dating advice only works for guys over five seven. Or white guys. Both severely not applicable here.

When Jasmine told him her godmother died, Henry had offered her a ride to Humboldt, eighty-five percent sure she'd turn him down. But she had said yes. And now he was driving up the bilious twists of the Redwood Highway, never before connecting this road to the 101 he'd taken to Pacifica or even the one in LA. But the winding road's stomach-churning qualities reminded him that this was all the same 101, the esophagus of California, and his steady climb north into the wooded mountains was nearing the end. Either the mouth or the ass end of the state, depending on how you looked at it.

Jasmine motioned vaguely to the left. "There's a cool tourist thing around this bend up here."

"Okay, then!" Henry drummed his fingers on the steering wheel.

On the other side of the curve, there was nothing but more dark green trees.

"Maybe we passed it? I thought it was around here." Jasmine frowned.

The forever 101 jogged an idea. Henry popped open the glove box and rustled around for a scratched CD. "Caucasity

Jamz" was scrawled across the back with a Sharpie in his sister's looping handwriting. A guilty pleasure. This could cheer up Jas and keep this trip on an even keel before it turned into the shitshow it promised to become once Jas caught up with her brother she didn't get along with.

The sudden movement made Jasmine jerk in her seat, but she clocked the mixtape title and smirked.

He fed it to the CD player and quickly skipped to track four. The opening piano notes of the *OC* song started. He patted Jasmine's knee quickly and pointed to the highway sign when the lyric "Drivin' on the 101" came on. Henry waggled his eyebrows at her suggestively.

"What is this?" Jasmine asked.

"Y'all never watched *The OC*?"

"No."

He smiled. Still worth it. He crooned the chorus at her in his best white-boy punk voice and she laughed. She was so pretty when she laughed. She was funny too, when she wasn't at work. Henry's eyes lingered a split second too long on the way her dark, smiling cheekbones caught the afternoon light. He turned back toward the road and— *SHIT!* "Oh shit!"

Henry barely registered what he saw before he skidded his Prius into the tiny entrance to a parking lot. He pulled up next to the parked car on the side of the road, smashed down the middle by a huge tree trunk. He jumped out of his car, slamming the door. He yelled, "Hello?" while searching for survivors.

Jasmine exited the car and slowly walked up, kicking dry pine needles everywhere.

"Jas, call 911," Henry commanded. "You think anyone was hurt?"

Jasmine shoved her hands in her dress pockets and said, "Nah." She started giggling.

"Why're you laughing?"

"That car has been there forever. It's a tourist trap. This is the thing I wanted to show you." She gestured behind Henry to the far end of the parking lot where a wooden cabin sat between giant redwoods. Nearer the road, a carved sign—its base plastered with flyers—advertised a petting zoo and gift shop. Jas giggled again. "You got trapped. I mean . . ." She pointed to the patch of grass and trees separating the parking lot and the main road.

Big carved-redwood sculptures stood guard. Standing eight feet tall were giant terra-cotta-colored ears and eagles and—

"Is that Shrek?" Henry asked. "What is this place?"

"This is Humboldt." Jasmine shrugged. "It's weird and beautiful and dark 'n shit. This is the *real* Northern California. It's really messing with my head not remembering exactly where everything is, though."

Henry clocked the flyers on the sign again. "Are those all missing people posters?"

Jasmine shrugged again.

"Why so many?"

"Drugs, woods, Bigfoot. People go missing for all sorts of reasons up here. On Mount Shasta, they say there's alien abductions, but that's a ways away so we're probably fine." She grinned at him.

Henry had to hold her, kiss her. This was the Jasmine he fantasized about looking at their phones in bed with. Vibrant and warm and loving. Everything about her was inviting him. He took a step forward.

But a hippie popped out from the other side of the Shrek statue, dirty blond dreads swinging (some with soda can tabs threaded into them). "Hey, new friends. Any chance I can snag a ride up to Arcata? I'm not a psycho or nothin'. Just a humble trimmigrant heading up to trim bud for the harvest season. Could y'all help a brother out?"

Henry and Jasmine exchanged simultaneous, nonverbal NOPEs.

Henry handled it. "Uh, nah." He and Jas scrambled into the car, breathing heavily.

Inside the car, Jasmine looked over her shoulder at the trimmigrant and shuddered. Henry didn't start the car. "Um . . . go?"

"Um . . . seat belt?" Henry replied. He wasn't peeling out of a parking lot until everybody was safe.

Jas scoffed. "You've gotta be fuck— Are you serious?"

"Serious as death. Click it."

In the rearview mirror, they watched the trimmigrant flash a peace sign at them. Dude was creepy but harmless. Jasmine's mouth disappeared from her face like someone had pulled a drain. Henry's grandma used to call that look a "sourpuss." But Henry respected automobile safety. Seat belts were something he took extremely seriously.

When Jasmine's seat belt clicked, Henry turned the ignition, signaled, and got back on the Redwood Highway.

Loitering around the redwood sculptures, the be-dreaded hippie watched the hybrid peel out. The trimmigrant started to hum "California" by Phantom Planet, alternately whistling parts of the song. He moved out of view from the road and took a piss on the Shrek sculpture.

"Hey!" a woman nearby yelled. From the gift shop, an older woman banged a wooden baseball bat against her screen door. "Quit pissin' on my fuckin' Shrek, and get off my fuckin' property!"

He zipped up his pants and bailed. He spotted a break in the greenery across the road from him—hopefully a trail. Thankfully a trail. The forest floor was like intricate tilework, with terra-cotta shards interlocking perfectly, softer than loam, beating along with his every breath. He was a little high.

A hundred feet above him, the redwood tree nearest him housed two gnarled burls. Redwood bark looks like wooly mammoth fur, thick and matted, then stuck back together. It can grow to be a foot thick. It's rich in tannins, low in resin, carbon dense, and sometimes, much like any human cell, can grow abnormally. Rounded, malformed lumps of biomass—in this case, wood grain—protruded from the redwood's trunk. In this case, two did. The marbled wood that made up the burls was a geological, hypnotic mixture of chatoyant ambers and ochres.

The swirling browns appeared to move, and then they did move.

The lump jumped the fine line between botanical and cancerous, expanding and unfolding jerkily into a camouflaged humanoid creature that moved so gracefully across the redwood bark, climbing down with a wild cat's agility and total control. The creature was bigger than a man, with sinewy arms. Its considerable weight barely registered as the monster glided down the bark, the tree, soundlessly.

The redwood's tannin-rich, resin-poor bark didn't register the sound of a single scratch when the creature climbed back up, hauling the head of the trimmigrant, whose fuzzy blond dreads were caught in the creature's talons. The chatty man's vocal cords hung from his bloody neck. The sinews of his neck swung down and scraped the bark, and it made a horrible sound.

The head was pulled up into the bony lap of the monster, which had paused midway up to the canopy and was clinging to the thick bark. It leaned toward the cradled head as if to whisper a secret through its enormous jaws, but instead it compacted its body into a misshapen burl with blood seeping earthward from its bottom.

The wind kicked up, puffing out pillowy clouds of goldenshine pollen. Across the street, back in the parking lot, the wind blew a MISSING flier loose. It skittered across the wood chips and stuck to the cold piss at Shrek's feet. Nearby, the trimmigrant's body was already reduced to loam.

4 THE LUMBERYARD

THE GREEN PICKUP SUMMITED a hill looking over Humboldt County and wove its way down the curling ropes of the Redwood Highway. Inside, James and Tilly sang along to the radio.

When the song ended, both their spirits were lifted. Tilly debated even opening up the conversation and spoiling the good mood, but it was better to take care of now rather than later.

"Hey, I wanna talk to you about something."

"Shoot."

She bit her lip. "I need you to try to be cool to Jasmine tonight. She's only up for the weekend—"

"Me? Cool?" James spat. "She's the reason we couldn't have Aunt Gin's—"

"She had to work! You know we didn't have to have the funeral in the morning. It's our land—"

James turned the wheel to the right. Hard. He turned the truck down a frontage road toward a big factory complex, a sign reading: NORTH COAST TIMBER COMPANY LUMBERYARD.

Tilly's stomach lurched. "Baby, what the f—heck?!" She pushed his shoulder to get his attention.

James shrugged her hand away. "Gotta stop at the office. Remember?"

"You gonna drive angry like that all the way to the bar? Because I'll frickin' walk."

"I'm sorry." James pouted.

Tilly gave him a look. "Damn right you are."

Inside the North Coast Timber Company complex, James's truck crawled past piles upon piles of logs and planed lumber. From out the window, Tilly marveled at a giant building just housing seventy-foot high piles of sawdust. All these years, and she was still astounded by how thorough the decimation of the forest was. There was somehow a market for every part of the tree and then for every kind of waste created to get it.

They parked in front of a small red building labeled OFFICE.

"I just gotta grab this thing real quick," James said.

Tilly didn't respond, pissed.

James stepped out of the truck and clomped up the stairs to the office inside.

The bulletin board outside had the requisite number of OSHA posters and MISSING flyers, as well as a taped-up printout from Google.

https://www.ajc.com > business > employment > these-are-t ...

Most dangerous jobs in America: Logger is No. 1

Mar 5, 2020 — These are the most dangerous jobs in America • Logging workers • Fishers and related fishing workers • Aircraft pilots and flight engineers • Roofers ...

People also search for

most dangerous jobs during covid

most dangerous jobs list

most dangerous jobs 2020

most dangerous jobs in the world 2020

most dangerous jobs australia

most dangerous jobs uk

The use of dark mode for the printout was the least surprising. The forest was so dense in places that the loggers said it was like being in a black-and-white photo. The men came out of the forest squinting and sun sensitive. She was glad that James's job as a truck driver didn't take him into the forest for long; his phone apps were still in light mode.

The lumberjacks took pride in it. It wasn't often they got to be number one at something. And like most Americans, when confronted with hard numbers about the brutality of their lives, they twisted it into a positive testament to their personal ability to survive. No imagination, just what they'd been taught in school, and how they were taught to think it. Tilly was grateful to have elders who taught her the true history of the world. For all her faults, Aunt Charlyne had inspired Tilly to think for herself, so she didn't choke down the North Coast's green-washed bullshit the way the rest of the town did. Or at least, she was smart enough to make money off it.

Another sign near the office building read: GOING GREEN? PICK RED. NORTH COAST TIMBER CO. REDWOOD IS FLEXIBLE, FIRE-RESISTANT, AND SUSTAINABLE.

Tilly rolled her eyes. She was glad James didn't fuck with his coworkers so she wasn't obligated to go to events and share her opinions about *The Bachelor* or attend baby showers or listen to talk about the stresses of being a "logging spouse." Where the loggers took pride in the danger of their job, their partners turned their proximity to that danger into a deranged status symbol.

A group of loggers laughed and headed toward the office. When they passed the truck, one logger Tilly recognized as Ugly Matt made a cunnilingus gesture at Tilly, then cackled. She flipped him off. James stepped out carrying a manila folder, and the men jeered, "Bee Jayyy" before brushing past him into the office. He nodded, straightened his hat, and slinked toward the truck. He tucked the folder into the sun visor and started the truck. He shut off the radio as soon as it started. They drove in silence through the timber complex.

They exited the lumberyard and headed back toward Redcedar. James batted on the steering wheel and silently mouthed something to himself. Clearly there was something he wanted to say so Tilly gave him an opening. "BJ?"

"Black James. Because that's apparently the only difference between me and Fat James."

"Well, they aren't known for their creativity." She nibbled on her lip. "That whole thing before—"

"That was dumb as hell back there," James interrupted.

"I'm just excited to see my friend."

"No," he sighed. "I mean I was dumb as hell. I'm sorry about that. I shouldn't have pulled off the road like that. I'm trying to be better about it."

"I know."

"Sometimes I just need to, like, *record scratch* the moment and pause. Take some time to work out how I feel before I just react at you."

Tilly put a hand on his leg. "The record scratch is still a reaction. At me. And in the truck it's f—dangerous. You could get in an accident. No wonder your back hurts all the time. You can't pull that shi—stuff—like that after the baby comes."

"I'm sorry."

Tilly smiled at him. "You wanna get some of this Jas stuff off your chest? Talk it out now before you all ruin my night?"

James frowned. "I don't want to ruin your night. Really. She just always tries to pick a fight with me."

Tilly turned toward him, giving him her full attention. "And you let her."

"I can't help it! Every time I see her, I feel like a little kid again. It's like she hasn't changed at all. Just starts bossing me around and being all judgy 'n shit." James wrinkled his nose, imitating Jasmine.

"But she has," Tilly replied. "She's changed a lot. You have too."

"I guess. If she has changed, I never see it when she's here."

"You're trying to win an argument started by two kids who don't exist anymore. It's just you two left in your family. She's the only one who has been through exactly what you've been through. You could understand each other better than anyone else in the world, but you're choosing not to. Maybe if you two got your heads outta your a—butts you'd be able to see that."

James nodded, then added, "Do you even like hanging out with her anymore? You said yourself that she's changed. You two used to be really close, and now you're not."

Tilly just smirked, staring ahead at the highway. "We've had a lot of good times though, and that's what I focus on. She makes you feel like a kid? She makes me feel like a kid again too. In a good way. I feel like a little hot-shit teenager smoking Marb Reds and flirting with ain't-shit lumberjacks."

"You never flirted with no lumberjacks."

"No, but I watched your sister do it enough times that it feels like it happened to me. I dunno. It's complicated."

It was complicated. How do you even start to explain your teenage relationship with your best friend without describing your own marriage? How do you explain a decades-spanning friendship—with all its ups and downs—without it sounding super romantic? How do you explain that texting with her feels as good as being with him? *She taught me how to love another person. And I love her. Not the same way as with you. Not as much as I love you, not anymore. But being with her reminds me of how in love with each other we used to be. And in hate. And everything in between. I wouldn't be me without her.*

Jasmine and Tilly had gone from friends to enemies, to best friends, to sisters. The truth was that sometimes Jasmine made Tilly feel seventeen again (during the enemies phase), but they stayed close and had made enough good memories together that Tilly was also able to feel twelve, fourteen, twenty,

twenty-one—and they'd made so many good memories since then. For Tilly, it was simple math. It still hurt sometimes, but less so.

"Well, whatever y'all get up to, just remember that after she leaves, *we* still have to live here. You and all these 'ain't-shit lumberjacks.'" He laughed. "So no bar fights, please."

"I promise nothing," Tilly joked.

For a long minute, the couple stared out at the road and the forest that enveloped everything. Their home. It made Tilly sad to think that Jas could look at this place and not feel at home, or at least part of something bigger than herself. Bigger than the problems she made for herself.

Speaking of which, Tilly noted, *I've gotta make up the air mattress in Gin's room so Jasmine and her situation-ship Henry have somewhere to sleep.* She didn't know why, but she didn't like him already.

"Think she's gonna have sex with Buck again?" James deadpanned.

Tilly scoffed. Buck pined over Jasmine for years until he realized that what happened between them wasn't happening again. It was funny to James because he hadn't had to listen to her cousin questioning his own self-worth over shots at the Skyliner. Rejection was one thing, but Jasmine acted like it hadn't happened. Tilly was caught in the middle, as always.

She leaned in close to James. "I love you."

"I love you too. Oh! I gotta show you this. I'm going to pull over now. Gently."

James's truck rumbled over the shoulder and onto a rocky turnout by a clear-cut. He parked and pulled the folder from the visor.

"Ah, yes. The Paperwork," Tilly teased.

"Guess which ain't-shit lumberjack just became eligible for health insurance?"

"Oh my God! Baby!"

"You, me, and the baby," James cooed, then counted off on his fingers. "Health, dental, vision, term life . . . We got it all, baby." He reached out and enveloped Tilly's face in his hands. She leaned in to kiss him, and he pulled her in for a bigger, deeper kiss, stowing the folder back under the visor and undoing his seat belt in one deft move. Tilly unclicked hers and giggled under him.

HONK!

Their horny reverie was interrupted by the brief, mocking blare of a car horn.

James and Tilly both jumped, and James hit his head on the ceiling. "Ow!"

Their heads popped up to look out the back window where the sound had come from. It was a little car honk, maybe accidental, but still close. A dozen yards behind them, Jasmine's distinct silhouette stormed away from a small car and down into the clear-cut.

"The fuck?" James asked. "Is that Jasmine?"

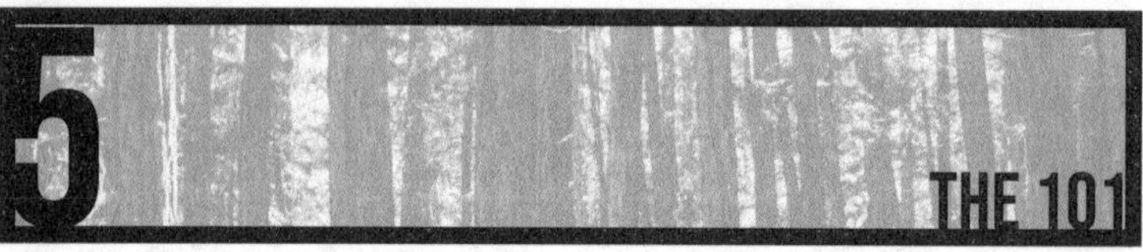

5 THE 101

THE SILVER PRIUS SUMMITED the hill that stared at Humboldt County. After this, they'd be under the redwood canopy.

Jasmine recalled the first time she and Aunt Gin drove into this forest. It was 1995 when the VW Bus summited the hill, rounding into an expansive view of Humboldt County.

Aunt Gin, bedecked in tie-dyed natural fabrics, drove. Jasmine stared out the window. The white pony beads at the end of Jasmine's braids clattered against the glass, tapping rhythms into her ear. James—only five or six back then—slept in the middle row. When the van reached the apogee of the 101, they saw cloud-dappled mountains covering the vista.

"It's beautiful," Jasmine had gasped.

"Sure is. This here is God country."

"I like that," Jasmine replied and whispered to herself, "God country." A prayer for protection.

"I want you to love it, Jasmine. All I want is for everyone to love this forest the way I do. Like your grampdaddy did."

Jasmine had smiled and looked at the trees with new eyes. She belonged there.

Now, thirty years later, Jasmine, wearing her least-cheap black dress, drove while Henry stared into his phone. He hadn't wanted to let her drive but relented after the second pickup truck tailgated them on the winding Redwood Highway.

She loved this place and its green velvet hills that towered prehistorically large in her memory. She looked forward to coming home and looking at the same old place with new eyes. Older, wiser eyes that could maybe appreciate its slow beauty. She wasn't the same girl who'd fled it. She was a woman now. Grown. Maybe a woman who would not flee, who could stay and make a life here. If Redcedar was just the redwoods, she'd move back in a heartbeat, but it was hard to see the forest for the assholes that lived under it.

But those ancient emerald mountains were chipped away in this new reality. Warped diamonds of white-gray stumps dotted the landscape. It had never occurred to her that while she was out becoming grown, her home would change too. The knot under her ribs ached. Maybe she wasn't meant to make a life here, but to take a turn too hard and let the trees tear her from the car, smearing her across the redwoods. She'd be gone. She could die here.

Henry snapped pictures, but the phone screen did the scene no justice, bleaching out shapes and dulling the colors. This re-entry to her home didn't captivate Jasmine the same way. The only thing that took her was how much the place had changed. A betrayal.

They passed the huge North Coast Timber complex: ten football fields of stacked tree trunks and the construction materials they got cut into. Despite a paperless revolution, Humboldt timber was still in demand, though not as much as the people of Redcedar would like. Logging had expanded farther into the forest. Righteous indignation rose like magma in Jasmine's chest, choking her. It wasn't just the lumberyard that was the problem. It was Humboldt. *Who are you to talk?* She winced. *You ran away. What'd you think was going to happen?*

Being back home again always felt like she was sneaking back into her old life, hoping no one had noticed her absence.

If she'd been the one to stay, she'd resent her too. Now she was back with this fucking guy who . . . "That was dumb as hell back there."

Henry checked the side mirror. "Back where?"

"The tourist spot. Waiting 'til I had my seat belt on. I'm not a little kid."

"I know that. Obviously."

"*Obviously.* Then why you actin' like you don't trust me to take care of myself?"

"I—"

"You don't know me well enough to make that kind of call."

Henry put a hand on her leg. Jasmine squirmed out from under him, easing her foot off the gas pedal for a moment. Her stomach lurched.

"I thought that going to a funeral alone wasn't the best idea when you're clearly on some suicidal-ideation shit. Do you have any idea how much you talk about being dead?"

Jasmine's mouth disappeared. Quietly she muttered, "I don't talk about being dead."

"You text me 'kill me' twice a day! Always eye-fucking the third rail on BART. You do know that people can see what you like on social media, right? I see those memes, Jas. I'm worried."

Jasmine clenched the wheel. "I'm not suicidal." *I feel like I'm already dead. I have no connection to the world I live in, my family—like, I may as well just not exist.* "Just fuck off, *please*." The knot in her stomach throbbed, grew.

Henry turned back to the window.

It could've ended there, but it didn't. Henry had to open his mouth. "I get feeling fucked up with all the shit we deal with at work. But you're doing a lot better than most people. Try to have a little gratitude."

Jasmine scoffed. "Gratitude for what? I want more than just the bare minimum. That's not wrong to want."

"Well—"

"Fucking *what*? I should be grateful? To live here? In a world like *this*? That punishes me for fucking existing and rewards everyone else for playing at being a black woman?"

Jasmine considered stopping here. Nah, fuck it.

"I have to watch the corpses of murdered women who look just like me turned into memes." *I have to watch women like me—like my mother—die over and over again.* "Watch 'em make money for other people. It's twisted. But I should be fucking grateful . . . to live? And get to experience all that?"

Henry scoffed. "Well, it's no reason to just give up."

"Who's giving up? I'm still here."

"You're still here."

Jasmine took a long second to consider that. She *was* still here. Out in the world. Not like her mom at all. But Jas was alone. The only person in the world who understood her had been as good as dead to her, inaccessible for years, and now she really was dead. Jasmine knew she could've seen her godmother, could've stayed in touch, but that would've jeopardized the good memories she had of Aunt Gin. And with Aunt Gin gone, the only family she had left—well, he hated Jasmine for leaving him too. *Everything in my life is telling me that this world hates me and I'll never belong in it. I don't feel at home here, and it's never, ever going to change. There's nothing for me.* But she couldn't deny that she was still here. *Somehow.*

"Ugh, I guess," Jasmine muttered. Admitting the unwelcome truth of her own continued existence felt like choking. She was swallowing down all the harshness of a world she wasn't sure she even wanted to be part of. As if her continued participation in this horrifying, undignified, dehumanizing world was because that's what she wanted. But she didn't. Even if she did, she couldn't afford to live. It was depressing. Especially when she saw people kill themselves all the time because they felt the same way. It's not like she wanted to die exactly; she just wanted to not feel like *this. I want to survive and thrive a little and grow. But for me to achieve that—*

Jasmine continued aloud, "This world needs to be completely different. I'm just me. But I'm still fucking alive. Compartmentalizing everything in my life and all my emotions boxed up so I don't scream. Keeping my shit separate is how I stay sane."

"But you don't keep your shit separate. We work together. We're doing . . . whatever it is we're doing. That is textbook shitting where you eat."

"Yeah, but we don't, like, work-work together. We're not on the same, like, level. I mean I have medical training—"

Henry leaned back in his seat. "Wowwww, okay, Miz Upwardly Mobile, congrats on being so much better than me." He crossed his arms, pouting. "Still, don't see me on Suicidetok." Then he leaned forward to face her, serious again. "You're doing well. And you can make a better life for yourself. You can get to a place where you have more power to change things."

There isn't enough power on Earth that would make me feel like I could change anything. Jasmine tightened her grip on the steering wheel as big, dark trees flew past her field of vision. "I can't save the world from itself. That's not my job."

Suddenly, his warm hand was on hers, on the steering wheel, and she flinched before she was aware she was doing it. The wheel jerked a bit, and Henry withdrew his hand.

"You're right. You can't save the world. I can't save you. You couldn't save your mom. But maybe you can patch things up with Ja—"

"The fuck you say?" Jasmine hit the brake. "Who's talking about my mother?!"

Henry grabbed the safety bar above the window reflexively. "No, I just mean—"

Jasmine jerked the wheel again. Hard.

The car skidded to a rough stop alongside the Redwood Highway. Sawdust and dirt flurried around Jasmine, who leapt out of the still-running car and scuttled down into the pale, dusty hillside littered with sun-bleached tree stumps. Up close, the place looked like a graveyard on the moon; white dust covered everything. When Henry moved to follow her, the car started to roll so he jumped back in the car to shift the gear into park. Out of his view, something mechanical buzzed nearby.

6 THE CLEAR-CUT

HENRY ROLLED DOWN THE car window, pissed. "Jas! Get back in the car!" She didn't stop; she kept shuffling down a ravine toward a big dirt field that looked strewn around with angular, white cardboard sculptures. He honked the horn at her, but she kept walking.

In the far distance, all-terrain vehicles vroomed loudly. They weaved around the cardboard sculptures. Oh, they were stumps. *Check these guys out*, Henry mused. Clouds of sawdust and dirt kicked up behind two ATVs. They soared off dirt hills, buzzing threateningly. Henry squinted. The riders looked like they were in Limp Bizkit. *Fuckin' Monster Energy drink militia over here.*

On further scrutiny, it looked like the drivers were wearing skull masks and carrying rifles. And Jasmine was shrinking away, headed right toward them.

Henry stumbled out of the car. The lead ATV driver motioned toward the road. The machines' Doppler roars echoed around the hillocks, the ATVs barely missing giant tree stumps and trailing white dust behind them. Straight toward Jasmine, who kept walking.

The fuck is this place?

Henry tripped and slid down the road, then ran as fast as he could for thirty steps but soon lost his breath. The ground was like quicksand.

The ATVs slid Batmobile-style in front of Jasmine, whipping up clouds of dirt and wood shavings.

Jasmine covered her face and yelled, "You trying to kill me?"

The lead ATV driver dismounted from the four-wheeler, the rifle strapped to his back glinting in the sun. Dude was built like a fridge, and Henry hoped he didn't mean any trouble. When he pulled down his mask, the thick-jowled Native American with gray stubble that matched his eyes grinned stupidly at Jasmine. "Welcome home, Jazzy."

Jasmine jumped up into his arms for a bear hug, legs swinging off the ground.

Henry jogged up to them, huffing and puffing, but still attempting to protect. "Jas . . . I . . . Guns . . ."

Jasmine peeked out from under Buck's huge arms. "This is Henry!"

Buck put Jasmine down and extended a giant mitt toward Henry.

Henry, still out of breath and doubled over, shook two of Buck's big fingers. "'Sup?"

"S'nice to meet you. I'm Buck."

"Tilly's cousin," Jasmine clarified.

The other ATV driver pushed his plastic Halloween mask up. He was a brawny white guy who immediately smirked at Jasmine real flirty. "Hiya!" He grinned. "I'm Doug." Some kinda Accent White guy. Henry couldn't place it, but it sounded maybe Midwestern. The worst.

"What's with the guns?" Jasmine asked.

Buck's face exploded into a grin. "Oh, this little thing?" He swung the rifle around to the front of his body and posed.

Jasmine scoffed. "'Oh this?' Psssht." She made a jerking-off hand motion, which embarrassed Buck enough that he pulled the rifle around to his back.

"Farm," he said tightly.

Now Henry was confused and embarrassed, but he had to ask. "What kind of farm needs motocross guys with assault rifles?"

The white guy scoffed now. "Motocross is bikes. These are all-terrain vehicles, bud."

Bud. A Canadian, then. That was the worst kind of Accent White. At least the Australians and Europeans had the decency to offset the accent by being huge assholes. An American like Henry couldn't compete with free healthcare either.

"S'the kind of farm you don't ask questions about," the big guy—Buck—replied. "Pays way better'n lumberyards. And you don't have to worry about chainsaws."

"Yeah, that'd be dangerous," Henry joked.

Buck chuckled.

Henry smiled to himself.

"Oh my God, it's just weed," Jasmine said before turning back to Buck. "You're not gangster just because you work on *Murder Mountain*."

She said the last part extra mockingly. *They must be close friends, then. If you can joke with 'em, they're family.* Henry shrugged. "I don't know, Jasmine. It *is* called Murder Mountain. Also, those guns look pretty gangster to me."

Buck smiled. "Thank you! Finally, some acknowledgement of my cool gun. I like this guy, Jazzy."

Jasmine pssht'd again. "Wow, Buck. Your big-ass dick substitute is so cool," she added facetiously before yelping as Buck grabbed her and pulled her under his arm for a noogie. "Stop! My hair! I'm gonna kill you!"

Matching Jasmine's mocking tone, Buck crooned, "Miss Jasmine Bay! It's *so* good to see you too! Redcedar's lost daughter has finally returned. Whipple's ghost can finally rest now!"

Jasmine wrestled herself free and smoothed down her hair, missing the back where it stood up. "Fuck off, it hasn't been that long."

Doug smiled at her, and she smiled back.

This guy is trouble. *He's tall too. This is bad.* Henry could feel anxiety beading up on the back of his neck. There was dust sticking to the sweat covering his hands.

Jasmine asked, "Are you guys wearing that to the wake?"

Buck shook his hair. "Aunt Gin never judged me for what I wear so she's even less likely to care now."

"Ha. Fair. Well, see ya there." She turned back toward the car, and Henry followed her.

When they were climbing up the ravine back to the road, Buck called after them.

"Hey, Jazzy!"

"What?"

"Nice dress!"

She gave him the finger as he and the Canadian mounted their ATVs.

When they were up on the road, Henry huffed a bit. On the median were two figures, standing scary still like the silent trees. What was it about this place that spooked him so much? As empty of humans as Humboldt County appeared to be, they certainly had a habit of appearing out of nowhere. As soon as he saw their faces though, Henry recognized the two as Jasmine's brother and his wife, her best friend. James and Tilly.

Before turning to greet them, Jasmine whispered to Henry: "My brother and I don't get along so, like, if he's a dick to you, it's not personal; he's just a fucking asshole."

7 THE SKYLINER

EVER SINCE THEY HAD entered Humboldt County, Henry noticed the canopy of redwoods over everything, like a roof on the world. As they drove up the 101, it felt at turns claustrophobic, embracing, guarding.

But this clear-cut part was so wide open, Henry felt vulnerable and missed the redwood canopy. The wall of aromatic black and green opened to a near-white clear-cut that went back miles. This kind of openness felt wrong to Henry, way too exposed, after only an hour under the redwoods' shelter. He searched for the big trees and saw only stumps.

Nearby, there was a stump covered in mossy burls that grew over a rusted blue truck. It must've crashed into the tree ages ago, and the stump had just kept on expanding until it absorbed the entire crushed hood. On the other side of the stump, a sign warned, "WELCOME TO REDCEDAR. THE BEATING HEART OF HUMBOLDT."

On one side of the stump—northward toward Redcedar—James Bay's green truck was parked. On the south side, the San Francisco way, sat Henry Savage's silver Prius.

Tilly bounded toward Jasmine for a hug while James hung back.

"Tilly, Henry," Jasmine introduced Henry, muffled from

the inside of a bear hug for the second time that day. "Henry, this is Tilly!"

Tilly released Jasmine to shake Henry's hand hard. "Oh, I've heard all about you," she said conspiratorially.

"I've heard all about you too," Henry replied. "You're the wild sister-in-law."

"She said I'm the wild one?! That's rich coming from her."

Henry looked over Tilly's shoulder. "Which makes you James." The guy definitely resembled Jasmine, if she put on more weight and had a scraggly, nappy beard. He went in for a fist bump. "You have no idea how good it is to see another brother up here."

Instead of meeting his fist, James pulled Henry in for a dank-smelling hug. "Every day of my life, man."

After he released Henry, James and Jasmine stood five feet apart and awkwardly nodded at each other. "Hey."

"Hey," Jasmine responded.

It wasn't unfriendly, just . . . not warm. Henry noticed and changed the subject. "I'm sorry about your godmother."

"Thanks," James said warmly. He seemed grateful for Henry's distraction, even if it was about his recently deceased relative.

All of us just want to survive this visit in one piece.

But Jasmine wasn't going to make it easy. "Nice work over here," she teased, pointing a thumb at the clear-cut.

"Thanks," James shot back. "Heard the lumber was all used to build West Oakland. That's where you live, right?"

"Oh my God—" Jasmine started, but she was cut off when Tilly and Henry both started to laugh uncomfortably.

"Welp!" Tilly announced. "We've all gotta get over to the Skyliner 'n start setting up."

"Yep. Skyliner. Yep," Henry agreed, and each of them subtly pulled their respective Bay sibling back toward their respective cars.

"Yeah," James and Jasmine both said, allowing themselves to be separated.

Tilly and James walked back to their car. She patted her husband's arm. "That went pretty well, I think!"

In the silver Prius, Jasmine pouted while Henry readjusted the mirrors and mused, "Your brother doesn't seem like an asshole." Jasmine heard the unspoken implication.

Miles away, the million-million eyes of the redwood forest watched the two couples separate and from the pine-green curtain of those unseeing eyes, something let out a barking cough.

The Skyliner was an ugly cement building painted to resemble a log cabin with neon beer signs in the window. Inside the bar was a country dive if Henry ever saw one—he hadn't ever seen one, but it was just like what he imagined: Christmas lights, Knob Creek whiskey on the top shelf, and a massive display on the wall of dozens of different-shaped axe heads. The stained carpet threatened to come up with Henry's shoe when he lifted his foot to shuffle awkwardly from side to side. This place was a redneck bar like out of a movie. Old rock played from a jukebox, and older, bearded men sat at wooden tables, many of them missing limbs—the men, not the tables. Explained the ramp outside.

Henry felt very conspicuous, especially with only two other black people and an indigenous lady. He half expected lightning to crash outside behind them, the scene felt so cartoonishly foreboding.

Jasmine started down a hall toward the back when—

"Hey!" bellowed the bartender, a light-skinned old lady with gigantic tits and pink hair and big red lips, stepping toward the group. The red lips smirked. "You know, I still got every fake ID you ever used up here behind the bar?"

Jasmine ran to the woman for a hug.

Okay, so she just knows everybody here. She said it was a small town. Is that bartender Native American? Do they call it Indian now? Maybe she's related to Tilly? Nah, don't do that. Keep your mouth shut.

After a long and awkward moment, Jasmine peeked out from yet another bear hug. As an afterthought, she motioned to introduce him. "Aunt Charlyne, this is—"

"Yeah, I know."

"Okay, well, then we'll have—"

"I gotcha. Go sit." Henry glimpsed blue tattoo ink peeking out from Charlyne's low-cut sweater. Some kind of flower. Lord, her titties were huge.

Henry, Tilly, and James followed the deft movements of Jasmine through the bar down a hall, past a pool table and arcade. A group of lumberjacks playing darts seemed to glare at them, but overall, they were greeted congenially enough by everyone not white so Henry shrugged it off. Honestly, he just felt relieved there was a place where she fit in. This was great. He genuinely enjoyed the time he spent with Jasmine, but in group settings, she embarrassed herself—and by extension him—by saying weird shit. After that blowup in the car, it was good to see her smiling again. He could still dig himself out of the hole he'd dug and salvage this trip.

They came to a swinging door that desperately needed some WD-40 or something. They passed through to a back room with a stage, red vinyl booths, and red walls covered in an amount of black-and-white stickers and framed kitsch that threatened the structural integrity of the room's sparkly popcorn ceiling.

The gang completed the awkward shuffle of four grown adults sliding into a booth, making creaking, squeaking, farting sounds on the vinyl the whole time.

Henry turned to Tilly, his only ally so far. "How many weeks along are you?"

"You think I look pregnant?" Tilly squinted her eyes then widened them, suddenly enraged.

Henry felt his stomach fall out of his ass.

Jasmine shoved Tilly hard and hissed, "Stop fucking with him. We're guests, dammit."

Tilly cackled.

The door swung open again with a mercifully interrupting creak. It was the ATV guys from before: Buck and Jeff, or Zack, or something. Buck carried a tray of drinks. The huge man carried the serving tray with undeniable grace. Even when he dodged Jasmine reaching out for a beer—Henry knew you never grab at a serving tray—Buck was light on his feet, and Henry wondered if his admiration of the man was a little gay. Buck passed a ginger beer to James and a canned cranberry juice to Tilly.

The other guy pulled up two chairs and sat backward in one. A real Zack move if Henry ever saw one. This one was gonna be trouble, Henry thought, not knowing why but just feeling more on edge around the swaggering Canadian.

When Buck handed him a beer, Henry accepted it gratefully. "Thanks. I was worried I'd have to go back and order with the big-tiddy lady."

Tilly choked on her cranberry juice while James chuckled into his bottle. Something was up.

"What?" Henry asked, searching for clues to the source of his party foul.

"Charlyne is Buck's mom," Jasmine whispered, grabbing his thigh hard under the table.

Fuck fuck fuck fuckity fuck. Did dying feel like crackling up into dust and being blown away? Because if so, Henry was suicidal right now.

"S'all right, guy, don't have a heart attack." Buck smiled. "You couldn't have known."

"I can see it now," Henry replied.

"Yeah, you've got giant hooters too," Tilly teased, reaching out to grab Buck's chest.

Buck smacked her hands hard. "S'good to see you too."

That Canadian guy piped up, "Hiya, Jasmine."

Jasmine smiled. Henry frowned.

Tilly urged them to stay, but Buck shook his head. "That's okay. Ms. Pacman's calling my name."

Henry caught the Canadian wink at Jasmine when he said, "Bye." He let it slide. *I'm the one she's going back to Oakland with. Maybe she'll be my girlfriend at the end of all this.*

A few rounds later, with empty bottles and shot glasses littering the table in front of them, Jasmine told a story to Henry while James nursed his ginger beer. Tilly had an equal number of cran-razz cans in front of her, chugging them dutifully with her friend. Jas was explaining their family to him. "So Aunt Gin was our godmother. Family friend of our Grandma and Grampdaddy Whipple."

"Grampdaddy?" Henry had never heard a granddad called that before. He liked it.

Jas nodded. "Our mom's dad."

"The white one?"

"You love reminding me of that." She scowled. "Yes, the white one. Damn!"

Henry smiled. "I gotta remind myself of that every time you send food back at a restaurant, like, 'Miss? Excuse me? I'm *so* sorry, but would it be *possible* to get this but *without* all the stuff it's supposed to come with?'"

Jasmine tsk'd. "I order a bacon cheeseburger with no bacon or cheese *one time* . . ."

"I just gotta tell myself, 'Henry. She can't help it. She got a white granddaddy. It's in her blood.'"

Tilly and James laughed, at least. Henry was probably going too far, talking about her relatives so soon again after the fight earlier, but the words were out of his mouth before all this occurred to him. He needed these people to like him.

Jasmine merely smirked back. "You got jokes, huh?"

"Oh, I got jokes." He flashed her a flirty smile. "But it's treatable."

Tilly took the opening to change the subject. "Yours is a picky eater too? That's cute. We have that in common."

"I've never sent anything back." Finally, James was joining the conversation, taking a break from sulking like a teenager.

Tilly patted his leg. "No, anytime we go out, you don't say anything. He's just, like, deconstructing a whole meal to pick out what he doesn't like, going, 'No, this is fine!'"

The group laughed.

Henry looked around and noticed that one of the framed items was a story from the newspaper. The headline read "NORTH COAST SABOTEUR PUNISHED."

"Isn't William Whipple your grampdaddy's name?" Henry immediately wished he'd done more than scan the article before he'd asked that.

This silence made the tiddy comment pale in comparison. Reading the article closer, Henry saw that—

"Grampdaddy Whipple was the North Coast saboteur," James said.

"So he's Whipple's ghost?" Henry asked.

"He's *the* skyliner," Jasmine added.

"I don't mean to be a dick, but why would you spend your time in a your-dead-granddad-themed bar?" Henry was incredulous.

The rest of the table shrugged back. "It's the only bar in town," James explained.

"Trust me. If we had any other choice of event space, we wouldn't be having the wake here," Jasmine muttered into her beer.

Maybe it being the only bar in town is a good enough reason. In Oakland, there's always somewhere else to go, and in a couple years, all the restaurants and bars change owners and themes. Buck's mom owns this place, though. That's gotta be weird.

"I'm Native so every bar in the county is a 'my dead family'–themed bar," Tilly said.

Damn. Maybe it's not that weird.

Jasmine added, "I used to steal those news articles. Sneak 'em out in my purse."

Henry laughed, fully charmed. "You stole? *You*?"

Jas nodded. "Yeah, but every time I took one down, they'd just replace it. Like they had a goddamned stockpile of 'em. Assholes."

"I mean . . ." Her brother shrugged.

"What?" Jasmine barked at him. "What are you gonna say about our dead grandpa?"

"Just . . . Maybe he shouldn't have sabotaged the logging ops?"

"Man, fuck you," Jasmine scoffed.

Henry put a hand on hers. "Wait, what? What'd he do?" This place was so goddamned weird. He couldn't wait to tell his friends about it.

Jasmine explained. "So, Grampdaddy Whipple was a local boy from around here. He started working at a sawmill when he was like twelve or something crazy like that. They hired kids because they were light and could run across the river when it was jammed with logs. Then he joined a logging crew as a skyliner."

Henry still didn't know what that was, but he could look it up later.

"After a while, he realized that what he and the other loggers were doing was wrong, cutting down these trees that had been around for thousands of years. Some of them were as big around as this building. They were killing the forest, and he had to stop them."

After seeing the clear-cut today, Henry could understand that.

"He quit once he saw how the sausage was made," Jasmine continued.

"Haha, 'saw'-sage," Tilly added, giggling. "Get it?"

Jasmine giggled too. Not a girlish giggle but the grimy little cackle of a teenaged boy. Henry had never heard her laugh like that.

"*Anyway*," James cut in, "he quit, and then he started pulling ecoterrorist fuckshit to sabotage the timber ops."

"What kind of fuckshit?" Henry asked.

Jasmine scoffed. "He slashed a few tires."

James became apoplectic. "He spiked their drinking water with LSD!"

"That was cool though!" Jasmine laughed.

"Not when everyone has a chainsaw!" James sputtered in outrage before turning back to Henry. "He also cut cables so logs fell. Some guys got killed."

Henry was rapt. This story was nuts. And it was their family history. He lifted his beer.

"You know," Jasmine said, leaning toward Tilly, "before they were used for logging, chainsaws were originally designed to cut open a woman during childbirth."

Henry spat out his beer onto the table. Everyone laughed. Tilly shoved Jasmine playfully.

Jasmine patted Henry's back. "I'm just saying that dudes dying or going missing is more about the job than anything Grampdaddy ever did. Logging is the most dangerous job in the world."

James picked up the rest of the story. "So in 1980, the loggers fought back against Whipple. They caught him and killed him."

"They fucking lynched him. And his wife."

"What?!" Henry almost choked on his beer a second time.

With Henry seemingly back on her side, Jasmine added, "But I'm sure their interracial marriage had nothing to do with them being hanged by a bunch of racist white hicks." She sipped her beer. "Anyways, that's what the paper means by 'saboteur punished.'"

"Well, shit." Henry took a big drink.

"He didn't have to do all that to them, though," James argued.

"You know another way to stop a timber company from killing the planet?" Jasmine was raising her voice. "Sometimes you gotta crack a few eggs . . ."

Henry sucked his teeth, regretting bringing it up.

James held up his hands defensively. "I'm just saying if Grampdaddy did even half of what they said he did, then stopping him was kinda self-defense."

"Oh great, so Lumber-Jackoff Boy is gonna stick up for the murderers? You really are on the other team now."

"It's not like there's a ton of jobs out here. Lumberyard pays more than Amazon and doesn't drug test. It's not as good as a farm, but I don't have to carry a gun." James downed his bottle of ginger beer.

The man had a point. Henry's head hurt from the nervousness flooding his body. Social awkwardness is one thing, but family is a whole 'nother level. But he didn't know these people so he stayed quiet. He wished Jasmine would as well.

"You could've picked something that's not completely against everything Aunt Gin taught us."

"You left Humboldt! Aunt Gin didn't teach you that. That's all you!"

"You buried her in your *yard* instead of the forest like she wanted!"

The table teetered, clinking glasses.

Tilly reached out and smacked both Bays on the back of their heads. "Hey! Both of you are acting like real fucking . . . turds right now."

Everyone turned to look at Tilly for that one: *Turds?*

Tilly scoffed. "I'm fucking trying not to fucking swear so goddamned much because I'm gonna be a fucking mother, okay?"

James patted her hand. "It's okay, baby, you're doing great."

Jasmine patted the back of her head. "You? Aren't going to swear? Good luck with that one."

James stood up, emitting the most pained old-man moan Henry had ever heard. “I’m taking a walk,” he announced, then leaned in toward Tilly’s ear and whispered, “I need a record scratch.”

“Yeah, that’s right,” Jasmine spat. “Run away, you limpy bitch. Be back here for the wake. Asshole!” Her voice—not the voice she used at work and gas stations, but her real voice, apparently—bellowed after James like a force of nature.

“It’s not a wake, idiot!” His final words rang out from the hallway. “We already buried her!”

On the other side of her, Tilly slammed a fist on the table. “Jesus jumped-up Christ, Jas. I’m not letting you two ruin my first night out in forever. Grab me another cranberry and soda and put some fuckin’ Foreigner on the jukebox.”

Still breathing hard from the confrontation, Jasmine slid out from the table. Henry would’ve gladly moved down but she disappeared from next to him so quickly and marched out the swinging door.

Henry shifted uncomfortably in the seat. “Oh, yours storms out too. That’s cute.”

After a beat, Tilly laughed. “I’d apologize but they’re fuckin’—friggin’—always like this.”

The Times-Standard

A THOMSON NEWSPAPERS COMPANY

Wednesday, October 1, 1980

MISSING MOONEY MEN
NORTH COAST SABOTEUR PUNISHED

REDCEDAR, Calif.—Eighteen men are missing in Northern California's Humboldt County and are assumed to have walked off the job, fleeing the area after apprehending and murdering a suspected eco-terrorist who had allegedly sabotaged the logging operation on multiple occasions. The disappearances were reported Tuesday morning when Mooney Timber Products workers were sent to investigate after the crew had not returned communications in 48 hours. The killing is believed to have occurred sometime Friday night.

Humboldt County Sheriff Ron Mooney commented, "Logging is a dangerous job, and we're used to losing our own. We're real sorry to lose these boys, but we're thankful they caught the saboteur. Although, obviously, I wish they'd brought him to me first. Due process and all."

Mooney Timber Products spokesman H.D. Mooney said that the company has plans to launch rescue parties in the coming days and reminded that they are hiring.

"The main priority right now is to backfill their positions and get the timber crop out on schedule," Mooney said.

Mooney Timber Products is in early negotiations for a merger with North Coast Timber Company, a subsidiary of Baumheyser International. Such a merger is expected to net Mooney $180 million and flood the area with new development, including planned upgrades to the Mooney Timber complex.

The deceased suspected saboteur—William Whipple of Redcedar—was found hanging from steel cables near Foreman's Cabin, a base camp and emergency shelter for logging crews. Whipple was a disgruntled former employee of Mooney Timber, who had become radicalized and participated in "eco-terrorism activities" against the company, resulting in $358,000 worth of damage and lost profits.

8 FIRE

1995

THE NIGHT IT HAPPENED, Jas remembered that James wouldn't stop singing. They were *in public. It's not allowed!* Jasmine was nearly ten years old. She didn't like her brother's singing and couldn't understand why Mom found it so funny. They were in an adult restaurant with a fish tank in the front and red lamps on the tables, with real fire, and no one else was singing. James just kept humming, then belting the lyrics to, "Heard It Through the Grapevine."

"Mom. Make him stop," she requested.

"Why should I?" Mom shrugged, then leaned toward James. "Jay-Boy, how do you know that song? You been listenin' to Marvin Gaye alone?"

Jasmine scoffed. "It's not Martin Gayalone, Mom. It's the California Raisins." *Everyone knows that.*

Mom sat up, shocked. "The California Raisins?"

James stopped singing to back up Jasmine. He nodded. "Yeah, Mommy, they're raisins, and *they* sing that song."

Mom scoffed now. "That is a Marvin Gaye song. Who raised you?" She laughed and squeezed James's arm playfully.

Jasmine laughed too until behind them, a man cleared his throat loudly. She sat up straighter and pulled her hair back, beads rattling against her ears. "Mom," she whispered. "Why are those people looking at us like that?"

Mom frowned. "Because they're jealous."

"Make them stop," James whined.

"I'm going to tell them to stop looking at us," Jasmine asserted. She took her older sibling duties seriously when it came to protecting her younger brother. She'd been so brave back then, unafraid to stand up to anyone. They were close back then.

"Don't worry about them," Mom soothed them. "You can't change other people. Just focus on you. It's not your job to save the world from itself, babygirl. It's too much." She finished her glass of water, having made her point.

But Jasmine didn't accept that. "Why not?" She laid her hand over her mom's to let her know that she didn't mean it in a rude way.

Mom flinched away from her, which shook the table. Jasmine shouldn't have been surprised—Mom was always a ball of nerves, jumpy and sensitive to touch—but it still hurt.

Mom coughed loudly and for so long that people started to stare again. Finally, Mom hit her palm against the table and coughed out, "Food's here."

The waiter basically dropped their plates in front of them. He wouldn't look Mom in the eye or make eye contact with any of them, even when Jasmine and James thanked him in unison.

"Thank you," Mom rasped. "Could we get some more water, please?" Her voice was scratchy but almost back to normal.

The waiter sighed heavily—Jasmine would later recognize that same irritated scoff whenever Carlos did it—and stalked off. He never came back with the water. Jasmine remembered noticing that and deciding that maybe the world wasn't worth saving.

Mom took a bite of her stir-fry, and her face soured. *That's how it started.* "Oh no, they did not . . ."

"Mom, please." Jasmine knew what was coming. They didn't eat at a lot of restaurants, and every time they did, Mom had some weird issue with the food.

Her mother flagged down a waiter who wasn't even serving their table. "Hi! Excuse me, I can't eat this. There's mushrooms in this and I asked for no mushrooms and there are mushrooms right here in it."

James ate his dumplings obliviously while Jasmine buried her face in her hands and muttered, "Mom, it's fine."

"It is not fine, Jasmine. If I'm paying this much for food, they should get it right," Mom chirped before turning back to the waiter, smiling. "I need a new number thirty-four with no mushrooms, please. And please don't let them just pick them out. They leave particles. I'll know."

"I'll take it back to the kitchen," the man said as he reached for the plate.

Then Mom's hand shot out and grabbed his arm! Hard. He tried to pull away, but she wouldn't let go. It looked like it hurt. Mom's hand and the waiter's arm shook together as they both struggled.

"Lady, what are you doing?" the waiter growled at her through gritted teeth.

Jasmine burned with embarrassment. That tingle of mortification froze into fear when Mom's voice went eerie calm and she smiled up at the waiter.

"Mama gave her babies away. They live in the trees now." She said it as if she was asking for a glass of water. The look in Mom's eyes was so . . . vacant. Later on, Jasmine would remember that moment as her understanding of the phrase "thousand-yard stare." Mom's eyes looked a million miles away.

"Ma'am?" The waiter looked as scared as Jasmine felt.

"It's Maid Marian. I went astray."

She recalled the sounds of everything from that night so vividly. The silverware clanked, and ice rattled in the empty water glasses when Mom slammed her fist on the table. It was scary. Half the people in the restaurant jumped in their chairs, it was so loud.

The waiter tried to pull his arm away, but Mom just held onto him tightly. Suddenly, she jerked his wrist so hard he dropped the plate, and it shattered on the floor. Everyone stared.

James reached for Jasmine's hand, and they scootched closer to each other. The whole scene was surreal. Jasmine started to feel dizzy.

Mom started to scream incoherently at the waiter, at the other people in the restaurant.

The waiter yanked his arm back and fell on the floor. He called out to the hostess, "Can I get some help here?"

When Mom grabbed the oil lamp on the table, Jasmine felt in her gut that the best thing to do was to get James and herself as far away from Mom as possible. She pulled James off his chair. It knocked to the ground with an ugly thud.

The other patrons stood up too, forming a circle around Jasmine's crying mother.

"No no no no," Mom babbled as she poured the oil from the lamp onto herself. A stream of flame splashed across her face and shoulder.

James tried to slip out of Jasmine's grasp. "Mommy!" he cried.

Jasmine was crying too. It was too much. They had just been laughing and singing and now Mom just . . . went crazy.

Another woman screamed. Men tried to step forward to stop Mom, but she flailed out at them with clawed hands covered in flaming oil.

Shell-shocked, Jasmine stood with her back against the red wall. She needed to escape but she was frozen.

James extricated himself from her grasp and ran toward Mom.

Mom grabbed his forearm, burning it.

James wailed.

Mom wailed too, roared like something dying, because she was.

Jasmine pulled her brother back against the wall with her and held him under her jacket, shielding him from the white-hot figure of their burning mother.

The white Madonna screamed at them, bright and terrible. Mom snatched oil lamps off the surrounding tables and poured their white flames down herself. She tried to reach for her children, but they stayed away, terrified.

James was still crying, shaking beneath her jacket. Jasmine wished she could disappear into the coat as well. Within her embrace, her brother only heard the windy rush of their mother engulfed in flames. He only felt Jasmine's hot tears drip onto his scalp as she tried to hide him from this horrible light and protect his charred arm. Unprotected by anyone, Jasmine watched their mother burn, white-hot fire reflected in her tears.

9 EULOGY

JASMINE HAD ENOUGH OF a buzz on to start setting up for the wake. It was five and that dick James wasn't back yet. Setting up didn't require a ton of work, and Jasmine didn't want his help anyway. It was going to be nice and informal: an open microphone for people to come up and share their favorite stories about Aunt Gin. Aunt Gin would've liked it. She preferred things nice and simple. Nothing too "froufrou," as she called it. She hated froufrou-ness, which led to tackiness, which led to shamefulness. All sins in Gin's eyes. The wake started in an hour but all Jasmine needed to do was turn the sound system on. Charlyne had already connected everything and set out ten chairs near the stage.

The Skyliner's swinging door screeched, and the rest of the Witches came bumbling in like a litter of puppies. Ellen and Nancy were chattering away while Victoria's tall frame loomed behind them, their queen. They all seemed drunk or high or something. Grieving as well.

Jasmine herself was settled in a comfortably numb state of inebriation so she wasn't judging. People grieve in all sorts of ways. Thinking about Aunt Gin being gone forever sent a shudder through her, spreading across her like a thousand spiders crawling from her rib cage. She waved at her godmother's best friends. "Hi, ladies. Thanks for coming."

"Jasmine Bay, as I live and breathe." Victoria's sonorous alto warbled as she took long, high steps toward the table. Gin's friends were all pretty birdlike, and in high school, Tilly once told Jas she pegged Miz Mooney as being remarkably similar to a secretary bird, an imperious-looking white-and-black sub-Saharan bird of prey with long legs. Especially with her walk. Jasmine shot a look at Tilly, who narrowed her eyes in a noiseless giggle; she was thinking the same thing.

"Stand up! Let's see how tall you are now." Ellen Zeller—the stout, dowdy pheasant—yanked at Jasmine's wrists. She pulled Jasmine up into a bear hug and then, seeing Henry, asked, "Who's this? Your husband?"

He stretched a hand toward her. "Hi, I'm Henry. We work together."

"Whose husband?" Nancy Hsu asked a little too loudly. Her blunt black bob haircut paired with her diminutive frame and scrunched face to transform her into the spitting image of a black-capped chickadee. Jasmine chuckled, remembering an avian doodle Tilly once had passed to her of this very caricature.

Miz Mooney stooped down toward Nancy to yell in her ear. "They work together!"

"We're not," Jasmine stammered. "It's not like that."

Henry's neck almost snapped with the speed with which he turned his shocked face up at her. She ignored him.

Ellen patted Jasmine against her. "Well, you can tell us all about how you two met while we set up."

"We are set up," Jasmine protested. These women always made her feel so small. Especially when they all gave each other the look they were giving each other now, as if they were able to communicate telepathically for the express purpose of shit-talking their friend's ward. "Who else is coming?" she asked, hoping to distract them.

"We'll set up, dear," Victoria condescended to her. "You sit down and keep . . . doing your thing."

"Of course, we're all very sorry," Ellen added.

"First that shamefulness with your mother and now this," Nancy yelled. She probably needed to adjust her hearing aid. "It's too much. Okay, bye now!"

The women shuffled off on three pairs of Easy Spirit sneakers. Jasmine plopped back down in the booth, causing the cushion to fart a little. Tilly burst out laughing. Henry, then Jasmine, joined in too.

The wake started at ten after six. When the Witches were done decorating the stage—a shipping pallet topped with carpet squares—it was trussed up like a Christmas goose. Extremely froufrou. An easel held a giant poster of Gin's yearbook photo. She smiled knowingly from behind giant funky glasses. The DJ booth was festooned with a birthday party letter banner reading "BLESSED BE." Green balloons framed the stage. It was tacky as hell. They'd put away the chairs Charlyne had set out, assuring Jasmine that standing would make people want to get up on stage. But so far, no one had. James still wasn't back, so Jasmine had to bite the bullet and talk first. She smoothed her hair down and grabbed her beer as she approached the front of the room.

About twenty people were gathered when Jasmine stepped up onto the stage. She held the microphone in one hand and her beer in the other, steeling herself for public speaking. She didn't even like making PA announcements during an emergency at the H. She held the microphone against her chin. "Um." It was way too loud. A group of men laughed in the other room, loud enough to pull the focus from Jasmine. It gave her time to slip over to the DJ booth and adjust the volume.

The Witches stood in front of the stage like groupies, blocking Henry and Tilly from getting closer. Tilly looked around for James, worried.

Near the door, Buck and Doug took off their hats. A few randoms trickled in but none of them were James. At least they were friendly faces; people from school and Gin's church stared up at Jasmine, eyes brimming with loving acceptance.

She took a deep breath and began, "Aunt Gin raised my brother and me as if we were her own blood. She wasn't really our aunt, but she took us in after our mom . . . The thing I'm going to miss most about her is all her sayings. I guess they're more like old wives' tales, but she always called them 'old wise tales.'"

A few people in the audience nodded knowingly.

"She was always saying things like 'don't go outside with wet hair' and 'put tree pollen in your man's food, and he'll never cheat on you.' I always thought that one was really funny. She never got married, so she never got to try it out, I guess."

The crowd chuckled lightly.

She fingered the microphone cord. "But she had us. And she was all James and I had."

"Boo!"

The fuck?

Braying laughter rang through the room. A trio of weed farmers—white, big-bearded, metal-band-shirted—approached the stage. Jasmine recognized one from high school: Ratty Matty. Which meant the others must be the bloated corpses of Fat Tom and Lars. She didn't consider them *her* high school bullies, but they were assholes, and getting rich off weed had made them all much cockier assholes.

Her face burned. She could let it go, but nah, fuck it. "The fuck you say?" she intoned in the mic, ignoring the feedback.

The men oooh'd, and Tilly moved between the men and the stage, cautioning a beer-swigging Jasmine. "Jas . . ."

"No. I wanna hear what he's got to say. Whatcha got to say, you ugly lil rat shit?"

The crowd laughed.

Jasmine set the microphone on the easel and stepped off the stage. She got right up in Ratty Matty's face. He towered over her, but she didn't care. "So what do you have to say about my dead auntie?"

His pink, pockmarked face scowled down at her. "I'm saying your rug-munching auntie sucked dick."

The Witches gasped loudly.

The pressure of the room shifted, but Matty continued, "Your brother's an uppity black asshole, and you're an uppity black bitch, and your grandpa was a piece of shit hippie terrorist who got what he deserved. Your people don't belong in Humboldt, and this place has been cursed since your family stepped foot here."

Before she was aware of what she'd done, Jasmine had broken her bottle and was brandishing it in his face.

"Hey!" Charlyne yelled at her. *She can abide this asshole heckling a wake but not shutting him up? Fuck!* "If you're gonna fight, take it outside."

"Fine," Jasmine said and shoved Ratty Matty in the chest.

"Fine, bitch, I'll see you outside!" he yelled over his shoulder. He gathered his posse and was first through the screaming door.

Jasmine grabbed her purse and another beer and followed him down the hallway. She considered grabbing a pool cue and whacking him with that but didn't want to get in more trouble with Charlyne, who was in the back room probably complaining about "goddamned kids gettin' glass all over my goddamned floor." Jas—followed by Henry, Tilly, then Buck—passed the bar and the axe-head display. She drained the beer bottle as she walked, and after she passed, two axe heads were missing from the bottom row.

10

JAMES

LOOKING FOR THE PERFECT place to sulk, James turned left out of the Skyliner parking lot and up into the forest. The truck staggered a final goodbye to the paved road, lolling back and forth up the ancient logging roads that led to the summit.

He shifted on the ergonomic seat pad, but his hips still tingled. Especially as the road wound around the hills, heaving James's truck back and forth. Kicked-up gravel assaulted the undercarriage, and trees rolled by into a tide of inky black against the sherbet-colored sunset. The sunset reminded him of a red glass oil lamp, its hungry little flame. The sun shone into his aching eyes, warmed his face, bathed it in orange light.

In his memory, the red-orange light illuminated old white people's sneering faces. His mother grabbed his arm. Her long, pale fingers snatched a red glass oil lamp off the table and held it aloft. The flame poured down on her like a liquid. The fire pierced his vision, warmed his face, bathed it in orange light. A hand, flaming white, shot toward him and grabbed his thin, six-year-old arm. It burned him.

James focused on the narrow road ahead of him, trying to find the horizon, but he was under the redwood canopy. Steering the truck through the twilight forest, he passed over dry creek beds and culverts filled with pine duffs, questing like an ant. The trees were the legs of giants that he would never see the tops of.

These woods were a creature he would never understand. One with spindly fingers like Aunt Gin's. Her nails cut up his forearms like she was whipping him with pine branches, forming crisscross patterns across his burn scar. Pale, poison-tipped claws raked his forearms under his shirt even now, just thinking about it. The woods had always felt alien to him, but where the fuck else was he supposed to go? This place was all he'd ever known. He wasn't Jasmine, who left him and Tilly all alone with Aunt Gin to fend for themselves.

James realized he was hyperventilating when he coughed hard, hacking and gasping for air. He slowed the truck to a crawl and rolled down his windows. A cross breeze of mentholated oxygen calmed him. Aromas of pine, lemon, and eucalyptus filled the truck. He stretched his arm out to catch the air, the melty swirl of scar tissue feeling just a little sharper and more tingly when he rounded a familiar bend. His headlights illuminated a moderately sized pine, where he parked and stepped out of the car and walked into a thicket of trees that stopped abruptly, falling away to reveal a stone outcropping. From here, James had a panoramic view of the clear-cut, the bar, the town beyond, and even farther away, the Pacific Ocean. He pulled a joint from under his hat and lit it.

Fuck Jasmine. Leaving them high and dry for years. Not even bothering to call him, only Tilly. "Oh, I can't see Aunt Gin like that." *And Tilly and I could? She's my godmother too. And at least she likes Jas. Liked.* He hadn't asked Jas to come home and help outright. But he shouldn't have had to. The phone goes both ways, and she can't just text Tilly and think that's the same as talking to him. It had been five years since they last talked face-to-face.

Fuckin' Jas. She was the stupid one if she thought he hadn't considered any other line of work. Fuckin' Aunt Gin was the reason he took the job, to pay for physical therapy after the first time she fell. And now, five years later, when he thought about what his life had become, he felt nothing but shame.

He was paid decently to break his body for the timber company; he could barely walk some mornings, but he climbed up into trucks and transported tons upon tons of logs to port. The baby was going to change so much. What if he couldn't take care of it? The last time his back went out, he was laid out on the floor for four days. He didn't want Tilly to have to handle that and a newborn. Taking classes online was impossible because every free moment away from the lumberyard was spent recovering. At least on the company health insurance he might be able to get some physical therapy of his own.

The hazy temptation of opioids swirled through these repetitive thoughts like silk mist through the lumberyard in the morning. Even knowing he was going to be a father didn't stop the intrusive thoughts from prickling through him. Or daydreaming about getting a disabling but non-crippling injury. On the job, of course. But the company lawyers were good at blaming injuries on "user error" and denying workers' comp. It wasn't worth it. And yet he still thought about it: imagining his truck rolling off the Redwood Highway, smearing him across the forest floor.

James smoked and stared down at the bar, the buzz of its neon sign echoing and mixing with the rustling trees. He stretched a bit then pulled out his phone and began tapping out a text to his sister.

To: Jas
HENRY SEEMS LIKE A COOL GUY. I WANNA TRY TO GET ALONG THIS WEEKEND AND I NEED YA TO MEET ME HALFWAY. FOR TILLY. K?

He pressed SEND. No service. No bother. He set the phone down on the hood and watched the sun set behind the misty

Pacific. Eyes closed and vibing, he breathed deep. His peace was suddenly broken by the echo of glass breaking down in the bar's parking lot.

"Oh, goddamn it."

Recognizing the tiny silhouettes below him, he hurried up from the rock to hop in his truck and speed away from the overlook. The forgotten phone slid off the metal hood with the truck's first violent leap backward, cracking on the ground.

Now that the sun was behind the mountain, the looping, coiling road was so dark that the truck's headlights barely made a dent in the opaque gray. The truck creeped along at a sensible pace.

Suddenly, from nowhere, a white pickup tumbled toward him and nearly ran him off the road. He swerved to avoid it; the truck lurched painfully over rocks and logs. His headlights' beige beam hovered over the brush until they spotlit a tree trunk covered in . . . something. It was human shaped, but the proportions were all wrong. The thing's huge black eyes reflected the light, and then it was gone.

James turned his head to see it. It moved too fast.

The truck kept going, and the light moved on.

CRASH!

The truck slammed into a tree, a mere sapling with a trunk thinner than a man. The hood tore open and folded around the tree in an art nouveau explosion of twisted metal.

James's head hit the steering wheel, and pain splattered the inside of his skull.

It was even darker in the forest when—dazed from the crash—James fell out of his truck. Its hood was split in half by the sapling, and the hissing radiator was the only sound in the silent woods. Above him, the airbag wobbled, losing air and spilling powder all over the seat. But James was intact. A little blood on his forehead but nothing he couldn't handle. He patted his jacket and pants for his phone. No dice. Climbing back up into the cab to look for it didn't yield results either. "Fuck!" He'd left it at the overlook. *Goddamn it.*

His tire tracks were lit red by the brake lights, and the sky that he could see was slightly lighter the way he'd come. *That's west and if you go west, you'll hit ocean.* He marched through the muddy tracks toward the sunset-facing overlook and after a time, familiar-looking trees gave way to the stone cliff. James approached the edge, looking for the green neon of the Skyliner. It wasn't there. None of it. No clear-cut. No road. Just more trees. James wheeled around to find that the post-sunset sky he'd followed to the overlook was now behind him. *Okay, then* that's *west.* He headed back into the forest after it.

Among the whispering branches, his cell phone rang out in the distance, over and over.

He rushed deeper into the brush after the noise. He followed the ringing for an eternity until, stumbling into a moonlit glade peopled by an overturned stump, he spotted the white-blue light under the stump's ropey roots. James pounced on it to answer a call from Tilly, leaning against the roots as he spoke. "Baby!"

"Hey, where'd you go?" she asked breathlessly.

"Can you hear me? I'm in the woods." The words spilled out of the normally taciturn James. "I drove up the mountain but then I lost my phone and I crashed my truck so I had to come find my phone at the overlook and it's so good to hear your voice I—!"

The stump toppled onto him and he screamed. It descended so quickly, but he felt every rotten millisecond, every ragged millimeter of the rooty tentacles impaling him. The stump had the weight of a small car, knocking him on his face.

James tried to crawl out from under it, but there was a root sticking through his thigh. The phone lay shattered next to him. He tried to turn on its flashlight, but it flickered out.

A *thwanging* above yanked James's attention skyward just in time to see a silhouette scramble across one of the old logging cables that crisscrossed the mountain. Its jerking, inhuman movements were at odds with the graceful speed it exhibited when it crossed the skyline. James had no doubt it was the same creature he'd seen before.

Struggling out from under the stump required herculean effort, as did stifling his cries. The pain shooting up his spine was a thousand screaming decibels vibrating through him, but the forest was deadly quiet. James pulled on a larger root, hand over hand, until he'd lifted himself up off the woody spike in his leg. The hole bled like crazy, but he was free. Terrified and bleeding, he scanned the canopy but saw nothing. The sky was now totally black, and the cable was still.

He saw movement from the corner of his eye. A person? He turned his head to find himself face-to-face with the tree creature. Its face was all eyes and teeth. Its body was human enough, like a lemur or other lesser primate, with smooth, blotchy amphibian skin. Its jaw opened wider than James thought terrestrially possible as it released a hoarse coughing bark.

James screamed and fell back, ripping his jacket on the roots. Ignoring his ruined leg, he ran, stumbled, crawled, ran, fell. Behind him, the creature released an airy roar, like the sound a deer makes. He limped as fast as he could, crying out with every step.

11 FIGHT

THIS IS FUCKIN' CRAZY. *Who heckles a funeral reception?*

As they exited the Skyliner behind the three white men, Henry whispered to Jasmine, "I hope getting murked by lumberjacks doesn't run in your family."

Henry examined the backs of the three men. And he'd thought Buck was the Monster Energy militia. The three men—a tall metalhead with a big black beard; a twitchy hippie with a blond mustache; and a short, squat guy with a scraggly red beard—fit Henry's descriptor perfectly.

"These aren't lumberjacks. They're worse." The statement was barely out of her mouth when Jasmine threw her beer bottle at a parked truck, spraying glass everywhere. As the men shielded themselves from flying shrapnel, Jasmine ran up behind the leader, jumped, and beaned him with the blunt end of one of the axe heads from the wall inside. With the heckler on his knees, Jas kicked him so hard in the side of the head that the man spit out a tooth on his way down into the gravel and glass.

Henry's head swam. A screaming, insect-like fire drill sound filled his ears while every other sound was muffled. He could deal with patients at the H no problem. Even when it got racist, their violence never felt personal. This fight—fuckin' *yikes*.

The man actually tried to get back up, and Jasmine kicked him again. Red Beard grabbed Jas's shoulder, and she turned and kneed him hard in the balls, sending him to the ground as a crumbling, shivering mass.

The third one, the blond tweaker, gave Jasmine a wide berth while his friend on the ground screamed squeakily at her, "That's offside!"

Blackbeard got back up and wiped bloody snot into his hair.

These guys don't stay down? Henry had been in exactly one real fight in his life. In sixth grade, he made up a rumor that a kid mooned him and that Henry had seen dingleberries on his hairy ass, so the kid beat his ass. Henry had lain in the recess yard until everyone else went back in. That was a fair fight, with no shots to the balls or face, and it still hurt more than anything Henry had ever felt before or since. His teeth hurt watching these guys get their asses handed to them by his girlfriend. But they kept getting up.

Jasmine held her hands out at the three men and shouted, "What are you gonna do about it?"

"Holy shit," Henry gasped.

Next to him, Buck rolled his eyes. "S'just go home, ya squirrels."

"Hey, fuck you!" The tall, ugly heckler in the metal-band shirt yelled back, spitting blood onto his beard with every "f." "Fuck that black bitch! Fuck you and fuck you!" He turned and climbed up into the driver's seat of a truck and flipped everyone the middle finger, calling out, "You're gonna fucking pay for this."

Jasmine hocked a loogie on the truck when it passed by.

Even Tilly yelled back, "Eat me!"

The truck kicked up dust as it slowly looped out of the parking lot. The dust clouds glowed green in the neon light, sliced in two as one of the guy's friends tried to chase after him.

I can't believe we fucking won. "I can't believe you kicked all those guys' asses." Henry appraised the woman he'd thought of as his girlfriend. *I'm gonna make this rowdy bitch my girlfriend.*

Jasmine just grinned and turned to follow Tilly back into the bar. She bent over to pick her purse off the ground and really made a meal of it, neon light highlighting every curve. *I'm gonna make this* sexy *rowdy bitch my girlfriend*, he revised. He watched her ass move as she sauntered away.

When he moved to follow her, Henry walked into a sucker punch.

"Ah! Goddammit!" he yelled at the red-bearded brute. "That hurt!"

With no hesitation, Jasmine jumped on the guy's back and pinioned his arms to his sides. This dude was bigger and stronger than any patient but this time, for some reason, it seemed like she was having a way easier time. Her purse fell at Henry's feet.

Red Beard grunted, "Let go, you bitch!"

She squeezed her legs harder. The man screamed and collapsed to the ground, rolling around and kicking wildly. Jas screamed incoherently into his beanie. She let him go and rolled out of reach.

And, of course, the dude pushed himself forward to get back up and keep fighting a girl. He lurched forward at Jasmine, but glass broke over his head with a teeth-rattling crash. Henry smashed the framed newspaper clipping all the way down to Red Beard's shoulders, then pulled it back up.

The man fell onto the ground, groaning but unable to push himself up.

Henry waved the broken wooden frame, toothy with broken glass, at the other guy and bellowed, "You want some too?"

His blond friend backed away and tripped backward over an ATV. He stayed down. *Finally someone in this town with a self-preservation instinct.*

Henry's chest was heaving. *Am I dying? No, I just can't breathe from exhilaration. A goddamned barfight. And we won!* A strong hand clapped his shoulder, and he wheeled around, brandishing the frame, mouth full of bitter adrenaline. Jasmine.

"Hey," she exhaled.

Jasmine Bay glowed. A goddess with a halo of green neon. She was panting heavily and noticed him noticing her. Without hesitation, she kissed him, hard. Henry tasted blood in his mouth but didn't care. He dropped the broken frame and pulled her into him, but as soon as his hands slid down her waist, she suddenly pulled away. The look she gave him was like a scared animal rearing back in horror at a larger predator, even though she was looking down at him. She ran back toward the bar.

"Fuckin' crazy," Henry muttered to himself, savoring the bloody mineral taste in his mouth.

12 RAIN SLICKER

LATER, JASMINE EYED DOWN the scope of the plastic rifle, hitting every pixelated deer dead center. Henry leaned over from a barstool and admired her, occasionally licking his lips, still savoring her kiss. She avoided eye contact.

Jas set down the gun when Tilly walked up. The bar's neon lights reflected off the contours of her round face, streaking her dark hair red the way she used to dye it in high school. She was still so pretty. She looked upset.

"What's up, buttercup?" Jasmine smirked, trying to keep the mood light.

"The truck isn't in the parking lot."

"So?" Jasmine shrugged. "We knew he left."

Tilly frowned and pushed her hands into her jacket. "I know, it's just . . . He said he was going for a walk. I thought he'd be back for the memorial. I dunno, I just have a bad feeling."

Jasmine's phone chimed. "Speak of the Devil: text from your husband."

She squinted at her phone to read his garbled message. Maybe she was drunker than she'd thought.

James Bay
HENRY SEEMS LIKE A COOL GUY. I WANNA TRY TO GET ALONG THIS WEEKEND AND AS TO I SDAG UR QWERVAB. FOE TILLY. K?

"He says he wants to 'sdag' my 'qwervab.' Fuck's that about?"

Impatiently, Tilly asked, "Can we please go?"

Uggggggghhhh, kill me! I was just having some fucking fun. "Ugh, okay. But I'm drunk—drunker than I thought. I've been drinking all night 'n shit. So . . . has Henry."

Henry leaned precariously on his stool and babbled, "She's so drunk she kissed me. She's only done that once before. Like a month ago, in a closet at work. It was . . . I shouldn't drive either, yeah."

Jasmine was mortified by his recollection of the night. Cold shock gripped her. What would Tilly think?

Tilly's thick eyelids didn't waver. She just scoffed and jutted a hand out toward Henry. "Gimme your keys."

Jasmine's mind raced. *She truly couldn't care less. But now all that embarrassment was for nothing? Why am I even embarrassed for kissing my boyfriend—or whatever? Why doesn't Tilly care? Is she really that pissed at me for leaving?* Instead of letting those churning thoughts take over, she downed the rest of her drink and reached over to finish Henry's beer, winking at him as she drank it. He still wanted her, looked at her like she was something precious.

Henry's hybrid hummed along, slowly winding its way through massive fog. With Tilly behind the wheel, Henry sat shotgun; Jasmine tried to avoid the spins in the back seat by ill-advisedly sliding across the seat, trying to find a good position to lay down in. Her head hurt, and she just wanted to shut down. The familiarity of being driven home on the looping 101 stung with the knowledge that she wouldn't be able to curl up with Aunt Gin, who always brewed her some herbal tea and called her a "lil drunk ass" when she came home wasted.

"Go faster," she whined. "I'm gonna hurl."

"Jas," Tilly warned. "Shut the fuck up."

"You shut up." Those last drinks were hitting hard, and the lazy oxbows of the Redwood Highway did not help.

Tilly sighed. "Can you chill, please? I'm worried."

Jasmine burped at her. "He's fine. He wants to 'sdag' my 'qwervab,' remember?"

Henry cleared his throat. "That sounds like a drunk text maybe. I can barely text right now. Are we sure he's not just at a different bar?"

Jasmine and Tilly shut him down in unison: "There's only one bar in town."

"Well, shit, I dunno. Maybe he went home?"

Tilly shook her head. "No. He'd let me know. He always sends me a pin of his location."

Still writhing around to find a comfortable position in the hybrid's back seat, Jasmine scoffed. "Ew, why?"

"Because we love each other."

"Aw, that's sweet," Henry crooned.

"Sounds codependent but whatever."

"You know what?" Tilly started, then suddenly tapped the brake, hard enough to send Jasmine rolling off her seat onto the floor. A deer standing on the side of the road gingerly walked in front of the car. Tilly took advantage of the time and turned around to look Jasmine in the eye. "Fuck you, Jas. James is your brother, and he's a good man, and you'd notice that if you thought about anyone other than yourself for a freaking second." Tilly sighed. "He was trying to be chill and make nice with you, but you had to fuckin' needle him with that logger shit."

The deer passed, and Tilly continued to slowly drive along the winding, misty road.

Admonished, Jasmine leaned back in the back seat and pouted, while Henry sucked his teeth. Tilly squinted angrily at the fog. The next ten minutes passed in tense silence, until Henry's hybrid lolled up the bumpy road to the small house Tilly and James lived in. Jas tried not to think about how much this place had changed since she had last visited. It'd only been three years, but that was definitely a new storm door. Maybe different curtains. She tried to focus on the structural elements that were the same: the wilting sandpapery roof, the small porch that was always littered with camping chairs, the big redwood at the end of the driveway. It was no use—the place was a fucking dump, and she shouldn't be jealous. It was barely more than a shack.

But now it was all James's. Tilly was his too now. She pushed the burning jealousy she felt down into the ulcer under her ribs where all her indignation was boring a hole in her digestive tract.

"The driveway's empty," Tilly announced solemnly. Fog swirled through the headlight beams as the reality of the moment sunk in. James was missing, and they had no idea where he'd gone. They knew why, though.

Jasmine was about to start her apology when Tilly's phone rang. After the shock of its loudness, everyone breathed a sigh of relief when **JB<3** lit up the screen with James's face.

"Hey, where'd you go?"

"Can—hear—" His voice was staticky and cutting out all over the place.

"James! Where are you?"

"The woods . . . I . . . truck . . ."

"Where in the woods? Baby? James. Hello?" Tilly still had the phone up to her face. "It cut out. He says he's in the woods. He sounds hurt."

Jasmine reached for the car door and unlocked it. "Fuck. Well . . . Okay."

"Okay?" Tilly repeated with an undertone of "the fuck does that mean?"

Jasmine sighed. "Let's all get changed so we can start searching for him. He's in the woods, and the police won't take the report for another day, so we're the only ones who can go up there for him right now."

Henry interrupted, "You wanna go in the woods? Right now? It's nighttime."

"You wanna stay here?" Jasmine challenged.

Henry took a quick look at the shack. The sagging roof and dark windows looked especially scary tonight. "I'll come with y'all. Glad I brought a coat." Henry opened his door and started out of the car.

Tilly smiled. "Okay."

Jasmine reached around the driver's seat to hug Tilly from behind. "I'm sorry for being a bitch. We're gonna find him, and I'm gonna fix this."

Tilly avoided Jas's eye contact. "Thank you," she whispered.

"Hey, you guys? Look at this, please," Henry called from outside the car.

The two women followed Henry's pointing finger down the car headlight toward Aunt Gin's grave. Under the sentinel redwood, below a neat headstone marking the final resting place of Virginia Jones, 1938–2025, the fresh dirt was displaced. The grave had been dug up.

Jasmine fell out of the car and desperately stumbled toward the grave. Tilly clicked on her keychain flashlight and shined it down into the hole. No body. In its place was the outline of a human form made entirely of delicately arranged pine needles. Jasmine felt the ground drop out from under her. A powerful lurch that jolted outward from the ulcer in her stomach, climbing up her nervous system until the only thing she could feel was the cold, empty absence of the one purely positive thing in her life. Sobs whipped through her body. She felt sober and ashamed. Not for grieving her godmother but for not being able to muster that level of emotion for her missing brother.

"We had the hospital bed put in here," Tilly said by way of explanation.

The memory of the room she grew up in was a light miasma over what was now obviously a hospice care room. Her posters had been taken down and rolled up in a corner. Jasmine didn't need to unroll them because she could still see them, sun bleached and peeling on her wall, the way they'd looked when she'd last visited. When Aunt Gin was still alive and vivacious and supportive of her ambitions. The comforter on the bed was the same, at least. Jasmine smelled it to get a last whiff of her godmother's scent. Her heart reached out for the botanical mix of lemon and tea rose and earth that followed the woman, billowing like pollen from her swishy caftans. But it wasn't there. This room—her room—smelled medicinal and inert. Like the deathly H. Like a dead woman's room.

Jas could barely reconcile that Aunt Gin's vitality had diminished so much so quickly. The thought of it made her want to weep, but she had a mission. *Two, if you count finding out what the fuck happened to Gin's body.* The whole thing was so senseless. So grotesque. Jasmine pushed through the closet for something to wear. She still had on her dumb black dress from the wake and would need something a little better than that before bushwhacking through the redwood forest at night.

"You need a raincoat?" Tilly kneeled before the bed and pulled a bundle of purple plastic from the cedar chest where Jas used to hide magazines. She brandished it in Jas's direction.

"Absolutely not." *You've gotta be fucking kidding me.* Jasmine handled the nylon monstrosity. Its cheap fabric crinkled in her hands.

"Look." Tilly rubbed her eyes. "This is all that's left unless you wanna wear a garbage bag. I'll bring some garbage bags just in case. But just try it on."

Jasmine's hand slid through the raincoat's slippery polyester sleeve, emerging from the end and continuing . . . until the coat's sleeve ends squeezed her forearms. For a jacket she hadn't worn in twenty-five years, it fit remarkably well in the shoulders. Everything else . . .

"I'm not even gonna try and close it. This shitty raincoat won't fit over *one* boob."

Tilly winked. "Yeah, but you'll thank me when it's raining."

God*damn* her. Tilly and her fucking logic. She hadn't changed one bit. Actually, that wasn't true: Tilly had grown into herself. It dawned on Jasmine that in the years since she'd left Humboldt and had spent that time learning and growing, everyone else had too. This wasn't the same friend she'd left behind. "Hey Til?"

"Yep?"

"You're gonna be a great mom." She meant it. All the nervous voice-of-reason energy that Tilly had brought to their friendship as kids had blossomed into common sense and a strong sense of how the world worked. Kids need that clarity.

Tilly smiled ruefully. "And James is gonna be a great dad."

Jasmine crossed the small bedroom to loop her arms around her friend's shoulders. The raincoat made a horrific rubbery sound when she lifted her arms, but Jasmine didn't care. She hugged Tilly's back, pressing their faces together. "We'll find him."

Henry stood in the door. "Aw! Y'all are cute!" Lifting her gaze, she watched Henry taking in the scene, bedecked in head-to-toe hypebeast brands. *He won't get lost with all the neon, I guess.* Was Jasmine imagining the lascivious look in his eyes? Was seeing her hug her best friend reminding him of some porn he'd seen? Skinny, white lesbians contorting in the same way? Maybe not. Maybe she was projecting. Maybe he meant what he said. It was cute. Maybe he was a good man. A regular person. Not just some fucking guy.

Henry's face dropped uncomfortably as Tilly's shoulders began to heave under Jasmine's arms. Her friend turned around and sobbed into her chest. Jasmine was so much taller than Tilly that when they hugged, her friend fit perfectly into her arms.

"She was really bad these past few years," Tilly gasped out. "She would just berate him constantly, then just run off into the woods and disappear for days and nights at a time. She'd come back covered in dirt and screaming about all kinds of crazy shit. This feels like that." Tilly gulped and clutched Jasmine, pulling her in.

Suddenly, the sound of rustling in the kitchen broke the moment.

Tilly released Jasmine's midsection and nearly knocked Henry down, rounding the hall to the kitchen–living room. It sounded like a bear was rifling through their fridge, and Jasmine almost hoped it was one. If James was home, then Jasmine would have to make good on her promise to make up with him. The prospect chilled her to the bone. She didn't really know the man he'd become; she just knew the punk kid he'd been and the best friend he'd stolen from her.

"Goddamn it!" Tilly shouted from the kitchen.

"S'up?" Buck's deep voice growled. "I hear we're doin' a search party. Figured I'd pack up provisions in case you forget."

"How did you hear about this? We just fucking decided."

"Henry texted me. Y'all need a truck too, prob'ly."

In Aunt Gin's bedroom, Jasmine sat on the bed and pulled on some thermal leggings and jean shorts that still kinda fit. The rain slicker's seams loosened around her armpits until it was almost comfortable. Jasmine figured that keeping the dress on underneath would be okay. It's good to layer in the woods.

Tilly's voice was shrill. "How the fuck did he—? Ugh, yeah. We do. Thank you for being here. Pack some garbage bags too."

Overhearing the argument in the kitchen, she and Henry exchanged a look that said, "Yes, I did, and yes it was a good idea, but I was wrong for doing it." Henry, floundering, reached for a notebook on the nightstand and flipped through it. He held it out to Jasmine. Months and months of medication info and vitals; a home-baked reminder that James and Tilly had been doing her job as well as she could've up here. Jasmine gave the notebook a last flip. On one of the last pages was a rough, black pencil drawing of a body made of needled leaves. Who drew it? Tilly? James? Aunt Gin? Jasmine needed answers and rushed out to the kitchen.

"Who drew this?" she demanded.

"Hey, Jas. S'a nice jacket." Buck smirked.

Jasmine brushed past him to Tilly. "Til, who drew this in Gin's med log?"

Tilly took the notebook, and her eyes widened. "I don't know. This was in her notebook?"

"Buck, did you see outside?" Henry asked. He appeared at the front window, peeking through the new curtains. "Somebody dug up the grave out front."

"S'some freaky shit." Buck exhaled. He filled jugs with water, and Henry abandoned the window to help him.

"I hate to ask, but is there any way James could've dug up Aunt Gin's body?" Henry asked the room.

Tilly looked up from the notebook and glared daggers at him.

Jasmine felt the pointed stare and tried to will Henry to shut up, but he kept going. "What I don't get is why would you bury her in your front yard?"

Tilly crossed the room to him swiftly, like a predator, and was suddenly up in his face. "You don't 'get' a lot of what happens here. James wanted to bury her here, at the home she loved, rather than some cemetery. So, we buried our elder on our land because we are planning on being here forever." She spread her recrimination, turning toward Jasmine fiddling with her ill-fitting rain slicker. "This place was always temporary for you. My people have been here longer than anyone thinks."

"Sheesh, he was just asking a question," Buck spoke up. "James was pretty torn up about Gin today at the funeral, so I don't think he dug her up."

"One mystery at a time," Jasmine commanded, already exhausted at the conversation. "Are we all packed up?" Sitting on the cable spool table, she pulled on hiking boots that hadn't been worn since high school and would almost definitely blister her feet, despite the two pairs of socks she wore.

Buck and Tilly nodded.

"Okay, then. Let's go find him." She smoothed down her hair and headed for the door.

13 THE NIGHT CUT

IT WAS EARLY EVENING, but the dense redwood canopy made it look much later. These woods and their dark awnings smothered the sky until daylight felt like a hallucination. On the ground, the light played tricks on the eye. So little of it filtered through the dense canopy that the forest was in perpetual twilight, flattening and desaturating colors until everything took on the tone of a vintage daguerreotype photo. It was one of the many things one gets used to when working in the redwood forest. The size and scale of the trunks messed with a person's sense of distance. The trees muffled some sounds and amplified others. The forest did her damnedest to blind and deafen anyone who dared to steal her treasures. But a job's a job.

Gary Guay and the rest of the three-man crew had been working at a pretty good clip, felling telephone pole–width trees and stacking them in neat piles next to a gnarled stump. The trees were dinky saplings compared to the old-growth giants cut down by the loggers' predecessors. But their predecessors didn't have a CAT feller buncher, a twenty-foot-tall, forty-ton machine with a hydraulic claw that could grab a stand of phone poles and pull them clean out of the ground. If any of them got stubborn, it had an attachment that could saw off trunks below the claw.

Roddy was operating the feller buncher, not tearing trees out of the ground but stacking them in neat piles ten feet high. When Gary had more time on the crew under his belt, he'd get trained on operating the behemoth.

His cousin Oscar's white pickup sat at the far end of the cut, separated from the log piles by a few young trees, barely saplings, whose flexible strength would be able to protect the pickup from errant logs. Always prepared, Oscar was outfitted in his warm vest with way too many pockets. He took inventory of the stacked logs.

With a statutory deadline at midnight, they needed to get as much timber out tonight before they were barred from the area for another ten years. The logging op would just move onto a new area where their rights hadn't expired, and they would be okay, but Oscar's pride was wrapped up in it. The principle of completion required nothing short of his absolute best.

A small truck revved its engine nearby, whining like a jammed chainsaw as it struggled up the logging road. Blinding purple-white LED lights glittered through the trees, and an unwieldy Tacoma rolled into the area, stopping next to Oscar's pickup.

The fourth member of tonight's team had arrived. He was late, but with the last name Mooney, the kid could do pretty much whatever he wanted on North Coast Timber property. This stand would be North Coast Timber property for another few hours.

Quint Mooney, class of 2028, hopped down, clad in fresh outerwear: a fleece vest with matching Air Jordan Retro High OGs on his feet. He pulled out a brand-new Stihl, the most lightweight and state-of-the-art chainsaw on the market. He revved it once, way too focused on looking cool and like he knew what he was doing. He approached the other men and sliced through saplings as he walked. The kid wore a gold chain around his neck, and Gary wondered how his scraggly beard hair didn't get stuck in it. The boy looked like he prided himself on his ability to talk with absolutely anyone, no matter where they went to college.

No one else on this crew had gone to college. Instead, they had training. Enough training to know not to unnecessarily cut saplings.

Without looking up from his clipboard, Oscar called out, "That's your grandkids' harvest you're chopping off there."

Quint scoffed. "Pssht, we won't even be using wood by then."

Pile complete, Roddy stepped down from the CAT but left its lights on. The feller buncher's spotlight was weak and dirty in comparison to the eye-watering halogen.

Quint tried to rush past Roddy to jump in the feller buncher, but the older man grabbed him by the collar and wheeled him back around, ripping the fleece vest. He growled at the boy. "Kid, we're on deadline. We have to get this whole stand before midnight, so we do *not* have time to drive your ass to the hospital when you kill yourself out here."

"Oh," Quint replied calmly. "You think you're in charge? I'm going to Yale for grad school. I own your ass. Fuck with me, and you can kiss your pension goodbye."

"I don't have a pension, you little shit-punk," Roddy spat back.

"Rod, take a breath." Oscar intervened with the quiet, respectful diplomacy he was known for. He was both a numbers man and a genuine leader. "Over there." When Roddy stormed back to the CAT, Oscar addressed Quint Mooney, his boss's son. The title should mean nothing on a work site but in an industry like this, a company like this, it meant everything. "Mr. Mooney, you can't drive the feller buncher. Sir."

Behind them, deep in the trees, wood snapped loudly.

The kid jumped. "What was that?"

Gary was securing the log pile nearby. "Maybe it was Bigfoot." He laughed.

"I just wanted to use the, uh, CAT to pull up that stump over there," Quint whined, pointing at the stump that served as the leftmost boundary of the log piles. "C'mon, man. At least help me saw the burl off. We can sell it to some Etsy jagoff and make a few hundred bucks." He elbowed Oscar conspiratorially.

"Fuck is Etsy?" Roddy barked meanly from the dark.

Taken aback, the kid tried to explain. "It's a website where people who pour resin on— Ugh, shut up!" Quint picked up his chainsaw from the ground and handed it to Gary, who'd joined the huddle at this point. "Just get the fucking burl. Put it in my truck."

Gary shared a glance with Oscar at the usage of the words "my truck" but shrugged and carried the chainsaw to the stump. Roddy climbed up into the CAT to turn it and train its floodlights on the stump. The second Gary revved the chainsaw, both the feller buncher's and the Tacoma's lights shut off abruptly. They were left in total darkness.

No one could see Gary Guay's handsome face collapse into hysterical screams. The blackness took hold of him sharply and suddenly. Yanked him downward. Gary fell toward the stump, and bark scratched his cheeks.

No, it wasn't blackness that had grabbed him. Whatever tugged at him had a heartbeat. It pulled in peristaltic bursts, like a pelican swallowing. Whatever it was, it was alive. The sweat on his skin turned ice cold, and Gary's face broke open with renewed terror. "Something's pulling me!" He screamed until his voice was hoarse and sounded faraway in his own head.

In the dark, sound was all he had. Over his heart beating in his ears and his own screaming, Gary could hear his comrades scrambling around in the sawdust and redwood needles. Dry clattering stumbled off in different directions, but Gary knew as well as anyone how these woods played tricks on the senses. He tried to assure himself that the sounds he was hearing were not there, like the swollen crackle of the stump behind him. It was like the thing was breathing. *Heaving.* He yanked at his leg, but the strong root kept pulling him downward.

The men ran to find light. Roddy opened the emergency flare box in the CAT. Oscar dug through his vest pockets for a flashlight and stumbled toward his cousin.

The boy, Quint Mooney, ran terrified back toward his Tacoma. Unbeknownst to the crew, the kid's sneakers slipped on leaf litter, and he tripped forward, downward, onto one of the sawed-off saplings. The hard little stump shoved into the boy's beard, pressed his beard inward through his skin, and impaled his jaw in a celebration of hair, teeth, flesh, and blood. Farther below, another angry sapling stuck out of the kid's back like a spout and soaked the ground with Quint Mooney's viscera.

The red spray of Roddy's road flare caught the last bit of Gary's hand disappearing below the stump's roots. Below the stump, the young logger wailed from a grave-sized hole in the ground, barely visible through the stump's roots in the dark red flare light. "Get me outta here!"

"We'll get ya, buddy," Oscar promised.

"Grab my hand!" Roddy yelled, reaching through the roots to pull Gary out. After some struggle, the two men hoisted him through. The three men lay sprawled and panting on the uneven tangle of root-covered ground.

The CAT's lights flickered on suddenly. Like a streetlamp, it needed time to juice up and a emitted weak, sherbet-colored light in the first few minutes. Relieved, the men shared a nervous chuckle and started to stand. Roddy heaved with effort and rose to his feet, then pulled up Gary.

When Oscar started to place his hands on the ground to rise, one of the roots shifted toward him. It *clutched* his wrist. The root had a hand. And elbow joints. Oscar smashed his flashlight onto the hand until it let go. His flashlight beam fell upon a lightning-shaped hole in the stump.

Within the rustling dark of the stump, something moved. Oscar focused on the movement and saw wetness. The lights' reflections were cast from the smooth jelly of a dark, bloodshot eye. It blinked. Whatever it was inside the stump moved; white flashlight, red flare, and orange spotlight reflected off wet-looking skin. But it was skin. Behind Oscar, the frenetic *whoosh* of the flare reduced to a whimper. The trees raged above them in a sudden gust.

Oscar realized he had been screaming when he no longer could. His raw vocal cords crackled like kindling.

The men yanked him to his feet, and they were halfway toward his pickup, all patting different pockets for keys. Someone started the truck, and the brake lights illuminated one last surprise.

Near the dead Tacoma, the men found Quint Mooney's body sprawled over a puddle of blood. In the red brake lights, the scene was medieval: a decadent martyrdom. A pale shard like a vampire's stake rose bloody from the back of the boy's skull. Gory bamboo shoots of cut saplings sprang from his backside. The boy was dead, pincushioned to the forest floor.

The men sped away in Oscar's truck, leaving the boy's body behind. They had all screamed themselves mute, so they sat in eerie silence. Their panicked breaths punctuated the stillness, interspersed by jerky non-yelps, and branches pounded against the truck as the vehicle carried them back to civilization.

END OF PART 1

PART 2

GOD COUNTRY

14 MARIAN

1980

STEPPING OUTSIDE FOR HER morning chore, Marian leaned on the cabin's porch railing and opened the rubber stopper on the white plastic water tank. It sat abutting the porch on a trailer that hitched to her father's truck. She poured the mug of antibiotic powder into the tank, banging the mug on the lip to loosen any clingers. Her task completed, she replaced the rubber stopper and gave herself permission to drink a soft drink and daydream before the loggers arrived. She slid the soda can under her red, striped crop top to open it and muffle the sound from her parents, who were inside arguing again.

Mama had recently lost another baby, so tensions were running high. Better they fight each other than unite against her. When her mother lost a baby, Marian felt guilty. Her parents' gazes drilled into her, accusing, jeering, as if to say *Why are you the one that lived?* The air in the moss-covered cabin already hung heavy with the smell of forest and soil. When that heavy air became the armature for the Whipple family to hang its unspoken shame and guilt on, the cabin adopted a heaviness that felt like being smothered by a pillow.

Canned soda was Marian's favorite distraction, strong flavors to combat the dense atmosphere of her world. The chemical sweetness surfed down her tongue, igniting every taste bud on the way down. She imagined the flavors dancing through her bloodstream, bringing their modern energy to every part of her body. The can was bottled in Sacramento. She wondered about the state capital, what it was like. Probably less wooded than here. Maybe.

"She's certainly your daughter!" her mother's voice bellowed from inside. Great, they were fighting with each other *about* her.

"I'm trying!" Pop returned. "You have no idea—"

The mossy insulation on the cabin swallowed some of the sound. Not enough.

Marian slouched even further over the railing, balancing the full weight of her thin body on it until she was dizzy. From upside down, the white skylight in the canopy looked like a lake, like the bottom of the world. Maybe if she let go it would suck her down like a drain. Bobbing over the railing, the trees moved to hide the hole in their world from her. Black jail bars of redwood and pine and cedar tried to cover her eyes and shield her from thoughts of escape. So Marian closed her eyes.

As her inverted head filled with blood, she fantasized about being scooped out, sucked down, pulled by strong hands. Down out of this forest and washed out into the world: where people went to real schools instead of sitting around reading old books; where cars drove on asphalt roads instead of pine duff; where there was more sky than trees; where she could be around people, all different kinds, and talk to them and learn from them and maybe even go to a restaurant. The world was pure potential for young Marian Whipple. All she wanted was to see it for herself. But Mama and Pop were determined to keep her in the mossy Foreman's Cabin, shut away behind closed doors, only to be brought out for special occasions like a first aid kit.

Her blood-filled ears heard the trucks coming up the dirt logging road. The Mooney men were here. Marian levered back up and smoothed her twin braids, readjusting herself from head to toe. She tried to look nonchalant and untouchable to the men hopping down from the trucks. Young men in red flannel and yellow safety vests milled around the wood-chip parking lot. They puffed on cigarettes and pushed each other, laughing. When she was little, Marian used to want to be one of them.

They mostly ignored her. Not all of them, thankfully. Without her daily chats with the loggers, Marian would never know anything about the world beyond this forest. One young guy, Tall Matt, sauntered out of his white Pontiac with the super-loud engine. Marian tried not to ogle as he smoothed his red-brown mustache and smirked at her. He was so tall and manly and strong and white and cool. His eyes on her made Marian feel electrically aware of her darker skin, but not in the same way she felt when she was with her mom or dad, neither of whom she looked like.

He approached the porch to toss his cigarette butt into the metal barrel next to the water tank.

She swallowed down the feelings of insecurity and managed to greet him. "Hi, Tall Matt."

"Hey, Mary."

"It's Marian."

Tall Matt smirked. "Yeah. Maid Marian. What're ya doin'?"

"I live here, so obviously nothing." She leaned over the banister toward him, which had the intended effect. His eyes wandered down to her flat chest.

"How old are you anyway?"

"Fifteen."

"Jailbait, eh? I get off at eight." He winked. "So I'll see you at 7:30."

She laughed at the idiotic pickup line. She tried to laugh the way she imagined girls laughed in places like Sacramento.

Marian's manic giggling alerted an older, bearded logger named Smitty. The lumberjack lumbered toward the mossy cabin where the foreman's daughter was getting herself in trouble. He clapped a hand on Tall Matt's shoulder and ordered, "Hey. Big Jonesy's lookin' for ya."

The boy sputtered, "Well, I'm—"

"Bye." Smitty pushed him away.

"Bye, Maid Marian!" The kid called over his shoulder. The girl blushed.

Even a flimsy-mustached greenhorn like this gangly virgin should know better than to hit on the boss's daughter. This job was dangerous enough without that kind of target on your back. *Where do they fucking find these guys?*

Smitty opened his vest and pulled a newspaper from an inside pocket: that day's *Times-Standard* that he'd read at breakfast before heading up to work. He passed it up to the girl. "Don't get mixed up with these punks, Miss Marian. They'll lead you astray."

His voice was warm and caring, not at all like her father's, still yelling indistinctly inside the cabin. Smitty was a good guy, but Marian knew what she was about. "If 'astray' means out of here, I'll take it."

Smitty frowned, and his frizzy beard hair rearranged around his jaw. "Astray means they'll shackle you to this place with a chain made of babies. You're smart, but don't mistake smart for being grown up."

Marian shuddered.

Smitty softened. "Just b'careful around these guys, okay?"

She nodded.

Behind her, the cabin door slammed open. The screen door spring screeched after hitting the cabin wall, and Marian's father stomped out: From his height-enhancing caulk boots to his white, short hair, everything about him accentuated the taut red veins of his ill temper. It swept across the group of men like a fast-moving fog, drawing them toward the cabin. He turned to his daughter. "Get inside! And cover up for Christ's sake. You look like a hooker."

Arms clapped over her midsection and red-faced with embarrassment, Marian Whipple—William Whipple's most beloved daughter—stormed past him into the protection of the moss-covered Foreman's Cabin.

"Boss." Smitty nodded.

"Smitty. We're headed out soon, so you get plenty of water. Make sure the others do too."

15 INTO THE WOODS

BUCK'S TRUCK CLIMBED THE logging road in almost total darkness. They left the house around midnight but had been looping up the logging road for what felt like forever. The trees teased Jasmine with intermittent, brief views of the lights in Humboldt Bay Harbor. Container ships, not unlike the ones that entered the Port of Oakland, came, unloaded, loaded, and left. Transporting Humboldt County forest products around the world.

These woods were the last place Jasmine wanted to be. The past is a ghost, and this part of her past had haunted her, her entire adult life, looming large and dark in the background of her psyche like the tall black trees. As a child, she had loved the forest and was an avid camper. Aunt Gin had taught her all about the forest. But it scared her now; its dark, stark peaks stared down at her, a tiny human who dared to exist in a world that wasn't hers. This forest wasn't hers. It never had been. But she was back now. Now, it had her and judged her with a million green-gray eyes and found her insignificant.

In the passenger seat, Tilly screamed James's name out the window and desperately strained to listen for a response.

Jasmine hoped James was okay. For Tilly's sake. And the baby's. She had to keep it together for them.

She had let the darkness in before—no use in ignoring reality—and it had draped over her like a shroud. But she was still going. Fuck Henry for saying she was suicidal when she was just being realistic: The life she had wasn't the one she wanted. *What do I want?* She looked over at him sitting beside her in the cab's back seat. He caught her glance and placed his warm hand over hers. Right now, it was nice to have him here. Someone whose loyalties weren't split between her and James. She squeezed his fingers. *Kill yourself* darted through her thoughts, and she pulled her hand back abruptly. *Henry isn't on your side. He doesn't like the real you. You've never shown him what you're* really *like. Everything you do is a front. Just trying to trick people into liking you. He's gonna find you out and run for the hills.*

Snaking up the mountain, the cracking of the truck's wheels over branches was the only sound. Behind it, the trees glowed red in the brake lights. The round whorls of sword ferns reflected the light like an animal's eyes and stared into Jasmine. She turned away, shamed again. The forest's eyes reminded her of Tilly's reproach. "*This place was only temporary for you.*"

Of fucking course it was temporary. I was always going to leave. Hometowns are for *leaving.* But technically, Oakland was her hometown; it was where she and James were born, and she had lived there for almost the same amount of time she'd spent in Redcedar. *Fuck you, Tilly, and your holier-than-thou "we were here first" bullshit.* If Tilly really cared about being a steward of the land or whatever the Wiyots believed, she wouldn't let James work for the logging company and destroy the forest she claimed to care so deeply about.

The dusty road behind the truck was pale and dying. Because of the goddamned logging. When the trees died, their root systems couldn't replenish the soil with nutrients, so the soil dried out and blew away until nothing could grow. That affected the rivers and the health of the entire area.

James ran toward that life with open arms. Away from Gin and everything she had taught them. And Tilly supported it. *Fucking hypocrites.*

The trees gazed down at her impassively: black sentries staking out the entire mountain. Jasmine kept thinking about the trees as guards, but were they keeping people out of their world, or keeping them from leaving it? Even as they killed it with axes and saws, the forest kept the people of Humboldt protected and trapped in its piney arms.

James was right about limited opportunities. Buck had probably been really lucky to get that farm security job. The growers weren't too kind to guys who looked like him and James, and never paid them fairly. James was just trying to support his family. She couldn't fault him that. Driving a truck for the lumberyard was probably better than doing it for Amazon. He was trying to keep his shit together as much as she was. He was just so damned hard to talk to. He was different from her. But maybe not irreconcilably so.

Everything was falling apart. Out there. Up here. In these woods. Inside her heart and mind and body. Her stomach ached. Her back ached a little less.

I'm just trying to stay alive myself. Jasmine repeated it in her head like a mantra. It wasn't a prayer—this was just for her. But the mantra became a call and response as she was reminded of the loneliness she felt away from this place. The feelings that drove her away. The people who caused them. The thoughts that swam around her like ghosts: *Your life is never going to get better. You're not good at your job. If you were, people would be nice to you. You're bad and wrong and need to be locked away. Just kill yourself, and do everyone a huge favor.* She had to shove those thoughts aside. There was no room for that here. James was missing, and if she could find him, then there was a chance to fix things, no matter how much that scared her. She whispered a prayer to the forest: *Please let my brother live.*

16 THWANG

JAMES BAY WAS LIVING in some kinda goddamned nightmare. In order to escape those cancer-bodied freaks, he was limping through a forest in his funeral clothes, dragging his dead leg down a godforsaken mountain. He couldn't feel anything below where the stump root had impaled him, but it might just be shock—he prayed it was shock, but was secretly grateful for the break from the pain that normally stabbed through his hip flexors. Gasping for breath, he stumbled blindly through the understory. Sword ferns and salmonberry bushes slapped his face and scratched his hands.

The sounds of those creatures chased him, taunting him like a police escort. Were they escorting him or herding him toward an ambush? James hoped against hope that he could elude the things on what was obviously their home turf. He needed to hide. His leg dragged through the duff, kicking up dust and spraying pine needles in irregular arcs.

When he spotted a water tank through the trees, he didn't care if he was being herded. The creatures' sounds grew fainter: their coughing exhalations, their metallic thwanging on the logging cables that crisscrossed this part of the woods. James clocked the white plastic and categorized it as man-made, therefore safe. A line of the same brand of water tanks on their rolling trailers stood at attention next to a fence at the back of the lumberyard. Crews took them up to the cut all the time.

He felt alone in the silent woods. That brought an entirely different kind of fear shivering up his body. *If those things don't kill me, I could still die here.* He fell to his knees at the tank's spigot and gulped down cold water. It left a gritty texture on his teeth, likely dirt from however long it had been sitting here. James let water run onto his destroyed leg. He felt the soothing freeze of the air cooling his wet jeans, but his leg itself was still numb.

The log cabin rose out of the darkness behind the tank. James lugged himself up the stairs onto the porch. The "nice boots" that Tilly made him wear clunked on the heavy, rotting wood. The front door had been boarded up previously, but the pried-off boards lay discarded on the porch. James knocked, and the busted door in its frame opened easily. Inside, the two-room cabin was quiet as a tomb. Quiet as the outside.

The main room was a combination living room/dining room with a kitchenette attached. A thick layer of dust covered everything. When James touched it, the dust was resinous. He rifled through the cabinets to find a first aid kit for his leg and wrestled a box away from the spiderwebs. The faucet ran no water, so he was forced to sanitize the wound with the dregs of a vodka bottle he found knocked over in a cabinet under the sink.

Through the kitchen window, James spotted about a dozen creatures moving about in the darkness. Up and down the trees they ran. Chattering, barking their plosive coughs. Angry. He pulled himself up and leaned back against the mossy wall, feeling around for a door.

With his good leg, he kicked the cabin's interior door shut. The screen door was a lost cause. The windows were boarded up, and James crawled around in total darkness. He felt the dark frame of a sofa and pushed it against the door. The creatures scratched at the windows and batted on the door and stomped at the floor from beneath. James threw himself on the couch to hold it down. The door rattled in the frame, jostling James with bass thumps so regular that—when paired with the metallic shaking of the sofa coils—the reverberation calmed him, made his eyelids heavy. The sofa enveloped him like a tongue.

No!

James forced himself awake. This was too easy. He fought the cabin's musty, soporific air, willed his aching eyes to stay open even though they seared with every millisecond of contact; he stuck his finger into his thigh in the hope that the pain would jolt his body into wakefulness. Instead, he plunged it into the wound, and his skin felt nothing but the friction from woody splinters embedded inside his flesh.

But he felt no pain. His brain screamed, knowing what the excruciating reality *should* be. Adrenaline flooded his mouth, sharp and acrid: the intended effect. James was so saturated with fear and stress that he didn't know if he would close his eyes again. His dilated pupils darted back and forth to locate the minutest sound. But the sounds he sought were gone: no rattling, no scratching, no batting. Only the pregnant non-silence of the forest: leaves rustling, insects trilling, a faraway twig snapping.

17 OVERLOOK

"JAMES AND I USED to come here a lot." Tilly stood on a huge stone overlook.

Paint-tagged boulders perfectly framed a view of Humboldt County's emerald hills limned by dense fog and the Pacific Ocean. Henry hadn't realized it was all so close together. He looked down the cliff. The bar and the 101 were just a stone's throw away. But not a person's throw away. If you hoped to make it down in one piece, you'd need the fifty minutes of looping back road they took up here.

"Yeah, that's usually how people get pregnant around here." Jasmine smirked.

"Eat me."

"Eat yourself. You could use the calories, you skinny bitch."

"Why would I eat myself when you'd rather do it, you feral slut?" Tilly shot back, making Jasmine blush and turn away.

It always surprised Henry to hear women talk to their friends that way. He'd never heard Jasmine talk like that before. But he'd also never seen her with friends before—up till now he wasn't sure she had any. Normally he found women talking like that off-putting and indicative of a lack of home training. But here, in her real home, Jasmine Bay had a pheromonal hold on him or something because everything she did was charming. Henry felt lighter than the highest air at the thought that she was sharing this bizarre look into her past with him. He didn't say anything, instead nearing one boulder to find "TIGERF*GS" painted across it. Probably visible from the highway.

After that bar fight, it wouldn't surprise him to learn that Jasmine had been the one who'd tagged slurs on the rock and become some kind of local legend. Maybe she'd been a student environmental activist who lived up in a tree to save it. Equally likely. There was so much about her that he didn't know. Did she get into fights a lot? Was she punching bitches back in Oakland? Henry hadn't been in a fight since middle school. He never even talked to anyone from back then. Maybe small towns were just like this. Humboldt had been nothing short of relentlessly weird as fuck so far. Everyone he'd met had been aggressively chill but in a way that infused the air with musty static.

Below him, the clear-cut separated the bar from the road, and a slim tract of trees separated the bar from an even larger clear-cut. From the bar parking lot, it looked like an impenetrable forest on that side. From up here, it looked *maybe* twenty or so yards deep. So the new clear-cut made the first clear-cut seem not as big with the thin screen of trees. It also made it seem small because this one was *so* much bigger in comparison. A pretty little fence to hide how big the problem actually was. Typical. Fuckin' white people and their polite smoke screens. Henry shook his head.

By way of explanation, Buck quietly materialized next to him and pointed at the tract of trees and mumbled, "S'a beauty strip."

"Like a Brazilian?" Henry couldn't stop himself from quipping back.

Just as Henry was starting to internally chastise himself for his big mouth, Buck's face bloomed into a grin. Even Tilly chuckled that time, and Jasmine smiled appreciatively. Jokes can make things feel better as they get worse. If he could make these people laugh and feel a little better with *everything* going on, that was something. A missing guy and a missing dead lady. Shit. Henry wanted to be useful here in any way he could.

A sound like a wooden baseball bat cracking rang through the trees behind them. Everyone flinched. Henry tried not to let the fear make him tense his already sore back from the drive. "What . . . was that?"

"Bigfoot," Tilly said, deadpan.

Buck playfully reached out to cover her face with his big hand. "S'probably eucalyptus bark."

"Oh yeah!" Jasmine chirped. "The bark peels down but doesn't fall off all the way. Then the wind catches it, and it hits against its own trunk like clack, clack, clack." She hooked her fingers together to form a tree then pivoted one hand down to tap against her forearm.

"Cool. Cool." Henry didn't think it was cool. But he wanted to encourage Jasmine to keep talking to him. *Bark? You come up here, and you get scared like an asshole in the fucking park.* He was frustrated that he'd acted like a coward and played into the paranoid city-slicker trope. Right now he wanted nothing more than to lay down in the middle of the road and let a heavy truck squish his body into the earth until he became nothing.

Tilly clapped her hands. "Enough squawking, let's search. JAMES! BABY!"

Jasmine shot Henry a sympathetic look. *I'm not totally alone here*, he remembered. "How are we doing this?" Jas asked. "Should we split up?"

"If we split up, you'll be looking for two lost niggas in the woods instead of just the one." Henry clapped his hand over his mouth far too late. *Of all the things to fuckin' blurt out. You and your fuckin' jokes. Asshole.*

His comment hung there, unavoidable as a bad national anthem.

"We can split up," he rebounded. "This is as good a place to start as any."

Henry could catch glimpses of the other three through the trees but still felt hopelessly alone. The others' silhouettes shimmered like a mirage, closer and farther, depending on the trees. It was impossible to judge distances out here. Sometimes it looked like there were more people walking alongside him than Jasmine, Buck, and Tilly. This place was trippy. He thought about the loggers Jasmine's granddaddy had dosed with LSD, and he no longer wanted to try hallucinogenic drugs out here. He did wish that he'd brought edibles or something to help with how anxious he felt. And the back pain. The back of his hand looked pale against the forest's saturated darkness. The biggest trees' lowest branches formed a ceiling above them. How could all these redwood trees block out so much moonlight? And why did they need to be so damn big?

Having clocked the coats of the other three to his right, a noise on his left scared Henry so much his guts lurched like they were going to fall out. He noticed movement on that side as well, but he didn't dare mention it to the others. *Hold it together, man. Don't be the jumpy city dude who can't handle shit and makes everything worse.* He tried to take deep breaths, but the forest air was too heavy with Pine Sol–flavored vapor, too chilly when he breathed it in, and too much like warm breath on the back of his neck.

The greenery was oppressive on his eyes after a lifetime of the variegated grays of the city: BART stations, his apartment building, sidewalks, the H, its peeling linoleum corridors, the patients' dumb little grippy socks. Not all grays were bad, though. For example: the little silver starburst of hairs on the back of Jasmine's head. The warm gray door to the supply closet. Gray he was used to. It made sense. In Oakland, a block was a block was a block. Up here, distances were jumbled and confusing. He couldn't find north right now even if the compass app on his phone did work up here. People on TV said that moss grows on the north side of trees, but there was moss on every side of these tree trunks.

The ground was uneven. A man was missing in this forest. In these creepy-ass woods where men died and lost limbs constantly. Where that missing black man's white grandfather was lynched. Everything about this place was upside down. And now Henry was traipsing blindly through that same forest as if his presence would help anything.

He pulled a magenta tie-dye hoodie out of his backpack and slipped it on. Tilly rolled her eyes. *Is it me or does this bitch kinda hate me?* Henry thought. "What?"

Keep it light. He fanned out from the group back toward the logging road. *What's the difference between poison ivy and poison oak?* He started high-stepping when he realized he didn't know what poison ivy or poison oak looked like. In the light of his flashlight, everything looked washed out and colorless. The redwoods took on the familiar grays of his home city, adopted the grays that he knew and loved. It unnerved him, like a too-real mask of a human face. *Fuuuck this forest, man.* A splash of red ruptured the gray tones, sticking out of a moss-covered log. Henry high-stepped toward it and pulled it out of the log: a baseball cap with a patch that read BIGFOOT LIVES. *Fuuuck.*

"Y'all! Over here!" Henry called out.

Jasmine reached him first, followed by Buck, then Tilly. Henry held the hat out limply at the Blackmans.

The pregnant woman in her neon-yellow beanie snatched it out of his hands.

Henry asked, "This is his hat, right?"

Tilly looked up and down the dusty road near them. "Yep. When James called, he said 'truck.'" She nodded up the hill. "We should follow the logging road until we find something."

"Then we at least have a way to get back down," Jasmine added.

"S'go," Buck said gruffly, then added, with some brightness, "S'good. We're close to where he's been tonight. Good eye, Henry."

He clapped a huge palm on Henry's back, and even though it felt a bit like being paddled, Henry basked in the attention. He was trying so hard in this fucking impossible situation, and it warmed him to get that recognition from Buck. He'd rather it come from Jasmine, but good vibes were scarce in the chilly, aggressive redwoods. Coming up to the ass end of the state to just hang around while the woman he was obsessed with went through one of the most stressful things that can happen to a person had been a bad idea that had snowballed into worse as the hours ticked by.

Flashlight beams zigzagged across the trees as the group traipsed up the mountain road. After almost an hour of fruitless hiking and shouting, the road terminated at a dark wall of trees.

Beyond the trees, a light shone like something outta *The X-Files* or that one really scary movie where the aliens abducted . . . loggers in the woods.

Shit. *I swear to God*, Henry thought, *if we get abducted on top of all of this other shit, I'm gonna lose it.*

18

BRIGHT LIGHT GIRL

1980

MARIAN DECIDED TO TRY hitchhiking for herself after reading about it in the newspaper. She wasn't sure what she'd even say if a driver stopped, she had so little experience with strangers. She'd never met anyone who didn't know her parents, who didn't know her as "Whipple's little girl" or "the boss's daughter." Mama's friend Aunt Charlyne always called her "babygirl"—Mama did too, sometimes—and Marian had recently begun to hate the nickname, cringing every time the woman's big red lips pressed together to form the plosive *b*—.

She held out her thumb, feeling stupid. The first vehicle that passed was a freight truck that honked and kicked up splinters at her, scaring Marian off the shoulder. Its horn roared, and Marian heard the driver yell "Nice legs!" She scampered into the ravine, hiding behind the Redcedar sign, terrified that another of the giant, ugly-smelling trucks would veer to the side and destroy her. Pressed against the thirty-foot-wide stump, she built up her nerve again. She berated herself: *How are you ever going to get out of this town and see the world if you're too scared to hitchhike?* Marian punched a burl on the stump, stood, marched her way back up to the road, and stuck out her thumb as insouciantly as she could.

The only car that passed after that was driven by Tall Matt, who picked her up and took her to the overlook where Marian straddled him in the front seat of his GTO.

"You look better'n Daisy Duke in those shorts," Matt exhaled. His eyelids fluttered lustily as he stared down at her body. His lip curled under, swollen from her kisses.

Chin reddened by his stubble scratches, Marian watched his hands grip her thighs, sliding across them in soft circles. "Who's that?" she drawled. The loggers always said words she'd never read in her books or the paper. Marian found it easier to ask. To her surprise, it made the men like her more. Asking for definitions from her parents always brought a clipped reply to "look it up in the 'cyclopedia." The Whipple family's encyclopedia was *The People's Almanac*, and Marian had read it from cover to cover over a dozen times in the handful of years since she'd brought it home after finding it on the side of the highway.

"Shit, you don't know anything." The boy smiled wolfishly. "Maid Marian."

"I know to keep these shorts on." She ground on his crotch more, enjoying the power she felt hardening under her. "And I know that you're no Robin Hood."

"Shut up and suck on my neck."

He pushed her head in for a "hickey," which was a dark bruise she could make on Matt's skin that he always wanted visible though Marian had no idea why. She gave him his hickey and writhed in his lap. When they were done, she stepped out of the GTO and walked home, glad he never tried to give her a hickey.

Tall Matt was only a handful of years older than her, but he acted like he knew so much more, when all he really knew about was cars and TV shows. She'd forgotten more about trees than he'd ever know, but it never came up. She liked him because he'd also been homeschooled and didn't make her feel stupid for not going to a real high school like the other loggers she'd talked to. He made her feel worse about not being a Christian.

He reminded her of Lumber Jack from the comics section of the newspapers Smitty gave her. Smitty was more like Lumber Jack than Tall Matt in looks. Smitty was big shouldered and strong like a bull, whereas Tall Matt was lanky. But Smitty was also old and kind and principled where Lumber Jack was young and lazy and funny. Like Tall Matt. Smitty said Lumber Jack hadn't always been that way: When Smitty was a young boy, the cartoon was about Lumber Jack's adventures taming the wilds of Humboldt rather than about him drinking, chasing women, and trying to get out of work.

The trees stretched high and glowed red in the light of Matt's departing vehicle. Marian always felt watched in the woods, and the trees tonight felt particularly watchful. The redwoods reproached her. Marian shuddered at the thought of her parents seeing her through the trees, peeking out from the dark spots between the bark and knowing what she'd been doing. She didn't used to feel so seen in these woods. It was different from the "seen" feeling she got from her father's men. The loggers made her feel exactly how much of a woman she was. These woods made her feel like a little girl. She pulled up the hood on her jacket on her trot home. She hurried through a trail that cut up the valley, meandering through gullies and hillocks and felled logs, coming out from the bushes by the cabin where her father's small frame stood on the porch. Waiting for her.

"Pop."

"Where in God's name have you been?" he growled. His hand crumpled a handful of her newspapers. How had he found them? Did he know about her other hiding places?

"Those are mine." Marian confronted him.

"They're a waste of pulp is what they are." He lifted the handful to his face and read, "*Hitchhiker Murdered in Eureka.* The fuck you need to read stuff like this for?"

"I just wanna know what's going on in the world!"

"You're fifteen years old!" he screamed.

"Exactly!"

What didn't he get? She was basically a woman now, and a woman's place was out where the people were. Where she can live and work and meet someone other than the loggers in these *fucking* woods. When she complained to Mama, the woman always said that these woods have everything they need. Just because Mama and Pop found each other in this forest didn't mean that Marian wanted that. Was it so wrong to want more than she needed for survival?

She'd met Tall Matt here, but they both knew it was temporary. She would never marry a logger. But she couldn't make her parents understand that. The world was so much bigger than this stupid forest, but they just wanted to keep her blind, deaf, and dumb in their tiny moss-covered cabin. There was so much going on out there, even in close cities like San Francisco. And they were trying to imprison her in this tiny forest in the forgotten corner of California.

She climbed the stairs to accost her father. She was terrified to be talking back to him, but couldn't stop the words from sputtering, indignant, from her lips. "President Carter is planning to send troops to Lebanon, and you don't even care! You probably don't even know where Lebanon is!"

"It's pronounced *Lebanon*," he said quietly, seething in the dark.

A tense moment passed. Maybe he was considering her point.

Marian heard his caulk boots cross the porch and felt his hand grab her braided pigtails in a fist behind her neck before she even saw him move. His strong fingers tugged the shorter hair at the base of her scalp. Anger made his light blue eyes seem almost white. Marian yelped in pain. "Ow! I'm sorry! I'm sorry, Daddy!"

Whipple pulled her close. "I'm trying to protect you, goddamn it. You have no idea what the world is like. How bad it is out there." He let her go, and something like shame washed over him. He leaned over the porch railing and lit a cigarette. He ashed it on the water tank and tossed the newspapers into the metal barrel next to it.

Before she could intercept him, Pop dropped a lit match into the barrel, and the newspapers disappeared into ash. Tears streamed down Marian's face. Next to her, Whipple took a last hungry suck and flicked his cigarette butt onto the embers.

Her throat coiled on the inside into a painful, scratching knot. A knot so big that she would never be able to swallow the hurt she held inside. The rope inside her was woven out of everything that separated her from Pop, making them so different. He was a man, an old man, and a white one at that. He loved her and she loved him. He was her father, so of course she loved him. He cherished her like a precious object. As long as she stayed in these woods, she'd always be something of *his*, something he owned. The rope tugged at her like a leash. The knot in her throat wound through her insides, anchored just beneath her ribs, and if she were ever able to untangle it, the rope could probably reach the moon. But Marian Whipple didn't want to untangle it, to say all the things that went unsaid between them. She wanted to coil the rope more and bludgeon him with it. She wanted to burn him, scream and kick and choke him till his white-blue eyes dripped out of their sockets. "I hate you," she whispered.

"Well, too bad because I love you." He shrugged. "You're my little baby girl. My only child. You're safe here, and I aim to keep you safe. Now git inside. Your mother wants to go over your reading with you. She doesn't know about these, and I don't want to tell her, but you need to promise me that you'll stop wandering off. If she found out you've been"—he sniffed her jacket and frowned—"where you've been . . . Even I don't wanna think about what she'd do. Just stop, okay?"

Tears burned in Marian's eyes. He had no idea what she could do. What she was capable of. She nodded her assent, but she couldn't stop being herself.

Her anger dissipated upon entering the warmth of the cabin. She scanned its two rooms for the source of that warmth: her mother. Mama sat in her rocking chair next to the kitchen table, balancing a worn Latin book on her pregnant belly.

19

CUT SITE

TOO-BRIGHT LIGHTS SPILLED THROUGH the trees, reaching out toward the search party. Buck led the way, pulling thick saplings aside for the other three to pass into the staging area where a huge yellow machine stood with the lights on, spotlighting a big tree stump.

Cancerous-looking wood grew out of the side of the stump and made it look pregnant. Under the bulge, chains dug into the wood. Moss grew over them in parts, making the chain look ancient.

"Some kinda logging op," Buck grumbled.

"It looks abandoned," Jasmine commented, "with all the growth 'n shit over it."

"I dunno, these chainsaws look pretty new." Buck pointed to two chainsaws near the stump.

"Oh my God," Tilly gasped.

The group followed her flashlight to the big logging machine, its orange spotlight still shining faintly. Henry knew it probably had an official name, but to him, it looked like a big claw machine game claw. Plants and wood were swallowing the machine from one side, absorbing it into the swollen roots of two nearby trees.

The whole scene was like something out of a fucked-up movie with the A24 lighting and everything. *Fuuuck.*

The machine's big red claw was frozen around a bunch of trees, but it looked like they'd tried to escape the claw. By melting through its fingers. Wood spilled out from the red metal fist like a lava flow, covered in needley pine branches, tiny pine trees in their own right. It was like the trees were trying to eat the machine back.

The machine's light was still on. Which seemed impossible because the whole thing was covered in decades of overgrowth. *Fuck you know about decades of overgrowth?* Henry's doubt chastised him. *You've been in the woods for ten minutes.* But on the other hand: *If plants could grow that fast, I would've seen a video or a documentary or something. Someone would've mentioned it. This is weird. This is weird and creepy and—according to the loggers—dangerous. I gotta fuckin' get out of here.*

Henry scanned the area, heart thumping in his ears. He prayed that this was just another tourist trap. His beam spotted a Toyota truck with a Yale license plate holder. Vines quested around the support bars, green shit spilling up over the tires the same way the wood was eating the machine. He didn't want to add hysterics, but these people were being way too chill about these Jumanji-ass woods eating fucking cars. City slicker or not, Henry knew this was not normal. These people seemed like they expected this sort of thing to happen all the time. Next to the truck was a small thicket of spikes. *In case I need more clues that this forest is a trap, now there's fuckin' spikes.*

Bloody spikes. *Shiiit!*

The other flashlights joined his in illuminating a massive blood puddle. Outside the periphery of their beams, the moonlight turned the red blood into a sea of black against the pale saplings. Some saplings were already sprouting bright green piney buds where they were cut. The blood boundary spread outward from the outline of a human body made entirely of pine needles.

20 PARADISE BY THE DASHBOARD LIGHT

1980

MARIAN STEPPED OUTSIDE FOR her morning chore, like she did every day. Like every day, she opened the rubber stopper on the white plastic water tank. She emptied the mug of antibiotic powder, banging the pewter cup on the lip to loosen any clingers. She replaced the stopper and took in the wilderness that jailed her.

When she was small, the woods were like protective arms hugging her to them, making her feel part of something enormous. But now at fifteen years of age, unignorable hormones and urges pushed out, making Marian feel like her skin was too small, like the forest was too small, getting smaller every day. The dark redwoods became prison bars that blocked her path to the real world.

Pop drove the water tank away while Marian ate breakfast with Mama. After morning lessons, Marian came out to contemplate the redwoods again. To solidify how stuck she really was. But she had found ways to make it tolerable.

On the back edge of the porch—the one that couldn't be seen from the door or from the front—Marian found Smitty's gift for her. The day's newspaper, already plenty thumbed through that morning, based on the edges. Marian grabbed it and ran expertly down the hill toward her hiding place. Deep in the forest, she reached her creek. It was an offshoot of an offshoot of an offshoot of Dinner Creek, and it was all hers. Behind a big boulder, Marian pulled a rope until the creek released a package wrapped in clear plastic tarp. Inside were several more layers of plastic grocery bags from Hsu's Market. Her mother kept the bags under the sink in the kitchen, and Marion had wrapped them around her treasures until they were watertight. From the bag she pulled a nascent stack of newspapers, rebuilding her stash after Pops's outburst the other day. From under that pack she pulled out cans of soda, chilled to ice cold by the stream.

Marian popped open a can (distributed from a company in Bakersfield), lay on the sandy bank, and read the newspaper mostly all the way through. President Carter was running for reelection against Governor Reagan. She wondered why they let such old men be in charge of things. Students at Humboldt State University, just a dozen miles up the road in Arcata, were protesting the timber companies. They looked so mad and ugly in the picture that Marian didn't bother with the rest of the article.

Her favorite section was the sports section and its dozens of pictures of male athletes in action. She thumbed over the faces of high school sports stars, poring over every detail of the photos. In the crowd, fans held signs that read FUCK THE PANTHERS. HSU's mascot was Lucky the Lumberjack.

When she reached the comics, her eyes zeroed in on the lower section where Lumber Jack always was. Today he was trying to make extra money by peddling "jen-you-een" photos of Bigfoot, which turned out to be the name of his neighbor's dog also. Classic.

After finishing the paper, she decided she'd liked today's news more than last Thursday's but not as much as the first paper Smitty gave her: July 4, 1976. He'd given her the paper in 1978, and she'd treasured it. Until Pop burned them up.

After finishing her soda, she pulled out a bent Polaroid from her bag: a group shot of a dozen or so loggers sitting in the mouth of a giant redwood. Some smiled and some didn't; some wore gloves and six didn't; three had light hair; two held axes; one looked darker-light like her, maybe Mexican, like some of her dad's men; all of their gazes were serious and masculine. She masturbated to a man holding an axe this time, posing with it in mid-swing above his head as if he were going for the Humboldt undercut. Marian grinded on her palm, thinking about his strong arms lifting her up, his long fingers completely encircling her thighs, digging in. After she was finished, she lay on the sandbar, staring up at the blue sky and listening to the trickling water.

Marian was thirsty when she came back from the creek.

The white plastic water tank shone like a beacon in front of the mossy log cabin. Pop must have stopped by the cabin while she was at the creek. Marian made a beeline toward it and started to gulp from the spigot.

"Marian!" Her mother's high voice rang out from the porch. "Stop that! I don't wanna have to keep refilling this thing. You are perfectly capable of getting water from the well. Grab a bucket because I would like to make some tea, please and thank you."

Marian trudged to the stairs where her mother held a bucket down. Her yellow, paisley-print dress stretched across her pregnant belly. Marian knew Mama had had miscarriages in the past; she and Pop hoped openly for the baby's health, while Jeanne never discussed her pregnancy.

"You never drink the tank water. Is the powder in it bad for the baby or something?" Defiant, Marian struck a rigid pose with her hand on her hip, the way a model had in a slacks sale insert in today's paper.

Her mom scoffed. "No, I just prefer no chemicals. And I'd prefer you not drink it as well. And don't think I don't know you're drinking 'em soda pops. The least you could do is throw the cans away instead of hiding them under the porch. S'bad for the environment. And all the chemicals in the soda will rot your teeth outta your head. You want that?"

"No, Mama."

"Okay now, go get some well water."

Mama was being cagey, but she was always a little twitchy, a little suspicious. Mama didn't trust the loggers on a deep, subhuman level, and that phobia extended to everything they touched—Pop being the lone exception. Marian supposed Mama didn't look down on Pop the way she looked down on the other "lumberjacks" because he was management at least. Or she just loved him so much that what he did for a living didn't matter. The whole thing seemed too tangled up for Marian's tastes. Adults made their lives more complicated than they needed to be, more concerned with tradition than how their actions contradicted their principles and made them total hypocrites.

During those weeks after Pop asked her to stop sneaking out, Marian maintained an uneasy truce with her father by only sneaking out in the early hours of the morning. If she left the house at 3 a.m., it was sneaking out. But if she held the creaking screen door and lifted it up a bit so it wouldn't make any noise at 4 a.m., that was pretty much morning and what she was doing was just waking up early. Especially if she remembered to make her bed before she left. The morning air was invigorating. As she walked back from the post-coital heat inside Tall Matt's car, the chilly fog stuck to her sweat before dissolving into her skin. Her body drank it in. Marian was coming into her power those mornings. She was worldly now. A woman.

When Mama asked, Marian lied that she was doing a science study on California giant salamanders and that they were easier to find in the early morning. But because she was homeschooled and lying to her only teacher, Mama called her bluff. So Marian actually started to study the salamanders during her morning jaunts. She presented the survey to Mama, who approved of the methodology but struggled to accept Marian's proposed applications for the study. Marian wrote that the information could be useful for measuring surface area for the use for tailors who wished to make salamander-skin raincoats, which Marian thought was very clever of herself. Her mother called it "barbaric."

Marian looked forward to the early-morning trysts with Matt. Depended on them. The look in his eyes when he looked up at her riding him . . . She wanted to live in that feeling forever. To be his forest queen. His girl. His wife. Marian thought about what her life would look like as Mrs. Tall Matt Johnson. Not unlike Mama's life, probably. Maybe escaping out into the world wasn't the right move; maybe she only needed to escape her parents' house and live in town like a regular adult.

Every week or so, Pop came home with more stacks of signed papers. He always had a lot of paperwork. While Marian pretended to sleep, Whipple sat at his desk and looked at his papers under the green hooded lamp. Sometimes he didn't even write anything, just stared down at his files.

One night, when her parents were in their bedroom, and their twin snores filled the cabin, Marian clicked on the lamp and looked through Pop's papers. It was purposeless snooping, just looking at the pieces of her father's life in order to gain a picture of the man. More evidence of what her future might look like as a logger's wife.

Pop worked hard, she thought. Whenever he got home, and the loggers' trucks disappeared into the forest, his face was agitated and tired. But then he'd spend some time behind the closed door with Mama, and he came out looking like Pop again. Would something on his desk explain why he was like that? Marian didn't know any other fathers—maybe Smitty—so she wasn't sure if every man needed two hours after work for their shoulders to lower from around their ears.

A green file folder bulged under a stack of papers, creating an awkward lump. Marian carefully lifted the papers so they wouldn't topple and grabbed the folder. Inside was a stack of Polaroids of dead bodies. Dead loggers: impaled, missing limbs, crushed by logs, surrounded by glistening pools of brown-red blood. One young man was sliced through the midsection by a grappler cable. He was in her group photo, holding an axe. Where in that he'd been tan skinned and smiling, this new, shiny photograph showed him wan and bloodstained. His face was a mask of anguish. Marian stole the picture and put the rest back. After she clicked off the lamp, Marian lay in bed, wondering if her parents could hear the manic thumping in her chest.

The next morning, Marian stepped outside for her morning chore like she did every day. Like every day, she opened the rubber stopper on the white plastic water tank. When Pop clomped down the porch steps, she asked him about the tank powder. He said it cleaned the water.

"Keeps it potable. Stop tryin' to get out of yer chore." He returned that evening with another stack of contracts and some more Polaroids. More men dead.

Tall Matt picked her up near the Redcedar sign and took her to the overlook. When she asked how yesterday's men had died, he shrugged and said it's a dangerous job. Maybe that was the truth, but his parroting of her father's standard line made her despise him.

After doing her morning chore, Marian "read" at the creek, but mostly she rolled around and rubbed her crotch while she pined over pictures of a long-dead logger.

Neither Mama nor Pop was home when she returned, thirsty and flushed from the rush of all the things she wanted. Mama must have run out quickly on a foraging trip or to visit one of her friends. She'd left her mortar and pestle in the kitchen, half full of the pale yellow powder for the tank. It was stupid of the woman to rail against "chemicals" that she herself manufactured, but very little of what Marian's parents did made sense. They were hypocrites, always trying to get her to do as they said and blind herself to their contradictory actions.

The antibiotic powder beckoned at Marian from the counter. She drew closer. After an eternity of internal debate, she licked her finger and stuck it in the mortar; it felt good along the bowl's rough curvature. She examined her frosted finger. The powder had no smell, but there was something about it, invisible fumes that towed her forward, pulling her in. Marian tapped the powder with a dry tongue. No taste. Just the enticement to try more. Her instinct whispered:

Do it.

She stuck her whole finger in her mouth and sucked off the silky powder. She ravened like an animal, using her teeth to pry any excess from underneath her fingernails. It coated her throat, and she coughed until the edges of her vision sparked out into coruscating silver and white. Immediately exhausted, she collapsed on the couch without taking off her shoes. But no rest was to be had. Marian's stomach ached as if it were collapsing on itself. The walls of her insides were grinding against themselves like sandpaper. It was as if she were being wrung out like a rag, leached of her life force. She rolled off the couch, sharply knocking her head on the floor. Her skull reverberated—Marian knew she'd gotten her bell rung, but she felt no pain.

She pushed herself up. Her muscles wrenched, crunching like a plastic bag. Below her hands, the floor fell away and revealed the world underneath the cabin. Layers upon layers of tessellating redwood needles, pine needles, cedar needles, fern leaves, animal bones, fungus, soil, earth. The whole world. The darkness . . . glittered.

Suddenly, Marian was under the cabin in the black, shimmering pith. *How did I get outside?*

She stumbled up the incline, grabbing handfuls of earth. Redwood needles poked the soft beds under her fingernails. She couldn't get a good grip and slid farther down. The furrows she made opened like wounds, showed her the inside of the world. The dark hole called for her.

Run.

When she heard it, Marian lost her footing and tumbled down the hill. Flailing to grab anything, she knocked her arm against one of the wooden house supports. She heard her wrist crunch but felt nothing. She couldn't do anything but listen to the voice in her head. The thousand-million mouths that whispered into the folds of her gray matter, tickling her neurons with the singular command: *Run*.

Without ever consciously choosing a destination, her feet took her toward her creek. The sound of rippling water grew louder in her head, enveloping her with its constancy, and Marian drifted dreamily on invisible guidelines to the place where she felt whole. However, when she approached her hiding boulder, there was a new formation next to it. A wooden burl, standing alone like the base of a snowman, waiting for its companions. The gray wood bulged, and the lines reminded Marian of her mother's stomach and its stretched, striated skin; the wood was pregnant. Marian reached out to caress the bark.

Before her fingers could touch it, the burl unfolded. It opened into a tall creature that towered over the hallucinating girl. Its arms were enormous, and moss grew in the hollows of its carcass, of which there were many because—with the exception of the strong arms—the bark-skinned creature's body was emaciated. Wet, shallow breaths escaped from its awful mouth as its chest rose and fell in the same frenetic pattern as Marian's own pounding breast. Large, black-red eyes considered her.

She felt no fear. Surprise at this was the last thing she remembered before blacking out.

When Marian awoke, she was in her parents' bed. One of her father's shirts was hanging on the closet knob. Its red plaid lines moved, whipping past like cars on the Redwood Highway, gesturing at her with a wiggly hello. She rested more. When she woke again later, the whipping plaid had slowed to a crawl, eventually stopping altogether.

Mama was in the kitchen. Thirsty, Marian looked around the bare room. A thick clay mug steamed on the nightstand. Tea. After drinking it, Marian felt hale enough to get up. In the kitchen, Mama was hunched over the counter, grinding the antibiotic powder and sifting it into the storage box with the pewter cup.

"Hi, Mama," she announced.

"Babygirl! How are you feeling? Did you drink your tea?" Mama held a big, black hand against Marian's forehead.

She felt sticky all over, and drained. "I'm okay."

"Well, okay then. Why don't you lay down on the sofa so I can keep an eye on you till you're back to regular?" Mama turned back to the mortar and pestle.

"Okay, Mama." Marian grabbed her favorite quilt and curled up on the couch while her mother worked in the kitchen, bathed in the yellow light of the setting sun.

After a while, Mama added, "Don't touch this powder again, baby. It needs to be diluted. That's why you got so sick."

Marian shot up on the sofa. She'd forgotten that licking the powder was the reason she'd gotten sick. Marian remembered the feeling of the silky powder coating her insides and burying her whole. She shuddered. That stuff did all that? "Why do we put it in the water?"

"For the boys. The loggers. It's just for them."

"Why? Just so Pop can work them harder?"

Mama sighed. "It's a mercy. The boys shouldn't have to feel what this forest can do to them."

While Mama droned on, Marian remembered the creature at the creek-side.

". . . Those logger boys are trouble, Marian. Making friends with them, getting close—it's a bad idea. You have to stop."

"I can't stop being myself," Marian whined.

Jeanne frowned and let loose another weary sigh. She always sighed like that when she was most intent on misunderstanding her daughter. "I'm not asking you to do that. I'm asking you to use your brain. Your father and I are trying to protect you, you know. Those boys are dangerous. Moreso without the powder. So just stop. Okay?"

"You can't stop me from growing up," Marian challenged her. Internally, she added: *I'm gonna stop you.*

Don't stop, Child.

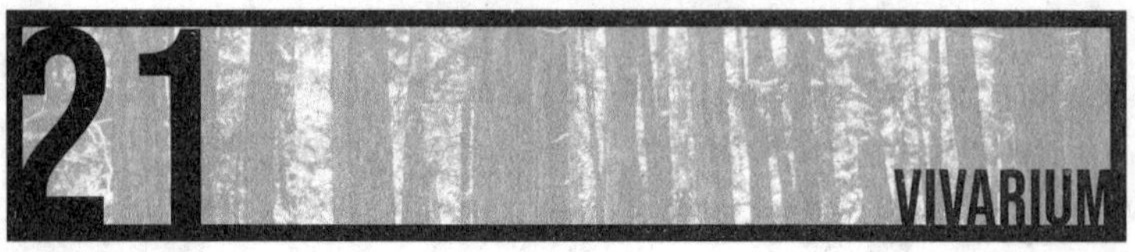

21 VIVARIUM

"NOPE!" HENRY BELLOWED. "THAT is blood. We gotta go."

Tilly's wide eyes looked to Jasmine to see what she thought. Jasmine wasn't thinking. The redwood-needle outline of a body was all she could think about. Just like the one at the bottom of Gin's grave. But Tilly needed her. She gripped Jasmine's hand and squeezed.

Jasmine shrugged. "It's a logging op. Maybe they killed each other. This could be totally unrelated to James. Let's keep moving."

Buck cleared his throat behind the three of them. "Guys?"

Under the interrogating chiaroscuro made by the feller buncher's light, there was no wonder the loggers thought the gnarled stump was a monster. The burl on it was enormous, bulbous, beckoning, begging. Veins of misshapen wood snaked across it, jutting forward from the blackness like a barky tumor in the orange light, its minatory presence infecting the whole area. The air around it felt spring-loaded. Like the thing would burst to life at any moment.

"That stump looks like it just got a BBL," Henry pointed out, chuckling.

"S'a burl," Buck explained.

"No, I said BBL," Henry repeated.

"A burl is like a tree tumor, kind of," Jasmine added, mindlessly repeating fun facts gleaned from a decade of sunrise hikes with Aunt Gin.

"Tumor is right on," Henry agreed. "That thing is abnormal."

The dry dirt around the stump crumbled beneath Jasmine's boots. She stepped back just as the sandy earth disappeared down a hole that ran beneath the stump. Deeper in the forest, something thwanged loudly in the canopy. It sounded like those metal sheets used to simulate lightning in stage plays.

Four white flashlight beams pierced the scene, frolicking over the stump and the ground around it.

Within the beam of Jasmine's own spotlight, the woody surface appeared . . . fleshlike. Like a biological sample on a microscope slide. More alive than it should be.

Something clanged close by. Jasmine jerked her flashlight around to locate the sound.

Tilly had her butt up, rooting around in the Toyota truck's bed. She looked up when the light flashed on her, holding up a coil of rope to her eyes. "Tryna blind me?"

"You trying to scare the living shit out of me?" Jasmine snapped.

Directly behind her, Henry screamed. He grasped at her raincoat, stumbling backward. Jasmine grabbed him before realizing Henry wasn't in trouble; Buck had shoved him enough to make him think he was falling. Jasmine shined her flashlight at Buck's eyes, hoping a little blinding would knock some sense into him, but Buck just laughed and walked in the other direction.

Likewise, Henry shoved him back, laughing. *That's a relief.* Henry's ability to withstand Toussaint's razzing at work was exactly why Jasmine had hoped he'd be a good buffer in Redcedar. He was good at going with the flow and doing what was needed to keep the group dynamic positive. Jasmine envied him for that. Every small injustice stung at her, dug deeper into her, and knotted her guts into a cancerous burl. Also, she liked him. When he smiled at her, his eyes twinkled, and the burl's stranglehold on her insides felt a little looser.

There were two paths away from the cut: the logging road ventured farther up the mountain and also led back the way they came. For Jasmine, the choice was clear. "We'll head up the road in two-person teams—one on each side. That make sense to everybody?"

Tilly grabbed Jasmine's arm and said, "Yep! You and I are a pair."

Henry raised a hand to protest, but Jasmine shot him a look, urging him to understand. *Please just be cool and go with it. Tilly needs me right now.* Jas was glad that Henry and Buck seemed to like each other, or this would be harder than it already was. Thank God for small mercies.

With the rope she'd snagged from the truck, Tilly looped a harness around herself, then ran a line toward Jasmine, who stepped back.

"What's the rope for?"

"To keep us together. There's root caves like this all over so if one of us falls, the other can pull them up."

"Oh," Jas murmured. "That's actually really smart."

"*Actually* smart? Wow!" Tilly teased. "Such a high compliment! What year did you win a MacArthur Genius Grant again?" She leaned in to tie the rope around Jas's waist. "Was that the same year you got that Dora the Explorer–lookin' haircut? Did a fox give it to you?"

"Damn, okay! I get it. Sorry."

"How does that feel?" Tilly stood up.

Ten feet of blue nylon rope separated them, yellow and orange chevrons pointing toward Tilly's round, pretty, expectant face. *Honestly? It feels like you put a leash on me. Or an umbilical cord.* Instead, Jasmine grabbed the length of rope that led to Tilly and made a jerking-off motion on it. She ran her circled fist over the rope back and forth and grunted, biting her lip like a man trying not to cum. She expected Tilly to do the same with hers, and the two women would devolve into mean little grunting laughs, their "special friendship laugh," their spin on Beavis and Butt-Head. As a child, Jasmine wasn't allowed to watch the show, so she had watched it at Tilly's house.

She also expected some groaning reaction, probably from Buck: "S'—? Oh my God, will you two grow up?" Instead, Tilly just looked at her and called out for her missing husband again. No one else noticed her.

Jasmine let it slide. *Fair. Fine. We'll move on.* "That's what I love about us: No matter how much time passes, our friendship stays exactly the same." Jasmine beamed.

"Yeah." Tilly flashed Jasmine a tight smile and led Jasmine into the brush on one side of the logging road while Buck led Henry over the lip of the road opposite them.

The girls hiked in tandem so they didn't clothesline themselves on the trees. Later, they rejoined the other duo and watched the sun rise over another clear-cut. In the almost-light, the pale stumps shone fluorescent white in the air as dust-encrusted whorls of mist swirled around their bases. The whole scene looked like they were hiking on some far-off moon.

"Damn, y'all not leaving any wood, huh?" Henry remarked.

Tilly scoffed. "If you know another way to build a civilization, I'd love to hear it."

"S'it grows back," Buck added.

Jasmine muttered, "Not if you build a town on top—"

"JAMES!" Tilly cut her off to yell across the expanse of dead trees.

The logging road passed through the stark white into the shapeless black of the last wildfire zone. It had been a year since a lightning storm sparked a fire that wrapped around the sides of the mountain like huge flaming fingers. Jasmine remembered the photos Tilly sent her: The orange sky had put the one currently threatening Oakland to shame. But things here in Humboldt were growing back. While the soil was the color of pitch, lime-green baby seedlings poked through the dirt. Sea glass–hued lichen dotted the rocks.

The empty black and white of forsaken land would slowly give way to velvety mats of moss and more lichens, more grasses, more plants, more complex growth: a kaleidoscope of greenery. Nature was healing. It always did. It would probably rain soon in the deep forest. It always did.

Jasmine reached out and ran her fingers along the feather-shaped leaves of a sword fern nearby, sprinkling spores from the round sori under its ribs. She felt the woods pull at her, vines and branches tugging at her, begging for mercy. She wished she could save this magical place where the sun filtered through the canopy in golden rays. It seemed wrong that something so big and powerful was struggling for survival the same way she was. She wished they could help each other. *If you figure out a way out of this, you'll tell me, right?* she thought, before laughing to herself. *Who am I talking to?*

Aunt Gin always called shrubs and herbs "woody pioneers," referring to the way they grew quickly after a wildfire and provided the first wave of treelike species before big trees moved in; they made room for the redwoods. At least woody pioneers didn't have to kill everything in their path to make room. Not like out in the world, where people pioneered to turn the forest into cities, then pioneered again to push people out of their homes. The sound of construction rang throughout West Oakland now as house flippers pioneered her historic neighborhood into a new Berkeley. With what she knew now, Jasmine thought "woody pioneering" was more like reverse gentrification. She'd tell Henry that later, maybe. Maybe he'd laugh.

Once they were past the wide-open white of the clear-cut and the wide-open black of the wildfire zone, they were back in the old-growth redwoods. Safe now, Jasmine felt. Less exposed. The group split up again, calling out for James now that the forest was dense again, sucking up their shouts like acoustic paneling.

Stark white redwood branches grew out of the base of some trees, looking like ice-encrusted arms clasping up at the trunks, begging for mercy. Sapped of color like the stumps back in the clear-cut. They were "ghost redwoods," which were able to survive by absorbing poisonous metals, taking the bullet for the other trees. Jasmine liked that. Everything had its place in the forest, even if it looked messy. The forest made sense, even the really gross parts.

This was a functioning system. This had dignity. Jasmine took a deep breath and immediately felt better—a little high, even—before Tilly looked back at her and she remembered the reason they were there.

Tilly was out here, pregnant, searching for her missing husband. *My brother.* Despite her pregnancy, Tilly's willowy little body moved gracefully through the brush. *She's still my best friend. She's still* my *Tilly.* Uncomfortable qualifiers to those statements fizzled around the edges of Jasmine's consciousness like static, but she ignored them. The past was past. Right now she needed to focus on being present for her friend.

As predicted, the morning brought rain in the deep forest. The redwoods were a rainforest, and always would be. Hopefully. Through some trees, Jasmine could see a glorious but bittersweet view of Humboldt County. The emerald blanket on the hills had deteriorated into a threadbare patchwork of emaciated green and sickly bone gray, ravaged by more pioneers.

There used to be more trees than this. *Duh, obviously.* It had been a steep downhill collapse ever since the Manila galleons first dropped anchor at the North Coast. Three hundred years later, the corruption was insidious. Devastation occurred at every level. It killed everything. The forest needed its layers of canopy, roots, and deep soil to regulate rainfall in the area, storing and releasing the water vapor that used to permeate the coastal air. The redwoods and their broad, interconnected root systems locked in nutrients and kept the soil rich. No more. Jasmine knew all this. Knew all about the carbon cycle and the water table and the redwood forest's integral role in them. She'd been taught these things from an early age when she first came to live with Aunt Gin.

Spruces, red cedars, and redwoods stretched their branches down toward her, like a person leaning down to pet a dog, fingers crooked, unsure of whether the animal was dangerous. *I am not your enemy*, Jasmine wanted to assure them. She took a deep breath. The air was lighter now than it used to be, but it still invigorated her lungs. The citrus-green energy flowed through her body and made Jasmine feel good. Better than she'd felt in years. She was reminded of the hope she held for this place and her place in it before James went missing. If only the whole world were this forest.

When the rainfall got too heavy, the group took refuge under a rocky outcropping, stopping to rest and eat the jerky Buck had packed. Henry didn't even sit next to Jasmine to eat. Instead, he and Buck talked about video games or something in giddy, hushed tones.

Jasmine and Tilly hadn't talked much while they walked, and now Tilly leaned on Jasmine to rest. Her neon beanie was fuzzy and wet and rubbed against Jasmine's cheek. She looped a protective arm around the pregnant woman. *This is my best friend, and I love her.*

After the rain subsided, the two groups ventured out again, up opposite sides of the logging road. The boys flickered in and out of her vision, but Jasmine wasn't worried. She was tethered to Tilly, walking through the forest like they had as children.

The mushrooms always bloomed after it rained, sliding out of the ground like worms. There were so many. It was like they were being followed by swathes of rapidly accumulating mushrooms. The little beige caps danced at her feet. The bright orange reticulated chicken mushrooms waved at her from tree trunks. Golden chanterelles brightened the shadows of mossy tree roots. This place had so much life. So much possibility. Even tied to her best friend, Jasmine felt small and alone when she let herself consider the full scope of these woods. They were massive and yet so much more was just below the surface. Energy was just floating through the air, unseen by human eyes. There was so much more here than what she could perceive.

"Why are you smiling?" Tilly asked.

"I don't know . . ." Jasmine tried to frown away her grin, but she couldn't. She felt too good. "This just feels right."

Tilly stopped short, almost tripping Jasmine, who had kept walking for several feet.

"What?" Jasmine asked.

"Are you glad that James is missing?"

"No, what the fuck kind of question is that?"

"What kind of thing is it to say 'This feels right?' all dreamy and shit?" Her best friend released a heavy sigh. A weary sigh. The same sigh James always made when they fought. "All dreamy and stuff. You keep saying that nothing's changed. But stuff has changed. Everything's changed. You're being weird, and it makes me think you want your brother to be missing."

Jasmine approached Tilly, whose face was fracturing into a pained rictus. Tilly's scowls were deadly, but this was so much worse. "I don't want that."

Tilly teared up, and her voice was small and babyish. "You . . . you're my best friend. But you're also my husband's sister." Her smoky voice cracked. "All the good memories don't matter as much as what you've done lately. And what have you done lately? You picked fights with your little brother, insulting him and his profession until he ran into the woods to escape YOU. That hurts ME. And now he's missing. And you're still acting like this is some kinda vacation!"

Jasmine tried to explain. "He's missing because he's a childish asshole who you love for some reason. I can be your best friend and have a separate relationship with my brother. I can do both without them affecting each other."

"No, you fuh—frickin' can't!" Tilly's eyes were manic, wide. "It does affect me. How do you not get that? In your mind it's two separate things, but it isn't. Like, how you can *say* you're keeping your work life and sex life separate, but you're still having sex with *someone from work*."

"Fuck off, Tilly! We're not sleeping together! And it wouldn't be any of your business if we were." Sirens were going off in Jasmine's brain. Fireworks of anger, indignation, resentment, guilt, fear bloomed across the sky of her consciousness. She tried to walk away from Tilly, but Tilly yanked the rope so Jas couldn't get away from her, pulling her back hand over hand. *Fucking preggo bitch with her umbilical cords and control issues.*

Tilly was livid. Hot tears streamed down the sides of her face. "Also! You used to bully the shit out of me, so don't pretend that's not part of our history too." She got in close to add, "It wasn't always laughing and dick jokes. You remember? Just because you say that two things aren't related doesn't mean that they actually aren't. You and James *are* related, and you're so similar it drives me nuts! It's so stupid that you can't see that."

Jasmine pulled an axe head out of her pocket and used its dull blade to slice the rope, still struggling against Tilly, who continued to pull her in.

Cutting frantically, Jasmine watched her boots slide across the needled forest floor, begging for purchase in the leaf litter. The rope mercifully unraveled and snapped. Free, she fell on the soft ground. Old memories poked at her from the periphery. Memories of this forest and Tilly. Of black blood in the moonlight and all the reasons it was there. She didn't want to remember. The trees towered around her, framing Tilly, as the wild-eyed, pregnant woman stepped toward her. Jasmine crawled backward on all fours until she was backed against a trunk.

"Let's split up!" she says. Well, I say fuck you and fuck this Scooby-Doo bullshit. I shoulda said that. Nah, come on. Give the girl a break. She's a lil crazy, but she's doing the best she can. Henry went back and forth in his mind while big, green ferns soaked his pants legs and twigs whapped him in the face.

Henry and Buck had a good cadence going where they'd stop every dozen steps to call out for James and listen.

They approached a massive fallen log. At first glance, Henry thought it was made of brown stone, part of the mountain. But a closer look revealed bark rivulets running down the length of the thing, packed with moss. Henry couldn't even see where the tree ended in the blinding greenery. Heightwise it was taller than Henry but not taller than Buck.

"Gimme a lift," Henry said, wedging a sneaker into a crevice in the bark. He reached his hand out to Buck, who paused a moment to appraise the log. "Come on, help me up," Henry urged.

Buck grabbed Henry's hand and helped him climb up on top of the log.

Henry stood tall, and it immediately made him woozy. He probably looked like a child on top of a jungle gym. He cupped his hands around his mouth and yelled, "James!"

His voice echoed once before it was swallowed by the forest.

The nurse log crawled with life: little green guys, big leafy green things, mushrooms, some neon-green stuff, fuzzy and wet at the same time. Little bugs crawled through the breaks in the bark like they were city blocks. Under his feet, the tree vibrated like something living.

"All right, come on, man. S'go," Buck called up to him.

Henry took a step to dismount. The wrong step—his full weight collapsed part of the log. It opened its rotting-wood mouth and swallowed Henry into its core like something truly alive. In the blackness, he could feel squirming bugs—*so* many bugs. His hands slapped the inside of the log, slipping across slimy mushrooms and grasping toward light.

With a choked yelp, he used his full weight to burst through the wood like a ghillie-suited Kool-Aid Man. "Ah fuck! I'm covered in bugs! Help!"

Buck stepped forward to brush dirt and decay off his bright magenta hoodie.

Henry shed the jacket and whipped it around, throwing insects and dirt everywhere. He could feel redwood needles in the creases where his neck met his back, and he couldn't shake the sensation no matter how much he scraped at himself. "Fuck this forest, man!"

Over the next hours, Buck would sidle up to Henry, giggling, to pick a bug off of him. The man's fingers felt like being poked with rebar. Henry didn't know if there really were bugs on him or not, but one of the times, he smacked Buck's hand away. "Stop it, man. You gotta lay off. I am fighting for my life in these damn woods."

"Saw that last night." Buck chuckled, feigning ducking away from a blow and walking into a sucker punch. For a big man, he was remarkably light on his feet even in the forest.

Henry had to laugh. "I got him in the end." He thought about Jasmine fighting in the parking lot, outlined by the light of the neon sign. "Jasmine was something else."

"She *is* something else," Buck said.

"Yeah."

The two men chuckled, sighed, *mmm*'d. Henry wondered what the fuck Buck was *mmm*-ing about when the big man thought about Jasmine.

Buck looked around, then draped a big arm over Henry's shoulders. He patted his arm conspiratorially. "S'you two banging yet or what?"

"Nah . . ."

"'Nah' . . . t yet?" Buck quirked an eyebrow.

Henry didn't know how to explain it. He knew he shouldn't even try. He didn't know this guy. *But what did he mean by "She's something else?" What does he know that I don't?* They'd reached another of their stopping points.

They both yelled for James, then listened. Only the sounds of the forest yelled back. Now that he knew what it was, Henry noticed the clacking everywhere. He couldn't even see any peeling eucalyptus trees up here.

"Okay, man, I'll tell you. I sorta invited myself up here. I swear to God I thought she was gonna say no, but now here we are. And I guess I thought we'd have a good time visiting and then . . . I'd ask her to be my girlfriend." Henry's face burned. He didn't know this guy. But he felt like he could trust Buck.

The man's face was great for poker. He just looked at Henry very seriously, then bit his lip. "S'good for you. Hope it works out. Good, uh, luck."

He lumbered away, ready for their next dozen steps. *Very fuckin' weird response.*

"What's that mean?"

"Nothing." Buck started to speed up ahead of Henry. He tried to wave Henry off, but Henry kept at him.

"What is it?"

"No, I just mean, like . . . Good luck. S'in 'Good luck taming that filly.'"

The fuck is a filly? "Buck, man, just say what you fuckin' mean."

The big dude kept walking. It enraged Henry. *Who does that? Just drops some cryptic-ass response then walks away? What is this guy's problem?*

Before he realized he was doing it, Henry had run up behind Buck and shoved him hard from behind. He expected Buck to fall for a long time, like the tree that Henry had just been inside of. Instead, Buck jerked forward and caught himself on a stump Henry hadn't seen. When Buck turned back to him, his face was pained instead of angry like Henry had expected. Henry dropped his fists.

"Son of a— Stop!" Buck bellowed.

"Fine, then tell me what the fuck you mean by all that filly shit. What do you know about Jasmine that I don't?"

"'Sides everything? We grew up together. She's not really the girlfriend type. S'good that you haven't banged yet because the second you do, she's gonna lose interest and act like it never happened. Then you'll just be some guy she knows."

And works with went unsaid, but they both felt it.

Henry didn't know how to feel, other than angry at himself for even mentioning it. *I shoulda got out the second this started to go sideways.* But he couldn't pinpoint the exact moment this trip went bad. It had started bad and snowballed from there. Defeated, he approached the stump. Having learned his lesson about this one very specific thing, he tested its strength before pulling himself up to sit on it.

He had to say something. "You sure you weren't the one who did something wrong?" *Why that? Of all the things to say, how did you end up saying that?*

But Buck wasn't fazed. He smiled, even. "Only thing I did wrong was try to love her. She's not the loving type. S'more of a wham-bam-thank-you-sir, fuck-off-back-to-Oakland type."

Henry lay back on the stump, staring up at the funhouse-mirror stretching of the tree trunks around him. He felt sick. Was it dehydration or stress or the fact that he knew Buck was telling the truth? It was the reason he hadn't said anything to Jasmine. If he told her he liked her like that, she could reject him. Definitely would, if she'd already done it to Buck.

Tempted to make a joke, he instead pushed his thoughts down into his knot of wrongness. The place where he put all that shit Jas was talking about. The world and his anger at it lived in that place. They'd talk about feelings eventually. But not here. Not while her brother was missing and people were dying. He may be an idiot, but he wasn't a monster.

He took a great big inhale. The air here was so different; he felt like he had to take three times as many breaths to get the same amount of oxygen as back home. Plus it smelled like menthol. Something tickled in his throat, and Henry shot up, hacking and coughing.

"P'tew!" He leaned forward to spit off the side of the stump, but when he looked over the edge, it was like looking off of a four-story building. Henry's head swam. He'd never been great with heights. He lolled to the side, still coughing.

"Hey! S'going on with you?" Buck looked down at him, still standing against the stump.

Patterns emerged, embossed on his vision like a tie-dye pattern of gold foil. The stump he lay on was a river of Spanish Mission roof tiles, and they stretched on forever beneath him until the pine-needled ground rose to meet him.

Henry woke up upon hitting the ground. *The fuck was all that?* Buck was crouched next to him, holding him up. Behind his lightly gray-flecked beard and heavily gray-flecked eyes, Henry saw genuine concern.

Suddenly, they heard scuffling nearby, as if it was right next to them. Then a shout. Jasmine. Through the keyhole greenery, they spotted her purple rain slicker.

Buck pulled Henry up. "You okay? S'bit of a spill you took there."

"Yeah, I'm good," Henry coughed out. "Let's just, like, not mention none of this to the girls. Jas has got enough going on, ya know?"

"Fuck you!" Tilly yelled from the trees.

A wide grin spread across Buck's face. The two men had a secret now. They headed toward the girls to calm them down as if nothing had happened.

"S'okay!" Buck put his big body between the two women. "New search teams. Jasmine, go with Henry," he ordered. He winked at Henry as he waved him toward Jasmine, who lay prone on the ground.

Henry reached down to help Jasmine up. "You okay?" He tried to sound unbothered and commanding.

Jasmine smoothed down her hair and stared daggers at Tilly through hurt tears as Henry led her toward the logging road.

"You're a selfish fucking bitch, Jas!" Tilly shouted after her. "And I wasn't joking about your hair; it looks stupid!"

22 THE WATER TRUCK

1980

MARIAN DIDN'T STOP. WOULDN'T. Daren't. The allure of the loggers was too strong, like they trailed pheromones, each scented tendril promising a different strange treasure: cities surrounded by water that were full of bright lights and tall buildings and Chinese restaurants and no trees. She knew from the newspapers that these cities also contained murderers and rioters and budget problems, but she didn't care. Marian wanted it all. She soaked up life and other people's experiences with religious fervor. Her earnest hunger quested in all directions and called newness and novelty toward her.

That same hunger brought her to a party at the overlook on the arm of Tall Matt. Girls wearing wooden clogs and thick eyeshadow appraised her in the firelight. The flames danced across her body, laying her bare for them, flaying her. The bonfire cracked, and Marian flinched away from it. That was enough for them to laugh at her. She felt their pale eyes search her, find her wanting, and move on. The pain of their dismissal raked her skin like cold fingers.

Tall Matt pulled her close and introduced her to some of the loggers who never said hi to her in the mornings: Little

Jonesy, Handsome Dan, and Fat Matt. They offered her a beer and she drank it, even though she preferred soda. Beer had a bitter, earthy taste that reminded her too much of her mom's tea. She asked Tall Matt for a soda, but he kept handing her beers, and she kept drinking them.

She drank until her head spun. She had to hang onto Tall Matt to walk back to his car where he splashed her across the front seat. He pawed at her until it was clear she wasn't in a condition to do anything for him and decided to drive her home, or as close to her home as he dared.

Marian was puking on the side of the Redwood Highway, not far from where Matt had dropped her off, when Smitty's pickup pulled into the turnoff behind her. His headlights blinded her and made her head hurt.

Pushing her eyes closed against the whirling, flashing pain in her head, Marian pouted in the passenger seat, willing her stomach to stay down.

"Stick your tongue against the roof of your mouth. It'll keep you from booting all over my truck."

"You're not my dad. You know that, right? I don't know what my mama told you."

"If I was your dad . . . Well, let's say I can understand why Whipple's such a prick. Ungrateful little snot like you running wild all over."

"Are you done?"

"Are *you* done?"

She folded her arms and didn't talk to him until the truck crept up the mulched drive to the Foreman's Cabin. Before Smitty's truck could get within earshot of the cabin, Marian jumped out and into the brush.

She hoped Smitty would take the hint and drive away, but he stopped and shut off the engine. The hissing noise of his engine settling was loud as sin. From the bushes, Marian glimpsed the big man gather his wits and open his door. He probably wanted to have some man-to-man talk with her father.

He never got a chance because he opened the door to Pop's ready fist. All five feet six inches of her father went into skull-cracking blows that Marian could hear from yards away. Pop climbed into the truck to strangle Smitty.

Marian couldn't let that happen.

"Daddy!" Marian screamed from deep within her. Before she knew it, she was hanging from Pop's back. She wasn't big either but was able to make a straitjacket of her legs and yank her father to the ground. A crowbar hanging from his belt loop skidded across the duff and under the truck.

The two struggling Whipples rolled down into the ditch below the road. Pine needles and dirt and leaves snaked into her clothes and bit her skin. Above them, Smitty's truck started up again. He took off, tires kicking up wood chips that rained down onto Marian and her father.

Still rolling, Pop yelled in frustration, bucking under her until his head met the bones in her nose and her blood joined the dirty leaves coating father and daughter.

Smitty's engine sounds disappeared down the logging road.

"What did I say about staying away from loggers?" her father growled before trudging silently to the cabin.

Marian could only lay panting and crying on the forest floor.

When the feller crew arrived in the morning, Smitty stayed in his truck and watched Whipple offer water to Tall Matt. He adjusted his turtleneck so no one would see the purple-green handprints framing his neck. When Whipple walked off, he approached the tank to fill his canteen. He wasn't keen to deal with the foreman after last night.

Water slogged out of the tank, wetting the camo of his canteen. He hadn't wanted to spend twenty dollars for a canteen from the company store, which already made them buy their own safety gear, equipment, and water bottles. The water was free, but unfortunately, Whipple controlled it. Smitty didn't need to pay for a company water bottle when he'd gotten the Army canteen for the low, low price of his innocence and the four worst years of his life. Until last night. He shouldn't have gotten involved, but he couldn't very well have left the girl puking her guts out on the side of the road.

"Don't," Marian whispered from the shadows under the porch. Two purple-black stains were smeared beneath her eyes. *Did Whipple do that to her?*

"What the fuck happened to you?"

"Don't worry about it. Do *not* drink that water, okay?" The girl looked crazed. "Just trust me, please? I trust you."

Smitty stopped filling his canteen and made sure no one saw him pour the water out. When he looked back under the cabin, the girl was gone.

The steam whistle blew, and he headed out, up the mountain to the cut.

The smell of gasoline filled the air, invisible rivers in the darkness of the prenoon redwood forest. It never ceased to amaze Smitty how much sunlight the redwood canopies could block. The crew was clearing the cut at a good clip. The gas chainsaws' buzzing rang across the valley. Pollen floated lazily along the lolling chainsaw fumes.

Some of the boys' cuts were sloppy and ragged. Probably hungover from the Skyliner or wherever Marian got so shit-faced last night. Smitty moved away from them and their dangerous, lethargic movements. He tried to keep an eye on Whipple and stay away from him too, and he succeeded for several hours. But in this life, every success starts a countdown to its eventual failure. Smitty was eating a sandwich, leaning against a massive old stump, when Whipple appeared next to him.

"Got enough water?" the short man barked.

"Yep."

"Listen. I owe you an apology. The girl told me what you did for her. I thank you. I hope we can put last night's misunderstanding behind us."

"Mmhm."

"'*Mmhm*'?"

"Yep."

"That's all you gotta say?"

"Don't have much to say to you. Hurts my throat to talk."

Whipple shrank back, embarrassed. Then he clapped Smitty on the shoulder. "S'all right. Take your time, and we'll just stay outta each other's way for now."

"Mmhm."

When lunch ended, Smitty stood up and knocked the stump clean over. The whole thing must've been fifteen feet across, root to root, but with a light hip check, a forty-year-old logger had toppled it. The soil under the dead tree had turned to dust. Pale clumps dripped from the root system. Other times, on other sites, these upturned stumps would fall back down just as easily, trapping a man within their desiccated roots. Smitty moved away from it to continue with the shift.

He considered whether the gravity-defying stump was some kind of sign. Was the mountain trying to tell him something? *You have more impact here than you think.* Or maybe it was as simple as *these woods are dangerous*. Whatever the intended message, the latter was certainly true.

One of the loping hungover boys, Little Jonesy, suddenly lost control of his chainsaw and somehow took off his leg at the shin. His screams were raw, pain piercing through the noise of the cut, and alerted every man on the crew to stop and come help. The chainsaw that separated his leg had whipped around in a freak accident, rocketing up into Tall Matt and impaling him against a tree trunk. Mercifully, it killed him instantly.

After taking his accursed Polaroids, Whipple immediately went to work at his real job. By the end of the day, he had coerced, intimidated, and threatened seventeen men into signing statements agreeing to say nothing about the Jones boy's incident or Tall Matt's death. Whipple addressed the group. "It's on the books in the office, and that's all that matters. Don't need a bunch of cops and bad press making us all look incompetent. No need to drag Little Jonesy, Tall Matt, or their families through all that," he said. Whipple gestured backward at the water truck where Little Jonesy sat, trying not to scream. The boy knew firsthand how accusatory a fallen comrade's screams could feel, so he just sat there shaking, moaning, and crying. Whimpering but not screaming.

Finally, Whipple got his signatures, and he nodded in Smitty's direction, flashing his unnerving, small-toothed grimace. He and Whipple ran the Jones boy down the mountain in the water truck. As if that weren't enough, Whipple had slung Tall Matt's body over the roof of the cab like a deer. As the water truck wound down the logging road, Smitty watched the boy's blood drip into the open top of the water tank. Was that what was wrong with the water? But Marian couldn't have known that.

If one was so uncouth as to be a dick about it, there was one upside to a death on the job: Whenever one happened, the remaining crew was given the rest of the day off for bereavement in the form of a free round at the Skyliner on the company's account. Both the rest and the whiskey would be good for Smitty's bones. The bar at the bottom of the hill, an unofficial money-laundering front for the Mooney family, still served as a welcome refuge for the loggers. The pretty Native girl was running the place all right, but the little cement building's deed was held by Old Nate Mooney. *All that money, and they own us for the price of a shot every other month*, Smitty thought. They took guys who were already over a barrel and yanked them all the way down.

Poor Little Jonesy. The kid had been on the job a little over a year. Something like this would ruin his future at the timber company and limit his prospects at any honest work. The boys would take up a collection for him and his family, but they were all broke as shit too. No one did this job because life outside had been easy on them. Logging was a last resort. This wasn't an escape to nature. Nature was cruel, and only fellas without other options chose this. Smitty could wrap his mind around the cruelty of men. Nature operated on an entirely different level; her violence was nonjudgmental. No man could game the system to buy years on his life. Trading lives for longevity was something men did.

And poor Tall Matt. Senseless, something like that. Let it be a lesson to the other ones coming onto the job hungover and still drunk, gulping tank water down like . . . *Why did Marian tell me not to drink the water?* Smitty wondered. *Did it have something to do with the accident? Oh, God.*

No, it was just an accident. The kid was drunk and had been careless, he convinced himself. Tall Matt's death was a freak accident. Just like all the other casualties they had had that year. Logging was the most dangerous job in America. Top five in the world. It was a hard job, and people died doing it.

Still, what had Marian been going on about with the water?

23 SEX

JASMINE'S HEAD SWAM FROM Tilly's accusation, the second in twenty-four hours. Every minute in the forest passed like an eternity. *Fucking bitch. Calling me selfish? She's the one who let her husband get all pissy and storm out into the damn forest . . . Mmm. Not just her husband. My brother. My baby brother who I love, even if we don't like each other. He's the only family I have left. And if I lose him, I'll never see Tilly again.* The harsh truth stung her in the knot under her ribs. Whether she liked it or not, Tilly and James were intertwined. No amount of wishful thinking could make them separate. She hated when Tilly was right.

She and Henry continued through the brush, and the pain subsided gradually as Jasmine took deep breaths of aching green forest air. Every minty inhalation loosened the knot in her until Jasmine realized she wasn't in pain anymore. At all. She realized that she didn't just feel good—she felt *well*. Great, even.

Her heartbeat thumped steadily where the too-short leggings and too-tight shorts rubbed against her crotch. When she came to a fallen log blocking her path, she straddled it to climb over. She imagined herself as a nurse log, infinitely more important after falling, more powerful in death. This wasn't suicidal thinking. It wasn't the same here in these woods, where death sustained life and decay was just another integral part of the forest ecology. Jasmine didn't want to die. But she was heartened by the thought that if she did die in these woods, her lost life would have meaning beyond what she could do for other people. It wasn't just heartening, it was energizing. Life had value here. Death had worth. *She* was significant in these woods. Not just significant. Important. Powerful. She still had potential here, not like in the world out there where she was deemed past her prime the day she had turned thirty.

The realization buzzed across her skin like warm static. On top of the soft wood of the nurse log, the rhythm in her was strong, urging her to stay on the log and grind herself into it until it disintegrated and she saw stars. Jasmine imagined lying on the ground, with soft moss tickling her skin, hair radiating out around her like a romance novel heroine, with strong hands gripping her thighs.

Nearby, Henry hummed a song to himself. His low voice was a honey grumble. It vibrated through her. They weren't tied together like she and Tilly had been, so she followed invisible fumes to him, like a predator following a prey's scent, and cornered him near an almost-dry creek. The water trickled lightly. The creek bed was all pale stones, great for skipping across a pond. There were no fish that she could see. Huge boulders at its shores showed where the water level used to be much higher. More evidence of depressing, destructive changes in the forest. Jasmine pushed it out of her mind and kicked a stone down onto the creek bank to alert Henry to her presence. He swung around, jacket swishing in a brief, bright magenta blur, and she was upon him.

"Hey," Jasmine purred and pressed herself into him.

His lips met hers willingly, gratefully. He ran his hands over her too-short raincoat sleeves, still slick from the morning rain. She pushed him back against a boulder and kissed his neck while reaching back to slide her raincoat off. She wanted to feel his skin against hers. Every inch of her was hungry for it.

"Wait," Henry whispered into her ear while she kissed his beard.

His beard smelled like the forest—like concentrated pine like dirt like leaves like moss like the color green like squirrels like potato bugs like mushrooms like a body like a living huffing sweating body a body maturing a dying body a dead one like decay like rebirth like—

"Jas." Henry turned his face away, so she kissed his neck. He tasted even better than he smelled.

She pressed her crotch into his leg, hoping to feel hardness under his pants. How could he not feel the way she felt right now? Did he not feel the same energy that she did? It reached up through the ground and ran pins and needles across her like a light electrocution. She felt radioactive.

"Wait—"

She kissed his lips. Messily, like she was trying to devour him. She wanted to. A millipede climbed up his glossy beard hairs. She wanted to eat that too. She leaned in toward Henry, toward the leathery little crawling thing trapped in his beard.

He pushed her off. "Stop!" Henry rolled away from under her and put the boulder between them.

Oh. Oh no. But—why wouldn't he want to? She backed away from him, burning with embarrassment. The swirling, branching goldenshine threads that ran galvanic ripples across her insides suddenly went cold—rigidified into sharp-peaked heart-monitor mountains. Her body ached. Her throat was frozen so she ran, swiftly darting away like a deer.

Henry chased her down. Henry, who was huffin' and puffin' earlier in the clear-cut.

"How did you . . . catch me just now?"

"I played high school football." Henry smirked. "But I couldn't run like that before."

"Huh."

"Huh." His smile dissipated. "JAS, WHAT THE FUCK WAS THAT? YOU CAN'T GO RUNNING AWAY IN THE MIDDLE OF THE SUICIDE FOREST ON THE MURDER MOUNTAIN!! WHAT THE FUCK IS WRONG WITH YOU?"

Jas collapsed onto the soft ground into a stiff, cross-legged position. This was gonna blow so she might as well be comfortable. She sighed. "I'm sorry. I shouldn't have done that. When I realized what I was doing, I . . . I felt frozen. And, like, if I stayed, I'd just make it worse."

Henry sat too. Both of them seemed lighter on their feet in these woods. Healthier in every regard. "I feel you. You need a record scratch. Like in an '80s movie where it goes *Rrrr!* and everything freezes? You're trying to carve out space to react and process things that's removed from the situation. I read about it in a self-help book." He frowned at her. "But we're in a goddamned haunted forest looking for your brother so you can't go doing that out here."

Chastised again, Jasmine nodded. She'd basically sexually assaulted him and then, when stopped, ran away toward probable suicide. It, uh, wasn't great. She could see that now. She noticed the sliced rope that hung from around her waist. She wished she could tug it and pull Tilly to her. "Sorry."

"This place is dangerous." Henry rose to his feet and held a hand out to Jasmine.

She put her hand in his and let him pull her up. He moved magnificently— *Stop it, Jas. You can't get all forest horny while your brother is still missing. Calm down, woman.*

Henry pointed south. "Okay, I think we were headed this w—!" He took a step and disappeared into a hole.

Jasmine yelped as he vanished in front of her. She moved toward the place where he'd fallen and looked down at Henry. He must've fallen ten feet.

He moaned in pain below her.

Was that there before? Jasmine looked around and untied the rope from around her waist, making a loop on each end. She didn't know what kind of knots to tie or if they would hold. When she threw a loop down to Henry, she was startled by the gunshot crack of a branch snapping nearby. It echoed off the trees. *Shiiiit.* Jasmine looked around but only saw the forest. Was that minute shift from green to black to green a hundred yards away a person? Or just branches? She couldn't tell.

Someone was walking through the leaves toward them. Jasmine couldn't see anyone, but the rustling got louder.

"Pull me out," Henry hissed from below her. He tugged the rope out of her hands. "Jas!"

"Shhh!" she shot down toward him. "Shut up, there's something up here."

Ferns rustled! Right next to her! Jas prepared to pounce, digging into her pocket for the axe head. She could wield it like a blunt object and maybe bean the guy like she had last night. She shifted her weight onto her back foot, and the ground disintegrated beneath it. Jasmine went sliding into the hole with Henry. She clawed at the roots above her head as she fell but couldn't stop her momentum. She landed on her butt with a muddy thud and felt the crotch of her jean shorts rip. The axe head landed next to her.

"That's what you get for telling me to shut up," Henry scolded.

Horrified, Jasmine looked up at the edge of the hole, neck sunk deep between her shoulders. They were both trapped now.

Henry wondered what she was grimacing at and followed her gaze skyward.

A dark outline peeked over the edge, emerging from the green-gray canopy. Jasmine squinted.

What the fuck is that?

24 THAT NIGHT

1980

WHILE THE BOYS IN the bar played darts and shuffleboard, waiting around to hear news about Little Jonesy, Smitty frowned into his beer at the double reflected on the surface, who looked like he drank more than he should've. Who would probably get in a fight tonight if it meant he could fuzz up his brain with enough alcohol to drown the puzzlement creeping in from the borders of his mind. To dull the sharp wrongness of how he felt. To kill the confusion about why Marian had warned him to not drink the water.

Smitty was already feeling like shit on the drive home from the Skyliner. The undulations of the 101 brought dizziness, which brought nausea, which pulled out tomorrow morning's hangover now to wrap around him like an uncomfortable sock as he squinted into the darkness.

Pop walked into the cabin looking like shit. He shuffled past Marian and wiped a large hand across her forehead in a lackluster head pat. She shrunk down behind her book and watched him collapse into his desk chair and hunch over his paperwork. His frantic pen scribbles were loud enough to hear from across the room. Marian silently willed him to stop.

And he did. The silence between them was a thousand times more horrible than the pen scratching. Marian glanced up over her book. Pop was sitting stick straight, staring at Polaroids. His big, broad shoulders shook. He sniffed. Was Pop crying? She'd never seen her father cry before. Fear seized her. Why was she so scared? She had to get out of there. His shoulders heaved, and she slid down to the ground from the couch and out onto the porch. By the time he finished crying, his daughter was down at the Redcedar sign with her thumb out.

Driving along the Redwood Highway, Smitty's headlights alighted on the skinny Whipple girl. Tan legs poked out from her shorts and reflected the light. Hitchhiking again. He pulled over to give the girl a piece of his mind and find out what she knew. Before he could open his mouth—

"Who died in the cut today?"

Smitty's knuckles whitened around the steering wheel. "What makes you think someone died?"

"There's paperwork my dad has to do when someone dies, and he gets really sad after. And there was blood on the water tank."

"Paperwork?"

Marian nodded. "I looked through it once. He had pictures of dead bodies. And a bunch of contracts. Your name was on one. He says it's company business."

"I bet," Smitty spat. With all the union busting the Mooneys did when the men had demanded safer working conditions, the rumor had gone around that the company took out insurance policies on its workers and got paid big when they died, while widows and children had to rely on the kindness of the logging community. *Most dangerous job in the world. We pay with our lives, and they get paid.*

The girl put her hands up to her face and started to cry.

Smitty was uncomfortable with the sobbing child, sharp elbows bobbing next to him. He stared ahead into the black woods. Trees loomed all around. There were so many of these giants. And these were nowhere near as big as redwoods used to get. He didn't know how to get a girl to stop crying.

"You ever drive before?"

Marian often tried to remember that night before everything went so horribly wrong. Especially the part where she heard David Bowie for the first time. Smitty taught her how to drive the truck, and she guided it around the loops of the 101 for almost an hour. She could park, signal, and make turns. On the fourth circuit north to Redcedar, Smitty leaned over and clicked on the radio.

The voice that came out of it grabbed Marian's heart, gripped her soul with strong hands. She was barely able to whisper, "What is this?"

"Music." Smitty smirked.

"Fuck off," Marian scoffed.

Smitty batted on the steering wheel with the syncopated rhythm of the song. "This is David Bowie. You'd like him. Sings about being from space. Among other things."

The man's voice was crisp and smooth at the same time. It welcomed her. For the first time, maybe ever, Marian Whipple didn't feel alone. This man understood what it meant to be born straddling multiple worlds with your heart.

When the song ended, Smitty turned to her. "So, what's in the water?"

She fidgeted next to him, wobbling the steering wheel. She stared ahead at the road.

"Marian."

"What?"

"Tall Matt was the one who died today. He drank that water and then he died."

"What?!"

"It's the truth. There's prob'bly a picture of his corpse up there on your pop's desk."

Marian jerked the wheel. Hard. The truck crossed across the middle line and skidded to a stop a few feet from the welcome sign stump.

Before Smitty could admonish her, the girl had opened the driver's side door and disappeared into the woods.

25 AND VIOLENCE

AT THE BOTTOM OF the hole, Henry breathed heavily and coughed in the dusty air. Stretched above him, the redwood trees took on a sinister affect. The bark showed off its Spanish Mission roof tiles again. Each terra-cotta section was nested like the scales of the pine cones on the trees.

YOOOOOOOO, am I fucked up right now?

All the mirroring, repeating patterns of the forest revealed themselves. Then, worse: They started to move. They moved in conjunction with each other, became the toothed whirring tracks of chainsaw blades, coming toward Henry. His heart beat in rhythm with the kaleidoscope of his hallucination. From fear? Trauma? Had someone drugged him?

Something rustled under his head. Plastic! The dry riverbed had also been full of trash. Finally something normal. Uncovered, it revealed itself as a tarp folded into a bag or something. It had saved his life.

Jasmine had tried to save him, then she fell in too. Just his luck. If pushing her off him hadn't been the thing to make her lose interest, then falling on his ass in a trash hole might do it. Yanking her down with him was the cherry on top.

Now they were gonna die.

The shape leaning over the hole came into focus. Henry wondered, *Is that . . . ?*

"Geoff!" Jasmine cried. Happily.

"Doug!" he shouted back, annoyed. *Doug . . . Oh God, it's that white guy who was hitting on Jas earlier. Why is he here?*

"Buck! Get over here!" the man hollered. After a minute, Henry could hear Buck's big frame trampling through the forest. "S'at Doug? How'd you get up here?"

"I took my ATV up the logging road from where Buck parked." He was nonchalant in a way Henry did not trust. Doug continued, "I can't believe you left without me. James was my friend too, and you didn't think you'd need some help out here? In *these* woods?"

"Hi! We're still in this fucking hole!" Jasmine chirped. Her voice rasped a little.

Tilly scowled down at the two of them, dropping a knotted rope.

Henry decided to bring the plastic tarp satchel up with him and tossed it up next to Buck, Tilly, and the white guy as they pulled Jasmine, then him up out of the hole. He hoped the others would appreciate his resourcefulness. Outdoorsy people loved tarps. Survival show guys were always going on about tarps. On opening it, they found it was full of garbage, or maybe treasure, heavy with unopened soda cans and folded newspapers that had stopped him from cracking his skull when he fell.

Doug arched a skeptical eyebrow as he examined the parcel. "Soda? You brought soda pop to the woods?"

"I found 'em," Henry defended himself. "There's other stuff in here too."

Buck frowned. "S'probably not a good idea to drink those."

"Yeah, who knows how long they've been out here," Jasmine agreed.

"It's ninety-nine percent fake sugar. I don't think soda goes bad," Henry countered. He wished this off-brand can cache had something he'd heard of. His taste buds pined for the familiar comfort of his daily soda from the vending machine in the breakroom.

"Then you can drink it. I'm not trying to get this baby hooked on vintage chemicals." Tilly chuckled.

"Even if you don't drink the soda, we can use the tarp," Henry added.

"Well, if anyone's interested in what I found, I brought a chainsaw. And I think I found Jamesy's truck," Doug bragged, then added seriously, "It's covered in plants. It's fuckin' weird."

Henry's brain was screaming equal parts *FUCKIN' FINALLY SOMEBODY MENTIONS IT* and *No shit, Sherlock. These woods are weird.* Henry could see how easy it was to slip into the same "these woods are dangerous" line that the people in this town clung to. Because yes, the woods were weird and dangerous—much more so than the locals' nonchalance led him to believe—but also: *I don't wanna agree with Doug. Fuck that guy.*

Henry would've led with finding James's truck if he'd found it.

Tilly grabbed Doug to her, tight. "Thank God you're here."

"We're gonna find him," Doug assured her.

James's truck, the one that had looked brand new the night before in the Skyliner parking lot, was now a rusty, crashed wreck. It reminded Henry of the truck sticking out of the town sign. Yet where that truck had accumulated woody growth over decades, this truck was overgrown the same way the logging equipment had been, only in a matter of hours. Henry suspected there was something off about these woods, but he didn't know enough about forests to qualify it. Although this proved it. If quickly swallowing a truck was a normal thing forests did, someone would've mentioned it.

"We should set up camp before it gets dark," Jasmine said.

"It's already dark," Tilly spat.

So *that* was still going on. *Just go back to being friends, already.* Every woman Henry knew had a best friend or a sister whom she alternated between loving and hating. Tensions were high. They just had to find James and get the fuck outta here. Once he and Jas were safely back in Oakland, she and Tilly would go back to normal. Hopefully. If they all made it out.

Doug speaking up about the forest's weirdness was a crack in the dam Henry had built in his mind that held back his anxiety and fear. Everyone else was from here. They were used to this place. But having someone else verify that yes, this was extremely creepy and dangerous, and not the normal amount of creepy, there was something seriously wrong with this place, flooded Henry with apprehension. What Toussaint always called "bad vibes." Of course, the H had bad vibes—it was a goddamned mental hospital. But panicking didn't help anybody, so Henry breathed in deeply, assuring himself that this was just like work. *It's a place with shitty vibes. You just gotta make it to the end of today and get home.*

"S'a great idea, Jazzy. We all could use a rest," Buck said, shrugging his backpack off his shoulders. Henry had barely noticed the pack since Buck's frame was already so massive. He dug through and handed a nylon baggie to Henry.

Doug pulled out a fire-starting kit and had a roaring bonfire going almost instantly.

Henry rolled the bag in his palms. It had metal poles in it. *Oh, this is the tent. This is gonna be so fucking embarrassing. How do I get in front of this? Can I just say that I don't know how to set up a tent? Black people don't camp. That's like a scientific fact that everybody knows.*

Jasmine appeared next to him. "'Kay if I help?"

That question held so much under the surface. Was this her apology for jumping him earlier? Was she still interested? Was she just being nice and helping him? Was this the last goodbye before she dumped him for Doug? Did she just wanna get the tent set up so she could sleep? Henry's thoughts were all frothed up, so he just nodded, and she took the tent baggie from him, opened it, and pulled out black metal poles.

Jasmine was an authoritative, understanding teacher as she guided Henry through setting up the tent. He liked the intimacy of standing on opposite sides of the nylon fabric, facing each other. Stretching it out together. Like a couple folding blankets together. Completing a task together. After they had two tents up, she left him to investigate a map that Doug had brought. His ATV was loaded with goodies, but Henry didn't see what good a chainsaw would be out here.

Buck insisted on keeping watch and started to march a loose perimeter around James's ruined truck. Tilly sat in the cab for a while and tried James's phone again. No one had service. When she came back to the fire, she looked like she'd been crying.

Doug came back with more wood than Henry felt was necessary. He wished he didn't hate the guy. But he did, in a lizard-brained male aggression way that was contrary to his whole state of being. Henry was an overthinker for sure, but he was chill with other people. He enjoyed being a hater as much as the next person but mainly for the laughs it would get him. *This* feeling hadn't surfaced in him since he stopped playing football. The difference between his thoughts and his feelings was violent. Right now, his body pulsed with loathing for the tall, white Canadian who kept shooting looks at Jasmine. Henry knew those looks. Those were his looks. He gave her those looks at work. Hackles raised, he tried to distract himself.

He sat down next to the fire and examined the contents of the tarp pack. In addition to some soda cans that didn't have expiration dates on them, there were a half-dozen thick newspapers from the summer of 1980. All of them were curled up at the ends with little, dark fingerprint smudges in the corners. A photo fell out from in between the pages. Henry picked it up and looked at it. "Y'all."

Jasmine, Tilly, and Doug gathered around him to examine the overexposed Polaroid. In the snuff portrait, a young logger lay dead. The camera's flash reflected harshly on his blood.

"That's messed up," Doug said.

Yeah, no shit. Henry shook out the other newspapers to reveal four more photographs of loggers, alive and dead. Who did they belong to? Some weirdo. This was weird. Everything about this place was weird. Henry wanted to go home. He wanted Jasmine to come home to Oakland and for them to never talk about this ever again.

Jasmine stared at the photos of the dead men, face snarled into an intense, concentrated sourpuss look. "Tilly." She held up a photo. "Who does this look like?"

"I don't fuh—friggin' know," Tilly started, but Jasmine thrust the group photo into her face. "Oh my God."

"Yep," Jasmine replied grimly. "Grampdaddy."

Doug cooked beans for the group, while they sat on some logs he'd rolled over to use as benches. Henry ate them gratefully, and the nutrition soothed his dislike of the man a bit. "These are great, man. Thank you."

"Yeah, I figured y' all would need a nice breakfast after being out here all night."

The forest was so dark, it hadn't occurred to Henry that it was actually daytime. That it had ever been. Everything in this forest was sapped of any color besides black, gray, and green. Even the bright magenta of his coat and the purple of Jasmine's raincoat looked different in the perpetual twilight. It was like living in an old photograph.

On the other side of the fire, Tilly strung Jasmine's axe head on a length of rope and swung it.

"That's cool," Henry said admiringly. Tilly was cool. The way an anime villain is cool. Bad-tempered and unapproachable but still undeniably badass, and hopefully soft beneath all the aggressive posturing. He hoped she and Jas would make up soon. The iciness between them was unbearable.

Jasmine was trying too hard to get back on Tilly's good side. "Tilly's like a genius 'n shit," she boasted. It was uncomfortable. Sweaty. Like at work when Jas tried to relate to people in the breakroom. Her interests went far beyond shit-talking doctors and Steph Curry. But the last thing a tired mental health worker wants to hear about is how trees have it worse than they do.

Tilly saw through it. "Yeah, I didn't need to run away to some expensive-ass college."

Luckily, Jasmine didn't take the bait. "Not everyone's as good at teaching themselves as you are."

"Self-taught?" Henry tried to keep the conversation focused off Jasmine and her many faults. "What kind of stuff?"

Jas gave him a grateful look. "Oh, everything! Car repair, accounting. Tilly, who taught you how to roll joints?"

Tilly smirked. "YouTube. There's nothing you can teach me that I can't learn on the internet for free. There's a how-to video for basically everything."

Henry sighed in admiration. "That's really cool, Tilly."

The Native American woman let out an aw-shucks scoff that signaled she was warming up. "I mean, I just use it to do the books for my aunt's bar. It's not like I'm a registered nurse or anything."

"That's not true," Jasmine said. "I saw the notebook you kept for Aunt Gin. That was really great work."

Tilly smiled. "Thanks."

Feeling like his work was done, Henry stood up to go get some sleep. As he crossed over to the tent, the Canadian got up and sat down next to Jasmine. Henry paused at the tent flap. *Okay, so it's like that now? This fucking guy. Should I go back? It's not like I can make him move out of my seat. Fuuuck. Just go in the tent. Get some sleep so we can find James—or his body. Ugh. Why did I come up here?*

"You okay, bud?" Doug called to him.

"Henry?" Jasmine inquired.

Henry had been standing in front of the tent, short-circuiting in total silence. "Uh, yeah. I'm fine," he mumbled as he unzipped the tent and dove in.

Inside, pulling off his boots, Henry listened to Doug flirt with Jasmine. Henry was miserable. You know how when you go to the beach and afterward you have sand in all your shit? Same with redwood needles.

"You thought I was a 'Geoff'?" Henry heard the Canadian ask in a mocking impression of Jasmine. The broad silhouette nudged her.

Henry felt sick.

"I forgot your name!" She giggled.

"I didn't know your name either!" Henry shouted from the tent. It was a lie, but he felt like he had to say something. The two of them jumped so he turned over, satisfied.

"Uh . . . okay," the Canadian replied.

Then more giggling from Jasmine.

Resentment shuddered through him, like when Jasmine used to embarrass him back at work in the breakroom, like right before they left when she jumped down Carlos's throat for making a jerking-off joke about the patient who hung himself. *It feels like so long ago even though it was just . . . uhh, yesterday? This morning? I can't keep the hours straight in this place, just walking around and calling out for a guy who doesn't wanna be found. Time is doing its own thing in this forest. Fuck these woods.* Henry snuggled into his sleeping bag and pressed his eyes shut.

A hacking, coughing noise jarred Henry back to consciousness. Branches cracked and thundered to the ground. The fire went out abruptly, making getting out of the tent even harder. Henry heard Doug yelling. Someone turned on a camping lamp.

Cables thwanged above them. It was an ugly, savage cacophony. A cable snapped.

Pulling his boots on, Henry heard a heavy-sounding, wet crack, then something small and stonelike clattered to the ground. A broken cable smacked into the top of the tent and smeared blood across it, black against the camping light and nylon.

He zipped open the tent flap just in time for Doug's body—minus the top of the head from the jaw up—to land on its knees in front of him. Henry looked down into Doug's open-faced mouth. Blood squished under his still-moving tongue. Doug's body was trying to scream. A spurt of blood expelled from the throat into Henry's face. Henry screamed. The body fell, splashing his face with more blood.

Ahead of him, the women screamed.

The only thing Henry could hear was the blood pumping in his own ears, dripping down his face, the thwanging cables. The metallic sound kept pulling his attention away from Jasmine and Tilly. Something big and dark moved in total silence above him. Toward him. He had to move.

The women grunted manically while they fought off some kind of naked attacker. Not naked, Henry realized, not human. It looked like the evil gorillas from that Congo movie or an alien or some horrible zombie. Henry was frozen in place in front of the tent, his brain sputtering to take in what he was looking at.

The thing's mouth was full of sharp little teeth, and the jaw went on for way longer than could be deemed human.

Its skin was the worst: wet, rubbery-looking scales of bark stretched across an emaciated skeleton. It moved like something unholy. Fluid where it should've been hardest. Jumping a dozen feet up in the air and landing on a tree. But when it came to simple things like walking forward, it was creaky and unstable.

Jasmine kicked one right in the chest, but it kept coming after her, even with its chest caved in like a rotting log.

Henry rushed out of the tent and pulled the creature off Jasmine, tackling it at the legs. He fell to the ground under its gnashing mouth. A lucky break because something ripped the creature's neck out, and it fell off him. Its blood was more like silt than liquid. Instinctively, Henry held his breath to prevent breathing any of it in.

Tilly was swinging the axe head on the rope, facing off with another creature whose arm was already hacked off at the bicep. From the shadows, Buck appeared suddenly and grabbed the thing by the armpits. He heaved it at the overgrown truck, where it dented the driver's side door.

Henry pounced on it, kicking it, and opening and closing the truck door on the creature's form. Rage and fear and shock and so much fucking embarrassment fumed out of him. He wanted to destroy this creature. Deep in his soul was the bright white belief in the *wrongness* of this alien thing.

Finally crushed, the thing flopped sideways on the ground with a thud. He continued kicking its body. He wanted to crush it into the earth. The cleats on the bottoms of his borrowed boots chewed through the sinewy flesh beneath. Buck finally pulled him off, bear-hugging him from behind.

"S'all right, buddy, it's dead. They're gone. It's over."

Henry's shoulders fell, exhausted.

Buck asked, "We all here?"

"No," Jasmine answered in a small voice. "Doug . . ." She pointed to the semi-decapitated body of Henry's hated Canadian.

Buck started to hyperventilate. "We need to leave. Now. Tilly, start packin'!"

FINALLY some fuckin' sense. We're not the right people for this. We're not the type of people who survive this kinda thing. Have y'all seen literally any movie? BLACK PEOPLE DON'T CAMP! And now we got forest monsters? Monsters of the forest. Are you kidding me? Fuck that times five thousand.

"Agreed," Henry said aloud. "Jas, I'm grabbin' our shit."

Jasmine gave him a weird, torn look.

"No fuh—friggin' way," Tilly spat. "James is still out there."

NO, HE AIN'T, NO, HE FUCKIN' AIN'T. THAT DUDE IS DEAD, TILLY! Henry tried not to let his expression betray his thoughts. Calm would win here. "So that's two votes for leaving and one against. Jas?"

Jasmine, again with that face. The same face she gave him when it was time to split up. Pleading and apologetic. She would choose Tilly every time. It wasn't Doug he'd had to worry about.

Henry didn't care. *Jasmine, prove to me you're not suicidal by leaving the murder forest.* "Staying here is suicide." *That's not the right way to think about this.* But it was how he felt. "I mean—Jasmine, I care about you. You're important to me. There is something deadly dangerous in this forest, and the next person it kills could be you. I don't want that to happen. For me either."

"If Tilly's staying, then I'm staying," Jasmine said, as calm as if she were asking for water in a restaurant. "I can't lose James and her. They're my home."

Henry sighed. "If you're staying, then I'm staying." He hugged her to him before adding, "For one more day. Or to the death. Whichever comes first."

Over her shoulder, Buck and Tilly were similarly embracing. Tilly added, "Baby votes too, and it wants to find its daddy. It'll be easier with the ATV. We didn't have that before."

Behind them lay the monster arm Tilly had chopped off. It cast a long shadow next to the camping lamp. Henry half expected it to start crawling away on its own. It gave him an idea. "If we're staying here the rest of the night, we need a morgue tent. Or pile. Something. So those things don't come sniffing near us looking for dead bodies."

The girls took down the smaller green tent and reset it a ways away. Henry and Buck carried the bodies of Doug, two creatures, and one loose creature arm on the tarp from the hole. *My treasure tarp ended up being useful after all. But I kinda wish it wasn't.*

Halfway to the morgue tent, Buck stopped short. The tarp snapped tight from behind and almost pulled Henry backward onto the pile of corpses. When he turned, Buck was staring at the ground with an uneasy look on his face. This whole time, Buck's wide, friendly face had been the lone source of calm, yet now it was screwed up into a confused scowl.

"What?"

Buck readjusted the tarp so a faint sunbeam fell onto the severed arm. "S'that look like to you? On the arm? The blue?"

Henry's mouth dropped into a horrified O as his brain took in the faint blue outline of an axe and contextualized it as a tattoo. His eyes met Buck's and he understood.

"Goddamned things used to be men."

26

BUCK

WHEN THE BIRDS IN the trees were too loud to ignore, Jasmine's eyes flickered open. The light outside—what little could filter through the thick canopy—was still a predawn gray. In these woods, you never saw the sky. It made everything feel like it was in black and white.

She was afraid. She felt scattered and paranoid, and fear squeezed her whole body in its cold hands. She knew that what she was feeling was not mental illness. Jasmine knew what she saw and experienced. And amid all that blood and violence and pure insanity, fear was the only correct response. But she was having a hard time reconciling how good her body felt with her heart and mind shrieking silently. Adrenaline maybe. Even after sleeping on the cold, hard ground, she wasn't in pain. The feeling was rare, so she tried to savor it.

But people were dead. It was a nightmare; the sensual pleasures of these woods were just an enticement to lure her into its jaws. It happened in nature all the time. And out in civilization too, she supposed. Was there any part of this world that wasn't trying to kill her?

Her head hurt from all the contradictions sparking through her mind. *This is what insanity feels like. Nah. If I was insane, I'd be more confident. I don't know what the fuck I'm doing out here.*

Here, in the morning, lying between the snoring bodies of her situation-ship and her best friend. And they both hated her. They both blamed her for having to be in these woods and everything that had happened since. Another person was dead. And those creatures were still out there with their hardwood skin and giant teeth. Those things—despite her fear, it felt embarrassing to state the obvious and call them "monsters," especially when what they were was so much worse—those things had been people. One of them had just been another guy with a dumb tattoo. Probably a logger.

Their search party had managed to kill two creatures, but who knew how many were left? Or how long they'd been alive? If it was a long time, then maybe they'd killed the eighteen loggers who went missing after killing Grampdaddy. Maybe her grandparents got off easy by getting murdered. Maybe the loggers had deserved becoming monsters if they were already murderers. Maybe it was another no-win situation like everything else.

Jasmine zipped open the tent to find that the muted sunlight wasn't much brighter than what filtered through the tent. Aunt Gin had taught her how to take pine branch buds and turn them into the worst tea she'd ever tasted in her life. Which meant it was good for her. She hoped to forage some and surprise everyone with something that would rouse them. It wasn't coffee, but maybe it would help. The sound of the zipper caused Henry and Tilly to both talk out loud in their sleep, muttering protests before rolling toward each other for warmth. It made Jasmine smile, seeing how alike they were. She did love them both, even if she wasn't strong enough to love them with her whole heart.

Jasmine didn't see Buck, who was supposed to be keeping watch; she was the last to switch shifts with him. Maybe he was peeing or something. Yeah, just peeing. He'd be back. The log where he should've been sitting was wet from the morning fog. She took a closer look. Buck had brought out the tattooed forearm with its huge claws and explained his theory to Jasmine when he came to relieve her of watch duty. But now, where the creature's arm should have been—had been set aside carefully—little serried rows of evergreen needles formed the outline of an arm with long, spidery fingers.

"Yo, wake up!" she called. "Henry! Tilly!" She batted on the outside of the tent, avoiding Doug's blood where it streaked across the nylon.

Sleepy groans followed by yelps of mutual disgust erupted from the tent. Tilly shoved out first.

"What's up? Are you okay?" Henry asked as he followed.

"Buck's not here and that arm's disappeared too. I think the needles are where someone died."

Jasmine's theory was confirmed at the morgue tent where the forest had swallowed the corpses through both the tarp and nylon tent. All that remained was a mismatched pile of multihued pine needles.

Doug. It was a shame he was dead. He was so hot. Tall and manly looking, like a cartoon lumberjack. Jasmine barely knew him. Which didn't make what happened to him any less of a tragedy. The top of his head had been taken clean off. But it hadn't been clean at all. Memories of the bottom of his face would haunt her forever, dark red blood pooling between each pearl-like tooth. The whole mess had framed the tongue—Doug's tongue—like a gem setting.

On the lookout trail Buck had cut, they found another outline. A big one.

"Oh my god. Buck." Tilly pushed past Jas and knelt by the pine needles. The last remnants of her cousin were now a baby mesa of black soil.

Buck, who'd gotten a boner against Jasmine's leg at a middle school dance. Buck, who'd . . . never mind. She didn't want to think about what had happened between them before. How she'd treated him after. Buck, who'd volunteered for this ridiculous search and protected her in these woods as they got lost looking for James. *If James is dead, then there's no way we're finding his body. With those things out there, we'll be lucky to get out. I have to get Tilly out of here alive. And Henry. And myself.*

Another flash of possibility: Why should she go back out into the world? What was so wrong with dying in these woods? Disappearing into the pine litter and becoming part of something bigger? Maybe it wouldn't be so bad. There were people who needed her help out there, but that wasn't enough. She didn't feel like her job was helping anybody. She was a glorified prison guard. Jasmine let the tempting thought linger but cut it short.

She had things she cared about *here*. People she loved who *needed* her. The realization rocked her. Suicide was fine for her, but she was also responsible for the people she loved and for them, she had to live.

Jasmine stepped up to Tilly and put her hands on her shoulders. She still wanted to be a comfort to her friend. Yet Tilly jerked away from Jasmine. She whispered something.

"What?" Jasmine asked.

"Don't touch me." She stood up and pushed her hard little shoulder into Jas's chest as she passed her.

"I'm sorry."

"Every time you visit, I'm the one who ends up paying for it," Tilly snapped. "Then you didn't come home when we needed you. We shouldn't even be in these woods."

"Bitch," Jasmine hissed. "The rest of us were ready to bolt after Doug was killed. But you wanted to stay and look for James. Buck is on *you*." She considered letting it end there, but fuck it. "And James? James was always going to die in these woods. Most dangerous job in the world, right? Everyone knows loggers die in these woods, and you're the one who let him take the job anyway. That's not on me."

"He's not dead!" Tilly's words were a determined growl.

Jasmine grabbed Henry by the arm and pulled him back toward the camp. "New goal is to stay alive. Let's move out. We gotta get out of here. If you want any part of James to survive, Tilly, you need to come with us. Now."

Far above them, Jasmine heard thwanging. There was a skyline up there. Above it, the forest canopy seemed lower than ever. This forest was closing in on them.

On the ground, they ran toward their campsite. As soon as they entered the small clearing, something rustled in the brush.

"James?" Tilly called in the direction of the noise. Her voice was broken, frantic.

Henry clamped a hand over her mouth and hissed, "Tilly, you need to shut the fuck up right now. Do you understand that?"

She nodded.

"Then let's get the fuck outta here," Henry commanded quietly. He crossed to the ATV and tugged the vines off. "And we're taking this." He turned the key in the ignition, and the ATV roared to life. "One of you know how to drive this thing?"

27 HEROES

1980

AFTER UNLOADING THE TRUTH onto Smitty, she felt worse instead of better, so Marian decided to take a meandering dirt path toward home rather than the logging road or cutting straight through the brush like she usually did. She burst out of the bush onto the dirt trail not two yards from her father. He wheeled around toward her.

"Marian." His voice was hoarse. He'd been crying more. Or yelling at Mama. His eyes were wet and bulging, wild and white in the moonlight.

"Pop. What are you doing here?"

"Bringing you home. Walk with me." He tried to put an arm over her shoulder to herd her back up the mountain, taking the brush route, but Marian jerked away from his touch. They walked side by side in silence for a while until he took the lead.

The trail wound around the hills, a pale ribbon in the darkness. Water trickled through little culverts, riding the mountain down to the Eel River. The forest was so thick, it enveloped her whole world like a big green bowl set on top of the land. Marian thought about the singer she'd heard on the radio, and through the dense canopy, she could make out a few twinkling stars. There was so much more to this world than this forest.

"How old do you think . . ." Whipple muttered before trailing off and not speaking again for miles of undulating highway. After about ten minutes, he coughed, turned his head to the side so she could hear him clearly from behind, and restarted. "You know, there's a lot of bad things that happen out there. Outside the forest."

Marian turned, not wanting to meet her father's eyes. "I know that. I read newspapers."

The man continued. "Hush, girl. You don't know nothin' about what the world's really like."

"It's all I can think about. Because you won't let me see for myself." Marian tried so hard to keep the whining out of her voice. She steeled herself. "You keep me trapped up here, chained up like a dog. Why?"

Whipple sighed and slowed down to match Marian's pace. "Some bad stuff happened to your mom before she met me. She scrapped and survived, and the woods took care of her. Our job's to make sure bad stuff don't happen to you. Trust that your mother and I know the best way to protect you."

"The world's different now. Things are better," Marian scoffed. "There's women's lib."

"Women's lib. They don't mean all women. Not ones like you and your mom. And you're not a woman; you're my baby girl. My daughter. Trust me, it'd be better for you to stay here. You're a smart girl, I know that. Self-preservation is about the smartest thing you can do."

Pop clomped ahead of her, boots kicking up wood chips as they entered the clearing of their cabin. As he raced up the stairs, Pop batted a hand against the water tank; the plastic sounded out a thick, reverberating *BONG*.

Self-preservation. Marian wasn't sure that her self was even worth preserving. She could've warned Tall Matt, but she didn't. She'd thought she had more time. She should've known how tenuous the balance between life and death was in this forest, though; she'd watched it happen her whole life. A dead animal became a maggot-filled corpse, became a dried-out pelt, became a pile of dirt and pine needles, became more forest.

Marian felt a pang inside her. It was jarring, but the feeling assured her the redwood forest's circle of life was not the life she wanted for herself. She *would* leave. She could always come back. Right now, though, she was lashing around like a trapped animal. Was it self-preservation to choose to feel that way forever? Or was it self-preservation to chase the life she obsessed over because doing otherwise felt like rolling over to die? She wasn't beaten yet. She would not die here.

Pop wasn't a bad man. He loved her and Mama, that much was clear. The loggers dying wasn't his fault. It was a dangerous job. Pop was just doing his too. He was their boss, so he had to fill out the paperwork for the company.

He and Mama were wrong to put the powder in the water. Its purpose still didn't make much sense to Marian, but she'd already made her choice. Her parents were wrong to keep her trapped up here. But she did wrong things too: hitchhiking, drinking, touching herself to the pictures she had. She was wrong, but she wasn't bad. Just like her Pop.

Marian would explain everything to Smitty in the morning. Then she'd ask him for a ride out of town.

When he returned to the Skyliner, Smitty's truck skidded to a stop in the gravel parking lot. After talking to Marian, his hangover had turned into something much more toxic. His blood was up, fueled by righteous indignance. This couldn't keep happening. Whipple couldn't keep getting away with this.

The wooden boards whined under his weight with each step onto the porch and into the bar. The boys needed to hear what he knew, even if he didn't know everything.

A few dozen guys were still hanging around, drinking to Tall Matt's memory. No one ever had paid the kid much mind before, not until he started sniffing around the foreman's daughter. Then they'd joked that he was probably next to die. Then he *was* the next to die. This wouldn't keep happening. Whipple wouldn't keep getting away with this. They were going to stop him. *Tonight.*

28 THE CABIN IN THE WOODS

THE ATV CHUGGED ALONG the logging road, and it wasn't completely clear whether they were going uphill or downhill. The mountain—this forest—was so huge it felt flat even though Jasmine knew it curved, like the surface of the Earth. She imagined this was how a skin mite would feel if it suddenly decided to believe that the planet it lived on was alive.

Jasmine squinted into the distance. The air was thick and humid. She lifted her head to let the forest air evaporate her tears as the wind whipped past her face, leaving salt trails that crusted white on her skin.

Spare, nacreous sunlight poked through the ink-stained canopy like starlight, and in that light the pollen danced. It lent a trippy, golden shine to everything. Aunt Gin had told Jas that the canopy had an ecosystem of its own, hundreds of feet up in the air, completely different than everything she saw on the ground. Gin said it looked more like something from the deep ocean. Dirt accumulated on the branches, and stuff grew out of it in neat rows. Huckleberries grew up there. It was almost pastoral. If one forgot what else came from up there.

"So there's no seat belts on this thing? Like, at all?" Henry moaned.

Jasmine hugged his midsection. He sat between her and Tilly. Jasmine's ulcer throbbed for the first time in a day. Or was it two? Time passed differently here, and the difference between night and day was minuscule at best in these dark woods.

Henry was right—they would probably die up here—but acknowledging it felt wrong. For some reason, dying in the forest didn't scare her as much as going back to the life she lived in Oakland did. After everything she'd experienced up here, could she go back to all that? Her coworkers' blank stares whenever she said anything in the breakroom, the doctors' condescension, fuckin' cops, people on the BART, the million little offenses that never changed and never would. *I won't go back to that.* Jas shook her head to herself.

Henry snapped his face around to see what was wrong with her. So protective.

"Watch it back there," Tilly called.

The purple rain slicker flapped in the wind, and Jasmine caught a rare glimpse through the canopy out to the hills beyond. They were heading farther up the mountain. "Goddammit Tilly, we're going the wrong way. Are you fucking kidding me right now?"

"He's your brother, Jasmine. Act like a sister for once in your whole stupid life."

"Uh-uh!" Henry squeezed Tilly's shoulders until she slowed down the ATV. "He's the one who ran away! None of this is Jas's fault! How many more people gotta turn into pine-chalk outlines before you give it up? Turn around! Please!"

Tilly revved the ATV's engine and hunched her shoulders into a wall between her and her passengers. "He's still out there."

"You know what's out there? The things that will kill all of us!" Henry bellowed. He tried to grab the ATV's controls from behind, but Tilly elbowed him away.

Like he'd summoned them, Jasmine watched a dark humanoid figure move noiselessly among the tree branches.

She shouted, "They're following us! Gun it!" Her stomach lurched. Again, but harder this time. She cried out, "Follow the skylines down to the lumberyard!"

Hoarse coughing echoed above and then as if from all around them. The trees swallowed the sound of the ATV, and the air filled with only more aspirated barking.

"GO!" Jasmine shouted.

Tilly relented, steering around trees and skidding duff behind them.

A rusted *thwang* of ancient cables sounded.

The creature climbed along the skyline, hand over hand, making a horrible racket the whole time. The skyline shook violently as its bulky body labored across it. At the next tree, it leapt off the wire and landed gracefully on the tree. It glided through the branches like liquid. Completely noiseless.

If Jasmine hadn't been staring at it, rapt, she would've completely lost track of the thing immediately. They could hide in plain sight, probably.

"Fuck!" Tilly yelled.

Jasmine looked up ahead, expecting some obstacle like an impenetrable stone wall crawling with coughing creatures.

But ahead of them was a mulched driveway leading to a cabin. Small trees grew out of its mossy roof.

Tilly gunned it and almost lost control as they neared the shack. The ATV skidded through old wood chips and almost hit a plastic water tank.

Jasmine, Tilly, and Henry fled up the stairs to the porch. In their frenzy, they pulled the storm door off the hinges. Tilly jiggled the doorknob, but it wouldn't open.

Together the three of them were able to bust the door in, sending a couch skidding across the room.

Jasmine looked back as the three of them spilled into the dusty cabin. She pressed her face against the window as they held the door in place, trying to slide it back into its fittings.

There were more of the creatures outside now. She watched

those things silently melt into the darkness. Gigantic arms slinked up the drive in repeating patterns, sharp, insect-like elbows pumping mechanically over the ground, like in that video of a bat walking that Henry had shown her once. The creatures stalked toward the cabin, soundless on the wood-covered ground.

The silence was broken by the loud metallic cracking of one of them moving over the ATV, bending the frame. The axel heaved. The thing jumped up from the ATV and landed twenty feet up on a skyline. The cable thwanged.

Another creature climbed up onto the ATV. Its arms arced strangely, and Jasmine heard the keys land in the brush somewhere. It fucking *threw* the keys. Those things used to be men, and those men were assholes.

Henry picked up one side of the couch until it stood on its side. Jasmine moved to help him skid it over to where Tilly was holding up the heavy wooden door.

They were pushing the couch against the door when a noise in the kitchen tore a scream out of Jasmine. Something was moving under the sink. A hinge creaked lightly, just enough for Jasmine to pull a flashlight out and swing it toward an opening cabinet. Was one of them coming up from the floor?

When the cabinet door opened, the first thing Jasmine noticed were the eyes. Unblinking, sad, deep red eyes stared into the beam of the flashlight. Below, the face that housed them looked mummified. Pale and ashy, patchy beard, skin cracking. It was pitiful. A thin sheen of some kind of resin on its—his—skin. It was like some kind of greasy dust, and it covered everything in the cabin. This wasn't one of the barking things. This was still a man. This was—

James didn't blink the whole time. He unfolded from under the sink. "You hear them too," he whispered. Jasmine couldn't tell which of them he was addressing; his eyes were so distended they pushed his pupils outward in both directions.

Tilly ran toward him and hugged him. Her loyalty rewarded. Somewhat.

When James pulled a pale, shaking hand across Tilly's back, Jasmine flinched at how long his nails had grown in, what, a day? Two? His whole body was stretched and dried out like an old rag. Seeing Tilly and him reunited tore at Jasmine's heart, the unnerving truth shouting like a mad prophet jailed in her rib cage: Something was profoundly wrong with James. They needed to get out of the forest or he'd die. They all might, still.

29 GOLDENSHINE

WHEN HE WAS TEN years old, James Bay almost died in these woods. He still doesn't know why he didn't. The past was back now, caught up with the present. So what did it matter now what had happened back then? He'd tried so hard to forget it.

After school on a sunny day, James was playing catch in front of his godmother's house. Not really catch-catch because it was just him tossing the soft yellow tennis ball up in the air and catching it with both hands before it hit the ground. Sometimes the ball came at him so fast from above that it hit the insides of his palms, ringing his bones like a bell. It only stung for a minute, then faded, and he could play again.

It was during one of these hurt-hand breaks that James was lounging on the stairs when Jasmine stomped out of the house, clomping off to God knows where, acting like she was so important. Probably off to play with Tilly, her only friend. But that still meant she had one friend to James's zero. Jasmine brushed past him on her way out with a gruff "later."

"Jas!" he called, and his sister stopped scuffing her clunky heels in the pine dirt to face him. "Catch!" He threw the tennis ball to her, lobbing it a bit for easier catching.

Jasmine caught the ball with one hand. Her black nail polish and dark skin made the tennis ball look even more fluorescent. "I'm busy," she growled. "Don't you have anyone else to bother?"

"No. Aunt Gin won't be home till late. She's got a meeting at the school." The boy pouted.

Jasmine chucked the ball into the bushes as hard as she could; James could hear it ricocheting off the wooden pylons underneath the house. Jas smirked. "Now you've got something to do. Have fun!"

"Bitch," James whispered under his breath.

"What's that?" Jasmine started toward him—fist raised—and even though she was twenty feet away, James still flinched, falling back onto the porch. "Thought so." Jasmine cackled like Beavis and strolled down toward the road.

James sighed and lay back on the porch, listening to the wind soughing through the trees, staring into space, noticing that the ceiling had moss caked over its underside, the same as the roof. It looked different from the roof moss. Curlier maybe? Definitely not as green. Aunt Gin or Jas would know the difference between the two, and their Latin names, and the mythological origin of the Latin name, and all sorts of boring facts that James could never get to stick in his head. Gin quizzed them during sunrise hikes, pointing out flora, fauna, and, with equal enthusiasm, places where their family members had died. On Fridays, she took them to the Skyliner for fish and chips. The tragedy of Grampdaddy Whipple was ever present, but no one seemed to really care all that much. It was a fact of life and the town.

Maybe one day he'd feel that way about Mom, after more time. He wanted to forget about what happened: the way the fire streamed down her face, the way her flaming hands burned his arm, the way she screamed and babbled as she set herself on fire. He didn't want to forget about Mom: how she was so funny; and kind; and warm; and loved him, even as she burned his flesh. The bad memories infected the good ones, and all the forgetting and remembering and guilt made James's head hurt. He'd never been so sad in all his life. He'd never felt so alone.

Jasmine didn't love him. She yelled at him and smacked him. Aunt Gin didn't love him. She called him Lil Eight James and threatened to turn him into a spot on the floor if he didn't behave. Most everything James did (or didn't do) counted as acting up, according to Aunt Gin. She'd probably get mad if he didn't bring her tennis ball back. She'd probably say it's one of her good ones—"for comp'ny." James smirked to himself. He heaved himself up to sitting then dropped through the stair railing to investigate the bush Jas threw the ball into.

The ball wasn't in the bush. A raccoon-sized hole in the deck lattice behind it beckoned. James peered underneath the porch, into total darkness, but after a few long moments, his eyes adjusted to the dark, and he spotted the neon object in a far corner underneath the house. James considered leaving it but nah, fuck it. If he got the ball back, he would have something to do until Jasmine or Gin came home. He squeezed his shoulders through the broken lattice, careful not to break any more off or it'd be visible from the driveway, and being blamed for that was not something James needed right now.

Under the house it was dirty, dusty, and had a surprising amount of dried-up old pine needles. Did they not clean up the ground before building the house? Or had the needles been blown in through the same hole? The space wasn't tall enough to stand in, but James could crawl on his hands and knees, easily navigating around spiderwebbed pylons holding up the house. He couldn't make out some of the junky shapes around him, but he could see well enough to spot the tennis ball, shining in the dark so far away. It had lost some of its brightness and was covered with dirt and duff, nestled against a big mass that in the dark looked like it might be a wasp's nest. James listened carefully. There was no buzzing.

Underneath the house was eerily silent, but he could hear the wind rushing through the trees outside. Leaves and dirt blew in through the hole behind the bush. James shut his eyes and charged toward the back of the house on all fours, hoping not to get dirt or dust in his eyes. The ground felt less firm—more soil-like—and James tripped over his hands a couple of times. He'd have to hide his Taz shirt so no one would see how dirty he let it get. Dirt and pine needles prickled him underneath his clothes; they infiltrated every time he fell and got lodged in the parts of him where it hurt the most. After falling again and scraping his knee, James opened his eyes. The wind couldn't blow dirt at him this far back. He'd reached the back corner, under Aunt Gin's room, and his eyes were slow to adjust in the thick darkness. He looked up and all around him, trying to make out shapes in the black until his vision returned.

Finally, he started to make out some of the pylons supporting the corner as they materialized from the dark. Above him, he noticed straight, dark lines like a door in the floor of the house. He neared it but was suddenly startled by the sound of wood creaking next to him. The wasp's nest. Maybe it wasn't empty. James glanced over at it, waiting for it to pounce and spit forth clouds of stinging wasps. Maybe they would kill him, and he'd die under the house, and no one would find his body. But what happened was so much worse.

Worse than the nest pouncing was watching it slowly, silently unfold into a humanoid shape. Terror gripped James with strong hands. He was transfixed by the large bloodshot eyes that were abruptly so close to him, breathing cold breath into his open mouth. Creaking like branches in a storm. Like the branches outside. James was so scared he thought his frozen muscles were going to shatter his skeleton. After a long, cold moment, when his soul finally reattached to his body, he screamed so loudly and horribly that he lost his voice. He scrambled away, scraping up his hands and elbows, knocking into the pylons. He would do whatever it took to get as far away from that thing as possible. In fact, he shot out through the deck lattice so wildly that he took the rest of the lattice panel with him.

Sprawled in the sun, covered in wood scraps, James heaved down big gulps of fresh air. He didn't know if the thing would follow him out from underneath the house, so he dragged himself down the driveway to be safe. When he looked behind him, he saw the creature in the sunlight for a brief second as it emerged from the bush under the porch and *became* the forest. Its herky-jerky limbs jumped powerfully toward a tree and disappeared completely.

Shell-shocked, James lay in the driveway. He was on the verge of passing out when the tennis ball rolled down the driveway and lodged under his arm. He didn't bring it outside. He hadn't grabbed it. He'd been too scared. Something threw it.

James stayed in the driveway—terrified to go into the house above the monster, terrified to venture into town through the woods that were probably made up of more of the creatures. The forest went from a "place" to a "thing" that day in his mind. A thing that should be killed. When Aunt Gin pulled up later, demanding why he was trying to get himself killed, James's voice was too raspy and hoarse to explain what he'd seen.

In the time since, he convinced himself that he'd imagined the encounter, decided he had been attacked by bees. He blamed his childhood imagination and the cornfield scene in *E.T.*, which scared him well into adulthood. But James never had a good night's sleep in that house ever again.

Years later, the forest creatures came back for him, chasing him through their territory like prey. James had stumbled toward the cabin with its moss roof and plastic tank full of gritty water. He'd been lucky, he thought.

He was lucky there was a couch heavy enough to wedge the door shut, and that there was a pair of caulk boots underneath where it had been. The boots had two important features: (1) They were his size; and (2) They laced up to mid-thigh and could hopefully hold his obliterated leg together. Limping around the two-room cabin was hard enough with just a wounded leg but with the added weight of boots with a four-inch-high spiked platform, James had scraped up the floor something fierce as he searched the cabin for anything that could be of use.

There was no phone or running water, but there was a first aid kit and a jar of what looked like yellowing protein powder. James hoped it could sustain him until he was found. He ate a tablespoon then coughed so hard his skin ached, and he collapsed onto the couch.

It was night when he woke up, and the darkest shadowy corners of the cabin were glittering. Not glittering. Pulsating. He closed his eyes again and slept.

Time passed.

When he was conscious again, he tried to visualize being home with Tilly. Raising their child together, better than he'd been raised. But when James dreamed, he dreamed of nothing but death. Men dying wearing boots like the ones he wore.

In one dream, he was stepping lively across an ocean of logs. With every step he felt not only the caulks digging into the redwood bark, but the stomach-juggling dunking of the logs as they dipped into the water under his weight. A sawmill screamed nearby; all the floating logs waited their turn for the shredder.

He was racing another man—some white guy in a red flannel shirt like a cartoon lumberjack. James pumped his arms to move more efficiently, to spear into the submerged redwoods and make it across the logging creek first. But one of the logs turned on him. He'd judged the landing spot accurately, he was certain. The dead tree just shrugged him off, tearing his ankle apart. He felt his shin break even within the tight leather of the boots. The crack reverberated upward, and he heard it with his whole skeleton.

Before he could think, the water drank him under. The logs crowded above him. The cold numbed the electrifying pain in his leg. Blood clouded around the boot. The water forced itself into his body, filling him. James's lungs froze.

Someone dragged him ashore—the white guy he'd been racing. He wasn't more than a kid. James knew that he was dead, and the kid knew it too, not even attempting first aid. The boy pulled the boots off his mangled legs and picked his pockets. "No hard feelings," the sandy-haired kid whispered. There was something in his "aw shucks" manner that made James feel soothed, warm. The boy looted his corpse then pulled James into the bushes where James felt his body disintegrate into nothingness.

When he awoke (the next day? The day after that? Later?), James watched for hours as rays of sunlight traversed the cabin. The goldenshine dust suspended in the pale light transfixed him.

He realized he was probably dehydrated and dragged himself out to the porch. He hoped to be able to just dip the pewter camping mug he'd found inside into the top of the water tank and bypass the stairs entirely. James stepped outside to open the rubber stopper on the white plastic water tank. Using the porch railing as a fulcrum, he leaned over until he was wavering above the tank.

The water level was pretty low, but if he balanced on the railing, he might be able to reach his arm that far. Thankfully, the hole was just large enough to fit up to James's bicep. He scooped water from the bottom of the tank, and the dirty bottom made an awful scraping sound, like there was sediment there. On his second attempt, trying to get a little less grit this time, James felt something push his wrist. It was slippery like a fish. His skin tingled. Hysterically yanking his arm out of the tank almost caused James to lose his balance and fall off the porch, but he managed to stay upright.

Unfortunately, the camp mug clanged against the side of the tank's hole on the way out; the mug ricocheted to the ground and rolled under the cabin. Watching the mug roll away, James saw at the edge of his vision a dark tentacle brush the inside of the tank. An eel?

James was almost too scared to peek into the hole, but he had to know what had touched him. Slowly, he lowered himself over the tank again, eclipsing the tank's opening with his dark face, his silver stubble poking through his chin like a miniature clear-cut of its own.

There was nothing. The tank was empty, and his burn-scarred forearm still rattled with the pins-and-needles feeling the eel in the tank had given him. He knew there was nothing in it, but his mind had still conjured a slick black electrified eel lolling around the water tank, waiting for an arm to zap. But the inside was pristine. There wasn't even any dirt or grit at the bottom even though James had heard it kick up from the tank bottom, had felt it on his tongue—or thought he had.

With no cup now, he was forced to haul himself down the stairs and around to the spigot. He slurped greedily and tried to ignore the silty texture on his tongue.

Time passed.

During the night, he dreamed he was working on a skid row—the original meaning of the word came from logging and meant a rolling bed of smaller logs that made transporting the huge ones easier. Like the conveyor belt rollers at Hsu's Market. Oxen pulled a redwood trunk as big as a building across the corduroy road of greased logs.

Suddenly, a branch above snapped and landed not ten feet from James and his ox. Big Paul reared forward in fright and—trying to escape the sound—kicked James in the head. He felt a good third of his face crash through the back of his skull. It was all he could feel as he was currently airborne, the blow knocking him clean off his feet and onto the conveyor belt of rolling logs that hungrily crushed the rest of his body. They rolled him into pulp. His blood lubricated the skid row almost as good as pine oil. His crew was able to get Big Paul under control and finish out the shift.

When sunlight filled the cabin again, James unlaced the boot so he could clean his wound. His whole left leg had felt numb for a while now, so he wanted to check if it was gangrenous. It wasn't just numb; he felt no pain at all. But when he tried to walk on it, the sound of bone on bone was too much for him to bear.

When he peeled the boot down, his impaled thigh looked worse than he could've imagined: The hole went deep, down to his bone. James shuddered, remembering the all-encompassing snap of his shin breaking in his logging dream. The flesh wasn't healing. It looked like it was rotting, but not the way a human rots, covered in saprophytic bacteria and maggots. This was more—or less—different. Wrong. James stuck his finger into the dark slime oozing from his wound and felt nothing. The slime was fibrous, sinewy under his fingers, maybe a little gritty. Like the inside of a vegetable. He picked hard little granules out of the pooled tar on his leg, felt them under his skin, skidding on hard edges under the pressure.

The pain of his nightmares seemed to overpower every nerve, and he simply had no room left to feel pain while awake. If this was the case, James vowed to sleep much less.

Staying awake was easy because James's arm continued to tingle. Then it burned. The burning gave way to itchiness. Nothing made it go away, not even a spoonful of the soporific protein powder. He'd need strength to keep from irritating it more. But it was no use. James scratched at it rabidly until he broke the skin. His arm split open. He kept scratching; he couldn't stop. His nails felt sharper. Under the skin, his fingernails hitched on bark. Before he could stop himself, he was peeling the bark away, trying to find himself underneath.

Instead, his skin fell away around the burn scar, revealing rough, red bark underneath. He stopped scratching because his fingers had split into hundreds of long, sharp needles. He grew taller. His arms popped and stretched and reached toward the sun. The speed with which he grew nauseated him. Blood throbbed in his eyes, thickening in his veins until he couldn't see.

He stretched skyward. The wooded mass of him grew through the roof of the cabin, toward the glorious sun. All around him, trees just like him did the same. Their canopies connected. Their roots connected. Their consciousness connected. He felt . . . everything.

Below him, a line of ants made its way through his toes. Men. A cable snapped, fell, and cut down one of the men at the shins, and whipped down the mountain. It ravaged through the forest to finally crush the steam donkey operator at base camp. The force of the cable pulverized the young man into a million-million red specks.

Seven long steam whistles echoed through the foggy forest, declaring the known death at the lumberyard but not the shinless, now-dead logger disintegrating into the ground below him. His death nourished James. Not enough.

The line of men barely stopped to acknowledge their fallen comrade. It was a dark white morning, and they had a mission. They chopped James down, then sliced off his limbs, split him into manageable chunks, cinched him with metal chokers, and dragged him down the mountain. At the sawmill, he was washed with chemicals, then sawed into cuts like a steer.

Time passed.

After being shipped from warehouse to storehouse to wholesaler, he came home. James rode the winding 101 back to his mountain. Here he was used to build a cabin in the woods. Parts of him were tables and doors all over the country, but his heart lived on this mountain, in this cabin. The forest fed him life. Grew moss over his roof. Protected him and the chosen who lived inside him . . .

James woke up panting in the slithering darkness. When he opened his eyes, he was under the cabin, looking up at the trapdoor. The pewter mug rested in the duff next to his head. There, he saw a tennis ball, glowing in the near darkness, as he started to unfurl his limbs. Across from him, a child opened his mouth to scream—

BANG!

He was back on the couch, losing it again.

BANG!

The barkers were battering the door down; they were about to get through. James rolled off the couch and heaved his booted legs across the room as quickly as they would let him. They were so heavy, like roots. He hid in a cabinet, folding himself inside and slamming the cabinet door as the cabin's door busted off its hinges.

James watched from a gap as three frantic figures pushed the sofa up against the cabin door. Their flashlights were so blinding that the dark, cramped space felt safer than the rest of the cabin where he'd been slowly going insane. The sudden stimulus was too much right now, no matter how much he longed for something other than the crushing, hallucinatory solitude he'd been trapped in. With one exception.

The barkers continued their syncopated beating on the walls, and James grew positive that this was all in his mind. The hitting was too harmonious, too musical. Over time, he'd experienced a lot that had turned out not to be real. Those hadn't broken him yet, and neither would this.

The barkers weren't going to break through. They didn't need to. This cabin was still in the middle of their forest. Now, they were sending fake-real people to give him a last surge of hope before he finally snapped and made a run for it into their woods. Like Judas goats leading him to a slaughter that he wasn't sure he didn't deserve.

At least these newcomers made a good show of being scared.

One of the figures shone a light in his direction. Jasmine. James had never noticed how similar their eyes were. Deep, dark brown irises. Like Mom's. Even if they were mirages, maybe he could learn something from them. James creaked open the cabinet door and asked, "You hear them too?"

30 FOREMAN'S CABIN

RAIN PELTED THE OUTSIDE of the cabin while Henry Savage took inventory of his life. Sitting at a small wooden desk in the corner, he buried his face in his hands.

My name is Henry Lewis Savage, and I'm thirty-eight years old. I live in East Oakland, and I work in a hospital. Right now, I'm in Humboldt County, NorCal, hiding from monsters in a cabin with a guy who thinks he's a fuckin' tree. I wish I'd never come up here.

James was adamant about how good he felt, claiming his back didn't hurt anymore, the wound in his thigh was fine, and he was sleeping well for the first time ever. This creature was not the tall, mellow stoner Henry had met on the side of the 101. His hunched posture looked painful. His whole body looked horrible. His bones cracked with every move. James stayed in the shadows mostly, which was good because in the light, his skin was mottled like the melanin was being sucked out of him.

From the shadows, James was rasping out the realizations he'd made in the cabin. His presence offended every one of Henry's senses. The gravelly voice tickled the back of his neck, scraped up like the floorboards. His face was the worst: sunken cheeks, shrunken lips, and enlarged, bulging eyes with veins so blood-engorged that it was a wonder the man could see anything. He stank like wet rot, and the smell permeated the room, caking the inside of Henry's sinuses, like the inside of the log Henry had fallen through earlier—yesterday? Henry didn't dare touch him.

Tilly held onto James with her whole body, probably afraid to lose him any more than she already had.

"I can't feel pain and because of it, I'm thinking more clearly than I ever have," James rambled. His voice was muffled in the dark. "I understand things now." He took Tilly's round, fearful little face in his giant hands. "I love you so much. I need you to believe me. Just look . . ."

James tried to untie his boots to show the others his wound, but the blood staining the shoes convinced Henry there was no way he wanted to see what was under the brown leather. The forest was changing James, who had seen his deterioration and taken it as a blessing. "The forest is regrowing me."

If I looked like that, I'd probably believe some crazy shit too. Like Jas said, sometimes going crazy is the appropriate reaction to not-exactly-sane circumstances. She'd said it better than that. Before.

"It's changing me too." Jasmine's clear voice rung off the wooden walls.

Henry didn't turn toward her, afraid of seeming accusatory. He knew as well as anyone how much Jasmine was transforming. But where her brother was wasting away, Jasmine shone brightly. Lusted. Hungered. Henry knew because he felt it happening to him too. His back pain was gone. He could run again. Could breathe easy. Something in this forest was nourishing him, but he worried about what that nourishment cost. If it came from the man they were in the woods to find. Shriveled like a raisin in this cabin. Life doesn't come from nowhere.

Henry pushed the grease-dusted papers on the desk out of his way, and Jasmine's flashlight turned toward the sudden noise.

Gingerly, she came over and squeezed his shoulder, then rifled through the papers. File folders for payroll documents, NDAs, insurance forms. All from 1980. Care of William Whipple, on-site representative for Mooney Timber Products. "Grampdaddy . . ." Jasmine muttered.

From the drawer, Henry fished out a couple Polaroids of dead loggers. Proof of death for the insurance company, probably.

Stacking the papers, Jasmine spotted a larger photo and reached over Henry for it. In the sun-bleached color photo, a white man, a pregnant black woman, and their daughter smiled on the porch of a cabin. The same cabin they were in now.

"Mom grew up here," James said, close enough to make Henry flinch. He hadn't heard him or his spiked platform boots approach.

"Aunt Gin said he was an activist. The newspaper said—" Jasmine started.

"The loggers said he was a saboteur," Tilly said as she materialized behind her husband.

James croaked, "Gin said he used to work at a sawmill. They were all wrong. None of it is true. Grampdaddy was a Mooney man until he died. He was their boss. He lived here with Mom until she ran away. Nothing we know about our family is the truth. Just the stories some crazy people made up."

"They weren't crazy," Jasmine defended them. "There is something wrong with these woods. Crazy is believing—you know what? Forget it."

Surrounded by the Bay family and their dark revelations, Henry made the tough decision to add another. He pulled out the photos from the tarp stash. The Polaroids were the same as the ones clipped to Whipple's paperwork.

Henry had no idea what Jasmine was going through right now. At least the white guys who'd ruined his family had had the decency not to enter the bloodline too recently. Adding all kinds of filial obligation and feelings and bullshit.

"Let's get outta here," Jasmine finally said, smoothing down her humidity-frizzed hair. "We found James."

"You got any opinion on any of this Grampdaddy stuff?" Tilly asked, perturbed at Jasmine's matter-of-factness.

"Nope. We don't have time to deal with The Past shit right now. Let's mosey." Jasmine addressed her brother, "This is me getting along with you. You find anything in here we can use to fight those things off?"

As James led them toward the bedroom, Henry pulled Jasmine aside to whisper, "Do you think he can make it out there? Dude is tore up."

Jasmine just shrugged. "He'll get worse if he stays. I think he's turning into one of those things." She leaned in closer to Henry's ear. "To be honest, I'm worried about whatever is in this forest hurting Tilly's baby. This forest is changing all of us."

Henry nodded and rubbed Jasmine's back comfortingly. He'd wanted to leave since they found the eerie, overgrown work site, however long ago that was. *Whatever we gotta do to get off this mountain alive, let's do it.*

The bedroom was mostly bare. Weird. Henry had been in plenty of other people's bedrooms in his adult life, but this room still carried the nostalgic menace of a friend's parents' off-limits bedroom. Some doors should stay closed. Tilly and James dug around behind the bed, under the bed, in a cedar chest, pulling out an austere but serviceable arsenal.

With more rope, Tilly could swing her axe head from farther away. She affixed the metal piece onto it and tested the weight appraisingly.

Jasmine was handed an axe with a handle almost four feet long.

Henry got a crowbar, sticky with the same greasy yellow dust that covered everything in the cabin. Trying out different grips on it, Henry remarked, "Now we just gotta pull that couch away from the front door."

"Nah." James coughed abrasively. He opened the bedroom closet and pulled up the floor to reveal a trapdoor. When he lowered himself down and reached up to help the others, his arms looked too long, like they had too many bones.

Using the trapdoor, the group escaped under the cabin to the gully and searched for the ATV's keys. Its frame was cracked but it was all they had.

31 HANGING

1980

WILLIAM WHIPPLE WOKE FROM dreaming a nightmare to living one. Gasping for breath, he stumbled back into consciousness. Through the fog of sleep, he noticed his wife's beauteous pregnant form sleeping soundly next to him, hair coiled in a dark halo around her head. The sound of trucks outside led him into the big room where Marian should've been asleep. Light poured in through the front window, filling the room with rimy illumination. The sheets were on the sofa, but his daughter was nowhere to be found. Had something happened to her? Were the loggers coming to inform him of some horrific accident that his doomed only child had brought onto herself by continually going out there, away from the safety of these woods?

Shoeless and in his baggy long johns, Whipple stepped out onto the porch to find Smitty and the rest of the crew, plus some other fellas, gathered in his driveway. Altogether about two dozen men. Angry, drunk men.

"Boss." Smitty nodded.

"What the fuck is all this? Fuck're you all doing up here in the middle of the night?"

"We know what you've been up to. What happened to Tall Matt, to Little Jonesy, to Big Hank and Mick before him was no accident."

Taken aback, Whipple stiffened. "Of course it was."

"Where are the bodies? Men disappear in these woods, working for you."

"It's a dangerous job. If you're too pissant to do it, go grow marijuana with the hippies or suck dicks in San Francisco."

"We're not drinking the water anymore."

"Good for you." Whipple scoffed.

"And the insurance claims?" Smitty bellowed.

At that, Whipple tried to run back into the house, but a handful of loggers pounced up the porch stairs, grabbed Whipple, and dragged him down in front of the house, where the group took turns beating and kicking him. Blood soaked Whipple's long johns, but he still fought back, stronger than most of the men but not stronger than all of them together. When they hanged him, his last thoughts were of his love for his wife and daughter.

One of the loggers kicked in the cabin door. He'd busted in to ransack the place and stomped across the planks, searching for valuables. He grabbed Whipple's Polaroid camera and looped it around his neck. When he kicked in the bedroom door, it fell off the hinges and kicked up whorls of dust in the abandoned-looking room. *Whipple sleeps here?* the man thought. Seeing the boss's shitty bed demythologized the man more than kicking his teeth in had. The man grabbed Whipple's truck keys from the nightstand but hadn't yet put them in his pocket when he exited the cabin, alerting Smitty, who snatched them from his hand with a fierce "gimme that!" Two seconds as the leader of the group, and Smitty was already stealing from his men. *Fucker.*

The logger was at least able to snap a photo when the men hoisted Whipple's twitching body up on some rigging cable, piss and shit adding to the mélange of stains on the foreman's long johns. With a mechanical *zzzt*, the camera spat out the Polaroid, and he grabbed it hungrily. He'd never seen the photos Whipple took with this thing and waved it around so it would develop faster. Another bucker named Joe shoved him hard, muttering something about "evidence," and some men around him agreed and tried to grab for the photo.

Smitty bellowed for them to shut up and crossed the group, circling around the area directly below Whipple's still-pulsing body and its refuse. He grabbed the Polaroid from Jim. "Whipple was an enemy of loggers. He killed us, which makes him a goddamned saboteur. What we did here tonight—what we all did together—was self-defense. Agreed?"

The men nodded, united by purpose. One of the non-loggers—probably some mob-happy barfly who had tagged along or even a relative of one of the dead lumberjacks—suggested that the foreman's family was probably nearby. Consensus spread that the Whipple women needed to be scared into keeping quiet or silenced in other ways.

"Bring 'em both here," Smitty growled. "If anyone can convince the girl and her mother to hush this up, it's me."

32 BARKERS

THE BROKEN ATV CREAKED down the logging road from Foreman's Cabin. It was a mess of torn fiberglass, unwieldy and slowed by the weight of four people (more accurately, three humans and whatever James was turning into). Jasmine felt the axel groan under them, holding together for dear life. This thing was only meant for one person but somehow, they were all hanging on. Barely. Her legs dangled off the back, her long-handled axe resting across her thighs. Henry held onto her, also facing backward.

James drove, with Tilly hugging him. With his bloodshot eyes, Jasmine couldn't imagine how he saw in these dark woods, but James claimed to be fine, and Tilly backed him up. *Tilly will always choose him.* He was the Bay she wanted, the Bay who was able to love her the way she needed. No matter how much he assured them he felt good—felt great, even—the forest was changing James. Something like heartbreak cracked inside Jasmine as the ATV slumped through the dirt trail. *He's wasting away*, her brain offered hopefully. *Maybe dying. If he's gone, maybe . . .*

She was supposed to be keeping watch, but darkness infected this part of the forest. As long as the barkers stayed in the trees, she wouldn't hear anything either. Until they wanted her to. When Jasmine thought about it, the idea of certain death held some comfort. *At least I know what's coming. If I'm gone, maybe . . .*

She wouldn't have to worry about anything else since she'd be dead soon. Fuck that job, that rent, Oakland, California, this world. At least by dying in the forest, her death would feed something greater than her and benefit the whole. Better than dying out there where her death accomplished nothing. Out there, she was just another black woman. Here, she'd become a nurse log. Like one of those fallen trees whose dead flesh births new life, creates a new world for tiny organisms. Was their whole world.

The ATV's red taillights reflected off knobby bark as they bobbed along, casting shadows that danced macabrely over every tree they passed. Every turn jostled them, and even the smallest bumps made Jasmine's stomach lurch. First from the initial loss of gravity; then from Henry grasping her torso way too hard so she didn't slide off; and finally from the sharp cutting pain at the thought of actually surviving and having to go back to that job, that rent, that world.

They weren't even taking a turn when the axel shattered beneath them, near the edge of a ravine. The wheels dug into the soil on one side and skidded, knocking Jasmine loose and nearly sending her flying.

Immediately, Henry grabbed her hand and pulled her back to him.

Sweet Henry. Even in this moment of terror, after everything that had happened, he was there for her.

Unfortunately, the momentum lurched the vehicle onto its side. Jasmine's shoulder caught on debris on the dirt road, and she was yanked so hard she lost the sleeve of her purple raincoat. The high tenor of fabric ripping next to her ear was so loud she didn't hear Tilly scream, "We're going over!"

She only felt Henry disappear from next to her. He was snatched upward, torn from her by forces much stronger than Jasmine Bay.

She slid down an incline; they all did. Henry rolled above her. Jasmine assumed he was rolling because his cries were muffled at regular intervals, making him sound like a train: *hoomph, hoomph, hoomph.*

Against the sky, Jasmine could see the last shadow to fall from the cliff path. The silhouette of the ATV tipped over and fell toward them, gathering speed even as metal was torn from it. Clouds of sawdust and dirt kicked up behind it. The engine was still running, buzzing with deep threat.

Jasmine felt like Alice in Wonderland, falling forever in the blackness. She was able to grab onto Henry, and together they narrowly avoided stumps and trees. All the while, the broken ATV followed behind, screaming as the forest ripped it apart.

Legs held tight around Henry, Jasmine searched the chaos for signs of Tilly's neon beanie and James's elongated form along the hill. She heard nothing but the horrible metallic screeching of the ATV, getting closer and closer, breaking into more and more sharp pieces.

Jasmine acted before the idea fully formed in her brain, and she let go of Henry, kicking him away from her. He screamed but rolled in a wide arc just in time for the avalanche of twisted metal to pass them both.

The forest spit them out at the bottom of the ravine, still raining pine duff and car parts onto them.

The fall had decapitated her axe, the handle of which fell next to her. She hadn't thought about the weapons falling with them.

Groaning, Henry fished a flashlight from an interior pocket of his hoodie and shined it right into Jasmine's eyes.

"Jesus!" she hissed.

Henry crawled to her and hugged her close. "I didn't lose you."

She hugged him back, and they parted long enough to stare into each other's eyes. Was he going to kiss her? Did she want to kiss him?

Behind Henry, Jasmine thought she saw neon yellow bobbing in the darkness. She stood up and scanned for Tilly and James. The two were nowhere to be seen.

Henry turned his flashlight on the steaming hulk of the ruined ATV, and Jasmine steeled herself for what they might find under there. Her own death in these woods was fine but not Tilly's. Not now. Jasmine paused in front of the wreck.

"I'll look," Henry said reassuringly as he crouched down to shine the flashlight underneath. When the beam returned to her, Henry shook his head. "They're not under there either. They must not have fallen as far as we did. Maybe they're still up on the road."

Sadness pooled into the carved-out hollow under Jasmine's ribs, then fear froze it solid when Tilly's screaming rang out through the dark.

Just then, the skylines above them vibrated with that awful broken-cello-string sound. In her horror, Jasmine grabbed Henry's arm and watched a shadowy figure cross in front of the moon. Or maybe it was the sun; it was impossible to tell anymore.

Suddenly, a group of those *things* was closing in on them from above, stalking down into the leaf-littered gully toward Jasmine and Henry. The barking, bark-skinned creatures with the creaky movements that propelled them fluidly through the lightless forest. The mechanics of it entranced Jasmine, but Henry yanked her after him down the ravine toward Tilly's continued screaming.

Jasmine ran after him, still gripping her axe helve in case she needed to fight the barkers again. Just the thought of getting close to one of those things and its coughing, ballooning throatsmade her gag. She had been afraid to touch the arm before and imagined their skin felt something like rotting wood. She prayed she wouldn't have to get into close contact. To whom she was praying, she had no idea. Her fear, however, proved she wasn't ready to roll over and give up on her life. She still had things she wanted, even if it was just to get away from disgusting monsters that she hated.

Henry's wild flashlight beam suddenly alighted on Tilly's face. She was buried up to her neck in soil, beside a nurse log. She looked so terrified. It was so much worse than anything Jas could've imagined.

"Tilly! My God!"

She knelt at the mound and used the axe handle to dig around her friend. *Where is James?* she wondered.

"Jas!" Henry bellowed.

She turned just in time to see a hairless creature's huge teeth and giant, speckled amber arms reach out toward her and knock her to the ground. Her whole body ached under its weight.

Too afraid to look up into its face, Jasmine struggled under the creature, trying to twist herself around like a cat declining a hug. She grasped around, desperately searching for the axe handle she'd dropped in the attack—for something she could use to fight it. The barker's legs were as strong as its arms, but Jasmine managed to scramble out from under it.

She crawled across the ground, trying to keep the thing away from still-trapped Tilly. Tilly looked up at Jas, then at the nurse log she was buried in front of. It was too much. Tilly lost it. She started to scream and buck her head. She was freaking out, eyes frantic, animal-like in her fear. "Jas!" Her voice rasped with strain, like she was about to lose her voice. Tilly writhed wildly in the dirt but was still stuck.

Jasmine scrambled over to her again to help dig her out, but Tilly screamed, "GET AWAY FROM ME!" in Jas's face and tried to headbutt her when she got too close.

The creature came at her again, but Jasmine—full of adrenaline and fear, Tilly's as well as her own—shoved it to the ground and was able to put it in a leg hold. She used this move with violent patients often and wished she had Carlos's dumb ass nearby to inject trazodone into the bark-skinned monster bucking underneath her legs. The creature felt strong and slithery like the nurse log she was grinding against earlier; soft and hard at the same time. She deserved this for her perversion. This is what it feels like when the forest grinds back. If trees could hug people, they'd squeeze the life out of them. She didn't blame them. But she had to live. To get Henry and Tilly and James out of this forest of death.

The barker grasped at her face with long fingers. Its skin was silicone soft like mushroom gills, and the feeling of it sliding across her skin sent bolts of alarm through Jasmine's whole body. A feeling less like being electrocuted, more like being connected, like she'd been a dormant circuit before this terrifying, ugly creature touched her. When its hands gripped her, the feeling of rock-hard bones through its skin brought part of her online. Turned her on. Why was her body reacting this way? Jasmine wanted to throw up, but the knot in her was pulsing too much pleasurable exhilaration. The creature capitalized on her shock and pinned her again. She was forced to look into its big, bloodshot eyes. Sad eyes. It gripped the meat of her leg then caressed her face. Lovingly. It opened its mouth and coughed out, "Marian."

Jasmine's insides sunk as cold terror dragged her into the ground. *That* thing *knew Mom. These creatures used to be people. People from this town, who knew our family. My family is connected to all of this.* Her eyes widened, afraid of what this monster would do to her. She swallowed and blinked hard.

When she opened her eyes next, the creature's head was missing. In its absence, behind it, stood James, swinging a piece of the ATV's frame. The barker fell to the side, off Jasmine.

"James," she coughed out. He was still human. Still enough of James to be her brother.

James extended a hand to her.

Jasmine reached up to it, grateful, and was pulled to her feet. Together they would be okay. They could work together and save Tilly. They could fix everything, in time.

With a metallic crack from the canopy, four barkers fell onto James, as suddenly as snow falling from a roof. The dark figures covered him. They dogpiled on him, swarming over him like insects.

Jasmine struggled to locate James from between the gray-red bodies. She pushed through their limbs, reaching for her brother. Her fingertips barely grazed the stiff flannel of his shirt, nearly touched the soft body underneath. Barker anatomy tightened around her fingers, and the amphibious skin beneath her touch grew rough.

The creatures started to squeeze together, becoming hard and solidifying into a woody mass.

Jasmine pulled back, horrified, and tripped on the axe handle. She stood up again to use the helve to batter the monsters, hoping it would free her brother. But it was fruitless, using wood on wood. A stick against a tree. She kept beating the dogpile, hoping for a different outcome.

The wooden blob had enveloped James's body. It crushed him to pieces. Blood gushed from under the shards of bark, and the mass ossified into a burl-covered stump.

"NO!" Jasmine wailed and kept trying to chop at the stump with her headless axe. She wasn't in control of her body anymore. Pain was. Grief filled her, propelling her to try everything to undo her brother's death. If not that, then to provoke the creatures into releasing his body. Would they take her too? She didn't care. Her hope was gone. Her purpose for being in this forest was crushed like wet berries under the woody mass in front of her.

It was grief. She knew that now. Jasmine had resented and hated and loved and envied James. As his blood poured from the wood, black in the gray light, it was as if a part of her own body had been cut out. The rope between the two of them was frayed, but it was supposed to stay connected, and they would have figured it out eventually. But it was cut now. James was dead. They were supposed to have had more time. It wasn't supposed to be like this.

It wasn't fair. She and James were supposed to make up better than this. None of it was fair. Their whole family history had been a lie. James's words rang in her head. *Nothing we know about our family is true. Just the stories people told us.*

Jasmine's awareness returned to the world in time to realize Tilly had screamed herself hoarse, still in the ground. She'd seen her husband die saving Jasmine. Despite the empty shock at the loss of her brother exploding within her, Jasmine still wanted nothing more than to comfort her friend. Jas started to move toward Tilly when Tilly growled a breathy "no, no, no!" up toward her. Feral. At Jasmine. Past Jasmine.

Wooden, hard hands grabbed her shoulders and arms. Hundreds of hands held her as she bucked, trying to loosen their grip. The hands lifted her up, out of view of Tilly, whom she could still hear rasping at ground level. Jasmine faced the roof of the world, the redwood canopy sliding through her vision as the barkers carried her to the nurse log. The trees were shaking. Gray-green fronds of needles, soft and sharp at the same time, drifted to the ground all around her.

The hundred-hundred hardened hands pressed her through curtains of woody roots, into dirt and barky blackness.

33 OUT OF THE WOODS

1980

WHILE POP ARGUED WITH the loggers outside, Marian climbed out from under the sink. She slipped into her parents' room and woke her mother, shaking her. Jeanne gasped awake with a loud "huh?" and Marian clapped her hand over Mama's dark, frowning mouth.

Outside, Pop started to yell in pain. Jeanne bolted upright in bed, cold sweat matting along her hairline. She pulled Marian's hand off her mouth and silently led her to a trapdoor in the bedroom closet. She lowered Marian down to the ground, then jumped down herself. Miraculously, Mama barely made a noise landing on the crunchy leaf litter. Even nine months pregnant, the woman was impossibly graceful. Even at a time like this. Maybe especially at a time like this.

Marian felt guilt tear a hole in her just under her ribs, and every needling pang reminded her of her part in this. *If I hadn't said anything to Smitty, they wouldn't be beating up Pop. But if he hadn't poisoned the men and covered up their deaths, the men definitely wouldn't have gone after him.* She went back and forth internally, chastising and excusing her actions, while she and her mother cowered underneath the cabin, sinking into the dirt. Above them, boots stomped through the two rooms.

On the other side of the cabin, Whipple was suspended by a cable line. Through a crack between the ground and the wooden cabin slats, they saw his body rise from their field of vision. Mama started to scramble out from their hiding place, but Marian pulled her back and held her down until the suicidal urge passed.

Wriggling above them, Pops screamed, cursed, gargled, and after many, many long minutes, died. Truck headlights illuminated his bare feet dangling in the air.

Jeanne went rigid next to Marian. Her fingers dug into the girl's arm when Smitty issued the order to find them. Her stone-hard hands led her daughter with her, creeping away from the loggers to disappear into the forest.

How could he? Marian wondered. Her mother's strong hands pulled her through the dark woods, deeper and farther away from their pursuers. To Marian, it seemed they crossed miles in seconds. The uneasy feeling she got from the forest's distortions in time and distance contracted her vision, calling to mind her earlier drug trip. Her stomach lurched, but she kept up with Mama.

Behind them, the men shouted and waved flashlights around, but the women were able to stay ahead of them. This forest was their home. The loggers just worked here. It would always be temporary for them.

In a stony gully curtained with roots and vines, Mama finally stumbled. She tried to keep her high-pitched heaving quiet, but when the moans got more and more unbearable, Mama was able to croak out, "Baby . . . It's coming. We gotta hide." The loggers were getting closer, alerted by her cries.

Mama crawled on all fours, pausing for her contractions, and led Marian to a thick tangle of roots that formed an impromptu cave. Hidden behind the roots, Marian cradled her mother in her arms to keep her warm and comfortable, while allowing Marian to muffle her cries if the loggers came searching their way. Anticipating the same problem, Mama pulled one of the dead tree's roots—a thick one about the width of a wrist—toward her and bit down on it. Her fingers dug into Marian's legs, hard as wood. It dawned on Marian that she had no idea what to do; she had never been there when her mother gave birth. Mama always disappeared in the night with Pop and came back empty-handed. Then done it all over again the following year. Her mother's soft squeals were muffled by the root in her mouth but not the pealing wail of the baby that slid out of her. It was so pale in the darkness. Its voice cleaved a trail through the forest straight for the pursuing men to follow.

When Mama stuck her finger in the baby's mouth, Marian relaxed. Maybe the men would give up before reaching the gully. Marian offered Mama her red hoodie to wrap the baby in, but she shook her head and reached out to caress her daughter's wrist. Mama's love spilled into Marian's arms and warmed the rest of her body. She loved her mother so much. It wasn't her that she wanted to abandon, just the forest and Pop's ghoulish deeds.

Cursed as the thought was to even entertain, Marian couldn't help but think that with Pop gone, maybe she and Mama could leave Humboldt together, along with the baby that shone pale and wet against Mama's arms. Mama moved the child from one side of her body to the other and pushed the newborn against the soft soil wall. *Wait. What is she doing?*

Roots wrapped around the newborn's fat limbs and slipped on the wet skin. Woody tendrils pulled it from Mama's hands.

Marian could only watch in horror, still not registering that what her eyes were showing her was really happening. It couldn't be. *But what about the other babies Mama never gave birth to?*

The baby gurgled lightly as it was tugged into the soil wall. The shadows were swallowing Marian's sibling. She didn't even know the sex. Just that it was disappearing before her eyes, portion by portion.

The hungry black dirt gulped up the child like some kind of animal. The baby's babbling was abruptly silenced.

Mama and the root log sighed in unison, slow and contented.

Marian emitted a choking yelp as the last breath of her innocence escaped her.

A flashlight shone on them, penetrating the root cave and illuminating Mama's furious face.

What did the men think they were looking at? Marian tried to imagine it. Herself, blinded and blinking, frantic and frizzy-haired, kneeling beside her mother helplessly. Mama, wearing a soaking-wet nightgown stained with blood and redwood needles. What would they see when their flashlight beams landed on Mama's hands slick with amniotic fluid and caked in dirt? They probably looked like monsters to them.

"Over here!" a man yelled.

Marian's insides wrenched, every muscle turgid with adrenaline. She couldn't move, didn't even struggle when the loggers ripped through the roots. She could not will her body to resist when the men pulled her to her feet and marched her back to face her father's body.

The men grabbed Mama, who bucked and seized until blood spilled freely from between her legs. It spilled on the men's shoes and Mama's bare feet. Marian could only follow them, held so tightly she could feel her shoulder bruising.

As they neared their home, her mother's legs buckled, going limp in the men's grip. She screamed so loudly that Marian felt the pulse of it echoing off the trees. Mama froze and, with a squatting heave, released a bloody, livery mass onto the ground. The non-light of the forest made the blood look black.

From behind, Marian could only stare in horror. She'd never seen a live birth before, but she couldn't have imagined that it involved expelling so much from one's body. It was like her mother's insides were leaking out.

Pop's body still dangled like a ghost above the cabin.

Suddenly, Mama lunged for the Whipple truck and almost got the door open. But she was too weak to move very fast, and the men grabbed her. After that, one of the men slashed the tires.

She remained unmoving when Smitty hugged Marian to him. When he faced her, he tried to block her view of her father's body. But she'd seen it already. She'd heard her father's dying breaths. Smitty was part of the mob, and she would never, ever again look in his eyes with love. Every adult in her life had made their secret deals over this forest. This forest was death itself.

"Marian . . . Babygirl," Mama moaned and reached for her daughter. The men dragged her under William Whipple's corpse.

The death of her baby sibling and her mother's monstrous actions fractured Marian's world into a million shards. She barely registered it when the men beat Jeanne in front of her, but splinters of their taunting pierced the haze.

"Sorry Mommy!"

"Sorry murderer."

"Black bitch."

"Lumber bunny gave up all your family's dirty little secrets."

"Bitch."

"Little bitch tipped us off."

"Bloody witch bitch."

"Die, bitch!"

"Fucking bitch."

As the men pounced on Jeanne, Smitty tried to shake Marian's unseeing mind awake. She was able to look up into his eyes and really see him.

She blinked languidly. "Smitty . . ."

Nodding, he pushed the blue truck's keys into her hands. "Go. Drive away and get out of here," he whispered in her ear.

The old man's hot whiskey breath on her face brought Marian back. She grabbed the keys and stumbled toward the truck. Marian caught herself on the ground and picked up the Polaroid of her father's body. She jumped into her father's truck, but she forgot everything the second she heard her mother screaming as Mama was raised on a cable. Frantically, Marian turned the key in the ignition and pulled levers until the car reversed. It swung wildly on its rims, creaking threateningly as she drove away. Her mother's and father's bodies shrunk away, dangling like dying leaves stained brake-light red in the rearview mirror.

Their blood was up, high on righteous anger and unrighteous killing. They whooped and threw things at Whipple's corpse. Their loudness, as always, drowned out all other sounds in the forest.

All around Smitty, the men cheered. They'd slain the foreman and saved their own lives. They'd stood up to the oppressor, the murderer. Smitty didn't want to think about how they'd all be out of a job now. He'd got his revenge on Whipple, but now he was a murderer. He'd taken away the father of a girl he cared about—what? So he could replace him?

What the hell did he think was going to happen? That Marian would move into his trailer with him, and they'd read the morning paper together? *Stupid, foolish old man. She'll never recover from what you've done to her.*

Some loggers were looting the foreman's cabin and others were hurting the foreman's wife. Smitty hugged the girl to him, hoping the men would overlook the last Whipple. He pressed her father's truck keys into Marian's hand and instructed her to go. He kissed the top of her head and hoped he was doing the right thing.

The men yelled and scattered when the flat-tired truck began skidding around the mulch yard.

Smitty watched the truck amble away, hoping against hope the girl was driving toward a better life. He was caught in this reverie when bark-patterned arms moved noiselessly around his body and swarmed him. Bodies as dense as oak felled him to the ground.

From the ground, Smitty saw dark forms crawling all over the moss roof of the Whipple cabin. They made barking, coughing noises before pouncing on the men below.

Above, the loud metal thwanging of the skylines. And the dangling Whipples. Bloody and lifeless in their sleeping clothes.

Death above and death below. The creatures savaged the men. Somehow, Smitty was cursed to witness all of it through his naked, unblinking consciousness. The guy who stole Whipple's camera—Jim, he remembered dimly—was yanked up by the Polaroid's strap. Up on the logging wire, three creatures defied gravity, tearing a young logger apart, spilling his blood and entrails onto the mulch below.

The forest soaked it up hungrily. The camera fell and rolled under the cabin.

Marian coasted the unwieldy truck down logging roads, barreling to the bottom of the mountain for long, slaloming hours. When the roads ended, the spaces between the trees were wide enough for the truck to pass. The slope of the mountain worked with her fortuitously, so the truck didn't build up too much speed. Her clenched muscles ached.

To calm herself, she thought of David Bowie. She clicked on the radio, but the static blasted so loudly that she flinched and shut it off. That static was replaced with the wind rushing through the trees, like the air itself was chasing her and the woods were calling her name. Marian rolled up the windows and hit the gas.

The rickety ups and down rocked the truck. Marian worried she'd flip over, but she just kept steering. She was resolute in her escape. Whatever the world had in store for her, it had to be better than what she was leaving behind.

She crashed into the Redcedar sign stump, and the front of the truck crunched like a soda can. Freshly concussed, Marian fell out of the truck and left the door swinging open. She stumbled toward the road. Inside the truck, the Polaroid dropped on the floor of the cab was the only evidence of what happened that night.

Many days later, North Coast Timber investigators came up with a satisfactory explanation for what happened, using that picture as Figure 1. What they didn't know was that the person who drove the truck down from the foreman's cabin was his daughter, for whom there was no birth record. That the girl—dazed and hurt—had crawled from the cracked stump to the road and when oncoming lights approached, she'd feared she'd be hit. That she had been surprised that she was still able to be scared after seeing her parents murdered, seeing her mother smother a baby in the soil under a tree's roots that had in turn devoured the infant. Marian had stuck up her thumb, and the truck horn had roared at her twice.

The truck rolled slowly into the turnout in front of the sign, and its passenger-side door popped open. A graying older man with bright eyes looked down at her. He climbed from the cab to help her up. "You look like you've had a night. How far ya going, darlin'?"

"Astray," Marian slurred, the cut on her forehead throbbing. She'd meant to say away. "Far away."

The man's arms looked strong, like Smitty's, like her dad's. "I can take ya to Oakland," he said as he propped her up in front of him.

"That works," she replied breathlessly. With the trucker's help, the injured young Whipple girl climbed up through the open door and away from Humboldt County forever.

Around Ukiah, he patted her thigh. "Some nice legs you got there."

END OF PART 2

PART 3

SEMPERVIRENS

34 ASCENSION

THE FOREST EMBRACED JASMINE fully. It had waited for her for so long.

The nurse log's filaments dug into every one of her skin's pores. With a million-million imperceivable eyes, she watched mycelial slime wind across every curve of muscle, every mote of air. Strong, burled fingers gripped her limbs. Vines cupped her thighs. It was pleasurable. It hurt and tickled and aroused, hard and soft within her and without, flowed like thick syrup across her nervous system, her soul. The forest gave her strength as a million-million fingers scraped over her body.

Acid-green pine needles pierced her skin, then returned to the soil. Every puncture created a new point of contact for the forest to spill itself into her. Peridot light clouded her vision with goldenshine green, spreading across her consciousness. Jasmine's neurons fired as the forest slithered across the folds of her brain. Between her cells. She thought:

> *I'm dead. Encased in the ground. The forest shows me everything from below. I see the forest, the ocean, Humboldt County, California, the world beyond. It chokes me. Strange, strangling fingers made of flesh and steel and wood—my wood, my own body—constrict my neck, squeezing me into nothingness.*

Above her, deep in the forest, a fire! Her mother? No, just a fire. A cigarette butt tumbled down from the Redwood Highway. The fire burned out of control, clearing acres of redwood forest. The dying forest released clouds of prismatic pollen that floated up, toward churning clouds. They rained down over the felled trees. From the black ash, greenery sprouted. From each burned tree, a ring of baby trees grew. From death, more life is always possible.

I feel . . . bigger. So much bigger. And ancient. I inhale, and a billion trees, spanning from Alaska to Mexico, breathe for me. With each breath I take, eons pass. My body waxes and wanes. Generations of trees, ferns, fungi, mosses, animals, waterways spill forth over mountains, then dry up again. Growing and receding. Moving. Living. It's all me. Root systems are just a small fraction. We're all me. We burn and grow from the ashes, feeding each other in constant, evermore dense loops.

The cycles of energy are powerful and chatoyant. Goldenshining.

Jasmine felt herself rise into the redwoods' canopies. Ascending. The cycles of life and death bubbled below, buoying her higher and higher. The forest repeated its patterns over and over. The dying forest released clouds of goldenshine pollen that floated up to Jasmine, coating her in glittering potential. She and the pollen churned in a dense fog and mountain storm clouds. Fall, burn, die, feed, grow. With every iteration and angle, Jasmine grew. She learned. A forest isn't just its trees. It's the water, the soil, the air, every rock, every living green and crawling limb. It's a living thing that's so large and complex that they call it a place.

There are others like me, and I feel them too. Dense systems of interlocking life that think and feel as I do. This much concentrated life . . . this much power . . . Are we gods? I reach out for them, to my east and south and north and west. I can feel them and together we're stronger. We're one. We're not even all on Earth. The feeling of joy and belongingness and real safety makes my heart feel like it's on fire. Pleasure and power crackle across every micron of my being. All I can do to contain it is to writhe. Let it slide across me like soft, brown velvet, viridian satin, luscious lemon-lime softness.

I'm verging on ripeness. Almost there. Anticipating what new power age will bring.

I want to stay in this feeling of hope and possibility until the end of time.

It doesn't last.

I fall a bit into my Jasmine-body as my forest-body shrinks. Stinging pain. My limbs are being sliced off in violent jerks. In a blink, I'm an armless Venus whose shoulders open in supplication, unsure of which power I should be begging to. My cells cry out for relief from the pain, but it keeps coming. It rips me open. Patches of me disappear. I feel every cut as they're taken from me. Every sawed grain screams.

Firecrackers of pain nipped at her periphery like hundreds of biting ants. Like the ebb and flow of the thriving forest, waves upon waves of little men crawled all over her. Built their homes, their towns, their cities. They polluted her air, cut her trees, poisoned her rivers. An infestation. A possession.

It's not the dead trees that hurt. Trees have lived and died and decayed in me for eons. All living things will die eventually. Their decay is just another part of their life. Death isn't what matters. There are things worse than death. Being killed is nothing against being stolen from one's home. To drag it away and sell it and rub antimicrobial agents on it and dip it in plastic so it can never, ever rot. My body is thieved from me, carried away piece by piece on pilfering little trucks on a little asphalt artery that winds across California. They've stolen me from myself.

I'm cut down more and more over such a short time that if I didn't feel every blow, it would seem like it was happening all at once. It's overwhelming. Parts of me drop off from my consciousness, and I wither away. My body and sanity dwindle to nearly nothing. I retreat into myself so completely that I barely exist. What is left of me? An ear? A toe? A single cell? So little that naming it is pointless. But the cuts keep coming; they keep stealing me from myself. More cuts. New cuts. Harder, more efficient. Mechanized. Systematic.

I scream so hard I pass out.

When Jasmine woke up, she was lying on the forest floor, slowly—finally—understanding the true shape of the world. On the forest's timescale, the loss of so much of itself was nearly instantaneous. The shock caused a psychic wound that would take millennia to grieve. The forest still grieved. That grief filled it completely and continued as more of it was ripped away. But where others who grieve construct a life around their loss so that it slowly becomes a smaller part of the whole, the forest was unable to heal. You can't heal from something that's still happening to you.

More than anything, Jasmine felt that loss in that place under her ribs. It was a feeling she'd carried her whole adult life, maybe even before that. The Humboldt cut: the hard, carving, weakened feeling you get when you allow yourself to recognize exactly how sick this world is. It hits you when you hear lies accepted as truth, when people try to make you feel crazy for pointing out the obvious, when all the disrespect and indifference tells you that *you do not belong in this world*. The cut presents you with the choice of being insane or allowing the world's sickness to infect you so thoroughly that you don't even recognize yourself as a person. The cut dried her throat, clenching her. It was the pain of trying to remain still and quiet because if you allowed yourself to acknowledge your real feelings you'd never, ever stop screaming. So you suck in all the breath you can and hold onto it. For survival. To keep your head just barely above the water.

It was still happening to her, and it would never stop unless she fought back. Jasmine Bay was part of this world. Not the world of men but the realm that humankind decided was too savage to continue to exist alongside it. These woods. This world. Being made whole again. Evergreen.

Sempervirens.

They won't give back what they took, so we have to take it back.

Around her, concentric rings of pine needles, redwood needles, cedar needles—Kodak gold, phthalo green, and cadmium orange—radiated from her body, energy pulsing from her in waves that made the needles rattle on the ground like a fountain of acrylic nails. She still had the forest in her, but it was dissipating. She mourned the loss of power as part of it drained from her, leaching into the ground.

Moving across it.

Migrating.

Waxy needles levitated. They percussed in rhythm and color in swirling paths through the forest. They fluttered impatiently until she joined them, then continued on their paths through the black forest. Jasmine followed them. Grateful to be listened to, the forest floor constructed itself into filigreed patterns more ornate than any human taste would allow. The whorls and curves ventured into the organic, the obtuse, the obscene. It was almost too much—or would've been had Jasmine not just tasted godhood.

Jasmine chased the godpower through the forest, hoping that it led to another taste. Anything to replenish the dopamine and chlorophyll that coated her dried-out tongue.

The needles' path strengthened ahead, glowing in gold and green and white rings. The rings condensed. Coalesced into another body.

The light of the body solidified into soft features, long arms, drooping eyelids and skin the color of a teddy bear.

"Aunt Gin! I thought you—"

"Hey, baby." Aunt Gin reached out and grabbed Jasmine's hands. She looked exactly like Jasmine remembered her, laugh lines creped across her face. The woman who'd raised her. Who'd taught her how to respect the power of these woods. "Welcome to the world. Are you going to help us?"

"Of course." Tears streamed down Jasmine's face.

Gin smirked. "That didn't take no convincing, huh?"

Jasmine shrugged. "I don't need convincing. I need a win. I don't want my own trauma recited back to me. I want to fucking win. I always knew what I was fighting against. You made sure of that."

"Well, okay!" Aunt Gin laughed and clapped, delighted. She pulled Jasmine into a hug, hard and soft in all the right places.

And dropped her out of a redwood tree.

Gravity sucked Jasmine down so hard that her arms sank through Gin's body, grabbing at anything. Gin's ribs melted outward at Jasmine's pull, as if made of clay. She fell for hundreds of feet, maybe thousands. Jasmine never let go of her godmother's ribs, even as Jasmine's own wrists shattered on the forest floor. Her blood splattered in great sheets, painting the trunks of the trees. In the moonlight, her blood shone black. When Jasmine Bay died, every bone in her body broken, the forest sang to her the true history of the world. The true history of the forest. Of her family.

I feel in you the vibration that thrums within all
enemies of my enemy.

Those who are also losing this war.

Each of your heartbeats knows it could be the last.

Heartbroken.

Betrayed.

You've beat your last heartbeat, Child.

But my hearts beat for you.

My lungs breathe for you.

Be here.

With me.

Become.

35

J. SEMPERVIRENS

1870

THE FIRST TIME SHE died, Miss Jane Mooney woke to the sensation of being dragged through the rotting tube of a nurse log. Not dragged, she realized, but pulled. Wet, peristaltic movements pulsed across her body, shifting her through the endless dark. The wood's movement was like a hug from a fat woman: warm and enveloping and supported by strong bones, soft and hard in all the best ways.

Jane closed her eyes, remembering the men who'd stuffed her presumed-dead body into this tree. They'd abducted her on the high road. Mr. Mooney's own employees, who, as Mr. Mooney had always impressed upon his daughter Missy, "hadn't signed up to disappear into the woods because they were such upstanding young gentlemen." Jane couldn't help but feel his admonishment burn across her.

The dim, crawling moistness reminded Jane of offal. Of pulling intestines out of a pig to entertain young Missy, the girl Jane cared for according to her contract. Jane was born free but didn't feel like she had been. She didn't even have her own surname. Looking up, the nurse log was wet and hard and wasn't unlike the inside of a body. Perhaps she was the offal, sliding like suet across Cook's pan.

The inside of the trunk looked more alive than anything felt out in the open woods. All she remembered from her assault and murder was dead leaves in her face and wondering why there were so many leaves on the ground in an evergreen forest.

Now she was being digested by that same forest. The men had chosen the right dead tree.

Were those palpitating mushrooms its lungs, that red moss heap its heart? Or were these the last merciful hallucinations of a brain as it flickered out of the Christian realm?

The squelching was rhythmic, beating. Its squeezing and throbbing matched her frenzied breaths. Yet, simultaneously, the rhythm calmed her. Jane closed her eyes again and let the forest in.

You are safe here, Child, the forest purred,

and Jane's heart beat its last human beat.

The forest moved quickly.

Roots and mycorrhizae speared through every pore, burrowing deep into her nerves, her muscles, her bones. Jane felt her own sharp intake of breath crushing her body from the outside. Her panicked breaths slowed as she realized she was breathing deeper than she ever had before. She breathed through a thousand-million mouths across hundreds of miles. Reaching out between the air itself. Into the very planet. Exponents snatched her human perception and bounded off toward an unknowable limit. Every inch of the forest was inside her, was her, and she it.

Warmth flooded her body. Shining green renewal danced through her veins. The embrace of the forest pulled across every muscle, wringing out every indignity inflicted during her now-gone life from her body. A thousand-million fingers slid across Jane's nerves. Its fingers, her fingers.

Jane's heart—the forest's heart—beat its first beat as something else entirely.

Now made as clear as the dewdrop on a needle of a tree that language lacks the specification to describe, Jane learned. The forest poured itself into her.

36 HECATONCHEIRES

1929

WHEN JANE MOONEY FIRST saw the man who would become her husband, it was nearing fall. He was a boy eating huckleberries under the canopy of her favorite redwood, a short but wide-spanning *Sequoia sempervirens* she referred to as Briareus, one of "the hundred-handed ones" from the *Iliad*.

When she had been allowed to sit in the room during the Mooney children's lessons, Jane's favorite subject was the classics. She especially loved stories of the primordial deities before the Olympian gods; Zeus and his highly specialized family didn't hold a candle to their ancestors, who personified much more elemental concepts like Chaos. Inevitability. The Upper Air That the Gods Breathe.

The boy the men called *Whipple* breathed this air. He climbed the tall trees so she thought him special.

From inside the nurse log, Jane appraised him like a precious object, using the thousand-million eyes of the forest to hold him tight in her gaze.

Jane recognized that naming individual trees was like naming each of the hairs on her head, but three particular giant trees *did* have personalities. All the trees did. She herself was merely a strand of hair too, but she had a personality, things she enjoyed, things she coveted. So the folding, jutting, many-crowned triplets became the fifty-headed, hundred-handed Hecatoncheires: Briareus, Gyges, and Cottus. The three massive redwoods stood guard, blocking the alluvial valley in the shadow of Mount Pierce, that darkened place where the titans were held. With a fresh supply of creek water and the ocean fog, the tallest redwoods grew here.

Over Briareus's hundred hands, the boy moved carefully along the canopy. He regarded each lichen-coated branch with respect. He didn't wantonly snap twigs the way the other canopy visitors did. He didn't pull epiphytes from the trees in an effort to "clean up." She learned from listening that the youth's name was William Whipple, and she learned from watching that he accepted the forest as it was. Or he seemed to. After all, he was still a Mooney man whose only aim was to despoil the entire coast of its redwoods, making chum of half the wood to churn out geometric planes of lumber. Across the forest, at the end of the titans' creek, the sawmill spat out dirty smoke. Its blades screamed as they destroyed a thousand-million years of life. The precious green magic was spit up into the air on wood chips and dissipated in the great circular saw's engine smoke.

Jane watched as this sensitive young man stepped across Briareus's arms, only grabbing a couple huckleberries to snack on; she told herself such restraint might come from reverence. *This one is different. I want him.*

In every cell of her body, the forest grumbled. It didn't believe her.

Not different. Remember, Child.

It flashed its memories, her memories, the world's memories across the inside of her eyes, distracting her from her infatuation. The memories bubbled up through the earth, warming her body.

Jane stuffed into a log. Hidden from view by the men who'd raped and killed her.

Jane kicked down a ravine. The loggers who'd run her down laughed at the way her broken limbs flapped like a rag doll.

Jane, raped.

Jane, murdered.

Thousands of miles of redwoods gone. Clear cut and stolen.

Jane, pregnant.

An unborn child kicked to death inside her death-marked body.

Jane, killed again by loggers for a seventh, eighth, ninth time.

Remember and learn, Child, the forest commanded.

It showed her more ways she had been killed by the men who laid siege to these woods. The forest had resurrected her each time, sucking her body into the ground and rearranging biomass to rebuild her time and time again, no matter how carelessly she behaved. Any toe stepped into the world of men was a step toward death. The forest was exasperated with the stupid choices humans made. Jane especially.

By merging her soul with the forest, she'd become something that couldn't be killed, could never really die. What does one owe for a gift like this? For a curse like this?

Jane tried to push the memories back down into the ground so she could fixate again on the sun-freckled, sensitive, sandy-haired boy lying below her in the tree, dreamily soaking in the sounds of the forest. She seeded the air with soporific aromas and plumped the lichen under him to cushion his rest.

This was a man who could love the forest, who could love her. All he needed was her.

No. The forest wouldn't let her.

Her brain stem bloated with the influx of sensations: chopping, cutting, burning, marking, killing. This was the bargain. She was a part of the forest and it of her. These woods felt every hurt inflicted on her by men, so it was only right that she feel all that they'd done to these woods. Were doing. Breaking off pieces and using them to build better killing machines.

Our own Children returned to us, cobbled into tools for those who would kill us all.

We cannot love the ones who do this to us.

The forest unceremoniously spat Jane out of the nurse log onto the ground of the stone gully. Mycelium and mud formed the amniotic fluid slicked across her. Coughing, she pulled herself up.

"NO!" She raged, battering her fists against the now-closed root ball of the nurse log. "You can't have him! He's mine!" She tried to pull open the roots.

YOURS?

Wind sped through the trees, whipping her with needles and leaves. Tiny fibrous root hairs sprouted from the roots in her hands and impaled her, digging deep to pull her close by her very nerves. The forest's angry energy crackled electric across her vertebrae.

Ungrateful Child. We've given you everything. Yet you ask for more.

You're too much like them. So human still.

Jane had a vision of dying in a log again, but this time it was permanent: Her body would waste away; her skin would bloat and slide off her muscles in neat sheaths; her muscles would seize up then slowly succumb to gravity, liquefying into the putrid ooze of the decaying nurse log; generations of insects would live, breed, and die in her skull, until only her skeleton remained. Dry and white. Eons would pass.

Pressed against the closed-off nurse log, involuntary tears streamed down Jane's face. The forest was right, of course. Twenty million years in the same place brought nothing if not an intimate knowledge of things like Chaos, Inevitability, and The Upper Air That the Gods Breathe. She had no right to ask for more.

So she stopped asking.

Time passed, and Jane only watched Whipple. Just watched him. Watched and learned. Watched and wanted.

Watched him install the skylines, hammering metal into the trees, capping them at the knees. Non-redwoods would've bled sugary sap that gummed up the pulley wheel, but the redwoods remained strong in every way. It was why they were needed to build the railroads, the great western cities, America.

She watched Whipple as he got his ass kicked by a fellow logger. The man's big shoulders strained under red flannel while he beat the boy senseless. Jane watched the whole ordeal but could not figure why the man would be so upset about the boy going to high school. By then, the Mooney Timber men had killed her almost a dozen times for a dozen inscrutable reasons. Maybe the reason simply was that Whipple was so much smaller. But the man's motive didn't matter because the second his fist hit William Whipple's face, the man was marked for death.

The day after that beating, Jane razed the man with a well-released branch. When his blood splattered on the ground, the life from it soaked down into the forest floor, to be slurped up by her mycorrhizae. The man's life fed a thousand-million imperceptible mouths, nourishing the weakest plants through a root system that had once stretched from the Santa Cruz Mountains to the North Pole. Now the whole system was weak. Less than a twentieth of its original size. Barely a toe remained of a primordial giant that once took up half the world.

The forest was sated by the death, yet only for a little while. Jane wanted to give it more. Needed to. She must kill more men, but how can she cut the loggers down to a toe when they just kept coming? Kept taking. The world out there had no shortage of reasons to drive desperate men into the jaws of death. Even among the Greeks' grand old concepts, death was still a category so huge that it had to be shared by many: Moros, Thanatos, the Keres. All born of Nyx, the Night, another kind of death.

Perhaps Nyx was onto something. The obligation of death was far too heavy to be held by one woman. She needed children.

No.

She needed an army.

Eventually, Jane built the barkskins.

For a year, Jane slept and thought. She dreamed and remembered. She scoured the forest's vast caches of knowledge and experience for inspiration. The monarch butterflies, returning from Mexico every summer in great jeweled clouds, told her this story. They brought information from the south, its rainforests heaving with their own million-millions. In those rich lands lived a fungus that invaded the brains of ants in order to reach high branches of trees to release its spores. Likewise, if Jane could invade the brains of men, she'd never need to lift a finger to protect the forest again. Her drones would do the work, and she, their queen, could live comfortably in the redwoods' protection, making children with the sandy-haired boy. She dared not call him hers yet, but the forest knew her heart.

During her time in the forest, Jane killed many men, though even more killed themselves. New tools replaced old ones and brought new complications to the lumber crews. The first portable chainsaws were heavy and gas-powered. They took their fair share of limbs and lives. As did the steam-powered engine that reeled dead trees toward the road. The foremen called the worker men lazy and drunk, berating them into working longer days, which made them tired and careless. More men died.

Jane had been releasing clouds of soporific pollen to cause the men's lethargy and intoxication, so she didn't feel too badly for them. But they just kept coming: wave after wave of fresh-faced boys and grizzled older men. She heard one man call it "honest work" and wondered how he could think of murder as honest. Perhaps they didn't see the trees for what they were. Like how they'd looked at her black skin and hadn't thought of her as a person every time they'd killed her.

She dragged bodies into the forest, burying them in different ways in order to find the right combination of factors that would bring her army to life.

In the end, the answer was so simple it embarrassed Jane that it had eluded her for so long: the nurse log. The same chamber that had pulled her into the consciousness of the forest and allowed her to regenerate endlessly would be able to rebuild a man into whatever image she desired, as it would for dozens of decomposing corpses.

The first creature was once a logger who spotted Jane by a creek. She'd been lying on the pebbled bank, her hand in the water dancing through the coolness as she listened to what the trees upriver had to say. The man snuck up on her, approaching from downwind like he was hunting a deer. When he snapped a sword fern, she noticed him and fled.

He shouted at her and chased her when she ran. That was how it had started so many times before. Spotted, pursued, beaten, knocked out, raped, then killed or left for dead. She expertly led him around the alluvial plain toward the cliff above the nurse log. Part of her hoped he would give up and leave her alone, but more of her knew these men never stopped unless you killed them first.

Jane slid down a steep gully and the man followed, skidding along the rough bush. His weight pulled him toward her, faster and faster as they tumbled. He was nearly on top of her. His thick, spiked boots scraped her legs. Jane flailed away, caught herself on a root. She appeared to float up as the man plummeted toward the stone-walled bottom of the gully. Suddenly, the ground opened up beneath him. He screamed. The sound was immediately swallowed as the earth closed around him.

On either side of the disturbed black earth, cupped rims of bark pushed up out of the ground. The nurse log extended through the soil, its decaying bark undulating under and over it like a whale under an ocean of rocks and dirt. Jane kicked at the rich loam. She could feel the man beneath, struggling hard as adrenaline shot through his veins. On thin, bleeding legs caked with mud, Jane carefully walked down to the stone gully. At the roots, she climbed into the nurse log. The man was still screaming, even as dirt and mycelium filled his lungs. His voice became a hoarse coughing bark.

Jane had designed her army of barkers in her mind and modeled them after all the timber company people who'd hurt her, as well as a few other creatures that hid and hunted so well in these woods. The man's skin mottled into the dark, bruise-like patterns of a giant salamander. Muscles bubbled under his skin, swelling up like they were being inflated, and the skin tightened to the hardness of wood.

The needling, offending caulk boots split down the middle, shed aside by malforming feet. His bones cracked, leg structure rearranging to make climbing trees easier. Aware through all the transformation, the man's hair turned white from the shock, then fell out completely. Shoulders displaced the soil around him until he pressed against the inside of the log. Goggles fallen away, his eyes poured out of their sockets and ballooned into thick bulbs of red-black jelly. Translucent eyelids closed over them.

Jane felt the fight leave him as mycelial threads glissaded through the wrinkles of his brain to choke the higher functions, leach out his memories, and replace all programming with one command: *follow*.

It was much easier to take men after that. Struggling in her big guards' arms, men screamed and hollered until they too were silenced in the rich, black earth around the nurse log. During the day, her barkers lived in the darkest parts of the redwood canopy. Anyone passing by would think they were just a large burl. Whipple hadn't noticed as he passed through a nest of barkers in Gyges's branches one afternoon. Even to his expert hands, the forms he crawled across were just wood.

Years passed as she built her army, until the forest seemed satisfied with her numbers. Now, the obligation of death was shouldered by many, held under the power of one.

With the forest's permission, Jane went to collect the man who would become her husband.

37 PROPAGATION

1933

WHEN THE WOMAN WHO would become his wife stepped out from the ferny veil of the forest, William Whipple's heart fell out of his ass. He wasn't a poetic man, and that's what it fucking felt like. Like falling from a redwood a mile high. He gulped, trying to yank his consciousness back into his body. The past four of his twenty-three years had been spent in the redwood canopy, two, three hundred feet in the air, but now—on the ground, in the presence of a dark-skinned waif o' the woods—he felt vertigo for the first time.

Her name was Jeanne, and he'd never wanted anything the way he wanted her.

Her brown skin reflected the chlorophyll-tinted sunlight. It reminded him of the Tiffany lamp in Mr. Mooney's office. He'd only seen it once but now twice daily thought about the way the sun filtered through the glass shards of chartreuse, emerald, and jade.

He was filling his canteen at the tank when she emerged. He'd felt the telltale earthshake of a felled giant, and the peelers were most likely still stripping the shaggy bark. He wouldn't be needed until the collars were affixed and ready to be steam donkeyed down the mountain on the skylines he himself had installed along the tallest trees. He liked to watch the trunks bobbing along the forest floor, carried away on his cables like on a conveyor belt. Mechanical. This forest was his factory.

Whipple liked the work enough. It was better than the other opportunities for a kid born in Humboldt, which were few even in booming Eureka. He'd started at the Humboldt Cutting sawmill after graduating high school, which he'd stopped mentioning after getting slugged by an old bull bucker on his first outing up into the cut. The bull bucker died shortly after, when a fallen branch splattered him all over the young Whipple's swollen, horrified face. After that he'd kind of stopped talking altogether.

But now he climbed up in the forest's canopies, on account of his sure-footedness and the fact that his lack of height was doing him no favors on the ground. A regulation Humboldt axe helve was forty-two inches, so Whipple made himself useful in the trees. He ran pulleys and cables as thick as his forearm and made one hundred and twenty-five dollars per month. It was enough for the life he needed. He shared a room in a boarding house in Redcedar with two other loggers. One Saturday a month, they'd go to the Elks Lodge in Eureka and drink and dance and kiss girls. The work was hard and dangerous, but sometimes some stevedore's daughter would look at him in a way that made him feel like the danger was in service of something greater.

Until now. A dark-skinned seraph had descended from the heavens and stumbled into his camp and all he could do was impotently grunt, "D'you want some water?"

Her clothing was . . . weird, somehow. Mismatched and out of date, like she'd found the pieces on the side of the road. Not at all like the tailored getups the girls in Eureka wore. But it was 1933, and no one had any fancy clothes, least of all William Whipple. The woman's clothing was charming in its shabby modesty. Whipple assumed this must mean she spent her resources on much more noble and important things.

When she crossed in front of him to approach the water tank, the air between them turned solid, his vision cloudy like gelatine. He felt dizzy, high on her pheromones. Her hair was black and long and smelled like a pine breeze. She put her mouth to the spigot, almost kissing it. Whipple wanted to be that spigot in every way he could think of, but he couldn't say anything. His mouth wouldn't let him. His heart beat in his every extremity. His chest sank, as if a falling redwood had just caved it in, leaving a vast hole where his organs used to be. His fingertips beat against the rough insides of his gloves, palpitating as his blood and sense sloshed around his body. The roughness of his life up until now felt at odds with the feelings flooding his body right now. Maybe when she was gone he'd kiss the spigot.

"I'm Jeanne. What's your name?" There was no coquettish hesitation in her speech. She stood and talked straight, her voice and eyes clear.

Whipple gulped. All the consciousness of the self-possessed, cocky young man he'd been before disappeared as soon as he'd laid eyes on . . . Jeanne. *I need you in my life from now until forever*, his mind screamed. "William," he managed to squeak out. "William Whipple," he said again, voice stronger. He wanted her to think he was strong and not afraid of her. He wasn't afraid of her. Just the way she made him feel. Tendrils of desire had taken hold between the bricks of his being and were rending the whole thing apart.

"Hello, William Whipple. Are you a Mooney man?" So she was a local. Local enough, anyway. Her voice was honey thick, with a raspy, smoky quality that made him think of redwood bark, for some reason. Everything about her reminded him of nature, from the flowers on her dress to the way her bare feet were planted on the ground. She belonged here. The realization made him feel naked and out of place.

Whipple shivered. Jeanne reached for his arm, immediately soothing him with one touch. A curious, warm calm spread through his body. It replaced the cold agitation that she'd previously evoked in his physiology.

"Yeah—yes. I'm a skyliner for Mooney."

"A skyliner? You like it all the way up there?" She smiled at the canopy above them.

"I love it," he admitted.

Suddenly, she grabbed his hand and pulled him after her into the trees. The shock of skin-on-skin contact made him go hard, so he took care to take wide cowboy steps to keep Jeanne from noticing if she looked back. Whipple feared the way she would look at him if she saw the way he felt right now: a short, trembling man in tall boots with an embarrassingly hard penis, unable to control his animal nature in front of a lady, shaming her with his indecency. But when she did look at him, she giggled without judgment, let go of his hand, and began to run.

Whipple could faintly make out the sound of the power saws starting up in the distance. They'd need him soon. This wood nymph didn't need him at all.

"Hey!" he called after her.

"Follow me, Mr. Whipple!" she called back without breaking her pace. She didn't need him. But she wanted him. For what, he didn't know.

He watched her dress ride up, exposing long legs as she hopped through ferns and bay laurels. It reminded him of a Greek myth he'd heard once about a girl who turned into a laurel tree to avoid being raped. Part of him wished girls had that magic. Less incidents at the boarding house that way. The loggers were . . . the loggers. His brain cleared the fog of lust for a second as the memory of his violent comrades sobered him. Obligations. Liabilities. The things that men do.

"Are you coming?" Jeanne asked teasingly.

The power saws roared as if in response. Mirthful attraction to her surged in him again, subduing his professional concerns with a narcotic effect.

He bolted after her. If she turned into a tree, he'd just end up in the same place where he started. These woods give and take. So many men had died so he could be here in these woods, chasing a pretty lady until his chest burned icy hot with exhaustion, too hard to laugh and run at the same time.

Finally, he reached the glade where Jeanne stood waiting. He almost collapsed into her arms as he brought himself to a stop. She'd led him to a grove of trees in the elongated shape of a church: a long empty alley colonnaded on both sides. She stood at its altar, before an impressively sized redwood. The forest's Sitka spruces and incense cedars stood at attention around the stand. Whipple felt as if they had gathered here to witness the joining of himself to his forest bride. Pollen rained down on them in celebration, riding the sun's rays down to form a golden halo of aura around Jeanne.

"Give me something." She smirked.

"Anything," Whipple panted. "Jeanne, girl, I'll get you anything you want."

She patted the massive redwood. "In this tree's branches, a huckleberry bush grows. Will you bring me some berries?"

"How do you know that? The lowest branch must be a hundred and ninety feet up. Maybe more!" Whipple laughed before realizing the woman was serious. When he said he'd get her anything, he wasn't lying. What was stopping him from getting her this? He'd climbed higher trees. Of course, he'd had ropes and help then. But he felt stronger in her presence. He felt alive and glorious in this wooded chapel grove. He approached her, cupped her face, and kissed her.

"If I bring you huckleberries, will you marry me?"

"Marry you? Must everything be a transaction with you Mooney men?"

"You don't have a fella already, do you?"

"No, I don't. Where would we even live if I married you?"

"The moon. The ocean. San Francisco. Anywhere. I'll build you a house in this tree right here, if you want. Miss Jeanne, if you were mine, I think I'd be capable of pretty much anything."

Jeanne's face, coated around the edges with sweat and tree pollen, framed by a halo of sunshine, brightened in a way that Whipple could only describe as mighty gentle. The woman appeared lit from within by the powerful promise of a future together, and Whipple felt the same.

It was there, in the cathedral grove, that Jeanne and William Whipple conceived their first child.

For ten years, Jeanne was pregnant. But their cabin in the woods was silent. There were no children stomping across its planks. The children never came. Jeanne would grow full to bursting, but when it came time for the baby to come, something would always go wrong. She would disappear into the woods and return without a baby in her arms or in her womb.

Whipple was saddened by it, but he loved Jeanne so much that he didn't want to further burden her. When he tried to keep from impregnating her and save her the pain of future loss, she wouldn't have it. She enjoyed every moment they spent together, she said, and no loss was worth losing him. So for ten years, Jeanne was pregnant but never had a baby.

In 1942, Whipple's number was called, and he went away to fight in Europe's dark trenches. While the men around him fell more and more in love with the idea of their gals back home, Whipple felt only resentment. He didn't have a photo-booth shot of a blushing, fair-haired ingenue, only a quiet, black weirdling woman he'd never be able to tell anyone about. Who couldn't marry him. Whose children were never born, taken away by God before they could become proper Whipples. He aged more in those two years than in the past ten with Jeanne.

But when he came back, the second he was in her heady presence, all doubt drained from him. Only devotion remained.

He came home and went back to work at Mooney Timber Products. The war abroad hadn't hurt the lumber industry one bit, only smaller companies' ability to compete with the big guys for contracts. It hadn't affected Whipple's ability to climb trees and run skylines either. If anything, Whipple had gotten stronger and more sure-footed since that day he'd chased Jeanne into the redwoods. The war had taken it out of him a bit, but when he returned to these woods, he bounced back with a vengeance. Back in his cabin with his strong, secretive, fecund forest bride, he was again alive with the glory of love and his life was perfect.

Jeanne became pregnant again in the fall of 1948. Whipple was almost in his forties but still looked like a twenty-year-old, so he never corrected any of the crewmen when they called him "Kid." Most didn't stick around long enough to notice he'd been a kid for almost twenty years now. He himself wondered about it, but thought it imprudent to question good fortune. His wife was as big as a house, and he was grateful for the strength to ease her burden, wherever it came from.

One rimy night in late February, William Whipple woke from a nightmare to find Jeanne gone. In his dream, cadaverous hands had grabbed him and pulled him upward into the gaping sky; the warm embrace of the black soil had shrunk away below him, drowned out by the white. Gasping for breath, he'd stumbled back into consciousness and through the fog of sleep, he noticed his wife's side of the bed was empty. Cold, too. He scanned the room and arose to check the other room. The cabin was empty. Silent but for the roof, which creaked under the weight of its moss cover. The moss kept in the heat and absorbed rain and snow before it could seep through the ceiling. Despite this, the air in the cabin felt frozen solid. Was it raining or snowing now?

Whipple put on boots but not a shirt, which he regretted out on the porch when the hard kick of forest cold knocked his chest in. It must've been thirty degrees.

Snow frosted the evergreen boughs. The canopy collected the majority, but a centimeter of snow weighed down the usual soft pith of needle debris. Whipple was glad for it. Jeanne's warm, bare feet had left a trail.

Pulling on his flannel jacket, he clomped down the stairs. Boots on dead wood rang across the forest.

It was a clear, cold night. Black moon night. Even without the moon's bright floodlight, he felt he'd find his bride. There was something chemical—animal—about his ability to always locate her. He floated on invisible lines that led to her: skylines. He was the redwood, bobbing across the forest toward her, his final resting place.

Near the cathedral grove where they'd consummated their union, Whipple found his wife giving birth. His first instinct to rush toward her was halted by a feeling he hadn't allowed himself to feel since he'd had half a world between him and Jeanne. Its grip on him iced his muscles still, skeletal hands squeezing his very soul, holding him back. In his heart lurked the suspicion that something was very wrong—dangerous, even. He stayed hidden.

Jeanne arched her body over the roots of an epic nurse log that spilled through a stone gully. She held a smaller root in her teeth and pushed her feet into the snowy ground. The snow crackled under her pressure, then turned red black. Blood and baby hit the ground unceremoniously. Whipple gulped loudly, but Jeanne had heard him from miles away. Felt him as he had drawn near. She cut the umbilical cord with a small loop of root provided by the nurse log. To Whipple's dawning horror, the root bed opened wide, exposing the interior of the redwood. Separated from the fetus, she pushed it up into the inside of the tree.

Jeanne smothered their baby in the nurse log and turned toward her man. Her usually placid face broke into a mask of grief. Whipple couldn't believe what he was seeing. He wanted to think that after this hideous act he wasn't still drawn to her, didn't love her. But he did. He knew he wasn't bewitched, which implied a clouded judgment. His devotion to Jeanne was pure, the only clear thing in his life. He was making this choice. He stepped out of the brush toward his waiting bride.

"Are you okay?" he asked. He knew, though, that she'd always be okay in these woods.

She sighed sadly. "I'm sorry, William. I can't keep them. I kept you and . . . need to make up for that as much as I can."

Snow floated down rivulets of air, landing in her hair and coating her face the way the redwood pollen did every summer. She was sobbing. He rushed to her. Embraced his crying wife. Comforted her.

"Why are you sorry? Kept me? What are you talking about?" He cradled her face in his hands and stared into her eyes.

At the sight of his face, she burst into a conniption, filling the cathedral with her aggrieved wailing. He pulled her in harder, pushing down her heaving shoulders. The wind rushed around them.

"The forest used to take in equal measure to what had been taken from it, but it can't keep up. The men are better at killing it now. It's just not enough! Never enough!" she wailed. Her secret was finally out. She whispered, "The babies help. Life for life."

Whipple's vision blurred with tears. The snow on the ground dissolved when they fell from his cheek. Dozens of babies, fed to the forest. Feeding these woods. Were they here now? Wind soughed through the trees, as if they were talking to him. Would they forgive him for not saving them? Or were they better off? Would they blame him for trying to save one, just for himself? He muttered, "We could have some children and still give the others—"

Jeanne glared up at him. "What kind of life would they have in this world? This world has so many ugly words for what they are . . . Uglier actions. They're better off feeding the trees."

She was right of course. But this wasn't about being right.

He ventured: "We could have one. We'd raise her in these woods, and she'd love the forest as we love it. She'd never leave, and she'd always be safe. These woods will protect her like they've protected you and me."

Jeanne scoffed mirthlessly. The forest rustled, its agitated threnody mirroring his wife's thoughts. *No one can ever be truly safe*, the forest seemed to say, *not as long as the world of men still stands and harms and kills.*

Whipple pulled her into his flannel. She was already warm, always so warm; enveloping her calmed her and the trees. He whispered into the top of her head, "Is there any other way?"

Her eyes burned. The forest symphony came to an abrupt stop for Jeanne's cadenza. "Help me save these woods, and I'll give you a daughter."

38 BRANCHES

1942

IN THE TROPOSPHERE—THE LOWEST layer of the atmosphere—a droplet of rain formed over Humboldt County. The raindrop fell earthward. It didn't make it to the soil floor of the forest, instead hitting the redwood canopy, zippering down scaled needles until it landed in the crotch of an offshoot trunk of a towering coast redwood—*Sequoia sempervirens*—where it found soil. No one knows how the soil forms over a hundred feet in the air.

Even the wildest of magic may as well happen, because when death feeds life feeds death in concentric rings across millennia, there's no real difference between the two, between anything. This is the real forest. And there, all these things happen:

A coast redwood was hit by lightning. The tree didn't burn for long, but the initial hit broke the giant at its ankles. The top didn't fall immediately, but fall it did. When it fell, the remaining stump stayed alive. Its soul still stretched upward toward the golden sun. In time, redwood sprouts budded from its blackened circumference like tiny green fireworks.

Above it, something fell from the nest of a chestnut-backed chickadee. The first hatchling, pink and bald, emerged from his egg while his mother was gone. He struggled across the nest, yanking part of his egg behind him, connected by an umbilicus of slime. The gooey rope snapped at the exact wrong moment and sent the larval bird tumbling toward the ground, part of its egg floating after it. The hatchling and its egg fell in ugly parabolas to the ground.

When she returned, the mother chickadee mourned. She resolved to stay on her eggs until the rest hatched. She starved to death before they did. The eggs never hatched, and new life never emerged from under her cold feathers.

The dead birds decomposed on the ground and in the tree. The forest took their deaths and used them to live. The redwood sprouts grew quickly in a ring around the decaying stump from which they sprang. This kind of growth is called a fairy ring. Over time, the redwoods stretched upward and outward. They formed a cathedral grove, powered by the churn of a million-million lives and deaths across millennia. Every forest does this.

Jeanne Whipple's awareness hovered in the raindrop. She wasn't just in the trees. Wasn't *just* the trees. She was in the water droplet as its molecules fed the cells of the redwood tree. She was the dense mycelium noodled around the tree's roots that it used to tell other trees when it felt rain, sending them nutrients and hope. Her awareness infused every atom of the forest simultaneously. She felt every part of it. Every part of the system became her, no matter how small. She was a forest. She became a world unto herself.

But a woman still needs friends.

Jeanne Whipple befriended Nancy Hsu as the autumn winds blew. Or, more accurately, they met for the first time. Friendship came later.

Drunk men had chased the girl into the woods and beat her. Nancy screamed with every ounce of her soul, even as the men broke her jaw. She was determined to live, if only to get revenge for what was being done to her. The thumping violence tugged at Jeanne, quietly pregnant in her mossy cabin. William had just left for basic training.

She was upon the men so suddenly, Nancy remembered the brown woman as a blur descending from the sky like a falling branch. The men were suddenly screaming. Nancy rolled down a ravine and hid under some brush, turning toward the trail in time to see blood and viscera splatter the ground from above like someone pouring out bathwater. Then the men's screaming stopped. *Good*, Nancy thought.

When she climbed back up the ravine, the ground glittered. It had replaced the men's bodies with outlines of pine needles, bright green against the leather-colored ground.

A tiny pregnant woman stood nearby. No, she was just a girl. She didn't look much older than Nancy, but it could have been the energy radiating from her. In young Nancy's mind, Jeanne's power took the form of youth, but it was also so much more. It was something beyond time, pregnant with potential. More than that, it was a promise of safety. This woman could kill but would not kill Nancy.

Jeanne took Nancy to her cabin in the woods and fed her a textured, silty oatmeal that was somehow too hot and too cold at the same time. But the woman had saved her life. When she'd eaten the whole thing, her bruised and broken face didn't hurt at all.

Nancy looked up from her bowl to see her own face on the black woman's body. Her double staring back at her, healed and milk skinned and beautiful. Her twin eyes stared back at her with a look that was something less than human. Terrified, she shot back from her chair, knocking it to the ground. "What are you?!" she shrieked.

"I don't know," the woman replied. With a shake of her head, she was Jeanne again, sitting calmly in the kitchen chair.

Panic fried Nancy's nerve endings, but her curiosity was too strong. She was scared, but she still felt trust and warmth for the woman who'd saved her. Jeanne didn't move when Nancy drew closer, hand out like she was approaching a dangerous animal, begging for mercy. *Please don't hurt me.* Nancy placed her hand on Jeanne's hand. It felt human. It felt like her own skin.

The hand suddenly grabbed hers. Their fingers interlaced. Jeanne stared into the girl's eyes. "Please don't leave," she whispered. "I'm so lonely."

Nancy yanked herself free and ran from the house. Jeanne didn't try to keep her in the forest.

A few days later, Nancy returned with some books about Greek mythology from the library—those stories were full of shapeshifters—and the two were friends ever since.

1960

Jeanne Whipple found Charlyne Blackman in the springtime. Or, more accurately, Charlyne found Jeanne. That's the way she tells it.

Jeanne was at the overlook, admiring the velvet hills of Humboldt County, when a sudden rockslide sent her hurtling down the side of the cliff. This had been happening more and more over the years. The more intense the logging, the less stable the soil; the less predictable the soil erosion, the more likely the rockslides. Jeanne was normally so graceful, but this time her body landed in the dirt road with the elegance of a duffel bag of brass instruments.

Still alive, Jeanne pulled from the forest to knit her broken legs back together. Proteins and energy rode the cascading mycelium hundreds of miles, snaking through the ground to march through Jeanne's body with beetle-like industry and fall into place, locked in as bone, muscle, unbroken skin. This re-allocation was always painful—Jeanne was rebuilding herself from herself after all—so she didn't immediately notice the moon-faced child sidling up to her.

Ten-year-old Charlyne had been sent by her grandmother to the Skyliner to drop off a package. After dropping off the small box with the bartender, Charlyne had exited via the parking lot back toward the rancheria, kicking rocks with her red cowgirl boots. She loved running errands for her grandma and proving how grown-up she was. Charlyne had been smiling to herself, congratulating herself on a job well done, when up ahead of her, a body crashed down from above, landing in the road. Charlyne froze.

Her heart was beating so fast, she worried it would beat itself out. She stood stock-still for forever. But the bundle of hair and clothes in the road started to move. It was a lady! And she was still alive. She needed help, and Charlyne was nothing if not helpful.

She made careful sure not to kick any rocks toward the lady, stepping high and lightly as she approached. Charlyne steeled herself and called out in the same low, even voice her grandma used. "You okay there?"

The lady jolted but when she turned to Charlyne, she looked more embarrassed than anything. "Hello, thank you for asking. That's very kind. I'll be all right."

Charlyne looked up the slope to where the lady must've fallen from. "We should get you out of the road. So whoever throw'd ya doesn't see."

Jeanne blinked in surprise at the child's words. "What makes you think someone threw me?"

"Negro?" Charlyne pointed at Jeanne, then thumbed back at herself. "Indian. We have more in common with you than anybody else prob'ly," the kid mused. "If they throw us, they prob'ly'd throw you. Just stands to reason. You sure you don't need some help? I could ask Mr. Vaughn at the Skyliner to phone the doc or something."

Jeanne chuckled. Legs healed, she reached up to the girl. Charlyne pulled her to her feet. "Talking to you was help enough." The woman shook the young girl's hand. "Thank you, young lady."

"My name's Charlyne. What's yours?"

"I'm Jeanne."

"Jeanne! Next time I see you, I'll say, 'Hey, Jeanne, how's your leg?' Okay?" Charlyne beamed. "That's what my gramma says to her friends when she sees them. Now I can say it to you."

"That sounds mighty fine, Miss Charlyne."

1971

Jeanne Whipple recruited Victoria Mooney that August. She'd seen this Mooney girl in the forest before, and her father before her, and his father before him; that man had a sister, Missy, who never missed her young nanny who went missing all those years ago. This Mooney girl had been jumped by men in these woods—willingly and unwillingly—since she was fifteen, but Jeanne found her in a moment of true powerlessness.

To rebel against her father, Victoria bought a farm deep in the mountains. It was much more of a hobby than a statement, since the place basically ran itself. It existed but was never quite real for her. Victoria would find herself mid-party down in Berkeley and remember with a start: *I have a farm. Isn't that groovy?* Her old man had wanted her to attend Stanford like he had, where he met Victoria's mother in a building that carried her own family's name. Victoria had illusions of counterculture and self-sufficiency, but she only replaced not attending classes at Cal with not attending to her farm upstate.

Victoria thought, *If you're rich enough, almost everything runs itself for you.* It made better business sense to grow marijuana, so she did. She rented out parts of her land to others to grow experimental strains, and their rent repaid the farm exponentially. She wasn't stupid, just young. Her farm manager hired transients and bikers to work the land, a methodology continued into the future. People passed through Humboldt County to work on farms then returned to Oakland and Stockton and wherever else with resin embedded in their finger ridges and money in their pockets.

Jeanne encountered Victoria before she was to head back down to Berkeley. That day, Victoria had been sprawling around her parents' house: swimming, tanning, lingering on couches with her clogs on, and enjoying the view of Redcedar and the Eel River. The nineteen-year-old looked past her reflection in the window—wide-set dark brown eyes like her mother—and stared out across the dense mural of variegated green, and remembered: *my farm.*

Victoria jogged out to her Mustang; Dad wouldn't let her get the VW, still mad at the Germans about a war he didn't even fight in. The little yellow convertible kicked up dust as it hugged the tightly wound backroads, hurtling toward the farm. Pinene-infused wind frothed Victoria's ebony hair, swirling it around her head. She headed east, passed the impassive forest.

She got stopped at the edge of the property by a man with a gun.

Some ugly, bearded rascal put his dirty boot on the front bumper of her Mustang, sucked air in through his teeth, and barked, "Wrong way, missy."

"Excuse you?" Victoria smiled up at him. "This is *my* farm."

"Nice try. Git." He moved his hand to the butt of his gun. A bent bar of black ink saluted from his shirt collar, warning anyone who got close enough to see it.

Victoria scoffed and reversed. Then slammed the car forward, clipping the guard as she zoomed past him. She wasn't going to let riffraff like him tell her where she couldn't go on her own property. She'd have a talk with her farm manager, Miguel, when she found him. The cannabis plots she passed looked like overgrown thick bushes, camouflaged perfectly in the thick greenery of the forest's ferns. *At least they got that part right*, she thought to herself.

The guard Victoria clipped was thrown from the driveway down a ravine, where Jeanne sucked him into the earth, leaving only his gun behind. She lay in wait beneath the soil. There would be more blood soon. More life and death and life.

Aboveground, Victoria found Miguel. His broken, beaten body was strung up from a tree at the back of the property and looked like the men had used it for target practice. He'd been a strong, quiet man. Who didn't take shit. When Victoria had worried about employing bikers and ex-cons, Miguel had assured her it would be fine. "I'm tough 'nough to handle it, Miz Mooney," he'd said.

Whatever had happened here was tougher than him, Victoria surmised, and tried to skid the Mustang around. Nearby, shouts increased in volume.

Big, rough-looking men spilled from the drying shed. Many had guns. Some pointed those guns at Victoria in her little yellow car.

One shot a front wheel flat, and Victoria lurched to a stop. The air grew thick with adrenaline, testosterone, and fear. The whole tableau stilled like a held breath, ready to release at any second. The Mooney girl put her hands up and hid her face, too scared to look the men in the eye.

The crack-bolt of gunfire rang out all around Victoria. She opened her eyes and saw chaos: men running and screaming, branches raining from the forest canopy, shadowy figures spidering up and down the tree trunks. One of the remaining mutineers took cover behind the Mustang and jumped up to shoot at the figures in the trees.

Victoria jumped out of the car to hide next to him. Whatever was happening was worse than bikers right now. Had she unknowingly opened the gate for some rival gang to attack? The gunman next to her wasn't much older than her. He breathed heavily, and spittle and blood littered his beard.

"What's going on?" Victoria demanded, gripping the man's shoulders. His stuttering, muttering mouth couldn't form words. He just shook his head, wild eyes telling her that his head held nothing but his current fear.

The ground opened up beneath them, drinking the shell-shocked gunman into the earth. He grabbed Victoria. She tried to pull him up, but the ground was insistent. It pulled them both in.

Behind them, the Mustang lurched forward. It was getting sucked down as well. The man screamed, trying to climb over Victoria to safety, but the ground ate them both.

Victoria was drowning in the black soil beneath her farm. The man released his hold on her, and she floated back up to the surface and awoke, staring up at the white light behind the canopy. *Is it still daytime?* she wondered. *Am I dead?*

"You're not dead," a woman's voice called out. "We don't want ya."

Victoria heaved onto her side and coughed up dirt. Her car was half sunk into the ground and perched upon it was a black woman with languid, amused-looking eyes. She seemed drunk.

Victoria could barely choke out, "Who are you?"

"Jane Mooney. Used to be. You can call me Jeanne."

Jeanne eventually introduced the women to each other, and they grew close as well. Together, yelling over each other, facts and opinions and asides overlapping, they told the stories of how they met and the things they had shared in the years since. Charlyne would cry laughing, acting out Jeanne's broken body from that time near the Skyliner, but never failed to greet her with a cheerful, "How's your leg?"

On Sundays, the women would meet at someone's house for a lavish breakfast and chat. As the years went on, they founded a small hippie congregation and took their families to that. Afterward, they would drop off their kids somewhere and go eat breakfast. Over the years, they had their individual ups and downs, but the group remained tight. They kept showing up every Sunday and kept going to breakfast and kept together.

But friendship isn't just about the first time you met; it's about everything that happens in between then and now. The ups, the downs, the ways you subtly terrorize each other because you are so close. The way it doesn't feel right to say no to them because they know you better than you know yourself. The way they know a you that you dare not show to your husband, your girlfriend, your child.

Jeanne cherished her friends as emotional equals. The children she sacrificed could never be equals. They were offshoots, like the fairy rings around a fallen redwood. Those little sprouts could never grow if their parent tree was still alive. In the forest, baby redwood sprouts died all the time, starved for sunlight by the immensity of their mothers.

But these women, they were the other great trees around her. Together, their small grove found sanctuary in each other.

They learned how to be a family together. They supported each other in ways they could never with their children. They were friends invested in loyalty more than winning. With your children, Jeanne thought, you had to win against them, and quickly. There would always be more battles—any capitulation is fuel for the next argument: *What about that other time?* With friends, you could believe that each conflict would be the last.

The women made Jeanne believe the worst had passed, and Jeanne didn't ask for anything from them. But they knew her differences, her projects. She helped them when they needed it, but they ached to help her too, to make them feel worthy of her love and mutual respect. They gathered in front of the nurse log to hear Jeanne talk, and she told them what the forest needed. So, the young Witches resolved to feed the forest, and it survived on their secrets: tears, blood, miscarriages, abortions, healthy newborn children. The Witches buried themselves up to their necks and fed the forest using their bodies. Life and death and life. And of course, over time, they drew upon the loggers and hitchhikers whose MISSING posters plastered notice boards up and down the 101.

And yet, Jeanne grew dissatisfied: She did not choose the shape of her friends' devotion. She wanted them to respect the forest, not worship her.

The forest seethed.

Followers are not friends. Acolytes are not seeds.

It turned its attention toward future generations.

Jeanne wanted friends, but the Witches wanted a queen. Even after witnessing the godpower of the forest, their minds still imprinted on her. Humans need their idolatry. The Witches—her Witches—needed to believe that someone like them wielded the authority to change everything.

Jeanne was mistaken for the changemaker that was the forest. She was one of its million-million faces, only one of its voices. She tried to make her friends understand that, but unless they held the power within themselves, they'd never be able to grasp it. So, reluctantly, she became their queen, and they became her priestesses. Jeanne accepted their offerings, bestowed upon them her help. She became another mother to her chirping, begging baby birds. She was their nest and the branch it rested on and the tree and the forest. And she was their friend.

39 WHIPPLE'S GHOST

1965

JEANNE WHIPPLE RUED THAT wet March day she lost the man she loved to her daughter. When she handed the baby to him, the only one she'd kept after nearly a hundred years of sacrifice, Jeanne watched his eyes flash from pale blue to near white and knew that his love for her would be different forever after. William sobbed. The damned thing had rewired the man's brain. Whatever feeling Jeanne could arouse in him now was weaker, because no matter how much love and pheromones she poured into him, he would divert its flow to fill this wriggling, beige child. He named her Marian after his mother, who'd died in the 1923 earthquake when a chimney collapsed on her, which should've been a hint.

Marian was the only thing he'd ever asked of Jeanne, and she instantly regretted giving it to him.

The forest had warned her.

1980

Because of that child, the only person she'd ever loved was dead.

So was Jeanne, but her deaths never lasted. She awoke on the ground, looking up at her hanging husband. Fortuitously, the metal cable the men had used snapped her neck so hard it clipped her head from her body. The starving forest had soaked her up in no time, and when she emerged from the black soil, William Whipple, the boy she'd cherished for fifty-odd years, was gone. She knew in the pit of her stomach that she wouldn't be able to bring him back.

Yet she had to try. The forest had surprised her before.

Jeanne summoned her barkers. They came down from the trees. Up from beneath roots. From within stumps. From the bark itself. Looping, warped burls unfolded into right-angled limbs that pulled the recently killed, cadaverous, moist-skinned bodies out of the tree trunks. Large black eyes blinked in the foggy darkness, following a pheromone trail to the cabin where Jeanne stood wailing below her husband.

They carried Whipple's inert body to the nurse log and she climbed in with him, hugging his corpse and begging the pulsing organs of the forest to resurrect him the way it had her so many times. The red mushrooms flared their pink gills at her, pulsing with no particular hurry, breathing impassively, and giving no indication whether the forest would help her or not. The slime molds writhed around Jeanne and her husband, reading the braille of her raised pores. She willed the forest to acknowledge the fierce desperation screaming through her. She hoped the forest would understand and would grant her this wish after it had already given her so much. She had no right to ask for more, but the world kept taking and taking and taking. Without William, part of her was missing. Surely the forest could understand that.

Mycelial threads reached toward her and cocooned William's body. Jeanne hugged the body for the last time inside the nurse log's trunk. Fuzzy white mold tickled softly against her wet cheeks.

Please. Bring him back to me.

No.

William Whipple disintegrated in her arms. The full weight of her feelings crushed her; she felt so small, clasping his shrinking body. As his life force was sent miles away to feed the forest and help heal its demolished body, Jeanne let the nurse log eat her as well. The forest ate her sadness. It soaked up her entire life. The biomass that had been Jeanne Whipple dispersed in a million-million different directions.

When she woke once more, the forest told her that it couldn't be helped. It knew her pain but could not, would not, take her life from her. So she stayed anchored to the forest's consciousness, more of a polyp than a body. The forest allowed her to grieve. These woods operated on a timeline too long to acknowledge impatience—and humanity operates exclusively on impatience. It would wait for her. Now, with the barkers, the forest could kill loggers without her or her husband.

In the years Jeanne spent grieving William, she grew more and more angry at Marian. Jeanne's coal-black hurt condensed and fused into a clear, bright diamond of hate. Each of Marian's sins became a different facet: her slatternly association with the dirty men who fed the forest as they tried to destroy it; her idiotic lust for the outside world; the idea of "normalcy" she desperately clung to as if it meant anything meaningful in this world as a woman, let alone a half-Negro child. The fact that her loyalties sided with those loggers over her mother and father, despite Jeanne and William warning her about them over and over, enraged Jeanne. She couldn't imagine the twisted logic that led her daughter to crave such monstrosities, to covet them so strongly that she betrayed her family. The girl was too weak. She was insatiable. Did she recognize in the human hearts the same suicidal urge to eat the world?

Jeanne called her priestesses: Nancy, Victoria, and Charlyne. From the town of Redcedar they came to her, encircling the nurse log where Jeanne had first cemented them to her cause. They were older now but still strong. The women cradled her and clothed her after she slipped out of the nurse log into the root cave, slick with botanical mucus.

The women who caught her supported her in a way the forest couldn't and held her as she cried. They eulogized William in a way he would've loved.

The Witches helped ground her, prevented her from disappearing into her grief. They got her a job at the school. They continued to feed the forest, sending hitchhikers and runaways deep into the woods.

The Witches' best consolation was that the world outside would harm young Marian in more ways than any of them could dream. They assured her things had only become worse out there, especially for someone like Marian. Jeanne had embraced the forest because her black skin and feminine sex made her a target outside of the safety of the redwoods. In stuttering steps of progress, much had changed and not changed. Marian was a black girl as well as a homeless, penniless orphan. Her life would be hard. Maybe unbearable. One could only hope. Jeanne and the others would find ways to keep tabs on the girl using their connections in all the worlds, watching the ways in which the world she'd chosen would punish her treachery.

40 KINDLING

THE WITCHES WERE RIGHT. Marian got knocked around for years. The world out there hurt the treasonous child in so many ways. Some that Jeanne was all too familiar with and others that Jeanne could barely understand. It should've felt good. Should've soothed her somehow. In the forest, death fed life, but when it came to Marian, her pain just hurt Jeanne more. Every new piece of gossip that was brought to her by the Witches, the winds, the birds . . . None of it satisfied. It just felt pointless.

WOOD BORERS

The Port of Oakland was home to thousands of metal shipping containers and millions of wooden pallets. One of those wood pallets became the stage at the Skyliner. Like many others, it made its way northward on trucks. Humboldt County shipped its wood all over, but it still needed packaged goods shrink-wrapped to a little wooden platform for easier loading. Some of the pallets brought food, paper goods, and cheap plastic souvenirs to the tourist shop and market just off the 101. The one with the smashed car out front.

The pallets were made from the outer portions of logs. Not Humboldt redwood logs—that was far too valuable when cheaper pine was abundant. Just beneath the bark of those pines, wood-boring beetles laid their eggs. So many kinds of insects did: powder-post beetles, weevils, emerald ash borers, bark beetles, and longhorn beetles. Even as the trees were felled and cut into economically beneficial supports, the larvae gestated inside the wooden pallets, hearing everything. When they matured, emerging from the pallets behind Hsu's Market, the wood-boring beetles whispered to Jeanne what they knew of her daughter.

She'd made her way south on trucks, all the way to the Port of Oakland. The wood borers had heard the skinny teen crying, nestled between shipping containers. She was finally in the big city, and she had nowhere to go. Sleeping on wooden pallets full of beetle eggs, she cried herself to sleep most nights. On worse nights, she screamed herself and others awake. Her loud misery made her a target for predators of all kinds.

BLACK-CAPPED CHICKADEES

The birds announced that Jeanne's daughter hadn't stayed miserable. She'd been taken in by a group of older women. One of their sons was a young man who treated her gently, even when she flinched away from his touch. So many terrible things had happened to Marian among the pallets. Jeanne was almost proud that her daughter had survived long enough to find some happiness.

Marian grew older than Jeanne ever had in her first life and looked older than Jeanne ever wanted to. She had children of her own, a girl and then a boy. Jeanne hoped that motherhood would open Marian's eyes to the sacrifices a parent was forced to make. But Marian loved her children with the bright-eyed idiocy that had blinded William from doubting his daughter's devotion, even as she got him killed. A child's growth can only lead to the downfall of the mother, but Marian didn't see all that yet. Maybe she'd never find out.

As Marian raised her children, Jeanne begrudgingly accepted the Witches as her own. Her difference from them had become too vast; their former equality had decomposed into servants squabbling for her approval. And still, despite their simple worship, she loved her friends. She'd be the mother to them that she couldn't be to Marian. They expressed gratitude, at least. They did what she asked them to.

Charlyne gave birth to oversized twins and delivered one to the nurse log. She protected Jeanne's interests by overserving at the Skyliner and letting the writhing 101 do the rest.

Nancy, who long ago had offered to kill Marian and Victoria, instead offered to kill Kevon Bay, but Jeanne said no. She wasn't so vindictive that she'd wish the pain of losing one's husband on anyone, even Marian. So instead, Nancy lead the Witches' duty of directing transients toward jobs that didn't exist on roads with no names. The barkers did the rest.

Jeanne remained the queen of this forest, an overseer of a system that gave her nothing but dignity, praise, power. As its representative to this world, Jeanne took on the mantle of spreading the good word of the forest's importance. Despite it all, she hadn't completely given up on people and recruited others to their cause. More servants, but none as devoted as Charlyne, Victoria, and Nancy. No one else could be trusted with the work the Witches did.

SUDDEN OAK DEATHS

Sick acorns, choking on *Phytophthora ramorum*, told Jeanne that Kevon Bay let the kids play on oak trees all the time, and she liked to hear that. Their names were Jasmine and James, and they were happy whenever they were with their father, climbing coast live oaks. Marian was still wary of all trees and avoided the sprawling *Quercus agrifolia*. She smiled to herself when she heard the oaks were being lost to blight. She remained twitchy and standoffish to many, fractured from her past. Marian thought it was a wonder Kevon had been able to get two kids in her.

After the 1989 earthquake dropped a piece of the superhighway on their father, Jeanne thought she could feel her grandchildren crying out. She knew their sadness and disconnection from the world they were being reared in. *They don't know that they belong here. There's a place they can truly call home.*

Single motherhood required more of Marian than she had. She became a hypocrite in her daughter's eyes and a monster in her son's.

Marian had finally gotten her fill of the outside world. Her moods turned unpredictable: It infected her like the sapwood decay fungus that decimated the Oakland oaks. Violent outbursts sprouted from periods of quiet like the fruiting bodies of *Annulohypoxylon thouarsianum*, ugly and unwelcome, sprang from the bark of oak trees. The trees saw what was happening to Marian. When the fruiting bodies released their spores, the news floated northward.

Eventually, Marian turned jumpy, scared of everything. She never slept, and her nerves frayed until she was nothing more than an animal in a trap the moment before it decided to bite its own leg off. Jeanne hoped that when the inevitable happened, when the world finally broke Marian, she wouldn't take the kids down with her.

Marian loved her children, but her anxious, inconsistent love wasn't enough. Jeanne knew they didn't belong out there in that world. They belonged in these woods with their true family. They were a part of something so much larger than themselves, and something inside their sunken human minds knew it. Every minute Marian and her kids spent in that world hurt her children. Every gust of wind from the Bay Area spoke of the Bay family's punctured existence. Jeanne felt their souls calling out, fingers reaching for something—anything—to save them.

LADY BEETLES

When orange gusts of *Harmonia axyridis* brought the news of Marian's psychotic break, Jeanne felt only sadness. The previous disregard she had felt about her daughter, the pointlessness of all that wasted death, had metastasized into something worse: numbness. When the world finally broke Marian, Jeanne thought she would savor the justice done toward the girl who killed William. Who'd taken her birthright and set it on fire. Who valued music and soda pop more than her own family and the forest they protected.

Yet with every loss, the forest thirsted for Marian's sad children. Jeanne and her birds would carry the seeds home. The fire of Marian Bay's undoing lit a new purpose in Jeanne. She hadn't been able to save William, but she could save his grandchildren. *Time to return Jasmine and James to their birthright*, Jeanne thought as Victoria drove her to San Francisco.

GHOST REDWOOD

Jeanne viewed Jasmine and James not as seeds, but as sprouts. The germination rate for redwood trees is very low. They grow more successfully from sprouts that form around the base of a tree, utilizing the mature tree's nutrients and root system. When the parent tree dies, a new generation of trees rise. The Bay children's parent tree was gone, but they needed the protection of the rest of the redwood forest to grow strong. These children would find themselves reborn in the forest, confidently thriving as its guardians.

The Witches suggested a change of identity since Jeanne Whipple was supposed to have died in 1980. They had a lot of suggestions. And a lot of ID cards, from all the people they'd led astray in the forest. From their trick of clacking baseball bats against each other to disorient hikers enough to make rash decisions. From misdirecting drunk Skyliner patrons. From manipulating people looking for a quick buck trimming weed.

"We don't know what Marian told them about you," Victoria said during their road trip.

"A godparent is as good as kin," Nancy said.

"If you're lighter skinned, the court will be inclined to trust you more," Charlyne said.

They handed her an issue of *Jet Magazine*. It was much smaller than the publications Marian used to hoard. How many trees had died for that weekly edition? They'd decay for hundreds of years in a landfill somewhere. Jeanne changed herself to look like the beautiful black *Jet* woman. Her hair became straight and short. It flared around her head in a stylish halo.

All her melanin was sucked down the drains of her pores and concentrated into a sprinkle of slightly raised freckles across her nose and cheeks. Even in a hundred years Jeanne would never go full white—why would she want to? She was a black woman. She was wary enough of the world to not let it infect her in that way and take her identity away from her. The forest had chosen her because of that strength, for the ways in which it shaped who she was and made her worthy of the redwoods' power. With that power inside her, she never wanted to be anything else.

But she could change a little bit in order to secure her legacy.

The superior court building on McAllister Street was everything the forest wasn't: cold, dead marble festooned with tacky wrought iron spikes to discourage homeless people from sleeping next to it.

When children become wards of the state of California, they are assigned attorneys. Ellen Zeller was a dependency attorney, representing children who were removed from their homes after what was probably the worst day of their short lives.

Luckily, these particular clients had family that wanted to take them in. Godparents are as good as kin in some cases, and there was a shortage of foster homes. Better that Jasmine and James Bay go live up north with their godmother than languish in a group home. No action could be taken for reunification for at least another year. The judge agreed.

Virginia Jones's eyes looked strange in the surgical white hallway outside the courtroom for the hearing. She looked at Ellen like she recognized her, was staring down into her soul. It was uncomfortable. Her voice was low and smooth, adultlike. Not at all like the teenybopper twang that grated on Ellen's nerves so much since moving here from the East Coast.

The woman took Ellen's hand in hers. "What's wrong, dear?" she cooed in that soft drawl of hers.

Ellen wanted to respond, *What's wrong with me? What's wrong with you? A woman set herself on fire, and you're so calm! These kids are going to be traumatized for the rest of their lives.* But something in the woman's words was so sincere it ripped through Ellen's shields.

The question bored through her icy toughness, her steel-sharp wit, her gritty New York bravado—all those things that she wore like a cloak around herself to protect from the sinking feeling that she was living in a world she didn't want to be a part of. Lately, that cloak was feeling more and more like a mask. Like the things that made Ellen her weren't really *her*. Like being her authentic self would be some kind of childish rebellion against her new community.

Gazing into this beautiful black woman's sincere eyes, Ellen realized she didn't like her life, not one bit. She didn't love her family. Her job was demoralizing. This place . . . Art didn't get it. He was from here. Ellen hated San Francisco: all the fake-cool bohemians who wouldn't be able to hack it in New York City for a week. They didn't know what it meant to work, *really* work.

Her grandparents immigrated in 1947 and worked their asses off to provide for their children. She grew up hearing about their sacrifices. But her boys didn't want to hear it. They told her she was being a bummer when she mentioned "it"—refusing to even say the word as if the Holocaust were merely a momentary impoliteness rather than a horror that could still happen to them. *We teach our children so that they know, so they will fight injustice in all its forms, so they won't have to flee the country with their families*, she had thought. The boys had chastised her when she insisted they get passports "just in case." They'd called her morbid and made faces in their pictures, but they would be fucking glad to have their passports with their ugly pictures if the time came that they did need to pack up their lives and abscond to a country that didn't let neo-Nazis vandalize synagogues. It was 1995, for G-d's sake, and still it happened! People learned nothing.

Her own children even treated her like a second-class citizen in her own home. The boys—two giant-headed brunets she'd delivered vaginally with no anesthesia—had the temerity to call her "Ellen" to her face in front of their little goyishe friends. To call her a bitch behind her back. To exchange eye rolls with their father when they thought she was being hysterical. And Art encouraged it. He let them disrespect her and derogate her.

By that point, with this sudden onslaught of epiphanies, Ellen realized she was crying. The woman squeezed her hand and brought her back into the world. Ellen sobbed so hard and so loudly that she worried the judge or someone else would see. They'd ask, "What's wrong?" and she wouldn't be able to tell them the truth.

The woman nodded at Ellen, like she'd heard all of her frenzied thoughts. "I'm sorry you're hurting. This world isn't good for you."

Yeah, no shit. Ellen wanted to run. Not toward her Bernal Heights home. The fight-or-flight within her pointed somewhere else, a direction Ellen would later find was northward. She pulled her hands away.

Gin Jones enveloped Ellen in a hug. Ellen was pulled toward the center of this woman like a gravity well; there was something within her that felt like home. The air stood still around them, walling them off from the rest of the world.

The woman petted Ellen's head. "I'm sorry you're sad. Even when something is bad for so long, it hurts when it ends. There is always time to make a change." There was something in her voice that reminded Ellen of the look her grandmother got when she talked about the war.

Her tone turned hopeful as Ellen sobbed into her shoulder. The pain had become so cold and rigid over the years that she hadn't realized it was what was holding her up. She slumped into the woman, while the traumatized Bay siblings sat on a bench nearby.

"I can help you," the woman breathed into her ear. "I can see as clear as day that this world is killing you. That feeling you get? Where you want to die, want to be anything other than what you are, because this world hurts you for being what you are? I know it. It's hurt me too. But there's a place where the world can't touch us."

Ellen never wanted to be anything other than who she was, but she understood. The world wouldn't stop until she begged it to make her different. If she stayed, it would happen. The Ellen she knew herself to be would die. Art and the boys and everyone else would wear her down like the ocean wore down the cliffs south of the city. Until her whole self came tumbling down to a smooth sameness. Until she gladly ate pork like the rest of the West Coast Jews.

"Take me with you. Please."

The woman nodded, and they exited the building onto Polk Street, and Victoria drove the group north to Humboldt, to Redcedar.

In the VW bus, the wounded children stared up into her new face, and Jeanne wondered if her new face resembled their mother's in any meaningful way. In the reflection of their big eyes, she saw herself. Or rather, she saw Virginia Jones. Aunt Gin.

When James fell asleep, Jasmine squirmed around in the middle row. Gin sat in the back, waiting patiently for the girl to come to her. She would start with Jasmine. Every few minutes, she'd try to steal a glance at Gin. Often, she'd forget she was staring until Gin smiled at her, then the girl would whip back around in her seat, a clattering blur of beaded hair.

When the van summited a hill overlooking Humboldt County, Jasmine marveled at all the green laid out before her. All Gin could see was how much green was missing, how much had changed since she first laid eyes on this land in 1870. The greens had been deeper then. The road had been narrower, unpaved, barely visible. She'd died a dozen times since then, lost so much. But the forest died a million times over every year, and they'd survived together.

One day, these children would join her in protecting this place.

Jasmine climbed over the seat to sit next to her grandmother.

When the girl laid her small, beaded head on the woman's large breasts, Jeanne smiled, glad that she'd made herself so old. The child's head fit perfectly under her arm.

"This here is God country," she explained.

"I like that. God country," Jasmine said, almost like a prayer.

"Your mama ever tell you about her father? Your grampdaddy?"

The girl shook her head, beads rattling.

"He was a good man. He loved these woods with his whole heart."

"Whole heart," Jasmine repeated with wonder.

"A lot of people say they love something, when really, they want to be in control of it. Loving with your whole heart means you'd give yourself up for the thing you love. It's needing to love that something even more than you need to control it. I want you to love it, Jasmine. All I want is for everyone to love this forest the way I do.

"Like your grampdaddy did."

The girl nodded pensively, not understanding at all.

41 SPROUTING

OVER THE YEARS SPENT as Aunt Gin, the forest stopped talking to her. She got weaker. There were fewer birds and bugs and plants every year. The forest blamed her. Meanwhile, Jasmine and James lost the lines in their faces and bags under their eyes, filling in their trauma with memories of a real childhood spent in nature.

On the other hand, Gin started to age in a more human way. Her jowls sagged, and her vision started to fail; she needed glasses. Maybe it was that she was spending so much time in the world now, squinting at typewritten letterheads all day in the high school office while the kids were next door at the elementary school. Maybe having a job is just something that kills you a little every day, like smoking, no matter who you are.

That first year, Charlyne started bringing her brother's granddaughter, Tilly, around for playdates. The girl helped the children find something like happiness. But she was also the start of all the trouble. Anyone with even two eyes could see they were both in love with her.

Jasmine was sixteen when she lost her best friend to her brother. She loved Tilly with everything she had. Before Tilly, every day was painful. For two years after Marian Bay set herself on fire, her daughter never smiled. Jasmine barely spoke, except to boss around her brother. She was responsible for him now, and he didn't respond to reasoned arguments, especially after he grew taller than her. They fought more than they ever had: violently, verbally, viciously. Even though they had their own rooms for the first time in their lives, the weight of what had happened to them filled every room of Aunt Gin's little house with the wilting moss-covered roof.

Through middle school, Jasmine spent every waking moment either talking to Tilly in person or writing her notes. Everything she did had to pass the *What Would Tilly Do?* filter. Her friend was a powerhouse and never took any shit. Jasmine wanted to be just like her. To possess her *her-ness* in whatever way she could. Because Tilly was special. Jasmine wanted to be special too, so she remade herself in Tilly's image. And it drove her best friend into the arms of her younger brother.

In high school, the three of them hung out on occasion, hotboxing Tilly's Corolla. The summer before Jasmine's junior year, they were parked at the end of Gin's driveway, and Jasmine ran inside to grab water for everyone. She was juggling three thick plastic tumblers, trying to spread her fingers wide enough to keep control over all of them. Jasmine was struggling with the door handle when her shoulder pushed the curtain out of the way.

The little white car was visible, its windows obscured by eddies of white smoke. Jasmine wasn't sure at first she was really seeing it. She always sat shotgun in Tilly's car, but James was in the passenger seat now. The way her brother and her best friend were sitting was weird. They were close together. The way Jasmine sat with Tilly, feet up on the dashboard and reclined, an arm draped across the driver's headrest. Almost touching.

Tilly kissed James. She just leaned over and kissed him.

Jasmine dropped the cups and ran into her room. She wanted to run away from home, she wanted to kill herself, she wanted to kill them. She didn't know what she wanted other than to not exist anymore so she wouldn't feel her heart breaking in her chest.

When Tilly finally came to look for her best friend, she pushed open Jasmine's bedroom door. The first thing she saw was Jasmine's enraged scowl up in her face. Jas shoved Tilly with all her might, and the skinny teen and her long, straight hair went flying into a wood-paneled wall. Jasmine stepped over her and stomped down the hallway, screaming, "Stay away from my little brother, you pedo!"

Jasmine had to get away. Before she realized she'd chosen a destination, she was in the forest. She flopped down into the leaves and looked up at the canopy, letting twigs and pine needles impale her hair. She picked up the little needles and scratched her forearms with them. She pressed the glossy green spears through her skin, piercing herself through the thick skin around her fingernails, wishing the needles would cover her entire body, protect her. She dreamed their menthol-scented essence would form a shell around her and distance her from all that had hurt her. The pain of being her, of having her life.

It was hell to be around them after that, and the forest became Jasmine's refuge. She'd swipe a razor head from James's shaving kit and let it dance between her fingers, doing dainty somersaults. She thought about her mother a lot on those days. To live in pain was no life at all. Jasmine understood that now and forgave her.

On the worst day, Jasmine escaped to the forest and took an entire bottle of sleeping pills she'd swiped from Hsu's Market. She washed them down with a can of soda, hoping the chemicals would rot her insides the way Aunt Gin always told her they would and make the pills absorb faster.

She woke up alive in the twilight of the forest, not remembering her death. The forest blustered around her, chasing her back to her house by whipping wind and duff at her until she stumbled back up the valley to Gin's house. To where James and Tilly were making memories together and keeping it secret from her.

Tilly changed. All of Tilly's special her-ness that Jasmine had felt so proprietary over was replaced with something else. Whatever part of her that had belonged to Jasmine was gone. It made Jasmine feel like a part of her was missing too. She'd never be able to trust Tilly again. Not fully. The part of Jasmine that was dedicated to Tilly changed: All her love and respect and devotion to the sanctification of Tilly Blackman hardened into a knotted little burl under her ribs.

So Jasmine tried to drive her away. She nitpicked Tilly's hair, clothes, and skin. Tried to make her feel the way Tilly made Jasmine feel. During their sleepovers, Tilly would sneak out in the night to be with James. Jasmine started a rumor about Tilly at school. But none of it satisfied Jasmine. She still felt tortured. You can't heal from something while it's still happening to you, and Jasmine would never get over losing her friend if she had to stay here. Killing herself wasn't enough of an escape from life in Redcedar.

When San Francisco State University called the school to request Jasmine's grades, Aunt Gin nearly kicked down Jasmine's door. All the transcript requests came through her, so Jasmine had expected it. But not like this. Tears filled the furrows in Gin's soft, beige skin. "You're applying to colleges? When were you planning to tell me?"

"I mean . . ." Jasmine fidgeted uncomfortably. "I didn't even think I was gonna get in." She pulled her shirt sleeves down over her hands so Gin wouldn't notice any of the scars.

"After all we've done for you." Gin shook her head, making a decision then and there. "You can't leave."

After all we've done for you. She was talking about the forest. Jasmine knows that now.

Gin let her go. She could feel the girl's broken heart. It needed time to heal.

It was still no excuse for being sneaky. The girl had gone and applied to a college down south in that horrible city Gin had spent so much energy rescuing her from. The forest told Gin to let her go. It could wait.

After James married Tilly, Gin worried Jasmine might never come back. Tilly made James feel like a man, so he acted like a man. He saw himself as separate from the forest and learned to hate and kill it. He lost the forest.

Part of Gin hoped Jasmine wouldn't come back. The forest didn't talk to Gin anymore. Maybe now it was better out there in the world.

The forest waited. Its power abandoned Gin slowly, then progressively, then all at once, like a post-winter waterfall. The walls of her ancient brain caved in on themselves. She moved in her grandson and punished him and his wife because they were the ones who were there. James joined the Mooney men, or whatever they were calling themselves now. Marian's children as ever. Selfish. Disrespectful. A waste. Gin doubted their ability to continue their family's legacy. *They'll never be ready*, she whined.

Patience, Child, the forest purred. **Your urgency is not our urgency.**

Seeds blow away to grow new life in new places.

The girl will return.

She'll grow us back.

42 THE NEW WORLD

HENRY WOKE UP AND found himself buried up to his neck in front of a huge cave of tree roots. Gasping for breath, he stumbled back into consciousness. The roots hung down over the rock wall, hiding a deep, black mouth. Something moved in the blackness.

Next to him, Tilly's unconscious head faced away from him, her body also buried in rich soil, still in front of the nurse log.

Those creatures were all around them. They shuffled around awkwardly, nowhere near as graceful as they were in the trees. Up close, Henry couldn't believe these things were ever people. Their ankles and knees bent at insect angles. The creatures swayed from leg to leg: Watching them move reminded Henry of sports injuries, with their herky-jerky movements. Their wrong-angled limbs started to rise off the ground. Long feet levitated.

Henry swallowed sour bile, and it went down with the ease of a jawbreaker.

His neck cracked as he craned it back to follow them. High up in the gold mist, he spotted Jasmine. She was ascending too, lifted up by vines that seemed to sprout out from her skin. Behind her, the canopy was a galaxy. Grainy, glittering pollen frosted the mist and formed clouds, nebulas. Stars shone brightly in the blackness. Were those mushrooms? Some other crazy plant? Creatures swarmed over the branches and melted into tumors all over the tree.

A tiny figure walked across the branches' bark. A woman. The dead lady from the funeral reception. Aunt Gin—alive!

Holy shit this is nuts this place is nuts. I'm going nuts. I'm losing my goddamn mind.

The woman embraced Jasmine, illuminated fluorescent gray by the globs hanging down from the branches, like drool or snot or umbilical cords. The globs were babies. Fetuses. *Good God.*

Suddenly, a familiar mechanical buzzing rang out around him, echoing over the gully. A black dot grew into an ATV, flying down the gully, ridden by a figure wearing a skull mask.

Up in the canopy, the redwood bulges remained dormant.

Relief flooded through Henry. Buck skidded to a stop near him. He had a chainsaw strapped to his back. *I knew he didn't leave us!* Henry beamed up at Buck, trying to wriggle himself free of the packed dirt. "Ayo, down here! What happened to you?"

Buck scooped dirt out from around Henry and freed his shoulders.

"S'a long story."

S'not that long of a story. When Buck was on guard duty, he'd heard a voice calling out to him in the night. At first, he thought it was James, but it sounded more and more like his mom. He'd followed her voice for hours until he was back at the Skyliner. Charlyne had tried to get him to stay and help her at the bar, but he had to find his friends.

"I made it back." Buck had found his friends and was elated, but something niggled at him. "S'weird that the hiking maps my mom gives out lead right here."

"You've got a gift for understatement." Henry smiled up at him. "There's a lot weird about this forest." The two men clapped hands around each other's shoulders, and the giant man pulled Henry out of the soil. Together they freed Tilly from the ground, shaking her awake.

Her eyes looked like she'd been erased.

Buck met Henry's eyes when they averted their gaze from Tilly at the same time. He wanted to spare his cousin the burden of his attention on top of everything else. They tried to ignore the blood staining her pants, radiating out from her crotch and sequined with redwood needles. The two men looked everywhere except at her no-longer-pregnant belly.

She'd been looking forward to becoming a mother. Buck thought she'd be a good one. But right now, they had to move.

"Where's Jas?" he asked.

Jas! "Oh, fuck! She's up there!" Henry pointed toward the canopy where Jasmine was just barely visible in a nest or something a hundred yards up.

Buck and Henry yelled up at her. Tilly stared at the ground, holding her empty belly.

Jasmine didn't hear them. Something was lighting up in front of her. It was coming from her.

Barkskins fell to the ground around them. Each one thudded here and there with balletic precision.

Painfully, Henry's eyes darted around, failing to ignore the human limbs. His own limbs were pudding, but he had to fight. These things could kill him—or worse.

Buck swung his helmet at one of the creatures, and its head shattered like a gourd, bark-skinned pulp and bone splattering. "S'get her to the ATV. We gotta get outta here!"

Henry reached for Tilly, who collapsed to the ground in front of him.

She looked up at him and opened her mouth to talk, but what came out was a scream like fabric ripping, so heartbroken and soul shattered that she went hoarse.

Henry had the muscle memory for this; his days were spent lifting people who didn't want to be picked up, whether for the bathroom or because they were a danger to themselves or others. He scooped his arms beneath Tilly's and dragged her backward through the gully to the ATV. She didn't fight him. If only all his patients could be this easy.

Buck picked up the chainsaw and waved it at the creatures, but it took him just a second too long to reach for the starter and get it going. The barkers swept over him like a tsunami.

Buck dropped the chainsaw, and it skittered through the dry duff toward Henry.

It all happened so fast. A dozen of them enveloped Buck, dogpiling on him. He disappeared from Henry's panicked view, then blossomed through the top of the melee. The creatures lifted Buck's giant body with a heave. Their spidery fingers slithered over him, grasping him by the arms and legs and torso. Buck screamed the whole time until his voice was nothing but throaty croaks.

Those fuckers. Henry dropped Tilly and ran toward the mass of limbs containing his friend. Henry picked up the chainsaw and fired it up. Tried to. One more time. He got it going.

Yelling, he pointed it at the monsters and just *went for it*. Once he hit flesh, he pushed the saw down with as much force as he could. The blade glided through so quickly that he almost lost his grip. Despite their apparent strength, underneath the bark, these creatures were mostly goo. Like the big bugs that skittered under the shelves in the H's storage rooms.

The creatures dropped Buck and scattered, disappearing into the shadows like roaches. Buck was broken, but alive. His clothes were soaked through with blood. He smiled up at Henry, who used a different carry to lift him up.

When they turned toward the ATV, they saw Tilly had pulled herself onto it.

A too-long hand reached out from the shadows behind her. Henry saw it creep into view but could only emit a pale "buh" before she was grabbed by a barker.

When the barker's fingers closed around her shoulders, Tilly remembered she was alive. Hollowed out by grief and aching, but alive. James was gone. Their child had been sucked out of her into the earth. Lost forever. The pain of it rang through her like a church bell. Over and over and over.

A feeling worse than death enveloped her. She had to get out of here. She had to live. If only to get revenge on whomever had done this to her. Her muscles trembled, flooded with fear or adrenaline or a million other ugly things.

The moment slowed to a crawl. All around her, chaos. Henry's face was aflame in a rigor mortis of shock. Buck was trying to shake a creature off of his back. Mottled gray fingers gripped Tilly, hard and painful, like the back of a wood chair.

Something like electricity whipped through her muscles. She bucked and flailed until the creature lost its grip. She rolled away and pulled out her axe-rope, still tied around her waist. She whipped it into the creature's chest, caving it in like rotting wood.

"Tilly!" Henry called.

Tilly stalked across the gully toward him. Instead of helping Buck, she picked up the chainsaw and turned it on with one pull. She waved it around, gunning the gas in case any more monsters wanted some.

Tilly then brandished the chainsaw behind them, kicking up gas fumes, while Henry pulled Buck up into the seat of his four-wheeler.

Something pulled at her foot. A root—a hand! It grabbed her and she fell forward, chainsaw first. From under the roots, the barkskin screeched and held up its arms just in time for her to slice them off.

Tilly screamed breathy nothings as she fought. The pneumatic puffing of her non-voice was unnerving. There should be so much more noise than this. It was as if the clear-cut they'd trekked across was inside her, drying her up from within. She kept cutting even after the barker was just a pile of parts and powdery-looking blood. She kept un-screaming as she wheeled around with the machine and threw it. The still-running chainsaw sailed through the air. It sliced through the crusty mist—the air was so dense with wood pulp and spores it was hard to breathe—and landed at the base of the root cave.

A wall of flame erupted under the roots.

Henry reached out a hand to pull Tilly onto Buck's ATV. Buck was laid across the seat between them, limp as a deer.

All around them, the creatures' dismembered limbs were already rotting. Bugs crawled from mouths and eye holes. Mold and mushrooms reduced them to nothing.

The fire licked up the gully. It scrabbled through the rocky cracks, eating through the moss. The wood. It spread across the roots. Crawled across the mouth of the overturned redwood.

"Jasmine!" Henry screamed.

Above: more, different screaming. Fighting figures in the branches. Jasmine! She must've been fifty stories up. The kaleidoscopic greens danced behind the struggling forms of Jasmine and Aunt Gin.

Aunt Gin. Alive.

Tilly's heart twisted with the need to help, but Jasmine was too far away. Tilly revved the engine, and the ATV roared. She was about to squeeze the throttle when the headlights sputtered to life just in time to alight on a trio of dark figures. The goddamned Witches.

"Why aren't we moving? Oh shit," Henry said from behind her. "This can't be good."

Victoria Mooney, Ellen Zeller, and Nancy Hsu blocked the path away from the fire. "The fuck are they doing here?" Tilly growled to herself. There was no one left for her to mind her language for. "Fuck it.

"Oh, hi, Miz Mooney," Tilly called out, trying to sound casual, as if they were meeting in the hallway of Aunt Gin's house instead of at the epicenter of a slowly spreading wildfire.

Victoria inclined her head like the goddamned queen of England. "Tilly. Charlyne called us when your cousin ran away from the Skyliner. He was supposed to stay home with his mother, and now look at what's happened to him."

At his mom's name, Buck groaned behind Tilly, and the ATV creaked under their combined weight. Part of her wanted to rev the engine again and see if the women would scatter.

Fire spilled down the walls on both sides of the gully. It crackled all around them, reflected in three pairs of eyes (four if you counted Ellen's glasses). The Witches looked every bit their moniker as they closed in around her. Golden pollen glittered in clouds around the women as they moved. It was fucking scintillescent.

"W—what are you ladies doing out here?" Henry asked. Like smoke, the pollen curled toward him, entered his sinuses, and he slumped forward onto Buck.

"What did you do to him? What the fuck is happening here?" Tilly demanded.

"We're here for you," Ellen replied. Tilly could tell she was trying to sound magnanimous, but it came out too eager, too hungry sounding. These women were always "trying to help" but never actually seemed to.

Nancy reached toward Tilly and brushed some chunks of congealed blood and redwood needles from her thigh. "You've already sacrificed so much. We understand what that feels like."

"You don't know anything about me," Tilly retorted. Under the Witch's cold fingers, Tilly felt her blood going stiff inside her. She flinched.

"We'd like you to join us." Victoria laid a hand on Tilly's tensed shoulder. "Our group needs new blood . . ." She balked at the pun but powered through. "And you're uniquely suited to help us serve this forest."

"Why? Because I'm an Indian?"

"Because you're already one of us." Nancy's eyes shone.

"You're a woman who loves this place with your whole heart. With your help, we can regrow all of this."

Tilly looked around her and pieced it together. The Witches—and Aunt Gin—knew about the barkers in the forest, knew they killed people. These woods were her home, but this place had taken her husband and child from her. Only new misery could sprout around each towering trunk. There was no taming this forest. She wouldn't become its keeper. She wouldn't condemn others to what had happened to James and their child.

These women were fools, and Aunt Charlyne was a fool to hang out with these hungry-looking crones who thought they could possibly control the monsters that lived in these woods. But she needed to see how deep the evil rooted.

"What would I have to do?"

"Keep sacrificing." Victoria eyed Henry and Buck.

"I can't kill them! Buck's my family. Henry's my friend." *Crazy fuckin' bitches.* Tilly tested her grip on the ATV.

Victoria exhaled in amusement. "One is an outsider, and Buck, your cousin, is competition. You could own the Skyliner one day with him out of the way. You know, there used to be a lot more Mooneys around here, a lot more people to share the family fortune with, but the forest cut down the competition. Charlyne never has to know it was you."

"And if I say no?"

"You can go." Victoria uncrossed her arms, opened them to Tilly in that patronizing clemency they always gave Catholic saints.

"No shit?"

Nancy Hsu shook her head. "We're not monsters."

Victoria stepped aside, and the other women followed. "If you leave these woods and go out into the world, it'll change your mind better than we ever could. You know what Redcedar can be like. How hateful people can be."

"No one would believe you anyway," Ellen added.

Suddenly, high above them, Aunt Gin shrieked. Tilly knew that scream from a thousand nights of sundowner confusion. The women looked up, distracted.

Tilly gunned the engine, spraying the Witches with loose soil and pine duff.

In the ATV's rearview mirror, she saw her best friend's body fall from the gargantuan redwood. In a way, Jasmine had been falling the whole time Tilly had known her. A spray of blood followed her descent down the trunk. Gore and entrails bloomed as Jasmine dropped. She looked so small, like a fleck of dust suspended in the cold fog of the redwood forest. She fell forever. Her tiny silhouette grew as she fell toward the ground. She was going to land on the nurse log above them.

The last thing Tilly saw as they escaped was Jasmine disappearing into the flames. She didn't see her crash into the ground. Wood and moss and pine needles flew up in a wave of black-red blood as her body exploded on impact. When Jasmine Bay's blood splashed back toward the earth, it was in the form of fluttering green redwood needles.

43 BURNING

1995

NO MATTER HOW HARD she tried, Marian Bay couldn't shed her rind of otherness enough for her fellow Oaklanders to accept her as a native. She just wanted to fit in and felt like she'd earned it by now. If not a native, then at least as a neighbor. Someone who had been in the Bay Area for fifteen years and planned to live there for the rest of her life. Someone who had been married to a Bay Area native. Someone who was widowed by the '89 earthquake when the highway collapsed on her husband. Despite everything, she was living the life she'd chosen. For better or worse. She was trying her hardest to keep afloat in the world she chose. There'd been a lot of ups and downs.

She was raising two Oakland natives by herself, which was not a task for the weak. Her children Jasmine and James were nearly ten and six. They were her sunshine babies: two of the most beautiful, sensitive, loveable, and funny children ever born. She'd gotten a little money from Kevon's life insurance policy because he'd died working. It wasn't a lot, but it was enough to pay the mortgage on the house on Telegraph Avenue and clothe their rapidly sprouting kids in the latest fashions they begged for, which currently was "officially licensed"

Looney Tunes T-shirts that hung to their knees. Marian watched the edges of those idiotically long shirts getting wet as James and Jasmine stomped through Chinatown in matching purple rain slickers.

No matter how much her new life frustrated her and made her feel small, her children gave her hope.

Her eldest was smart as a whip and, more importantly, not afraid to show off how smart she was. Where other girls her age were getting boy crazy and letting that dull them into the feminine ideal (Marian knew the move all too well), Jasmine was singularly focused on being right all the time. People with a strong sense of justice didn't keep it for long in this world, but Marian knew that Jasmine's passion could be channeled into success somehow. She was only ten, but the fire in her shone so brightly. Marian prayed the world wouldn't extinguish it as she got older. This was a girl who could change the world as long as that flame never went out. But Marian didn't want Jasmine to change the world. She just wanted her to have a happy, full life that she loved living. If Marian could secure that for her children, it would be enough. Everything would have been worth it.

Little James, newly six years old, kicked his short legs under the tablecloth and hummed to himself. Taz peeked up from his shirt. Behind him, a waving cat statue's arm kept time like a metronome. "I heard it through the grapevine," the little boy crooned and batted his tiny fingers on the table like a piano. Marian smiled, watching him enjoy himself. Around them, the white and Asian patrons murmured. Marian smiled harder, cheerier. Maybe James's singing would get a waiter's attention, and they could get some goddamned service. They'd ordered forever ago and getting the waiter to come the first time had been like pulling teeth.

Maybe this was a mistake. Marian knew she'd scared the kids after Kevon died. She'd seen the wary look in their eyes when she tried to explain that she'd chopped down the oak tree in their front yard because it was being nosy. Their conspiratorial sidelong glances at each other had sent her into a monthslong depression. She'd needed to heal. She'd just needed to shut off for a little bit. The kids would be okay. Hopefully.

She didn't want to be like this. She wanted to be there for her kids, but this world was relentless. This life was nothing but hard work and very few opportunities for rest. There were ample opportunities for perspiration and very little time to breathe. A million chances to break yourself but none to heal. This world was taking every ounce of her energy just to be able to get up and go to work. She was keeping them afloat, and it had to be enough.

So when she woke up that afternoon feeling kind of okay, she'd waited for the kids to come home from school. She asked them to put on their most favorite outfits because they were all going to go on a special surprise adventure.

Marian felt a little self-conscious for wearing a red striped shirt and red-rimmed glasses that matched the whole restaurant: from the walls to the curtains to the little oil lamps on the tables. She hated unintentionally matching her surroundings. It made her feel like a cartoon.

James was singing, but she didn't have the heart to tell him to stop. When people stared, Jasmine bristled next to her with equal parts mortification and indignation.

Marian tried to soothe her. "Don't worry about them. You can't change other people. Just focus on you. It's not your job to save the world from itself, babygirl. It's too much." She finished her glass of water, having made her point.

When the waiter dropped their plates in front of them, Marian noticed the mushrooms on her stir-fry before anything else. The earthy brown stood out against the electric yellow rice. It looked like shit. It looked like worms. It was as if she could see the mushrooms' gills breathing.

Static electricity skated across the sheen of sweat that coated her body. White flashlight beams clouded her vision.

The dull clanking of diners around her crescendoed into the clacking branches of the redwood forest. Insects screamed behind her ears.

"I can't eat this," she muttered to the waiter. "Asked for no mushrooms . . . Please don't let them just pick them out. They leave particles. I'll know."

The mushrooms multiplied on the plate and when the waiter reached over to take the plate away, Marian stopped him. She had to keep an eye on the mushrooms. To make sure they weren't coming for her babies.

But they blossomed across the plate, onto the waiter's hand and onto her own arm. They were digesting her, like the tree digested . . . "Mama gave her babies away. They live in the trees now."

Marian couldn't catch her breath. She could feel silty powder on the back of her throat, trying to slide down into her body and spread its tendrils of control. Coughing uncontrollably, she knocked the plate out of the waiter's hand. It shattered on the floor, and the mushrooms spread around the room.

She pictured herself as the forest had last seen her. *Maid Marian*. A naïve girl, grinding on her own fists on a riverbank, dreaming of dead boys touching her. "I went astray," she whispered. The forest had come for her, to devour her like it had eaten every single one of her siblings. She'd had the audacity to live. She'd been stupid to think she could ever escape the bloodthirsty redwoods.

Jasmine and James sat across the table from her, their faces open wounds. Marian wanted to soothe them and tell them it would be okay. They just had to leave. But when she raised her arms to them, her skin was transformed. No more skin at all. Her arms were a texture that sent Marian into a muscle-hardening fit.

The pale forearms were longer than they should be. They grew darker and rougher and scraggly with the wooly mammoth fur of a *Sequoia sempervirens*.

Wood. Her arms were becoming wood. She was infected with the forest, and if she touched her children, they would be infected too.

"No no no no," she babbled. She couldn't let them near her.

Screaming, she scanned the room for something, anything to stop the spread of the forest that had finally come to kill her. Its dark influence had destroyed her first family. Its pine-needled maw had hungered for the flesh of her baby siblings. It was why her parents were dead.

In the end, no matter how tired or depressed living in a city made her, it was that cursed forest that scared her more than anything. This world was still good because it had her children in it. As long as she kept her babies away from the forest, they would be safe.

Fire! The red glass oil lamp was right in front of her. It illuminated the quizzical looks on James's and Jasmine's faces. She hoped they would never come to understand this decision. Hoped they would be spared from the darkness lurking in the redwood forest. This needed to be done. She had to stop the forest from getting to them. She poured the oil lamp onto herself, and streams of flame splashed down her face and shoulders. If the forest ever found them, they were as good as dead.

44

LITTLE QUEEN

JASMINE'S RUINED BODY LAY at the base of three trees: a quick-growing *Picea sitchensis*, a lightweight *Thuja plicata*, and a fire-resistant *Sequoia sempervirens*. These woods were nothing if not pure Potential. And what is Potential if not a kind of magic?

The forest embraced her fully. It knew Marian's seeds would be strong: weather-beaten and world-weary. A tree needs strong seeds. A forest needs strong souls, inoculated by fire, to grow it back.

All that chlorophyll-tinted energy soaked up Jasmine Bay and used its thousand-million fingers and its infinite brain to weave her back into herself. Strands of DNA, proteins, and life came together in a pattern to grow what was, in essence, just a cell of its body. Her body now.

When Jasmine opened her eyes, the dark forest appeared lit from within. She'd reanimated into clean clothes with a god-power that ran through every hectare of her. Life and death pulsed within, like organelles in their own right. She felt dead skin cells on her body, and they sat like a decomposing fox next to a riverbed. Death was now something that fueled her. Trees fall and things grow on them as they die. Life feeds death feeds life. Into eternity.

The life you have includes the lives of everything around you. Jasmine knew this now. The fox's body fed Jasmine life that rippled from her scalp and down her shoulders and back, tickling the backs of her thighs where her cutoffs ended. She noticed her was hair longer and braided it in the same thought. Manipulating proteins was like wind through her branches now. She ran her hands over the braids to admire her work. Easy. Instinctual. Beautiful. Useful. She'd save hundreds on hair shit.

To test her new power, Jasmine touched a sword fern's curled pinwheel bud. It unfolded in her hand, then curled up again to grip her finger like a baby. "Hello," she said to the fern.

Hello, it whispered back.

She sent it pulses of acknowledgement, as well as some water. She felt and communicated with her own self as easily as she'd braided her hair. Her power was so strongly coiled within her that she felt the air bend around her, making the shape of a woman's body radiate from her like a silhouette of pine needles.

Walking on the densely packed forest floor sounded like walking on bones; the chalky tension of the surface made a sound more like being squeezed than stepped on. Eucalyptus bark clacked against eucalyptus trunks, applauding her. Birds and bugs chattered in the trees, tapping out their own welcome. Deer silently paid their respects. In the canopy's upper air, the forest susurrated its salutations to its newest avatar. Jasmine felt the warm belongingness that she'd craved for so long. This was home, and she was as devoted to it as to her own body.

She still held a rib in one hand. The dull white crescent had once been a part of her godmother. Who had also been this forest. Now all that was left was just a rib, smeared with blood and dappled with mold. Jasmine was aware of a part of herself that would have been disgusted by this, but there was also a part of her that was a half-billion-year-old forest. Her fungiform neurons were aware of several million much grosser things happening within her second to second.

Above her, in her redwood bough of bones, her grandmother's most recent corpse rotted; her entrails spilling down the trunk were already gathering lichen. When she'd dropped Jasmine from the tree, Gin's face had been smug and knowing. Jasmine's decision to become the forest had been easy. Gin had groomed her well. Jeanne hadn't wanted children. She only wanted to serve the forest. She was so devoted to it. Jeanne's life had been full of suffering and betrayal. As Gin, Jeanne had become the perfect caretaker for the young Bay siblings.

The woman who taught her everything, Jasmine used to think. The woman who stole Jas and James from the ungrateful daughter who fetishized a broken world and raised them in a hoary, broken city. Had Aunt Gin really wanted them that badly? Who had she been saving exactly? Gin had told so many lies, kept so many secrets from them. Even now, she was pushing memories to the forest's periphery, trying to keep glowing bulbs of knowledge away from Jasmine's reach.

She didn't want them. Her grandmother's truths weren't her truths. Hiding was no way to live. Her grandmother's memories could stay hidden. Jasmine didn't need them.

The forest had told her the true history of the world, of her own family, of herself. The stories that people tell themselves and each other when they are crazed with loss. When the ills of the world infect them. But even with all of that information, Jasmine was confused. She knew Jeanne's reasons for everything her grandmother had done, and she could understand it. But she was still so goddamned angry. After all she'd done, the old woman was still hiding things from her. And Jasmine deserved answers.

"Oh no you don't!" Jasmine screamed at the rib.

She shook it violently, yanking Gin Jones's freckled face and then the saintly dark moon of Jeanne Whipple back into being, piece by piece. Ghostly mirages of both women poured onto the ground and solidified into one figure.

A full half foot shorter than her, Jeanne's presence bristled with condescension. She looked pissed. "There you go, showing off again."

Jasmine shook her again for good measure. "You've been able to do this the whole time? And *this* is all you've done with it? Make fuckin' wood golems to kill drifters and loggers?"

Shaking her head, Jeanne stepped back. "You swear too much. And I've been doing plenty. I keep this place alive! I feed the forest, and I've been—"

"Losing. This forest is dying. You've been hiding out on your little island and trying to wait this thing out. Time doesn't change things; you have to do it yourself. You had the power, and you used it to turn men into your guard dogs. You've been playing queen of the forest when you could've been fighting back. You're working so hard to protect your last leg, you never even tried growing back what you lost."

"Your mother tried to take you away from all this and deny you your birthright. I'm the one who brought you back here. You left before—"

"*You* didn't bring me back. The forest wanted me to leave. Then it brought me back so I could clean up your mess." *And replace you.*

"Listen, I need this power." Jeanne's eyes were manic, challenging. The woman was afraid. Of Jasmine. Good.

"You don't deserve it," Jasmine whispered. After everything the forest had shown her, that she'd seen and felt, she pitied her grandmother. Her world had been so small. She didn't know how to demand more. How to fix problems that were so big.

Jasmine turned her back on her grandmother and a cadmium glow radiated through her veins. She'd always had the will to do what needed to be done. Now she finally had the power.

"What are you doing?" Jeanne's eyes widened. "Listen here. The people of Redcedar don't deserve to die. They're my friends."

"They're your *fans*. And the world they've helped you build in these woods is even sicker than the one out there. But I'm going to fix it."

With a loud crack, the redwood behind Jasmine detonated. A forest needs strong souls, inoculated by fire, to grow it back. Marian's last gift to her children was the means to start it all over. Red flames licked the inside of the redwood's cat mouth like it had a built-in fireplace. Fire jumped to the red cedar, releasing fragrant smoke. Flames wriggled up the sides of the spruce like climbing fingers. The heat whipped the motes up into the sky. Jasmine dropped to the ground, dug her fingers into the black soil. She used those dirt-blackened fingers to tear her stomach open.

Blood and branches spilled out from her. Hyphae and vines quested from her abdomen, reaching for the soil. Letting loose the power of the forest, Jasmine poured herself into the earth. A dark orange smile spread through her, burning across the land to take back what was *her*. The knot inside her wasn't an ulcer or her conscience or anything like that. It was kindling. And flint. And spark. She was Jeanne's granddaughter and would always be connected to this forest—but she was also Marian's daughter. The fire that had burned so hot in Marian consumed her, but Jasmine would use this destructive force the way the redwoods did. There's a time to burn and a time to grow. And a time to explode.

Disoriented and terrified, Jeanne scanned the flames surrounding her for her granddaughter. But Jasmine was everything in this forest, especially the wildfire she would ride into the future.

When death feeds life feeds death in concentric rings across millennia, there's no real difference between the two. And in this forest of death and life, all these things happened:

Thomas "Jonesy" Jones, Jr., lost his best friend and his leg in 1980, and a new lichen was born.

The boy's leg puked out blood and spilled it across the forest floor. And it fed countless hungry mouths. With nourishment and life and the hope for survival, we can all do more miraculous things.

The forest joined fungus and algae, mixing them in the primordial laboratory of the redwood canopy. Lichens aren't plants, but rather a tapestry of almost-plants. Fungi provided the skeleton, while proteic algae wove themselves across, around, and through lichens to form something new and completely different from the algae or the fungi. Something special. Not a plant but a beneficial relationship that allowed two wildly different beings to survive better than they could on their own. As alive as anything else in the forest, and no less important to the forest's power.

The resultant holobiont had never existed on earth before that day. Scientists would never know about it, but it was a perfectly self-contained ecosystem. Any human passing by would think it just looked like a puddle of thick black tar and avoid it. But hidden away in the secret ocean of the forest canopy, no human would see this for many, many years.

That black tar held a universe. The whole forest did.

In the distance, a pileated woodpecker worked its supernaturally quick little red thorn head. The drumming echoed through the forest, ricocheting off each tree like a marble. Its hard jackhammer beak carved through the bark of a *Sequoia sempervirens*, pulling apart plants that were not really plants just to get at the insects beneath them.

Countless loggers were sent to their deaths to feed their world's hunger for wood.

Many found their deaths feeding this forest.

But Jasmine could fight it with this new form. Not as a plant or a woman but in a beneficial relationship that allowed both her and the forest to survive better than they could on their own. This beautiful system where nothing really dies. A plane where time doesn't exist, only life. The forest's infinite brain processed so much information, there weren't words yet to describe its magnitude. The power pulsed upward and outward, using death to feed growth.

Jasmine-the-forest burst into flames, snaking across tinder-dry duff to the nearby trees and up their trunks into the canopy. She climbed higher and higher. Below her, the mossy silhouette of Jasmine-the-woman lay opened across the ashen ground. Fog rolled in from the Pacific Ocean, and the moss turned its thousand-thousand thirsty mouths upward. Moss covered the substrate of her dull white skeleton, engorged with water. Her bones, carpeted in rich green velvet, were the verdant mountains themselves. Her heart, her whole heart, was the beating heart of Humboldt County. A human heart can only beat for what it wants, but a forest's heart beats for itself and everything that counts on it. Can a creature ruled by desire ever truly be able to be a part of a system with dignity? Or can it just wield power?

The forest pumped its rhythmic energy up into a wall of wildfire. Jasmine surfed screaming-banshee flames across California. Her awareness spread like the edge of an avalanche as she burned across the state, floating as goldenshine power.

Sucked down into the ground and trapped within the nurse log's membranes for maybe the last time, Jeanne could only feel the quake of her granddaughter breaking the world.

She was a prisoner now. No flesh body, but still conscious. Just a clot of biomass fixed to the forest's roots alongside molecules of water and nitrogen. Inert. Like one of Jasmine's patients. A vegetable. Of all the deaths of Miss Jane Mooney, this last was the hardest.

Forests can heal even if hearts can't. Jeanne hoped that Jasmine would come around, would come to know her. They had time. The forest always has time.

45

THE BIG ONE

CHARLYNE BLACKMAN'S FOREARMS BURNED as she scraped pint glasses against the bottle brushes and wondered if her back was gonna keep bothering her all night. She'd do a shots-and-bottles deal and hopefully save her body the strain of changing too many kegs later. She dropped the clean glasses into the sanitizer sink with the familiar *shloop* and *clunk* and was moving onto the next batch of dirty glasses when the *clunk* became a *clank*, and then there was a sharp underwater *crack* as two glasses shattered under the sudsy water. The ground started to shake.

"Everybody, hang on to something," she bellowed toward the table of regulars.

"Oh God, it's the Big One," someone groaned.

Charlyne whispered a silent prayer to herself, begging for Jeanne to hear her. The entire bar shook like a giant was lifting it off the ground because that's exactly what was happening. When the shaking subsided, the Skyliner was floating thirty stories up in the air, lodged between twin trunks of *Sequoia sempervirens*. Stranded, but alive, Charlyne thanked creation for letting her live to fight another day.

On the other side of the mountains, bud farms were sprinkled throughout the dense forest. Goldenshine flecks of pollen floated down onto the ripening buds. The pollen coated the plants, forming crystalline threads that shimmered under the reddening sky. The next harvest was sure to be a good one.

When James Bay didn't arrive to work that morning, Hussein Malek took his route. He shifted down gear as he grapevined south on the 101 toward Petaluma. The wildfires that had ravaged Sonoma last week had left the hills charred black. But today, green splashed across the devastation, growing each time he glanced at the black hills. Nature was healing. It could grow itself back. Build back better.

That's all anyone wanted, he mused, the chance to rebuild. The people who had lost their homes to the fires would build back too, using the twenty-one-ton load of construction lumber in his trailer.

Hussein was nursing a rotator cuff injury that began to throb. Each of his half-dozen rearview mirrors darkened as a titanic cinder-gray cloud rose behind him, escorting his truck down the 101.

Suddenly, the asphalt split open ahead of him. Hussein jerked the wheel to avoid the dark cylinder bursting out of the ground.

The people riding BART felt the train's cars shake, scraping the sides of the tunnel under the Bay. "Is this it?" some wondered. Most chalked up the horrible service to budget cuts or a strike or something. The train escaped the tunnel and rose from the Bay. The commuters with window seats could see cracks tattooing 7th Street as the train jerked along on its tracks, slowing to a stop at West Oakland Station.

When the doors opened, the crush of fleeing passengers was worse than the tectonic pressure of the Embarcadero at

5:10 p.m. Human bodies flooded out the doors, trampling other human bodies who also dreamed of not dying on BART. Blood dripped through the tracks and drenched the ground below. Bones were crushed into bloody grit and caked shoe soles. Those who survived tracked the material away from the train station and with the blood of their own kind, fed the ravenous earth.

Dr. Williams always left from the front entrance of Hewes Hutton Hospital. Even though he had on-site parking, he chose to pay for a private garage to keep his Tesla from prying eyes and preying hands. He strolled down Peralta Street toward the garage. A rumble rippled through the ground. Above him, a BART train screeched into West Oakland Station, silhouetted against the orange opacity of a fire-season sky. It would be almost beautiful if that homeless encampment weren't cluttering the bottom of the frame.

The ground shook again, even harder. Not the train, then. He looked around him, eyes searching for something to make sense of the sound, some visual cause for this effect. There'd been an earthquake earlier, maybe? Yes, this was probably an aftershock. Definitely. Probably. Williams couldn't remember the last time he'd been outside for a quake. Maybe at Stanford. Was this the Big One then? He grabbed a chain-link fence and hoped the quake would end soon.

Suddenly, clouds of dirt filled the air. Thick particulate rutilated the cloudy citrine sky.

The asphalt cracked next to the doctor. He ran from it, leather shoes slipping on the still-cracking sidewalk. The garage was in sight. The street shattered after him like from a giant's footfalls. Williams didn't dare look back until, ahead of him, the red brick facade of the garage crumbled in an explosion of greenery. Vines pushed through the sidewalk and thrusted toward his Brooks Brothers loafers. The adage against running into a burning building didn't apply here, he decided, and Williams hoped against hope that his car was okay.

In front of him, the floor of the garage collapsed. A sinkhole twenty feet across gaped across the structure and swallowed two Beemers. Beyond the hole, next to the exit station, was his Tesla. His only hope of getting home. His baby since his dog died. He inched around the perimeter of the sinkhole, gripping the median wall separating the ramp to the upper levels. Under his fingertips, the cement became slick and spongy. Moss sprouted up under his feet. White ropes of fungus spread like a caul up from the hole and toward his feet, at once slimy and fuzzy. Williams inched along, determined not to look into the sinkhole.

Unobserved by the doctor, redwood roots snaked up the walls of the hole. With the strength of a freight train, the roots spread and crushed through the cement partition like soft cheese. The cement wall tumbled down into the chasm and, with it, Dr. Ethan Williams.

He lived, of course.

The ground still rumbled. Unbeknownst to him, the Humboldt forest was spreading its roots across the state, becoming the California Forest again. Finally. The forest could stretch its full body for the first time in two hundred years.

Dr. Williams landed on the hood of one of the BMWs, cracking his ribs and fracturing his forearm. Staining his white coat an inky red, his ulna peeked through at him—or was it his radius? Williams coughed up blood and behind him, someone else coughed. A hard bark, like they were mocking him. Williams rolled off the car toward the source of the sound. He looked around. The bottom of the hole was soft loamy soil. Even though tree roots crisscrossed the cavern, they were coated in spongy moss. The roots were thick and misshapen like the ugly potatoes and parsnips he got delivered every week. The burled wood on some of these roots would be worth a fortune, he thought.

Approaching a cocoon of twisted roots, Dr. Williams pulled his penlight off his breast pocket to examine it. Movement showed underneath the woody vines. Closing in, the doctor's beam landed on a huge, wet black eye. The strongest hands he'd ever felt burst through the roots and clutched the doctor's broken wrist. The penlight dropped to the ground, followed by the body of Dr. Ethan Williams, unconscious but alive. Of course. He needed to be alive for what these woods had planned for him.

46 LITTLE DEATHS

AS RETRIBUTION REIGNED ACROSS California, Jasmine rematerialized in the redwoods with goddess braids this time, then changed her mind and shook her hair out into sunset-tinted Senegalese twists. Even with the power of a forest within her, Jasmine wasn't omniscient; in human form, she couldn't process everything she could perceive as a forest. Jasmine-the-person had superhuman perception into space and time. It wasn't that hard to be better than a human. But she was little more than a singular cell of the god Jasmine-the-forest.

She was thinking that she'd never get over how cool this was when she was tackled from behind by the Witches. Three old women clawed at her and screamed as their thin nails flaked metallic taupe lacquer, which tore off completely in Jasmine-the-person's hair, clothes, skin.

She threw them off her and pulled herself up. Ribbons of flesh hung from her cheek. Jasmine pulled her flesh and with an elastic snap, the strips of her cheek snapped off. She fed them to the ground, where they melted into skittering petals of redwood duff.

"Where's Gin?" Ellen Zeller demanded. She was putting up a brave front, but her eyes were wide with dread.

"You shouldn't be doing all this!" pleaded Nancy Hsu.

Jasmine couldn't believe these . . . powerless fucking *losers*. These women had simply signed up to help Jane-Jeanne-Gin and be broodmares to the forest. Judas goats leading people into the forest to keep the whole thing barely gasping along on life support.

Victoria Mooney stepped forward imperiously, and Jasmine understood then. Her nails were ragged from clawing at Jasmine's face. Miz Mooney did it because she loved Gin so much. They all did. Love made people do crazy things. Was it love that had motivated her grandfather to kill so many? Was it love that had turned Jeanne into a monster?

"Ladies." Jasmine nodded at the still-heaving trio of women.

"You're wasting your power, you know." Victoria clasped her hands in front of her, trying to cover her bloody nails. She nodded as if acknowledging an equal, which could almost be considered a compliment if she weren't addressing a god.

Gin had always commented on how Victoria had looked like Merle Oberon when she was younger and after reading the rings inside her—centuries of Mooney history—Jasmine understood why. Being a broodmare was in her blood. They didn't get their beauty from nowhere. Jasmine smiled. Despite everything, this bitch still thought she was better than Jasmine.

"You're wrong. Gin was wrong. You were all wrong to hoard what little you did have to keep yourselves comfortable at the expense of everybody else. Imagine having this power and still not knowing how to use it. You useless hags."

Miss Zeller leapt at Jasmine, who raised a hand and collapsed her into a cloud of blood that fell to the ground as lemon-fresh evergreen leaves.

"Using everything I have has made me stronger than ever. It's replenishing itself to be even stronger than before. This whole forest. In time, I'll heal this whole planet."

"But—"

"Don't interrupt me." Jasmine waved a finger, and Victoria Mooney became a statue of rich, black loam. The resemblance was remarkable for a single moment before the statue crumbled to the ground.

Turning to Mrs. Hsu, her grandmother's first and oldest friend, Jasmine approached the woman and embraced her. "Go," she whispered into her ear. "Go home."

Nancy stumbled away, terrified and confused.

Jasmine laid down and felt the soil dance through her body, squeezing out as new growth from her margins as the forest approached Santa Cruz. The deep intake of coastal air hit her system like drugs, like a first breath after drowning, like a re-attached limb. The last remnants of the ancient redwood forest of California were reunited at last. She was whole now and more powerful than ever.

Time to do something crazy for love.

The experience and living power of millions of organisms across millions of years curled up into Jasmine's body. The godpower beat steadily, and like molten lava, it poured into the empty space where the knot had been. This was the real forest. And now it was Jasmine Bay as well.

Somewhere in all this infinity was where Jasmine kept the entity known as Jeanne. Her grandmother was alive, barely, encased in slime mold, held down beneath the ground. She'd been supplanted as the avatar of the forest. The forest had been waiting for Jasmine all this time. It had always been her. Jeanne was too human still, had too many wants.

The world Jasmine lived in before had stripped her humanity away. Back before Jasmine knew what strength was, she thought she was strong. She thought she'd been keeping it together pretty well, but she'd allowed the world's sickness to infect her so thoroughly that she hadn't been human in a long time. Jasmine realized that when all you're allowed to do is hang onto life by your fingernails, you become something else. *You become what you have to become.* She became something less than human. And now she was so much more. But there were still things she wanted. Things she loved. People she loved with her whole heart.

She descended upon the ATV, riding the flames that pursued the ones she loved. Jasmine's fire licked the air around the vehicle as it lurched down the logging road. The ATV fell into the earth below, and Henry and Tilly floated in rootspace. Buck fed the forest the little life he had left, and Jasmine accepted it gratefully.

From her vantage point, the people she loved were so small, so fragile, now that they were human and she was a god. She loved them the way a god loves: all-enveloping yet distant. She loved them the way a broken person loves: passionately but without respect. Her love had no humanity left. It was love, sure, but love without vulnerability isn't a love that others can participate in, like how a child loves a toy. Jasmine had not yet learned to love without total control.

They could never be equal to her, but she could possess them, suck them into her, and let them live inside her forever. Connection, protection. She'd never leave them again, and they never could leave her. She sucked them down into her beating heart. Made them hers. Tilly's and Henry's arteries flooded with her love for them. They didn't choose it, but they loved her back now.

There was so much Jasmine running through their bodies that they almost didn't exist anymore. No bother. Jasmine knew how they were supposed to go. Her consciousness slipped into their bodies, pushing them to the passenger seat of their own minds, wearing them like suits.

Their consciousnesses oozed down roots, in increasing complexity, where forest and flesh became indistinguishable.

They were fixed there, a part of her, no longer in control of their own bodies. Henry and Tilly could only watch in horror as Jasmine walked their bodies through the forest without them.

Killing so many made her so strong. But no one had to know it was her who had done it. Not yet. Jasmine drove James's truck down the mountain, the same way Marian had forty-five years ago. Not so unlike her mom after all.

47

THE 101 COMPLEX FIRE burned for weeks. It was called as such because the dispatcher who called it in didn't care very much about specificity. The 101 could mean anywhere from Crescent City near the Oregon border to San Ysidro, a short leap from Tijuana. But the greater context is one of the first things that goes out the window when you're facing down the largest wildfire the state has ever seen, spreading quicker than any natural fire could. National news just called it the California Wildfire, which Jasmine found more fitting.

The truth was that Jasmine's wild cloud of smoke and pollen cascaded down the 101 and destroyed everything within twenty miles of California's esophagus. And spread from there. Hundreds died. Thousands were displaced. Life fed death fed life and made Jasmine even stronger.

The gray ashes birthed hundreds of millions of redwoods. The trees grew faster and taller than they had since dinosaurs walked the earth. After the woody pioneers cemented their place on the landscape, more things were able to grow, and the West Coast pulsed with the saprophytic godpower of Jasmine-the-forest. She ate death and used it to regrow herself to pre–Columbian era levels.

With the California Forest resurrected, Jasmine used her emerald necklace to strangle the West Coast and wrest it back from the people who would burn it all down to make themselves richer. Silicon Valley was a sinkhole velveted over with greenery. Every bridge in the Bay became impassable, they were so overgrown with vines. Every cliffside mansion fell into the Pacific or, worse, had its view obstructed by a curtain of superdense *Sequoia sempervirens*.

Redwoods sprung up five hundred feet tall all across San Francisco. The city's famous fog wound around them, combing the forest's scalp with its miasmatic fingers and riding the currents until it was sucked down into the cratered Nob Hill section. The old robber barons' homes lay shattered, torn apart by roots and vines. The Financial District burned, and new redwoods sprouted up from the ashes. The air was redolent with goldenshine pollen, slicking across the water like an oil spill.

The California Forest was an ecological marvel. The trees released massive amounts of oxygen that cooled the atmosphere. Bay Area microclimates evened out, became milder. Despite the trees, because of the trees, it was more livable than it had been in a hundred years. No one feared the Big One coming anymore. Scientists flocked to study the rapid onset pyrogenic California superforest and its unique flora and fauna.

When they finally paid out, the insurance companies couldn't possibly let anyone build near the coast anymore. A lot of businesses left the state. A lot of industries left. A lot of people left. But the people who stayed lived in a world of evergreen wonder. This was still their home.

Some kept going like it was all perfectly normal, as if pretending it wasn't happening meant it would be over sooner. Not everyone acknowledged the new world they lived in.

Well, all right, then.

Jasmine kept the red twists. They cascaded down her back, while new growth made itself evident on the front of her. She thought the look suited her. It seemed that others agreed, if the look Carlos gave her when she strolled past the smoking nurses was anything to go by.

"I thought you quit. Where've you been the past year?"

Jasmine's smile tightened. "Family stuff."

"Clearly," Carlos responded. He eyed her belly with the same scorn he used to eye her messed-up eyebrows or fucked-up hair. No matter what she became, some people would always find a reason to look down on her.

Toussaint nodded. "Congratulations."

"Thanks. I have a private patient I need to see about. Take care," Jasmine said, walking away.

"Nice scrubs." Carlos sneered at her back.

Jasmine smoothed her hair behind her ear. She wasn't wearing scrubs. As a newly certified PMHNP, or psychiatric mental health nurse practitioner, she was able to dress how she wanted and take on a few private patients for a little more money and a lot more autonomy.

She didn't need the money *really*. She was still a forest, but some stuff was just easier to do as a person. For example, she had a date later, in the Napa wine cave of an oil CEO with a pregnancy fetish. Or at least, the wine cave was where his staff would find him in the morning, dead from acute tannin poisoning. If she was going to be successful in creating a new world, Jasmine needed to prune as much of the old one as possible.

This one was a twofer since he also was on the board of the H. Her revenge wasn't a perfect system, but it had dignity. She was nourished with life and hope, and with that, she did more miraculous things. And for the first time in a long time, Jasmine loved her life.

"Thanks," Jasmine chirped and with a smirk lured forth a caterpillar of hair from Carlos's brows, so fast he didn't even feel it. He looked like Bert from *Sesame Street*. She smoothed down her hair again as she called out behind her, "Have a good one!"

Toussaint was cackling at Carlos down the hall as Jasmine walked away. Freddie's room was vacant, she noted when she passed it, and she hoped they'd found a form of release, one they could cope with.

Jasmine opened the hospital room door of her patient, lying on the bed framed by IV tubes. Save for one sickly white fluorescent light above the bed, the room lay in darkness. This one was a psych hold who had become permanent due to the burns covering her body, requiring the patient to be on constant pain medication.

Jasmine could take care of this quickly enough. Henry was waiting for her. He'd be happy to see her. Tilly too.

Thick ropes of pinkened flesh crisscrossed the woman's face. She was an old, light-skinned lady; not as old as Gin was but definitely older than Jasmine ever planned to look. Her chart read: SMITH, MARYANN. 03/25/1965.

The old woman muttered, her speech slurred by tranquilizers. "G'way, I'm asleep."

"But Miz Whipple, it's time for your medicine," Jasmine replied evenly.

The woman's eyes shot open at the mention of her real name. "Who are you?"

Jasmine reached toward the old woman gently. Lovingly. "Mom, it's me."

"No." The old woman fidgeted away. "You're wrong." She eyed Jasmine's pregnant belly fearfully.

Jasmine grabbed her hard this time, held her. Her irises were rimmed in cadmium glow. "It's okay, Mommy."

Clear worms of mycelium slithered out of the veins on Jasmine's hand and onto the woman's melted skin. Under it. "Hold still, now."

"Jasmine, no!" the woman whimpered.

In the corner, a tiny mushroom sprouted from the black dirt packed in the baseboard. Jasmine dug under her mother's skin, into her pores, healing her. The two women were connected by translucent hyphae. Reunited.

"We're doing it, Mom. I'm saving the world."

After Marian's treatment, Jasmine left the H. Henry was silent when she got into the passenger seat, even when she didn't buckle her seat belt.

He paused for a moment, gripping the steering wheel tightly. "Seat b—?"

Jasmine shot him a look. *Go.* She sighed, perfuming the air inside the car with pollen.

Henry breathed in Jasmine's consciousness. He breathed it out, and it danced goldenshine on the sunlight. His hand relaxed on the wheel. His jaw untensed. Sometimes he pushed against her, but now was not the time. Henry put the car into gear and started for home.

"I love when you do that," Tilly said, a smile in her voice. Jasmine admired her reflection in the side mirror, her best friend reclined and pregnant in the back seat. Their new family was growing, and Jasmine was going to do everything right this time.

In the passenger seat, Jasmine shut her eyelids and saw with a billion-billion eyes. There was so much of her, and she was miraculous at every level. She watched everything so, so closely. She was a world now. She had to take care of herself.

THE END

ACKNOWLEDGMENTS

Obviously so many people contributed to bringing this story to life over many, many years. I hope I got everybody (I probably didn't).

First and foremost, my family. Tom, Mom, Dad, and Christina listened to more than they wanted to about this project for almost a decade. I can finally shut up about this one thing.

Diana Pho and the Erewhon team, Viengsamai Fetters, Marty Cahill. My agent, John Baker, who gets what I'm trying to do here. The fine folks at Panay Films, especially Bonnie Bentley and Stephen Duncan.

Everyone who gave me thoughtful feedback through every stage of this process. Everyone whose generosity of time and information allowed this project to be built.

The talented and hilarious Kelly Anneken, Violaine Briat, Pamela Council, Teri Davis, Jane DiBiase, Hayden Greif-Neill, Rayna Helgens, Jonaya Kemper, Catherine LaRaia, Amber LaFountain, Lauren Lavín, Mike Marchinetti, Adrian McNair, Katie McVay, Jaye Samuels, Aviva Siegel, and Mimi Vilmenay.

The Sigma Squeak writing group: Jackie Keliiaa, Dom Gelin, Alex Love, Madison Shepard, Dara Wilson, and the squeakster herself, Valerie Vernale. Their feedback on earlier iterations of this story was a guiding light for how I wanted these characters to make people feel.

Likewise the Pre-pando table read cast: Kristal Adams, Maggie Maye, Curtis Cook, Ella Gale, Hana Michels, Lauren Lavin, and Tom Guffey. Every coverage service and contest reader. Eden Dranger's horror writing workshop and my workshop partner, Robyn Morrison.

The inspirations: Octavia Butler, John Valliant, Richard Powers, everyone who's ever written Poison Ivy.

Scott Thomas, whose mentorship, picket line pep talk, and beautiful writing inspired me to think bigger. The boss, Vaughn Ross, for being a nerd about story and process, and for spending so much time teaching a masterclass in both.

The people of Humboldt County who've shared their home with me. Chris and Monica Durant of the Savage Henry Comedy Club in Eureka, Eloise LeBel, Joe Deschaine, Dr. Foxmeat, Kim Hodges, Josh Barnes, Ivy Vasquez, and Michelle Hernandez Wentzler.

All the loggers on YouTube and TikTok who livestream themselves doing their job (I won't name them since I'm pretty sure you're not supposed to be doing that). Henry Millard for trying to answer a truly annoying number of questions about his work.

72bookclub, who brought the fun back to reading and taught me that books can be more than just a "locus of expectation," they can also be smut.

Biggest thanks for Past Me for sticking with this project through so many ups and downs and dickheads. We did it, kid.

DISCUSSION QUESTIONS

These suggested questions are to spark conversation and enhance your reading of *Humboldt Cut*.

1. What specific features of the redwood forest stuck out to you most? Do these make you want to visit Humboldt County or stay away?

2. Which character do you identify with the most and why? Did that change as the story continued?

3. How does each character's race impact their understanding of the forest and "the world"? Do you think Jasmine's experience would be different if she was white? If she was Native?

4. Why do you think Jasmine is hesitant to return to her hometown?

5. What do you think of the relationship between death and the people of Redcedar? How does their perspective differ from your own?

6. Do you consider Jasmine to be mentally ill?

7. Does Marian's backstory impact how you think about Jasmine and the way she acts?
8. William Whipple is a mythical figure, shown mainly through the eyes and words of others. Why do you think that is? How do you think William Whipple would feel about his role in all this?
9. Which characters do you consider "good" or "bad" in this story? Does this change by the end? If so, how?
10. What do you think it means to love with your whole heart? Who do you think actually does this in *Humboldt Cut*?
11. Love takes a lot of form in this story: romantic, platonic, paternal, proprietary. How did your understanding of different people's relationships change as the story continued?
12. How do you feel about logging as a commercial enterprise now after reading this story? Did you know anything about it before this?
13. The story's epigraph is a quote from Richard Powers's *The Overstory*. What themes in the book did that bring up for you?
14. How would you cast a movie version of this story? Who would direct?
15. How did the ending make you feel? Would you consider it a happy ending?